Persia Woolley is a journalist and scholar specializing in the Dark Ages. This is her first novel, the first of a projected trilogy. She lives in northern California.

PERSIA WOOLLEY

Child of the Northern Spring

GRAFTON BOOKS

A Division of the Collins Publishing Group

LONDON GLASGOW
TORONTO SYDNEY AUCKLAND

Grafton Books
A Division of the Collins Publishing Group
8 Grafton Street, London W1X 3LA

A Grafton UK Paperback Original 1988

Copyright © Persia Woolley 1987
Map by Jean Yee Wong

ISBN 0-586-07469-4

Printed and bound in Great Britain by
Collins, Glasgow

Set in Times

To Autumn and Sharon, John and Nick,
without whose support this story
might not have been told,
and to Mama Dee,
without whom the teller
would not have been

King Arthur's England

Edinburgh

The Mote
THE WALL
Carlisle
SOLWAY FIRTH
Appleby
Ambleside
RHEGED
Ravenglass
IRISH SEA
York
Ribchester

Chester
NORTH-UMBRIA

The Wrekin

WELSH KINGDOMS

Gloucester
LOGRES
Caerleon
London

Sarum
THE SAXON SHORE
CORNWALL

N

0 20 40 60 80
MILES

0   40   80   120
KILOMETERS

Author's Note

There are few stories better loved or more often told than those which make up the legends of King Arthur. What began as the tales of a Dark Age warlord have gradually developed into one of the great story cycles of Western civilization, full of archetypal themes and personalities. Over the centuries it's taken the form of folk history, morality story, grand romance, swashbuckling adventure or high fantasy, generally reflecting both the social climate and the personal bias of the particular teller of the tale. This adaptability is part of its charm and probably one reason it has survived so long and well.

In recent years there has been a growing interest in looking behind myths of all kinds and retelling them in terms of human, rather than legendary, perspectives. This has led to some fascinating historical fiction, in which the cultures and climate of the times have a notable influence on the unfolding of the story.

I have made specific use of this technique throughout, but most especially in the development of Guinevere, who in the past has been presented too often as a two-dimensional character: either the shadow substance of a king's ill-made choice or the wilful and spoiled beauty who ruins the kingdom without compunction. (This approach to Arthur's queen seems to perpetuate the Victorian view of her character and provides a handy scapegoat for authors who need one.)

The tales of Arthur's remarkable kingdom grew out of the Celtic Renaissance which rose as the Roman civilization deteriorated and the Anglo-Saxons began their

7

invasions. From the scattered clues found in modern archeological studies, ancient folklore and the writings of Gildas (the only contemporary author we have from that time), there appear to have been more elegance, diversity of trade and education in the royal households of the Dark Age kings than was once thought.

Many of these Celtic kings were descended from the tribes who had resisted the coming of the Romans four hundred years before, and they rallied to oppose the Saxon invasions when the Empire crumbled. They were a rugged, wild, stormy lot, with a long tradition of queens who were co-rulers with their husbands. The activities of these vital and exciting women were recorded in both Celtic legend and Roman history, and any daughter of theirs was likely to be an independent and remarkable person in her own right. It is within this context that I have explored the background of Guinevere.

These pages won't offer the dragons and jousts that Malory presented, but rather times of change and evolving thought, external threats to civilization as the Britons knew it and internal bickerings such as even modern-day countries experience.

Like all other Arthurian tale-spinners, I owe an enormous debt to those who have told the story before, and to the various scholars who are engaged in serious pursuit of the Once and Future King. The specifics of Gwen's childhood are largely my own invention, based on what I thought would explain her actions and behaviour in the later story of her adult years. Cultures and ideas may change over the centuries, but the basic psyche of mankind evolves much more slowly. No doubt that's why archetypal tales remain popular through the centuries.

It is easy to become very picky about language in a work such as this. For instance, would these people use slang? Can one use the term 'lunch' or 'book' when the word itself wasn't invented for a number of centuries to come? If this principle is carried to its logical extreme, one couldn't even use the Anglo-Saxon and French words which make up such a large body of our vocabulary, since technically they weren't part of the Celtic tongue. In the end I decided that the purist should view this book as a translation; the characters themselves would have been speaking Brythonic or Latin or Goidelic anyway, and whether they called it lunch or the midday meal, book or tablet, the concept remains the same.

For ease of identification, I have generally used modern place names to denote specific locales, even though the name itself may be Anglo-Saxon. Where an earlier historical name indicates a political division more appropriately (such as the kingdom of Rheged), I've incorporated that. What we call Old Sarum I allowed the less ponderous name of Sarum simply because it was so much younger then.

The problem of the Welsh and the Cumbri is a bit stickier. The word 'Cumbri' means 'companions,' and it is the name by which the British Celts have referred to themselves down through the ages. When the barbarians finally overran Britain these people were driven into the mountains of the north and west, where they gave their names to such areas as Cumbria and Cumberland. The victorious Anglo-Saxons referred to these regions as Wales and North Wales, meaning 'the land of the strangers.' Thus, ironically, the natives found themselves branded as aliens by the newly arrived interlopers, a situation they thoroughly resented.

I've referred to the specific geographical area of Wales by its popular present-day name, but speak of the people as the Cumbri, in part to show the kinship between the various petty kingdoms and at the same time to indicate the extensive range of their holdings, which were far greater than modern Wales.

As to the spelling of personal names, they mostly follow the Malory version unless there is an equally well known Celtic form.

Since both legendary and historical characters run throughout the tale, I have occasionally opted for the historical reference as put forth by John Morris in his *Age of Arthur*. Theodoric is a real character, as are Urien, Gildas, Agricola Longhand, Cunedda, Maelgwn and probably both King Mark and Tristan. One of the great delights of Arthurian study is the interweaving of the verifiable and the mythical, for each contributes a kind of magic far more lasting than simple spell-casting.

Because this is a work of fiction, I've presented things as colourfully as possible while still trying to stay within the pattern of thought or behaviour that was probably prevalent.

When I began this project I had no idea it would involve so much research, or grow into a trilogy. Yet getting acquainted with the characters in this first book has been a wonderful experience, and I hope you, the audience, enjoy reading it as much as I have enjoyed writing it.

Mountain View, California
1981–1986

1

The Departure

I, Guinevere, Celtic Princess of Rheged and only child of King Leodegrance, woke to a clatter of activity in the stableyard. The sound of gruff orders and jingling harnesses was accompanied by swearing and grunting and the occasional stomp of a large, impatient hoof.

I scrambled out of bed and ran to the window. Sure enough, down by the barns the yard was filling with people and animals. Arthur's men were strapping pack-frames on the ponies, and before long even the travelling horses would be saddled.

Too soon tomorrow had arrived, and a surge of panic rose up to choke me. It was all happening, whether I willed it or not, and I struggled to keep control of my destiny even while I searched for a way to change it.

'I can't go . . . I can't leave Rheged,' I'd cried defiantly last night, tugging on a pair of heavy breeches while Brigit stared at me dumbfounded, the unlit lamps forgotten in her shock at finding me half-dressed for flight.

'What do you mean you can't?' Her voice was incredulous, and she tossed her head back defiantly, the red hair swirling like a shadow in the twilight gloom. 'No Celtic queen whimpers she can't face a challenge. Of course you can!'

Her words were more proud than angry, and for a moment she sounded so much like her cousin I could swear it was he speaking.

'That's what Kevin used to say . . .' Tears leapt up behind my eyes, and I blinked fiercely to keep them back.

'And right he was, for once.' She relaxed then and

11

came over to the bed, where I had piled the things I planned to take with me in my bid for freedom. 'But that's no cause to be talking of running away. You know no one survives in the forest; we'd be eaten by beasts, or caught by bandits and sold as slaves, or worse.' Her green eyes brimmed with terror, and she shivered suddenly and made the sign of the cross.

Her assumption that where I went, she went too was typical. At any other time I would have smiled at her loyalty, and I began to weaken in spite of myself.

'God forbid I let you do such a thing, Gwen. If you truly won't accept this marriage, tell your father. You know he won't force you to marry someone you don't want, even if you are a princess.'

The hot tears of anger and frustration and heartbreak broke loose then, and Brigit gathered me in her arms and let me sob out my anguish against her stalwart shoulder. If we both remembered the other time I had cried thus, neither of us spoke of it. This night held enough pain without bringing back a grief that was best left peaceful in its grave.

When the first crest of my emotion had subsided, a hiccup caught me unaware, and fishing a handkerchief from her apron, Brigit handed it to me without a word. I dried my eyes and, turning to the window, stared out over the fort.

Like most Roman things, it was half in ruins; patched and mottled and left to decay. Usually I disliked such places, but here a double-storied tower had been set aside as 'women's quarters' after Lavinia joined the household. The top room had a fine view of the lake and fells, so whenever my father held court at Ambleside I settled in like a swallow returning to her favourite nest.

Tonight Windermere lay serenely sheened with silver, while above it a new moon hung misty in the pale sky. A

12

fish sent ripples outward in silent beauty, and the little murmuring quacks of a mother duck calling her offspring drifted up to me. Somewhere in the village a child was trying to drive a noisy old hen into its coop for the night. It made me think of the one-eyed biddy who used to flap and squawk whenever I shooed her towards the roost at Patterdale, and the poignancy of so simple a memory threatened to bring back the tears I was trying to control.

'I think you're suffering more from nerves than from a real dislike of Arthur,' Brigit suggested, calmly returning to the task of lamplighting. 'Though I'll admit, he certainly picked a forbidding emissary to come and fetch you.'

'Merlin?' I shivered a little at the thought of the distant, unbending magician. He had given no more than a curt nod when my father presented me, and throughout the evening meal had avoided so much as looking in my direction. Even in the past, on those rare occasions when he had visited our court during my childhood, he was always strange and aloof, reeking of the magic Archdruids are known to have. It was said he had made himself indispensable to the young High King, and if his attitude was an example of the welcome I would receive in Logres, I had good cause to regret the loss of my homeland.

In the end I promised Brigit not to run away, but to face my father on this morning. And the last thing I did before going to sleep was pray long and hard to Epona, begging the Horse Goddess for help in breaking the marriage contract without bringing dishonour to our family.

Now the morning had come, and with it the mists that covered the lake so that even the stone jetty was hidden and the mountains seemed to float between earth and sunrise, their feet lost in the pale, shimmering fog. I

13

searched back through the bits of last night's dreams, looking for a sign from the deity. But like the veiled lake, whatever wisdom Epona could give me was hidden from view. The only picture that lingered was that of Mama, who seemed to be watching me carefully, with a worried smile.

That was no help at all, for Mama had been a regular part of my dreams ever since her death five years ago. Last night she had not said or done anything notable, and no other image rose to offer me guidance.

Pages began to appear in the courtyard, dashing about with bundles which the High King's men sorted into different piles. I turned away and headed for the wash-stand. Clearly any effort to avert the fate which stamped and pawed at the gates of my life would have to come from me.

Dressing hastily, I hurried down the stairs, all too aware of how little time was left. Unless I found some chink in my father's armour, we'd be on the Road before the fish had finished feeding.

In her first-floor room, my chaperone Lavinia was fretting over hampers and baskets, and I tiptoed past her door as quietly as possible; this was no time for one of Vinnie's flurries. I ran across the courtyard and darted into the Main Hall with a sigh of relief.

Our guests milled around a trestle table, picking up bannocks and cups of hot cider while the servants scurried back and forth. Gladys was crossing to the kitchen when she caught sight of me and steered her way through the crowd.

'I've taken your breakfast to the King's chambers,' she said, picking up an empty pitcher from the end of the table. 'I assume you wanted to eat together in private?'

I nodded gratefully, thinking how lucky we were to

have a household that recognized royalty's need to get away from the eager eyes of the court.

The King's chamber was the one quiet place in the fort this morning, and my father was already eating as I came in.

'Well, Gwen, all packed and ready to leave, I expect.'

The comment was a statement rather than a question, and without waiting for an answer he gestured to me to be seated in Mama's chair. It had been pulled up near the window across from his, and Gladys had set a tray of food on the folding table between them.

I perched on the edge of the seat and reached for a bannock. The window was unglazed, and though the day's first sun splashed through the open shutters and played along the carvings of the furniture, there was little warmth in it. In April the snows still linger on the peaks of the fells, and the clean cold nip of winter is often present in the northern spring. I was not surprised to see a thick plaid robe tucked over my father's knees.

'I had a long talk with Arthur's man Bedivere last night,' he commented. 'Seems to be a fine fellow; has his wits about him. He should be able to get you safely to Arthur in no time, provided there're no late storms.'

My parent went on with a discourse on this year's weather, its effect on the crops and the apparent late blooming of the apples. I ate my breakfast in silence, watching him with a mixture of fondness and admiration while I waited for a chance to speak.

Never what you would call a robust man, Rheged's King had grown lean and gnarled with age. His beard was more grey than brown now, and the angular face that used to break so readily into laughter had long ago been ploughed with furrows of sorrow and pain. But dressed in his best tunic and carrying the dignity of his years as a monarch, he was a presence to be reckoned with in spite of his infirmities.

'You know what they say,' he continued. 'If the apple tree blooms in May, you'll eat apple dumplings every day! With the buds still not open yet, we'll be seeing a full harvest this autumn.'

My father went rattling on about all manner of other mundane things, never once coming back to the subject of my departure. I noted how tired he looked, and wondered if he too had spent the night searching through dreams.

Finally, when I had finished a second bannock, he leaned forward and spoke slowly. 'Are you terribly disappointed, child?'

'Disappointed? No . . .' I said carefully, licking the butter off my fingers. Here was my chance, and I wanted to lead into it tactfully. 'I would prefer to stay here, however, and find a partner who will come to my lands and share my kingdom.' I glanced hopefully at my sire, praying he would understand what I was about to say.

'Ah, if only that were possible,' he interrupted, brushing a crumb off the lap robe. The patch of sunlight had been creeping farther into the room and seemed to spring into his lap like a cat.

He shifted uneasily in his chair and hurried into the list of reasons for my marrying the new High King.

We had been over the subject so many times before, I listened now with only half an ear and stared at the rich colours of the robe glowing in the pool of sunlight. My father's knobby fingers lay stiff on the soft wool, and I wondered if the warmth helped ease the pain in his joints.

At last he paused, rubbing the knuckles of one hand with the other and staring at them in order to avoid looking directly at me. 'You know I would never insist you marry someone you didn't like, and I worry that

16

you're not happy with this choice. I suppose it's the dream of every young girl to marry a man she loves . . .'

His voice trailed off uncertainly, for though we had discussed many subjects together over the years, things of the heart had never been among them. His fingers laced and unlaced themselves nervously, making the jewellery he wore shine and glint in the sunlight.

'Love is something that grows with time, child. With respect, with commitment to build something together. Your mother and I had more than a fine romance . . .'

He stopped then and stared down at the small enamelled band Mama had given him long ago. Compared with the official Ring of State it was light and frivolous, but I suspected he would gladly have relinquished the power of the one to have the donor of the other back with him.

It was the moment I had been looking for, and the words came tumbling to mind like bubbles in a spring surging to the surface. Love and hope and respect and caring: to have what he and Mama had shared; to stay here among my own people, and marry a man of my own choosing. Any scullery girl or dairymaid had that right; was it too much to ask, when I must be queen as well as wife?

They were all there, the words by which to regain control of my life, and they lodged in my gullet like a fishbone, refusing to move either up or down. I tried to clear my throat, and strained to make my voice heard in the silence, but all that came to me was Mama's whisper on the morning of her death . . . 'Once you know what you have to do, you just do it . . .'

My father looked up, the depth of his concern and worry over my future showing naked in his face. 'If there were any better solution . . .' he said helplessly.

With a gulp I reached over and put my hand on my

17

parent's arm, stricken by the realization that this was as difficult for him as it was for me.

'I understand, Father, really I do,' I reassured him. 'The High King seems to be a fine man, an honourable leader and worthy of much respect, and I am not unhappy to be given this honour. Whatever sadness I feel is from leaving you and Rheged, not from the prospect of marrying Arthur.'

My father nodded, relieved to have got through so awkward a moment. 'And he's right well lucky to have you, too,' he averred. 'It's no easy business, being queen of any country, and I should imagine a High Queen has more demands made upon her than most. I know you'll handle them well, girl . . . and be a good mate besides.' For a moment he covered my hand with his own. 'You're too much like your mother not to.'

It was not like him to mention Mama at all, much less twice in the same conversation, and his voice cracked slightly. He was twisting the enamelled ring about on his little finger, and now deliberately tugged it over the stiff knuckle and handed it to me.

'I think,' he said huskily, 'that she would want you to have this to take south with you.'

I looked at him in astonishment, a wave of love and gratitude welling up inside, but he glanced away hastily and held up his hand as though I posed a physical threat.

'There are a few last things we should discuss, Gwen.'

His voice returned to normal, and I listened quietly as he went over the list of people who might be named regent should something happen to him while I was away with Arthur in the south. This too had been discussed many times of late, and it bothered me to be going over it again when there were so many other things I would rather be sharing with him; things we had never told each other before and, in light of his ill health, might never have a chance to say again. But he overrode me when I tried to break in.

'These are matters of State, my dear, and must be considered no matter how painful. The needs of the people come first, always . . . surely you know that by now?'

He was right, of course, so I bit my lip and remained silent. The sun had slid off his lap, and the noise in the courtyard was increasing as the horses were brought up.

'The best thing you can do,' he finally concluded, 'is give Arthur such an excess of sons that I shall live to see one of them be chosen king of these good people.'

I smiled at that, since of all the things expected of a queen, childbearing is the most natural and easiest to fulfil.

There was a brisk knock at the door and Nidan stuck his head around the curtain, signalling it was time to leave. I slipped off my chair and knelt quickly in front of my sire before he could rise, determined to express at least a portion of my feelings.

'You've given me a fine beginning, Father, and for that I will thank and bless you, always.'

'Well,' he said, shifting awkwardly in his chair, 'it may have been a bit rugged, growing up here in the north, but I hope the things you've learned will stand you in good stead. You've become a strong, beautiful young woman, and I'm proud to have such a daughter.'

A lump rose to my throat in the presence of such unexpected praise. He put his hands on my head in benediction and when he lifted them, gave me a brusque pat as though I were one of the dogs. 'I suppose it's time to be off . . . mustn't keep the people waiting, you know.'

The courtyard was full of household members and villagers, as well as Arthur's men. I hung well back in the shadow of the archway, momentarily unable to move

19

towards my new life. In front of me both past and present seemed to interweave, as though I were being sent on my way by all the people I had ever known. Mama's spirit smiled encouragingly, and I prayed quickly that she would stay with me wherever I might have to go.

Even Nonny's ghost was there, seated in a warm corner out of the wind. Wet nurse to my mother's mother and governess to Mama, Nonny used to say she'd raised three generations of queens and wasn't about to see me disgrace the line with messy clothes and hair like a hayrick! I wondered what she would have thought about this change of fortune; most likely she would not approve, for she had decided opinions on anything Roman. 'The Cumbri owe nothing to the Empire,' she'd told me often enough, 'and should walk prouder because of it!' I could see her shaking her head sadly as the last of her fledglings prepared to go marry that Romanized king in the south.

There was a tug at my sleeve and I glanced down to find Kaethi peering up at me, her wrinkled face askew as she squinted against the sunlight.

'What I wouldn't give to go off on this adventure with you, Missy!' she exclaimed softly, the old mischief crinkling her eyes. 'But this time you'll have to do the travelling for both of us, I'm afraid. Just remember, life's a wonderful panorama wherever one lives, and only a fool laments what cannot be changed.'

I stared at Kaethi intently, wondering if she knew how close I had come to running away. Seer of the future and guide of my childhood, perhaps she could make a spell to set me free. But even as the thought came to mind, I knew she would refuse. It was she who had taught me that the moira of one's life spins out in its own way, and the best one can do is work within its pattern.

Kaethi reached into her apron and brought forth a small pouch which dangled on a leather thong.

'Since I can't come, I thought you might take this along,' she said cheerfully. I caught a glimpse of a strange embroidered symbol, faded and mysterious, and recognized the talisman she usually wore around her own neck.

'It's kept me safe for well over threescore years, so I washed and patched it yesterday, and put a piece of mistletoe in it for you, to ward off barrenness.'

I stood there in silence, unable to match the banter of her tone for the tears that were threatening to start again.

'It's time you were off, my girl,' she added firmly, reaching up to tuck the amulet into the neck of my tunic. 'Rhufon won't hold your mare all day, you know.'

Bending down, I gave her a quick hug. Then, holding myself as tall as possible, I walked through my people to where the Master of the Horse stood waiting. He greeted me with a crooked smile.

Rhufon, rough as coarse wool, who had let me tag after him for as long as I could remember. It was his sturdy arms that had swung me up onto the back of a dray horse for my first riding lessons when I was barely old enough to walk. I could still smell the scent of freshly cut hay and the tang of sweat as we came solemnly in from the fields. Or recall the richness of the leather shop where he made and repaired the tack. Or feel the bits of tallow disappear into a harness strap under my fierce rubbing when he taught me to dress the gear. 'No place for idle hands around horses,' he would say, setting me to sort out scraps of leather or polish the bronze bosses on a bridle.

He was bending over now, this man who embodied the very sight and sound of childhood, offering his knee and hand to help me mount my mare.

'No need to look so woebegone, Missy,' he growled. 'It's a fine day for riding.'

His manner was so courtly and grave, you would think this moment was the triumphant result of many years'

21

work and he was lifting me into a future long hoped for instead of grimly accepted. When I was settled in the saddle, I smiled down at him while he held my mount steady until my father rode into the yard.

Astride his warhorse and garbed in the royal cape, Rheged's King didn't look as frail as he had at breakfast. There was a flurry of movement as the people pulled back to make room for him, and he nodded solemnly and began the ritual of presenting the bride to the men who would escort her to her new home.

I barely heard the words, clinging instead to the encouragement he had given me over the crumbs of a cold bannock. At last the King gestured to Rhufon, who carefully led my mare forward and handed the reins to Arthur's lieutenant.

'King Arthur would have you know,' Bedivere announced, 'that the Princess Guinevere will be much cherished and well cared for.' He went on, assuring the people that Arthur would be mindful of the needs of Rheged in the future. I paid scant attention, for somewhere in the back of my mind the notion of rescue was beginning to take shape. Perhaps, with a little luck, the Gods would intervene on this journey, as they had on my mother's.

With a start I realized the people were cheering, and we began making our way slowly through the gates of the fort. My father was in the van, with his warriors ranged behind. Arthur's men surrounded me and my women, and the baggage train brought up the rear.

It is a proud moment when a king leads his daughter from her home to begin her wedding journey, and the villagers came scrambling down the steep paths to the lakeside with joyful excitement. Dogs and children and geese tumbled out of thatched house and farmyard, barking or shouting or hissing according to their natures.

The ragged goat girl was rounding up the village animals to take them to the meadow, and she paused now to stare at us and wave a wild farewell. Her charges jumped and leapt away, startled by her motion or simply pleased to have an excuse to bound off up the high mountainside, and she went scrambling after them with a grimace. I smiled at the sight in spite of my sorrow, caught by the bright edge of life's caprice.

On the far side of the village, where the path takes up beyond the sweet splashing stream, my father moved to one side and sat proudly saluting us as we filed past. By then the little crowd was waving and cheering uproariously, tears and good wishes all mingled together. I followed my escort through them, nodding and waving to all that had come to see me off.

It wasn't until I came abreast of my father that I saw, for a moment, the glimmer of a rare smile.

Talons clamped hold of my throat, and I fought to stifle the sob that pushed against my teeth.

Smiling gravely in return, I waved farewell and hoped the tears upon my face might be taken for those of joy.

2
The Messenger

The path out of Ambleside follows the eastern shore of the lake, curving and dipping with the land. The sun had not yet topped the peaks, so there were cool dark shadows where the woods came down to the water's edge. Dew hung heavy on the grass where the dark woods began to open into meadows, and it scattered in a silver shower when a young hare streaked for cover. A morning mist lay on the lake and trailed from the trees crowning the islands. It blended the seen and unseen worlds seamlessly, and a family of swans disappeared into it without a sound as we approached.

Gradually the beauty of the day overcame the anguish in my heart, and I turned to survey the procession. We rode two by two, spread out in a long bright ribbon of colour like gentry going to a fair. Arthur's men ranged before and behind us, chatting comfortably among themselves. Bedivere moved up and down the line, sometimes heading our procession, sometimes dropping back to check on the wagons and pack animals.

Ahead of us, Merlin plodded along on the aged grey gelding he had ridden up from the south. My father had offered him the gift of a younger, more noble horse, at which the Magician had snorted and allowed it would be a terrible waste of a good steed. Now he seemed to have sunk into a kind of trance that shut out everything around him; if it was true that as a shape-changer he was used to flying in bird form from place to place, I could see how he might not enjoy plodding along with a train of pack animals.

I studied him cautiously, this man who was the most feared and revered in all the land. With his austere face and inward glance it was easy to see why people said he'd been sired by one of the Old Gods, though in his present guise one saw not so much the terrifying sorcerer as the shadow of a man who has given his life over to the needs of his country. In that sense he was not unlike my father, and I wondered if leadership always takes such a toll.

Brigit and I came next. I glanced appreciatively at her, glad of her company and thankful she was willing to be silent and let me pursue my own thoughts.

Behind us was my governess, Lavinia. A proper Roman matron, she had insisted we must bring along a litter in order to show we had some sense of civilized living. I hated the thing, and had gained a day's reprieve by pleading that I could not bid my father a proper farewell from inside a swaying box. She rode in it now, happily ensconced upon its cushions and enjoying, in her fussy way, all the pomp of our procession.

Out on the lake a fisherman called a greeting from his coracle, his voice booming hollowly as it came across the water. He held up a string of fish for us to admire, the delicious char promising a tasty feast at his steading this night. It seemed like an auspicious sign, and I gave him a wave in return.

We had just reached the ferrymen's dock when the messenger caught up with us. He came on at full gallop, and when the King's men swung round to fend him off he all but crashed into them. He wore the white robes of a druid, and after a moment's hesitation the soldiers allowed him to make his way to the front of our procession.

'Is this the party containing Merlin the Sorcerer?' he inquired urgently.

25

Bedivere came to a halt and looked the intruder over with great thoroughness.

'Who asks?'

'Cathbad, with a message for the King's Enchanter.'

'On whose authority, sir?'

'It's all right, Sir Bedivere, I know this man,' I said, and the gathering knot of soldiers parted to let me through.

I had not seen my past tutor for several years and had no idea how much resentment he might still harbour for the events at Carlisle. Lavinia was sputtering in confusion about the delay, but there were enough horsemen between the litter and our group that I hoped the druid wouldn't even realize she was there.

Cathbad was flushed and excited as though from a hard ride, and his horse stood with head down and sides heaving. I wondered what was so important as to risk foundering a good animal.

He gave me a long appraising look, and apparently satisfied that I had grown into womanhood with some semblance of grace, nodded politely and murmured, 'M'lady.'

There was an awkward silence while we waited for the Wizard to make his way to us.

'My Lord Merlin, this is Cathbad the Druid, come with a message for you,' I announced when the Enchanter finally joined the group.

Merlin sat his horse with the unresponsiveness of a bag of grain, but I saw his tiger eyes go bright and sharp to the druid's face. 'Yes?' he mumbled, sounding more asleep than awake.

'I have a message for Merlin, greatest of sorcerers in the whole of Britain . . .'

Cathbad was studying the figure beside me, trying to decide if this was indeed the man he had been sent to find. There was a long pause, during which a flock of tits hurtled through the scrub between us and the forest, their high chattering filling the silence. I wondered if the Magician had gone deaf.

The druid shot an inquiring look at me, a fact that did not escape Merlin's quick eye.

With a sigh the Wise One pulled himself upright in the saddle and intoned majestically, 'I am he. What is it you wish?'

The transformation was instantaneous. The woods rang as though with the echo of a great, reverberating bell. I stared in awe at the source of that wonderful, compelling voice, and Cathbad bowed respectfully and reached for the purse that hung from his belt.

'I have come from the Lady of the Lake, who requests that you wait for her to join your party, as she also plans to attend the royal wedding and would like to travel with you. She sends this token,' he added, pulling a small packet from the purse and leaning over to put it into the Sorcerer's hand.

Merlin's wrinkled face took on the puzzled scowl of an elder asked to look at something his eyes can no longer easily make out; but when he'd unfolded the linen envelope and realized what was within, he laughed so heartily that I smiled too, though I had no idea at what.

After a minute he carefully closed the wrapper again and stowed it in the pocket of his robe, then turned to face the druid. 'How long before the Lady could join us?'

'She says she will leave the Sanctuary tomorrow and it will take her another two days to reach this place.'

A chill slid over me at the idea of travelling with the Priestess. Merlin's presence was unsettling enough, and he could be supposed to be well disposed towards me; the Lady was quite another matter. I remembered all too well the rage and scorn of which she was capable; to invite

27

that to be my travelling companion on such a fateful journey was enough to curdle milk.

'Ah well . . .' A small amused smile played around the Enchanter's mouth. 'Please tell the Lady that I am under orders to escort the bride south as quickly as possible, and cannot wait for anyone. If she can catch up with us on the road, she will be made welcome. Otherwise I will look forward to seeing her at Winchester for the festivities.'

My mare was growing restive, and I steadied her in order to watch the little drama that was unfolding. I could not tell whether Merlin was still smiling at the present the Lady had sent, or because there was something about rebuffing her request that pleased him deeply, and when I looked at Cathbad I saw that he too was puzzled.

'The Lady will be most disappointed.' The druid cleared his throat, as though at the beginning of a speech. 'She was specifically interested in getting to know the young bride after all this time.'

Merlin's good nature had dropped from him, and he brought the full force of a severe and sombre countenance to bear on the messenger. Just as his voice inspired awe, his displeasure created fear, and I withdrew, not wanting to embarrass Cathbad by my presence at whatever Merlin chose to say.

I made my way slowly back to Brigit's side, and let the reins go slack while I sat watching a woodpecker working at an anthill by the edge of the woods. Lacy patterns of light dappled the bird's green back, so that he looked like a bundle of leaves come to life as he tapped here and there between quick sidewise glances at our group.

When the matter of the messenger was settled and we took up rein again, the bird flew away, its yellow rump flashing briefly between the shadowing trees. A raucous laugh flitted behind it, and I shivered with apprehension.

28

It was inevitable that the Lady and I must meet at the wedding, since she would soon be my sister-in-law. But now once more a formal meeting had been put off. Fate? Poor timing? The whimsy of the Gods? Who was to know? I just hoped she would not see this most recent rebuff as a personal insult. The last thing I wanted was to start my new life with one of the most powerful women in the realm as my enemy.

We turned onto the Road, moving sharply away from the lake, and I took one last look at the misty, veiled beauty of the scene, hugging it to me as though it could fend off the cold stone of a court so far away.

I had assumed that when we reached the Road our pace would quicken, but though the way was broader and the length of the cavalcade became shorter, we didn't move any faster. The presence of Arthur's soldiers, now that they rode abreast of Brigit and me, was a constant reminder that I was more a prize possession and prisoner than a joyful bride. I had to check the impulse to break away and dash headlong in any other direction.

A royal progress is always slow, I reminded myself, and even on the best of days it tries the patience of those who long to race ahead. The memory of other such trips swirled up around me now, drawing me back into the bright times of childhood, before my first encounter with the Lady . . . back to a time when I was nothing more than a daughter of the Cumbri.

3

Appleby

Autumn arrived in a shower of gold the year that I was nine. The morning sky arched clean and deep blue above us, and the wind was nippy but not threatening as we moved out on to the Road.

It had been a peaceful year, with the Picts and Scots content to stay within their northern realms, and the Irish busy making up for the bad harvest of the year before instead of mounting raids against our coast. As a result, the warriors had not been called to battle and our household had accompanied my father all year long.

On May Day, the Beltane had been celebrated at the great rock they call The Mote beside the Solway Firth, with the bonfire at night and the circle dance in the morning, gay and lighthearted, on the hill high above the waters. Later we had stayed in Carlisle while my father and Rhufon reviewed the horses in the stables at Stanwix, deciding which to take with us and which to put out to pasture, which to break and which to trade away. Summer was spent in leisure along the Irish Sea, moving from one baron's steading to another, seeing to the crops, the war bands' strength, the needs and desires of the people. And everywhere we went my father settled quarrels, gave advice and bestowed bounty, as a good king should.

In between there were the festivals; happy and merry, solemn and fearful, or simply marking the turn of the season and the gathering of the people to pay homage to the Gods and see once more that their king was actively guarding their safety. Midsummer Night had found us at the Standing Stones of Castlerigg, and for Lammas we stayed with the people who live in the ancient settlement at Ewe Close.

Most recently we'd held court in the Roman fort at Penrith, and now were making for Appleby, where we would celebrate Samhain and spend the winter in the large timber hall atop the long hill by the Eden. Of all the places I called home, this one and the village at The Mote were my favourites, and the pleasure of our destination added to my excitement.

I rode at the head of the household, bundled warmly in a sealskin wrap, proud beyond measure to be perched on the back of a dun coloured pony instead of confined to the wagon with my little brother and Nonny. It was the first time I had escaped the slow hours of travel among the smaller children, and I reached out and patted the shaggy neck of my mount. Squat and sturdy by nature, he was fat from the summer pastures, and already boasted the thick coat he would need when winter came. He bore little resemblance to the fine creatures that my parents rode, but he was a horse of my own, and I had named him Liberty in gratitude.

The Road ahead rose with the land, going straight as an ash spear's shaft through the gap in the fells known as the Stainmore. Like the towns and harbours, the roads had gone untended since the Legions left, and now hazel and crackwillow, blackthorn and brambles grew right to the edge of the pavement, reclaiming the verge that used to be kept clear. Between that and the weeds which came up between the paving stones, it looked as though nature herself were trying to erase the arrogance of such work.

Nonetheless, there was ample room for our procession; banners and bodyguards, warriors and their kin, servants and freemen crafters (my father would have no truck with slavery) and all the cooks and smiths and others that make up a king's household. Edwen the Bard rode in one

31

of the wagons with the women because of his lameness, and Rhufon brought up the rear with the stableboys and baggage.

The moving of a king's court is a lively, noisy affair. When the roads are good and the weather fine it takes on an air of festivity, for the rhythmic jingling of harnesses, squeaking wheels, laughter and rustling pennants become a kind of music. This day it was the song of my world as surely as the ring of an axe is anthem to a forester's bairn.

Up ahead rode my parents, my father on the big Shire stallion he used for war and Mama riding her Welsh Mountain Pony, Featherfoot. Said to have come from the line started by Julius Caesar, the sorrel mare was the most beautiful animal I'd ever seen. This morning she pranced and sidled in the clear crisp air, playful and full of high spirits. Her coat was the same burnished copper as my mother's hair. Once I had risen early and stolen out to the horse pens just as the sun was coming up, and there were my parents, out in the dawning light, trotting back to the steading after some private adventuring of their own. Mama's hair was loose and free, hanging well below her hips, and where it fell across the horse's back you couldn't tell the two of them apart. I watched her now, riding with the easy style which didn't depend on having a saddle, and wondered if she was twin half of that horse, so much did they move as one.

I could not hear the conversation, but from the way Featherfoot tossed her head and Mama lifted her chin and looked sidewise at my father's face, I knew there was laughter and teasing going on. At one point Mama turned and gestured beyond the verge to where the hills burned with the copper fire of autumn.

It was my father's turn to laugh then, shaking his head and holding his mount steady with his thighs. Apparently they reached some compromise, for of a sudden they were leaping ahead along the pathway of the road, bolting beyond the formal leaders of the troop, racing each other in the simple joy of being alive. I watched them disappear over the top of the next rise and thought how nice it would be to be grown up and able to ride free against the wind, instead of plodding along with the rest of the caravan.

Shortly after that Kaethi came trotting to my side, pointing to a Great Oak which stood atop a nearby ridge.

'They say in the Old Times the Gods themselves lived in the wild-woods,' the Medicine Woman said, trying to tuck a wisp of her white hair under her veil. 'In those days the Gods would not come inside buildings and small, dark places. So the most sacred spots were in the open, under the high heavens. But that's all changed now. The Legions came with their little square temples, and the followers of Mithra dug out dark holy places like caves. Even the Christians put their god in a structure,' she added, thinking no doubt of the monastery at Whithorn. 'I don't know that it makes much difference. Indoors, outdoors, belowground, in the tops of the trees . . . I've seen enough of holy places to think they are made for the worshippers, not the god.'

Kaethi knew more about the world than anyone else at court, for she'd been born in a trading town on The Wall, back when the memory of the Legions was still fresh. Growing up an orphan in the alleys of Vindolanda, she'd been captured and sold into slavery as a young woman, and shuttled from one end of The Wall to the other through various owners and quirks of fate. Only her quick wits and a stubborn will to survive kept her alive, and everywhere she went she came away with new stories of strange gods and foreign ways still followed by the descendants of Legionaires from half the world away. But most of all she learned the healing practices of many lands. She had been an old woman, though surely not as old as Nonny, back when my father bought her and gave her her freedom in return for her medical skills. It was a bargain well made in other ways as well, for she never grew tired of sharing her knowledge.

She grinned with the bright, wrinkled smile that mocked a world which took itself so seriously, and narrowed her pale gaze in an effort to see the oak on the ridge better.

'Is that a clump of mistletoe, there to the side of the crown?'

It was a game between us; she would point out things and I'd tell her what I saw, for even as a child her hair had been white, and her pale, watery eyes too weak to make things out clearly. She looked so strange in this land of high colouring and dark, piercing eyes, some whispered she must have come from Saxon stock. But the very thing that set her apart had also protected her during her days of slavery, for none dared harm a creature so obviously touched by a god for fear that that deity would take vengeance for her life.

'Mistletoe?' I repeated, staring at the dark mass that hung netted in the branches of the tree. 'Perhaps. Or maybe it's a squirrels' nest. There's something up there . . . shall we go see?'

'Nay, nay, child! I'll not risk Nonny's scolding just to satisfy a moment's curiosity. Besides, we can ask a druid, next time one comes to court. They always know where the sacred herb is to be found.'

Druids, like all the other holy men, were in short supply at that time, moving from one end of the country to another as the need arose. They belonged to the people at large, and came and went between the kingdoms in perfect safety, no matter who was fighting whom. I did not feel comfortable with them, with their secret incantations and solemn pronouncements, and much preferred to learn about the Gods from Kaethi.

So we rode along in animated conversation, and I didn't even notice when my parents rejoined us until Mama reined Featherfoot in beside me.

'How's my girl?' she asked, pushing back her hood and nodding to Kaethi at the same time. Her cheeks were glowing and her eyes sparkled happily. 'Aren't you tired from a whole day on horseback?'

I shook my head emphatically while Kaethi laughed.

'She certainly is her mother's daughter,' the old woman averred, 'and comes by it from far back, it would seem.'

I knew she was referring to our ancestor who had marched down from the north and subdued the Irish on the coast of Wales. Sometimes in the hall Edwen sang of him: 'Cunedda of the lion's pride, Cunedda of nine hundred horses . . .' I had not known him as my mother had, but I took pride in our heritage nonetheless.

By the time we topped the last ridge the wind had turned chill, and the horses' breath came in soft, steamy puffs. Great clouds were scudding in over the forest, and I was glad we were almost home.

The river spread out below, and on the far bank the villagers came out to greet us. A cheer went up as we reached the edge of the ford, and I saw Llyn, the cheesemaker's daughter, squirm into the front ranks and wave frantically in my direction. I had playmates scattered around the whole of Rheged, but none I was more glad to see, and I waved back joyfully and would have spurred Liberty forward if Kaethi had not spoken up sharply.

'It's for the King and his Lady to ask permission to enter first, and you'll not go barging across ahead of them just for high spirits.'

So I pulled up on the reins and held my place in line with sober propriety, following my parents through the

35

ford and up the hill. The banners whipped bright against the darkening sky, while the harpers and pipers and local musicians marched along with us, keeping cadence with their music and adding to the festive air. People stood on either side of the track, waving or smiling, and I grinned broadly at Llyn when I rode past. As those along the roadside spotted friends or relatives in the procession, they too fell into step, and soon the entire populace was escorting us to our winter home.

The official entry of a king is often like this, but in the past I had watched it from the cart and had no idea how thrilling it could be when one was an active participant. I have made many grander entrances since then, riding more elegant mounts, but none with more pride and pleasure. It was perhaps my first real taste of what it means to be royal born.

Once we were inside the courtyard gates all sense of formality vanished, and noisy welcoming laughter mixed with hoots of surprise and groans of relief as the ladies climbed down from their wagons. Nonny handed over the young Prince to my mother, and Llyn came running through the crowd when I slid off my pony. We started for the barn together, where I was going to rub down my redoubtable steed, but Rhufon took the reins from me and shooed us off.

'No point in having a couple of giggling youngsters underfoot,' he grumbled, and Llyn shrank back and hung her head.

'Oh, don't take him seriously,' I said as we made for the kitchen. 'He sounds much gruffer than he is.'

It was a typical first night, when bone-weary travellers collide with cheerful celebrants glad to see them home again. Everywhere there was laughter and confusion, and we threaded our way around the noisy knots of people and darted through the doorway of the Great Hall itself.

The fire had been banked to coals on the centre hearth, and huge pots of steaming stew hung by their triple chains over its warmth. Trestle tables were being set up and the carved chairs brought out for the Council which would begin once the meal was through. Llyn and I found a quiet spot among the shadows under the loft and settled down to exchange our news.

'I broke my arm,' she said, pulling back her tunic sleeve and extending a slightly crooked limb for inspection, 'trying to set a snare in the woods.'

Not even adults venture into the forest alone, and I stared at my friend admiringly and ran a curious finger along the satinlike scar. 'You went into the woods?'

'Not by myself. My brother was with me, and it was only by the edge of the cow pasture. But the bone was showing and it hurt a lot, and Mum talked about taking me to the Lady for help.'

'Did you see the Lady of the Lake?' I was both shocked and delighted at the idea, for I had never known anyone who had actually met the High Priestess, though of course everybody knew about her.

'No,' Llyn answered, shaking her head as she dropped her sleeve over the scar. 'Mum set it and wrapped it with elm leaves and it got better by itself, with only 'a little twistedness, so I didn't go to the Sanctuary.' She giggled and ducked her head to one side. 'Daddy made a terrible scene when Mum suggested it. He grabbed a cheesecloth and put it round his shoulders like a shawl, then hobbled up and down the room making fun of the Lady all the while. Mum was shocked, and really frightened, and made the sign against evil just in case.'

At this Llyn herself made the deft little hand motion and I did the same, for ridiculing the Priestess came awfully close to blaspheming the Gods.

'Anyhow, who wants to see a worn-out old druidess,

too weak and frail even to go out among her people?' my friend concluded.

I wondered if she'd been listening to the Christians, who denounced any god but their own, but before I had a chance to ask she began telling me about the two-headed kid the goat had dropped that spring, and the rites that had been held after it died.

I told her in turn about Liberty, and the yearlings Rhufon had set out to break over the summer, and the merchant ship that had got stuck in the sands of Morecambe Bay.

It had come gliding into the estuary like some creature from the Otherworld, looming up out of the water and grounding itself firmly on a sandspit. All day long the monster lay there, unlike any boat I'd ever seen. Our bobbing coracles would have long since cleared the spit and been on their way, but this thing towered above both man and sea, leaning over them like a floating fortress of wood and hide. It had tall, straight trees growing from its centre, with flapping aprons tied to cross-branches, and was filled with sailors swearing in a language no one could understand. Finally the captain brought his cargo ashore to lighten his load and make what trades he could. Mama chose some jewellery and a length of shining fabric the colour of green apples in return for a side of salted meat and a pannier of cabbages.

'The stuff is all shimmery,' I said, trying to think how to describe the silk. 'Sort of smooth and soft and . . . and like a butterfly's wing. Kaethi says it comes from a land beyond the sunrise. Mama bought a green piece and promises she'll line my hood with the scraps if there are any left over after her dress is done. And she got a necklace made of ivory as well, with amber beads.'

'Amber?' My friend's eyes went round with surprise. 'Are the beads really magic? Can you call the Gods with them?'

Llyn's eagerness to meddle with the Gods was making me uncomfortable, and I shrugged her question aside with relief as a serving woman all but tripped over us.

'Get on with you, young'uns! Can't you see the King and Queen are arriving?' the servant cried, thrusting the wooden platters laden with oatcakes into our hands and shoving us towards the nearest table. 'No time for children to sit around and chatter when there's a table to be served.'

And so the day mellowed into night with all the usual richness; the Hall filled with the sound of freemen and women laughing and joking as they ate, and when the bowls were cleared and diners had wiped their knives and licked their fingers clean, the mead was brought out and the tables dismantled. The circle formed and the business of the Council began in earnest.

This man had news from the Strathclyde group, and that one had kept an eye on our Northumbrian neighbours. As usual, King Urien's men roamed back and forth across our Pennine border, claiming this farm or making off with that cow. A shepherd from Alston had lost his entire flock to a strange malady, and there was some debate as to whether it was punishment for leaving the Old Ways unattended. Emerys the Miller reported on the nature of the crop this year, how much grain he had ground and how big the yield had been. And the horsemen talked about their animals, while some sought to make arrangements to have the King's stallion service their mares.

Mama sat in her own carved chair next to my father's, listening carefully and sometimes entering into the discussion. But all the while I knew she was keeping an eye out for Nonny, and when the old woman came and nodded that the young Prince was ready for bed, Mama stood up and thanked the people for greeting us so warmly.

'It is always a pleasure to be with you,' she said gracefully, excusing herself from the circle and making her way towards the stairs to the loft. She moved softly through the shadows, being careful not to disturb those people who were wrapped in their cloaks for the night and already half asleep. I smiled, remembering how, when I was tiny, she had always come to kiss me good night and sing me a lullaby.

A pair of fresh logs, well aged so they would not smoke, were put across the embers for the night, and Llyn and I moved up to the hearthside and snuggled in among the pile of puppies there. We whispered and nudged each other sleepily while the grown-ups discussed the rumour that Uther, High King of Britain, planned to mount a spring offensive against the Saxons in the south. There was speculation as to whether our neighbour Urien would join the High King on such an expedition or stay here in the north and harry us with border raids.

I drifted into and out of sleep, little caring what the bigger, more powerful monarchs might do. It was enough to be back in Appleby, and I smiled contentedly when Edwen took up the harp and the familiar songs of history engulfed us all.

4

Samhain

We had been at Appleby for nigh on to a fortnight when a druid came striding up the hill and through the double gates of the stockade. I was down in the kennel, helping to dress the wounds of a dog that had been pronged during a stag hunt two days before, and so missed the excitement of his entrance. But by the time we had finished and were washing up at the trough, even the stable hands were talking about the visitor, and there was much speculation as to who he was and what he wanted.

The hall was crowded that night, for news of a druid's presence travels on the wind, and after dinner the Council circle formed. Those whose position did not warrant a chair spread out rugs or pillows and made themselves comfortable between those who were seated. I found Kaethi on the far side of the hearth and had just snuggled down next to her to watch the happenings when one of Mama's ladies touched me on the shoulder.

'You're to go to the Queen's side,' she whispered.

I stared at her blankly and she tweaked my tunic, adding firmly, 'Right now.'

I had never approached my mother in the Queen's chair before and did so now with a combination of caution and excitement. Discipline was handled within the family and not in open court, so I didn't think I was in trouble, but there was no explanation as to why I was being singled out. To judge from the aloofness of Mama's expression, however, this was no time to ask questions.

She gestured to the footstool next to her, and I sat

down as my father called the meeting open and a hush fell on the group.

'We are privileged to have a special guest tonight,' he said, looking around the circle and nodding welcome to the stranger. 'Cathbad the Druid has requested permission to bring the Council a message from the High Priestess.'

The newcomer rose and moved into the centre of the circle. He was lean and fair, and could easily have been taken for one of Nidan's warriors had he not been wearing the white gown of a wise man. Most druids were old and crabbed, and I watched with fascination as this young one acknowledged my parents with a formal bow. When they nodded in return, he turned to face the council and looked carefully at each of the freemen gathered there before he smiled.

'It is a pleasure to be among you.' He spoke in a rich voice well tuned to capture attention. 'And I bring you greetings specifically from the Lady of the Lake. She is in good health and sends you her blessing, glad that so many are returning to the Old Ways. The bounty of this recent harvest is proof that the Gods are pleased with their people, and have bestowed a plentiful crop on us all.'

He paused, and looked down at the coals of the fire while the listeners shifted happily in their places, nodding in comfortable agreement with him. Llyn was making faces at me, and I looked quickly back to the druid in order to keep from giggling. The pressure of Mama's hand on my shoulder was all the reminder I needed to watch my manners.

'In fact,' our visitor went on, the golden voice warming to his audience, 'the Lady sees it as proof of the Morrigan's approval of the school which has recently been reinstated at the Sanctuary.'

At the mention of the triple goddess of war and death

and bloodlust, he made the sign to ward off blasphemy and many in the Council did likewise.

'In the Old Days it was the custom to send the finest young men to Her school, where they learned the arts of war. That was long ago, before the Empire, when heroes and great warriors were visited by the Morrigan Herself. There was no better training anywhere, and even the princes from the Continent were sent to the Lady to be taught at the Sanctuary.'

He was well into it now, weaving a spell of glory and times remembered from the far past, and we drank in his voice like honey brew. Favourite heroes and much-sung battles formed in the firelit shadows, and one could catch the glint of golden torques and decorated shields in the magic of his words.

'Those,' he said, bringing the voice down almost to a whisper, 'were the days before the red-crested Legions came, with their marching armies and orders to wipe the Old Ways from the land.'

The people in the Hall were silent, as if brooding on some old wound, and a little tongue of flame shot, hissing, from the log on the fire.

'But those druids who escaped the massacre at Anglesey would not let the legends die, or give over to the Roman thought. Through generations of the Lady's protection they've kept the wisdom intact, have passed the memory on and held fast to the dream of one day reawakening the power the Old Gods offer.' His voice had lifted, full and majestic, and was ringing with triumph. 'Now, at last, the wheel has turned round again. The time has come to acknowledge our inheritance and rise to glory once more!'

'Hear, hear!' cried one of the warriors from the other side of the fire pit, and the druid turned, picked up his goblet and raised it in silent tribute to the congregation. After pouring out the first few drops for the Gods, he drank heartily, and a wave of approval rippled around the circle, then faded away when he lowered his cup.

'What better way to ensure success for the coming generations than to re-establish the School and send our young royalty to study at the Sanctuary of the Lady? This time the teaching will be more general, not shirking the lessons of the Morrigan for battle but also including the wisdom of the druids, the history and science and literature of many years' gathering. Even the arts of healing will be taught, so that every leader of the future will be versed in the secret ways of the Goddess' knowledge. The Lady began to gather students for this great endeavour when King Ban of Brittany sent his son Lancelot to her, and the number of students has grown with each year since. Now,' he said, turning slowly to face my parents, 'she requests the honour of your children's presence at her school.'

Mama's fingers tightened on my shoulder in the silence that followed the druid's invitation. All of us in the Hall were holding our breaths, and I heard a coal crumble and fall into ash on the hearth. Mama relaxed when the druid moved to put his cup down by his chair, and after he straightened and turned back to her, she was smiling. Whatever fear had caused her to grip my shoulder so hard had passed, and her voice was calm and firm.

'My good sir, you are well talented for your calling. It is easy to see that you will be, or possibly already are, a fine spokesman between the people and the Gods. And we are fortunate to have such a one visit our court. We have long felt it an honour to have the Lady living within our kingdom, and to benefit from her blessing and knowledge. Indeed, by protecting our land from invaders, we have also protected her, and willingly so.'

She paused and reached for her own goblet as the

implication of her words sank in. We were all following her now as closely as we had followed Cathbad, for the powers of the Lady were legendary and one refused her request at peril. Slowly Mama raised her cup and saluted the druid.

'Please tell her that we thank her for the offer to educate the Princeling, but he is still only a babe, not even past the toddling stage. And I would keep the Princess with me for there are many things relating to the running of a court which she has yet to learn.'

'The Lady had hoped . . .' Cathbad began, as though the matter were still open for debate.

Mama cut in, her tone gracious but still firm. 'I am sure the education of the young in history and science and healing is much to be desired, but we will have to do the best we can here within our family. With times still as unsettled as they are, I trust the Lady will understand.'

For the first time Cathbad looked to the King for his reaction, and my father nodded gravely in accord with my mother.

'It is as has been spoken,' he said, putting an end to the matter. 'Perhaps in some future time we can consider it again. Now, we have yet to hear your other news, and the Council is eager to know what has been happening in the farther kingdoms. Did you come up from the south, perchance, and do you have any knowledge of how matters stand with the High King?'

So the moment passed, and with it my chance to go live with the Lady. I leaned back against Mama's knees, full of wonder and curiosity about what life at the Sanctuary would be like. Rhufon had mentioned it once, saying that it had been the home of all great men when they were children, but this was the first I'd heard that girls could attend. I wondered how many others had been invited, and whether my parents might reconsider. The very idea of studying at the Sanctuary filled me with excitement; at the least I might have learned the art of shape-changing under the Priestess' guidance, and at the most I could have become a warrior.

I wondered why my parents thought it was necessary to turn down the invitation, and decided to ask Kaethi about it in the morning. In the meantime, the druid was continuing with his news.

It had been a quiet summer in the south, with the Saxons staying within their holdings along the eastern edge of our island.

'King Uther patrols the area closely, but there are rumours that there are others on the Continent who are massing for a major invasion. He wants assurances from all the client kings that their warriors will be ready if the need arises.'

My father's men nodded eagerly, and there was a general air of assent, for though we had no contact with the Saxons here in Rheged, they were said to be cruel victors and worse slavers. I didn't think they could surpass the Irish, however, for Nonny said the Irish still collected heads, a habit we in Britain had long since given up.

Either way, it was a subject I didn't care to pursue, and I was glad when the talk moved round to Samhain. My father invited the druid to join us for the year-end festival, and he accepted, provided that he had finished his errands for the High Priestess.

With the first light I was up and dressed, running off to see if the Medicine Woman was in her quarters by the kitchen. There was a muttered response to my knock, and I was through the doorway and plopped down on the three-legged stool by the bed before the hanging curtain had ceased to sway.

'Kaethi, did you know the Lady of the Lake was going to summon me to come study with her?' The question was out before we even exchanged greetings.

My venerable friend finished tying the herb pouch to her belt before she turned and peered at me with a crooked smile, as though to ask what had kept me so long.

'Well, let's say I'm not surprised, though I don't think "summon" is the right term. She's not powerful enough to command the attendance of kings and queens upon her own word.'

'Did she used to be? In the Old Days?'

'What do we know of the Old Days, except for rumours and the stories bad memories embroider to make them more lively?'

The old woman came over to the bed and sat down to put on her soft leather boots.

'Here, I'll do that,' I offered, and when she lifted her foot to my lap I concentrated on adjusting the strap. 'But why won't my parents let me go?'

'The deeper question is why did the Lady ask for you at all? There's more behind this than a friendly concern for your mental development, make no mistake, child.'

Kaethi dropped the finished foot and slowly lifted the other. The buckle had got bent on this one, and I had to coax the strap to get it into position. My mentor didn't even notice, so intent was she on her musings.

'The Lady and her priests are a small group, known more in stories than in person after all this time. But now that the peaceful days of the Empire are gone, every religion is gaining new recruits. They're all looking for new blood, and new political advantage. What a feather it would be for her to train a fine young princess so that when you are a great queen someday . . .'

Kaethi's voice had become soft and dreamy, and her gaze was hazed with seeing things that I could not. I held my breath while she probed about in the future, and after a bit she sighed and shook her head.

47

'Your parents are doing the wise thing, Missy. You aren't meant to be a pawn in someone else's game.'

I finished with her boot and she stood up and shook herself like a bird settling its feathers, as though putting everything to rights that way.

'What else did you see, Kaethi?' I asked hopefully.

She gave me a fond glance, then grinned. 'That it's a grand day dawning right now, and one shouldn't miss the opportunity for freedom and light spirits when they are available.' She paused in the doorway, holding the curtain for me while I skinned past her. 'But maybe, just maybe, it wouldn't hurt for you to be tutored by the druid here at court. As for the Lady, it seems she will have to wait a bit to make your acquaintance.'

After that the days passed like a scatter of bright leaves, full of colour and activity. The cheesemaker's daughter and I were inseparable: nipping into and out of each other's households as if we were fosterlings . . . climbing through the tall apple trees to gather the last of the fruit that still hung there . . . running to the gate as the hunting party brought in a full-sized boar, slung on a pole between two warriors . . . milking the cows as they grazed in the field or skimming the risen cream from the flat stone basins in the dairy yard.

And everywhere we turned there were apples: spread out in trays for drying or packed in barrels for the cellars, cooked into preserves with honey and spices or pressed into casks of cider for winter use. Their fragrance filled our days with heady perfume, and we romped through it as blithely as a pair of kittens through catnip.

When the harvest drew to a close, preparation started for Samhain, that day when the old year dies and the new one begins. It is a gathering-in against the season's change, and while it is the highest, most holy time of the year, it is also the most taxing.

Throughout the whole of Britain, any animal that cannot be fed over the winter must be slaughtered by the end of that day, and all the preparations have to be concluded by sundown of the day before, since Samhain begins at twilight. It is the time when the spirits of the dead return to warm themselves before winter and the line between this world and the Other melts away.

Of course the Old Gods and the Fair Ones are always near; sidhe and sprite and spirit mix all around us every day. But on the night of Samhain there's a difference, for then they tempt, steal, buy or barter with the souls of men, and anyone caught outside the circle of the hearth is likely to be lost by morning. Everyone knows that the Otherworld is a place of beauty and delight, as in the Land of the Ever Young, but it is filled with danger and terror as well, and always it is ruled by powers that are beyond the control of men. So we would all observe the ancient rites and stay indoors that night.

Down in the water meadow, where the river curves round, the men had been checking the cattle pens and tethering stakes for several days, and the smith was honing butcher blade and fleshing knife as well. The great caldron was brought out to the kitchen courtyard, and the women set about scrubbing it with soft fleeces and polishing clay. It stood on its tripod gleaming dully in the October sun, a symbol of the fullness of life and death.

'How old is it?' Llyn asked, wriggling in between the workers in order to get a better look at the figures that marched around its side.

'No one knows,' said a servant, buffing what appeared to be the relief of a stag's head.

'I'll bet Kaethi knows,' someone else offered.

'Kaethi wouldn't have anything to do with it,' I announced proudly, convinced the thing was evil and foreboding.

'It is not wise to speak for other people, Missy.'

The familiar voice came from behind me and I turned, startled, to find her standing in the archway to the kitchen.

A hush stole across the yard as the women made way for her, and she walked slowly towards the monstrous vessel.

The rim came up to the Medicine Woman's waist, and she bent close to study the carvings more carefully, squinting her eyes to make out the shapes. She made me think of a whitethroat peering inquisitively from the tangled underbrush of a thicket, and I would have giggled but for the solemnness of her expression.

'Many of the Old Gods have caldrons,' she muttered, as much to herself as to the gathering. 'Once I heard of another, even larger, somewhere on the Continent. That one is big enough to stand a human in, head first.'

For a moment I thought she was going to reach out and trace one of the designs with her fingers to better understand what it meant, but instead she shuddered and tucked her hands back into her sleeves and turned away from the vessel as one turns away from an adder, not wishing to provoke it. 'They appear to be gods and sacrifices . . . and some questions are better left unasked. It's enough to know its presence satisfies the Old Ways.'

Her voice echoed with some unspeakable knowledge, and the women returned to their work in silence as though each were filled with a hollow, nameless dread. The day before Samhain was no time to tempt the fates, and everyone concentrated on getting ready for the morrow, for there would be no time then to catch up on tasks undone. I caught Llyn's attention and we quietly slipped away.

That afternoon we repaired to our favourite spot on the steep hillside that falls sharply down to the river, and from the shelter of its wooded slope stared out across the rumpled land. A flock of noisy crows had gathered at the Sacred Grove near the top of the hill across the river. Special to the War Goddess Herself, their harsh voices and strutting ways grated on my nerves.

'Mum says the druid still hasn't returned from his trip to the Sanctuary,' my friend commented. 'She says it's a bad omen to celebrate Samhain without a druid.'

'My father's been leading the Samhain rites since before you and I were born,' I retorted. There was a prickling under my skin and I felt decidedly cross. 'I don't think it matters much whether a druid is standing around watching or not.'

'Shush, shush,' she answered, lowering her voice. 'I was thinking about tonight . . . when all the spirits are abroad. What's to keep them from coming to our beds and taking away every one of us?'

Something had disturbed the crows, and they scrambled upward through the air, clacking and clattering in alarm, and I wished I had the druid's art of reading what their movements meant.

'Have you ever heard of them stealing a human from inside a house?' I turned to look at her, hoping my voice sounded more confident than I felt. Llyn was tracing a little pattern on the ground, and when she realized I was watching she brushed the dirt smooth with a grin.

'What was that?'

'Nothing.' She shrugged. 'Just a sign Daddy showed me that a travelling fellow had taught him.'

'The Christian sign?'

'I guess. Daddy said the traveller spent some time with the holy man who lives in the caves down by the Eamont, so maybe that's what it is.'

I drew my knees up under my chin, wishing I had my fur wrap because the afternoon had suddenly turned chilly.

51

'Think it will keep you safe tonight?'

'Maybe, but I'll still be abed before the dark comes!' She laughed, and I knew I would too, so I laughed with her.

We left our perch and climbed back up the trail to the stockade at the top of the hill. The sound of the cattle being driven into the slaughter area drifted up, and we looked down the long slope at the dozen or so animals milling about in their different pens. The tanners had arrived, dragging their empty sledges behind them, and those who had no friend or kin to stay with that night were busy setting up a leather tent to share against the prowling of the Others. I thought it wasn't much more than shelter from the weather, but perhaps the magic of Samhain lay in being with kindred people rather than behind stout walls.

Llyn and I parted then, giving her plenty of time to return to her family's dairy before the dusk crept up, and I hugged her once just for good luck. We had never known anyone lost at Samhain, but there were some at court who could remember bodies found in the woods, faces stiff with death and terror, their spirit gone without any sign of wound or fight. And some, they said, disappeared entirely, without even a trace.

This year the sacred night was calm, with neither wind nor howling banshees to disturb the peace, and tucked away snugly under the fur blankets I thought how glad I was to be safe in our sleeping loft. The soft glow of a rushlight cast a wedge of warmth through the crack between the curtains that partitioned my sleeping niche from the big room where my parents were talking quietly. In her own niche Nonny began the rhythmic snoring I had known since I was a babe sleeping by her side. I thought of the tanners in their tent by the river, and like many

52

another that night, prayed that nothing would disturb their slumber.

Sometime in the dark hours I woke when the baby cried fitfully with a dream. Nonny's snoring stopped abruptly while she saw to his needs, then began again when she drifted back to sleep. The light was out, so I knew it was late and was surprised to realize my parents were still talking. Their voices were low, and at first I was unaware of specific words, but as everyone else went back to sleep I could hear them more clearly.

'Put it before the people, then,' Mama was saying in her most logical voice. 'You know they wouldn't hear of it when you were first wounded, and I don't think they'll consider it now. You are the king they want, and as long as you can rally the men in war and offer them wise counsel in peace, they will follow you.'

'Oh, I know they'll follow. I don't doubt that.' My father's voice was weary. 'But sometimes I think they should have a king more' —he paused, searching for the word— 'more whole.'

'Leo! How ever can you doubt your "wholeness"?' Mama was so shocked she forgot to keep her voice down. 'Lame, yes. Crippled even, if you must. But a leader's power doesn't live in his bones, and many a man has grown lame from old wounds poorly knit. They don't care that you walk with a limp; most of them don't even notice it, if you ask me. It's not as though you had been born deformed, after all.'

There was a quiet chuckle from my father. 'Sometimes, my dear, I think you don't even see how much I've changed. I'm no longer the proud young prince who stole you from your intended groom on a wild summer night, and claimed you as my bride by right of possession.'

'We all change,' Mama said hotly, more intent on the present moment than on the memories of what seemed to

53

me the most romantic elopement in the world. 'We're both wiser and much, much more knowledgeable now. But the best thing I ever did was refuse to go home after you'd made peace with my father. As for daring adventures in the dark of night, there's no need for that anymore. What's needed now is a king with a clear head and sense of organization; a keeper of justice and a man who envisions more for his people than another cattle raid or the collecting of booty from a neighbour's treasure.'

My father's reply was low and thoughtful, but it carried through the dark to me. 'The people have a right to a king who can walk tall and proud among them . . . who can stand upright for more than a few minutes without sweating in pain and fighting off the fatigue. They are restless these days, and frightened, and there is always the memory of the Old Ways haunting them. They may begin to feel that a younger, more vigorous monarch would be more pleasing to the Gods.'

Mama snorted disdainfully, and I heard her sit up on the pallet of bracken. 'And the druids don't help, with their whispered talk of 'proper' sacrifices. But the people won't turn away from a proven leader just because he grows old and gnarled in their service. Why, old King Coel was in his dotage and they still followed him!'

'But he had Roman tradition behind him, at least in memory,' my father reminded her. 'And that memory is fading fast. The elders have died off, and among the general people there are few now left who have travelled in body or thought even as far as Chester. So they fall prey to tales of great times in the past, and lose sight of what is possible for the present. And those old, past stories require a king who inspires fear and awe and admiration for his physical strength, not his mental prowess. I tell you' —his voice dropped almost to a whisper—

'I have no doubts about governing my people. It is the rites, the traditions, the "trappings," if you will, that I dread more than any battle. A ruler must spend his life for his people, and offer it up, if necessary. And that I am willing to do gladly. But if one day I should falter in some ceremony, should stumble or fail to make a clean sweep of the sacrifice, the muttering will begin. And with it will come talk of the older, darker sacrifice as well.'

He sighed heavily, and I heard Mama lie back down next to him, clucking soothingly as one does to a fretful child.

'You're just overtired tonight. Wait and see; when tomorrow comes you'll march down the hill with all the majesty anyone could wish, and every man there will watch you with love and admiration.' She must have added something else, because I heard him laugh softly, and there was no more conversation.

I lay awake for a long time after that, thinking about my father and, for the first time, about his crippledness. I had always known he was twisted and bent, but on seeing him astride his horse or seated in a Council one did not notice the deformity. Indeed, I had never considered it a liability till now, and the very notion that men might turn away from him because of wounds received in their behalf made me indignant. That his lameness itself could become a threat to his life came as a shock.

Drat the druids, I thought fiercely as I snuggled even deeper under the covers. Pesky creatures always meddling in people's affairs . . . as far as I was concerned, they could all go back to that Lady of theirs and sink into her precious Lake!

5
Winter

In spite of my father's doubts the sacrifice went well the next day, and while the bullock's blood flowed into the caldron the people chanted the old songs and took great pleasure in how fruitful the year had been. There was no restlessness or dissatisfaction, and we all began the new year with high hopes and joyful feasting.

Winter came soon after that, earlier than usual and bringing with it the Great Crown of the North which glimmered and sheered across the night sky in sheets of brilliant colour. Often when the days were stormy or Llyn stayed home I would go to Rhufon's tack room and take my place by the mending box.

I spent hours there, watching the sturdy older man thoughtfully chewing on a straw while his strong hands tugged and pulled and stitched away at bridles and harnesses, straps and saddlebags. He'd shown me where to look for the first signs of wear and how to splice in a new piece of hide, and I took pride in doing work that met his exacting standards. And always he talked about the animals.

Once he told me about the warhorses that were shod for battle and trained to lash out with their hoofs as weapons.

'Did the Legions use warhorses like that?' I asked, fascinated as well as repelled by the ghostly presence of Roman ways.

'Not that I heard of. The Romans weren't much for horses in battle, I guess, though they certainly used 'em along The Wall. Mostly they say the Legions fought on foot, same as we do now, but with them it was like an entire country on the move, there were that many of 'em.'

I used to try to imagine what the Romans were like. Once I'd asked Nonny, who snorted and said they were fiends, as any good Celt could tell you. Kaethi only laughed and allowed that we had all been Romans, back before the Legions left and the Time of Troubles began. Rhufon said he just plain didn't know and didn't much care; as far as he could see they had no sense about horses, and therefore weren't worth bothering about.

One day when I came into the kitchen from the barn I found Mama rummaging through the spice cupboard. She looked over at me and wrinkled her nose.

'Goodness, child, you smell like a stable. What ever have you been doing?' It was a casual remark, and she went back to her search before I answered.

'Helping Rhufon,' I said with a shrug, wondering what we were going to have that required spices. Herbs were plentiful in every garden and dale, but the pungent bits of nuts and bark in the spice cupboard were much less common. Nonny said it was barbaric to cook with twigs off a tree that didn't grow on one's own soil, but Kaethi said it would be poor fare indeed if we were limited only to onions and garlic to flavour our food. In either event, the spices were reserved for special occasions, and I was curious why Mama wanted them now. 'What are you making?'

'Starting the cakes for Midwinter's Feast,' she answered absently, frowning at the rear shelf. 'You spend much time with Rhufon these days?'

'I guess,' I temporized, eyeing the baked apples Gladys had set out to cool. 'He says I'm getting as good at spotting a weak place in a harness as he is.'

Mama lifted out the box she'd been looking for and turned to stare at me directly.

'I thought you were with Vida in the weaving room.'

Too late I saw my tongue had got me into trouble again; now all I could do was look away and keep my mouth firmly closed.

I hated spinning. It put me in mind of the times when enemy raids sent the men off to fight, and the women and children would be hustled into the hidden reaches of the Lakes until the danger was over. Those were times of dread, when the women went about their chores in silence and no one was willing to play or laugh or go romping down to the lakeside. It seemed to me those days were made of the heavy grey wool we children learned to spin with; coarse and greasy, it scratched my hands and rankled my nerves until I came to hate it. Even the odour of raw fleece reminded me of fear and imprisonment in gloomy houses.

'Well, Gwen, I think I'd better talk to Rhufon,' Mama said with a sigh, 'because starting tomorrow I want you in the loft with Vida.'

My dismay must have shown on my face, for she put her arm around my shoulder and gave me a hug. 'I know . . . I know how much you want to be down at the stables, but there are things you must learn about running a household, and they start with the distaff and fleece. Without spinning there would be no clothes, no bags, no hangings for the walls, no banners or fishnets or string for the kitchen. And you'll never be able to manage a weaving room's schedule in the future unless you learn what's involved now.'

I glared up at her, angry and trapped and miserable, and she burst out laughing. 'Oh, child, it isn't as bad as all that. It doesn't mean you can't be with Rhufon and the horses sometimes, you know. Only that you need to start applying yourself to the things all young women have to learn. And tomorrow you're to report to Vida first thing, so that she can get you started. Now you go out and wash; I don't want you coming into the Great Hall smelling like a dung heap.'

That's all very fine for you to say, I thought rebelliously as I splashed about at the water trough. You're grown up and free to come and go as you please, while I'm the one who'll be cooped up inside with all that smelly wool and the chatter of women every day!

But the next morning found me reporting dutifully to the weaving quarters, where Vida looked with dismay at the lumpy, uneven sample I spun for her.

'Well, there's nothing wrong with it that practice won't cure,' she said, pointing to Gladys' daughter, who was proudly producing an endless, even thread with just the barest motion of her fingers. 'She's only been at it since last spring, and her work was no better to begin with than yours is now.'

I stared at the girl and thought uncharitably that she was probably also afraid of horses, but held my tongue and tried to control the fibres of the fleece as well.

So I settled into the women's world of carding and spinning, weaving and sewing. Unlike the paddocks or the sweep of the hill where Llyn and I generally played, the weaving loft was close and stuffy and I found the women's talk of babes and broths to be incredibly dull compared to Rhufon's conversation.

They nattered over the quick onset of winter, with its blowing snow and icy winds; even the hardiest sheep had to be brought in to the inbyes lest they be lost for weeks under a peaceful, freezing blanket of white. But it seemed to me I could just as easily have learned that from the traveller who arrived one night and reported that Lake Derwentwater was already frozen over, and both cold and hunger were making the wild animals brazen: he had been

59

stalked by a pack of wolves during the whole day past, even though he'd stayed on the Road.

Gradually the year darkened. As the days grew shorter the light in the spinning room dwindled, and the tallow lamps burned all day long. Their heat and pungent smoke added to the already stuffy atmosphere, making the days wretchedly long and dreary. I dragged off to my task each morning as if under sentence by the Council and began to look forward to the Midwinter holiday much as an exile yearns for her homeland.

As the winter festival approached, the hunting parties increased and Mama gave my father packets of food to be left by the spring that the Ancient Ones used. These were the little people, dark and small, who lived within the heart of the wildwoods, away from Roads and steadings. Nonny said they were related to the sidhe and therefore fey. Kaethi said that might be, but they were also the first people to have lived here, back when the whole of Britain was known as Albion. Some even said they were the children of the Old Gods, and every prudent landholder left food in the forest for them when the winters turned bad.

With the holiday's arrival the court came alive as people gathered from all over the countryside. Some wanted to help call back the sun in the traditional way, and some looked forward to the best eating they might have for several months to come. But most came for the laughter and hunting and competitions that were held in the courtyard or down by the river.

I woke on the feast day to the special stillness that follows a new snowfall, and peering through a crack in the shutter, caught my breath at the sheer beauty of it. Scrambling into my warmest clothes, I ran off to find Llyn, and before long we were standing at the top of the hill looking out over a familiar world turned strangely wondrous, for it rarely snowed this much in Appleby.

The day was bright and brittle so that everything sparkled and I put up the hood of my sealskin wrap, which now had a lining of soft green silk. The rest of the children were taking advantage of the holiday as well, and they soon joined us in sled races down the hill road. There was much laughing and leaping about in the chilly air, what with snowball fights and pushing one another into drifts, and we all worked together to build a figure for the Gods. It was a fine Winter Dragon crowned with holly, and even the druid smiled at it when he came past on his way to the court. This was the first time he'd been back since Mama had refused to let me go to the Lady, and I wondered just what his smile meant.

Before the feast that night, Nonny was dressing the little Prince while Mama fixed my hair. I fidgeted restlessly as she drew the comb through my tangled locks until she gave my shoulder a shake.

'For goodness' sake, child, your hair looks like a rat's nest. Now just hold still while I try to do something with it. I've never seen such a girl for getting messed up.'

'I have,' said Nonny, glancing over at her. 'For getting into mischief, you used to set a pretty fair example, you know.'

Mama laughed and shrugged her shoulders. 'I suppose you're right, Nonny. But I never was comfortable sitting by the fire like a simpering kitten. There were always so many more interesting things to do down by the boats, or at the fishermen's huts. And of course, with the horses . . .'

I turned suddenly, knowing I'd caught her out, and that in fairness she would have to listen to me. So I made my case for escaping from the weaving room, including the fact that even Vida said I was getting better at spinning,

61

and couldn't I now please go back to helping Rhufon in the stable?

Mama grinned and went on braiding my hair, listing the many things I'd have to learn before I'd be able to run a household of my own, and raising horses was not among them. When she had finished with the hairdress, she turned me around to face her and studied the result of her work.

'You look well enough to bring honour to your father tonight, child, and he should be right proud.' For a minute she smiled down on me, playful and serious at the same time. 'Cathbad's brought some news I think will interest you, so be sure to pay attention at the Council after dinner.'

Downstairs, the feast was laid out with the little hard spice cakes soaking in mead and hunks of game turning constantly on the spits over the hearth. It was a grand meal and afterward, before the dancing began, my father called the Council to order.

Cathbad had returned from the Lady with an offer to stay and tutor the children at Appleby, and Mama announced that any parents who wished could send their youngsters to the court to be taught in all those things which the druids offered at the Sanctuary. A ripple of comment ran through the assemblage, and more than one head nodded in approval. Whatever reservations Mama may have had, the idea seemed to be a popular one, and naturally it delighted me, for it meant I could spend part of each day away from the spinning room with a clear conscience.

Once the Council was over, the dance to call back the sun began with much ringing of bells and clappers. All of us were garbed in our most colourful dresses or tunics and bedecked with torques and other bright finery. Mama wore her new silk dress and all the gold pieces from her jewel chest, and when she began the dance, moving gaily in and out around the circle and inviting each person to follow after her, I was sure she was the most beautiful woman in the world.

So we danced and sang well into the night, grown-ups and children and elders all circling about the hearth. It was a grand celebration, loud and colourful, and even the faces carved in the pillars that held up the lofts grinned happily behind their painted leaves. No matter how far away the Sun God had wandered, I was sure He'd hear His people and return.

Next morning Cathbad came to join me at the table where Llyn and I were eating our porridge. I eyed him cautiously, hoping his company would be more interesting than that in the weaving room.

'There are many things to learn about the world; about the habits and uses of plants, and life in the streambeds, and the stars in their cycles,' he announced as several of the stableboys sidled towards the table uncertainly. 'But I think we'll put off studying the things outside until the thaws come, and concentrate now on religions and ideas and history, since they can be learned about anywhere.'

His would-be pupils nodded silently and I noticed Gladys' daughter had edged into the group, sitting quietly across from the druid and staring at him in the same vacant way she stared at the fleece when she was spinning. It was clear she was either a monument of patience or not very bright, but as yet I wasn't sure which.

'Does anyone have any questions?' the druid asked, scanning his growing flock with a benevolent eye.

'Mama told me not to ask too many questions,' I blurted out.

Our tutor laughed, his young face creasing with amusement.

'There was once a very special man in Ancient Greece

63

who thought questions were the best way to learn about anything, Missy. He was considered very wise, but the leaders were afraid of him and told him he mustn't go about the market questioning things all the time. Few people now recall the name of those who caused his death, but Socrates' fame has lasted a thousand years, and we still honour him as a fine teacher.'

'What did he ask about?' Llyn's voice was clear and quick, and I suspected she hoped it was the Gods. As Cathbad explained, we slipped into our first lesson without even realizing it, and the rest of the morning went by in talk and tales and curious queries. By the time I headed off for the weaving room in the afternoon, I was sure the new arrangement was going to be very satisfactory.

The druid turned out to be an admirable teacher, though I was disappointed that our education didn't cover the magical things I suspected the Lady would have taught. In general, he delighted us with the stories of other peoples and countries, particularly the ancient gods and heroes of Greece.

We spent a lot of time talking about the Trojan War, and the strange, twisted fate of the family of heroes who lived out their lives of loyalty and treachery in that distant, sunny time. I was particularly fascinated by Helen.

'The legendary Helen,' he remarked, one hand stroking the gold beard of his chin. 'Her very name conjures up the destruction of men's souls. Have you ever noticed,' he added thoughtfully, 'how there are two kinds of beauty . . . that on the inside which cannot deceive, and that on the outside which often misleads?'

He went on to point out how something ugly is not necessarily bad, though we recoil from spiders and toads because we think them distasteful in shape and motion, and how beauty in itself is not an indication of good, for many poisonous things have a fair appearance.

It was typical of the time we spent with him, for while Cathbad seemed to be talking about one thing, we generally ended up thinking about another. And often I climbed the stairs to the weaving loft mulling over matters far different from the domestic concerns of the women I joined.

Perhaps that is the reason I was unaware of the disaster they were already scenting.

6
Death

As winter wore on, more children came to join us in the
Great Hall each day; with the snows so high and the
temperature so low, there was little to be done outdoors,
and often nowhere warm to stay except near the hearth.
Tales of tragedy and hard luck filled the talk around the
fire at night, and everyone agreed that it was one of the
worst winters in memory. The feast of Imbolc was held at
the beginning of February, but only those who lived
nearby could join us and the merriment was fitful and
measured out against the cold.

Food and fuel grew scarce in the households of the
freemen and they began to appeal to their king for help,
though usually it was Mama they spoke to.

'Your Highness,' Gladys said one day, her consternation showing in the use of the full formal title, 'you just
gave that woman half the salt meat we'd set aside for the
King's dinner.'

She gestured towards the bent and bundled figure of
the thatcher's wife, who plodded towards the Gates with
a small load of sticks and precious meat clutched in her
arms.

'I know, Gladys, I know,' Mama replied. 'But they
have such a large family, and are so low on fuel, they'll
barely squeak by as it is. At least we are comfortable in
the Great Hall, even if we're eating porridge. And we can
make do with soup instead of stew tonight.'

Gladys shook her head and muttered as she went about
her chores, and later that night I heard Mama talking with
Nonny.

'We can't let them go hungry, Nonny, you know that. It may mean our not being so elegant for a while, but that's a small price to pay to keep one's people from starving.'

Pretty soon there were so many requests it became easier to have the people share our food and warmth under one roof than to give it out piecemeal. So many folks crowded in to sleep around our fire, by the time mid-March arrived we were full to bursting and looking forward to a break in the weather as the days grew longer.

'I don't know where else to put them, Leo,' Mama sighed one evening as she and my father prepared for bed. 'We've got whole families staying in the Great Hall, and with the people who've come in this week, we've filled every corner and closet. What do you think about billeting some of them in the barn?'

I peeped out from between the curtains of my niche. Mama was seated at her dressing table taking the pins from her hair and my father came to stand behind her.

'Not the barn itself,' he answered, removing the enamelled barrette and letting the long copper tresses tumble down through his hands. 'The stock and what's left of the fodder are too precious to risk having people and fire close by. More likely we should have the stable hands double up in their quarters, and let the next few families use a part of the bunk area.'

'You think this cold's going to last much longer?' She leaned back against him and looked up at his face, tired and concerned and hoping for encouragement.

'It's hard to say, love. But I think we have to be as prepared as possible in case the good weather dallies too long in getting here.'

Mama nodded, and when he bent down to kiss the top of her head I sank back into my covers, reassured that our future was in such competent hands.

The very next day the temperature rose and the rains began, pelting down from heavy clouds and filling the brooks with thick muddy water. The snow turned to slush, grey and ugly under the thawing torrents, and there was much rejoicing that the season was about to change.

But the deluge continued for weeks on end, sometimes only a drizzle, sometimes pouring whole floods out of the sodden sky. One woke to the dim grey light of another sunless day and watched the afternoon slide into evening without a sign of twilight. Without the sun, spring would never come.

Water ran everywhere, sheeting down from above or dripping endlessly from soggy thatch, puddling between the paving stones of the courtyard or standing, stagnant and stinking, in the lower meadows.

Farmers who had seen their stock devoured by the winter cold now found their fields awash with muck and mire. Seed for the spring planting went to stave off hunger, and sheep died of starvation, their poor stinking feet too rotten to bear their weight while they searched for food.

Each day the line of supplicants at the gate increased, swelling like the river itself. They came with wives and children and grandparents, turning to their king for help when they could no longer help themselves.

Tents and awnings were strung up within the courtyard as makeshift shelters from the rain when there was no more space within the buildings, and a kind of grimness crept into house and barn alike.

'As if short rations and doubling up weren't bad enough,' grumbled the narrow-faced man who worked with Elidan the smith, 'now there's brats everywhere you turn.'

'I'll have none of that,' Rhufon said sharply, pulling a guy rope taut. 'There's trouble aplenty without your moaning and complaining. If you had any sense, you'd be thankful we've got a king who cares. Now wedge that post up here, or we'll never get this awning in place.'

While Mama tried to provide shelter for all who came to us, it was my father's task to feed them. He took hunting parties out daily, slogging through the wet woods or braving the rawness of the moors, and they considered themselves lucky to come back with a scrawny hare or perhaps a badger pried from his sett. Too often they returned empty-handed, for the animals of the wild were in as much trouble as those of the hearth, and always there was the rain.

Finally, one of the old workhorses was butchered in order to feed the masses. It was the black-and-white gelding Rhufon had nursed through infancy after its dam had been killed by wolves, and he spent a last few minutes with it alone, stroking its nose and trying to make some kind of peace with it, or perhaps himself, before the butcher's knife was brought out.

Mama and Gladys made huge pots of thick soup and served it in the Great Hall all day long so that everyone would have a chance to get out of the cold and wet for a few minutes at least.

Yet for all the fuss over having meat again, it provided little solace. The skies remained overcast, and even when the rain let up there was still no sunshine. Children came down with colds and one of the elders died. And at some point a baby cried from fever, rather than hunger, and by nightfall was dead in its mother's arms.

After that great numbers of people suddenly took sick, struck down between one hour and the next, and those who didn't die outright lay about weak and apathetic. Within days the number of bodies outstripped our ability to bury them, and despair skulked in the corners.

From the beginning Mama was everywhere, turning the

Great Hall into an infirmary, helping Kaethi make potions and trying to bring hope and comfort wherever possible.

'M'lady,' the Medicine Woman whispered one evening, 'we're getting way, way low on herbs.'

'Well, do the best you can,' Mama answered. 'Aren't there some in the chest upstairs in the family's room?'

'Aye, might be,' Kaethi answered guardedly. 'But those are for you and the King and the little ones here, in case of emergency.'

'I can't think of any greater emergency,' Mama said curtly. 'There's no point in keeping them back when there's so much need for them now.'

Her voice was more weary than harsh, as though she had been struggling across an endless bog all day, and she sent Kaethi upstairs to fetch the rest of the pharmacia with a sigh.

So there were new batches of brew made from the last of our reserve, and Kaethi leaned over the pots, shaking her head and muttering special words as she tried to save the whole country.

By the end of the first week of illness, less than half the usual number of people were well enough to gather for dinner in the Great Hall. We clutched our bowls of barley broth and crouched around the fire, for the pallets of the sick took up too much room to allow for the tables.

When the meal was over Nidan, as leader of the King's warriors, signalled for attention, and the group fell silent.

'We are doomed,' he began, staring at the haggard freemen seated within the fire glow. ''Tis the work of the Gods, angered by something we have done or left undone. And if we are to survive, we must find a way to appease Them.'

A murmur of assent greeted him, but someone else spoke up with a mixture of despair and anger. 'How are we to know which god, or what rite?'

There was a wrangle of ideas then, from followers of every god Rheged had ever known, and finally my father called for silence.

'It is abundantly clear that we need guidance. I, for one, am willing to ask the Old Gods, and' —he paused and looked directly at Cathbad— 'I hereby swear to do whatever is deemed necessary to protect my people.'

There came a sudden hush, as if each person had taken a soundless gasp of air and now held his breath. Those who had been watching my father when he spoke gaped at him in amazement, and others turned to stare as the meaning of his words reached them. I did not know exactly what this wordless awe foretold, but a terrible foreboding knotted my stomach.

In the silence, the druid rose and bowed before the King. 'You have always been both wise and just, M'lord. I hear you now offer to make the most sacred of sacrifices . . . the one on which all kingship is founded. Am I right in understanding this?'

'You are right,' came the answer. 'I make the pledge without reservation.'

Mama had gone very pale, as though she had not expected this, and I glanced between her and Cathbad, but saw no hostility.

The druid stared at my father with respect and admiration, and then looked round at the people. 'You are most fortunate to have such a leader. But I do not believe the old ritual will be required; at least we should consult with the Lady before any such decision is made. The Beltane is still ten days away, and if I can borrow a mare, I'll ride to the Sanctuary to confer with the Priestess. With luck, I'll be back before the fire must be lit.'

There was some discussion of details, and in the morning Cathbad and a small group of Nidan's men rode out. The druid was astride Featherfoot, which probably saved

71

her life, for all the other animals, except my father's stallion and two of the workhorses, were driven out into the wilds the next day in the hope that they would be able to forage something for themselves. If any of them survived, we would try to capture them come summer. I never saw my pony again, but begged Epona to see that he made it through the terrible spring and wandered into someone's steading later in the year.

One last horse was slaughtered, and for a while we had a broth with bits of meat in it.

Seven days after Cathbad left the little Prince took ill, and that night Mama was not at the hearth, though she came downstairs once the bairn was sleeping.

She looked worn and drawn as she moved slowly among the people, stopping to comfort this one or chat with that. I caught up with her as she approached Gladys, who was seated next to her sick daughter.

'How is she now?' Mama asked as the cook looked up at her.

'Still alive,' the stocky older woman said, 'but not any better. Not any better at all.'

'And how are the stores in the kitchen?'

Gladys shrugged her solid shoulders. 'About two barrels of oats and a half-barrel of barley left, a few more bags of pease, and the men brought in two grouse today. I used the last cabbage in the soup tonight, and we've still a few old turnips. There's lard, too, but with everything else almost gone, I don't know what we're going to do.'

The older woman's lumpy frame sagged in dejection, and Mama knelt down beside her.

'Why don't you let me sit with the girl while you go get a bowl of fresh water, and we'll bathe her face and neck to make her feel better.' Mama gestured towards the feverish form on the pallet and patted Gladys on the shoulder at the same time. 'I think you've been so busy taking care of everyone else, you haven't had a break yourself.'

At first the cook protested, then went off to fetch the water, and for a while Mama and I sat beside the girl I had never liked. I remembered the unkind things I'd thought about her in the weaving room and prayed she would get well soon. And I reminded the Goddess of Llyn, for no one had heard from her family for days now and I was afraid they too were stricken.

Later I was curled up next to Kaethi by the hearth when Mama stopped to ask how the supply of medicine was holding out.

'Can't tell anymore how much is thin medicine and how much plain water with a lot of words said over it,' Kaethi grumbled, reaching out to take Mama's hand. 'I don't like those circles under your eyes, M'lady. How long has it been since you've had any real sleep?'

'Oh, I'm all right,' Mama reassured her. 'I'm going back to our rooms once I've checked on the rest.' She made it sound as though that would be momentarily, but she was still seeing to other people when I climbed the stairs to bed.

I crawled under the covers and lay listening to the water dripping from the eaves, my stomach aching from fear as well as hunger. Spring and hope and even the Gods seemed a long way away, and I entreated every one I could think of, from the great Brigantia to Cernunnos the Antlered God, begging that no more sacrifices would be demanded of our court.

Next morning I woke to find Mama dozing in a chair beside my brother's bed, huddled in a fur robe next to the brazier which had long since burned out. She looked so tired and forlorn, I slipped out of bed and crept over to her, curling up on the rush-strewn floor and leaning my head against her knees. She stirred sleepily and reached

73

down to stroke my hair with fingers that were hot and dry against my forehead.

'Is it ever going to end?' I whispered.

'Of course, child, of course,' she assured me, coming more awake. 'All things come to an end, both good and bad.'

'But if it doesn't . . . if it keeps on like this . . . what is the ritual Cathbad's gone to find out about?'

I half-hoped she'd gone back to sleep and wouldn't answer my question, but after a silence she began twisting a lock of my hair round and round her finger. And when she spoke, it was in a whisper as faint as my own had been.

'It is said that in the Old Days the King was offered as a human sacrifice at Beltane, like the bull at Samhain. Such rites were done away with in the time of the Empire. But still the idea is there: a king must be willing to do whatever is demanded for the good of his people . . . and in very bad times that may mean being sacrificed himself.'

The knot in my stomach tightened as the words took form. In some way I'd known it all along, but like many terrible things, it had no shape until someone gave it a name.

My voice was a bare rasp of fear. 'In the weaving room, the women say it's never been this bad before . . .'

'They always say that when things get difficult,' she answered softly. Then she sat up suddenly as though coming fully awake. Reaching down, she took my chin in her hand and tipped my face up to look at hers. 'Remember, Gwen, no matter who says what, the important thing is to understand what needs to be done, and then do it. No matter how hard it is, or how much pain you feel. It's as simple as that, really. Once you know what you have to do, you just do it . . .'

A shiver ran through her, and for a moment she smiled

gently at me. Then she threw back the robe and got wearily to her feet. 'Here, you bundle up while I go down to the kitchen and see what I can do to help Gladys. Heaven knows how we'll manage Beltane in the midst of all this . . .'

So I crawled up into the chair, and she tucked the robe around me before going over to check on Nonny and the babe. Once she was satisfied nothing had changed, she tiptoed towards the door.

'Tell Nonny to relight the brazier when the baby wakes up,' she admonished, pausing at the doorway and putting out a hand to steady herself.

I don't know how long she stood there swaying before her body crumpled and slid slowly to the floor.

'Mama!' I screamed, forgetting the sleeping household. 'Mama . . . Mama!'

My father was stumbling out of the big bed and moving towards her, and Nonny came groggily to her feet while the baby started to cry. One of the serving girls from the Great Hall raced up the stairs, and by the time I reached the threshold where my mother lay, there was such a crowd around her I couldn't get near.

They laid her on the big bed, and Kaethi spent the day padding back and forth between the herb closet and the bedside, trying everything left to save her Queen. I ran what errands I could for her, or helped Nonny with the baby, who cried most of the day. My father sat by the brazier, staring at the woman who had been the delight of his life, and praying, I knew, to whatever gods he hoped would pay attention. From time to time he moved to the bedside or spelled Kaethi in applying cool compresses to Mama's forehead, but she only moaned and twisted in her delirium and he was helpless to reach her.

She died the next morning, with the dawn, and the little Prince followed her within an hour.

7

Beltane

I huddled in the hay, rocking back and forth with my hands clapped over my ears. Nonny's wailing went on endlessly, echoing through my head like the cry of the dispossessed.

More than anything else I wanted a warm, sweet embrace to curl up in; to be held and protected and cuddled until the cold weight in my chest melted and went away. But between the keening of the women and the stricken silence of my father, there was no solace to be found. So I sought sanctuary in the barn, desperately trying to shut out the thought of a world without Mama.

In the next stall my father's stallion nickered as someone tugged gently on my hands. I opened my eyes just enough to see Kaethi squatting next to me, her tear-stained face peering at me through the gloom. Reluctantly I let her pull my hands down from my head.

'There, there, child . . . you can't spend all day hiding,' she crooned gently. With deft caresses she began to smooth the ache from my forehead.

'She isn't really dead, is she?' I whimpered, and when the Medicine Woman nodded I shut both eyes tight and retreated into a ball of misery.

'Nay, there'll be enough time for grieving after,' the crone said, taking me by the shoulders and shaking me with surprising vigour. 'There's the Beltane to complete. You must come out for the rites, Missy . . . there's no choice but to follow the ritual.'

'Ritual!' The thought squeezed the last of my breath from me and I stared at her, suddenly very still inside.

Terrible pictures prodded me, of the caldron, the druid and vague forms performing unspeakable sacrifices. 'What ritual?'

'Why, the lighting of the bonfire. You know there's none can stay away from the Beltane rites or the Gods won't provide the fire, or spring, or crops growing rich in the fields come summer.'

'And Mama?' I asked, pushing the thought of the Beltane tradition as far away as possible. 'What about Mama?'

'Her body will be buried tomorrow, after the May Dance around the Pole. They've taken a log and hollowed it out, just as in the old days, for there's no time to build a fancy coffin.'

I nodded, thinking dully that at least it wouldn't be a cold stone box like the ones in the Roman cemetery outside Carlisle.

'So we must go in . . .' my friend persisted.

The howling in my head had subsided, but I hung back, still unwilling to leave the safety of the barn.

'It's late, child . . . the day's almost over, and it's time to help Gladys.' Kaethi's plea was becoming urgent. 'Gladys needs your help . . . and your father needs it!'

Somewhere I could hear Mama whispering over and over, '. . . No matter how hard it is . . .'

I gulped and nodded mutely.

In the Hall people moved with hollow step, speaking softly against the low moaning that came from the upper chambers. No one seemed to notice that the rain had stopped, though the outer door of the Hall stood open without water pouring in. Nature now confined her tears to those within the court.

Comments passed quietly from one to another; yes, the logs for the bonfire were well laid and waiting; no, the druid had not returned from his trip to the Sanctuary; and

77

perhaps it was most fitting for the young Queen's body to be buried in the old manner after all, rather than consigned to the Need-fire, as someone had suggested.

I started at that, my shoulders twitching at the thought of flames licking around Mama's form. Kaethi had her hand on the back of my neck, and she gently pushed me into the kitchen where Gladys was already working at the hearth.

In the past, we children had made a game of helping to extinguish the life-giving fires, searching out every spark in hearth or brazier, lantern or torch. With it came the security of knowing that all other peoples between the two rivers were doing the same as we trailed behind Gladys like chicks after their mother, scattering the ashes with mock seriousness.

But today it was in deadly earnest, for even a single ember hidden away in the corner of the hearth would keep the Need-fire from lighting, and this year, of all years, we must have that sign of the Gods' blessing. I dared not think of what would happen if the smallest coal were overlooked, and silently sifted each patch of ash through my fingers lest any hint of warmth go undetected.

Afterward I made my way back to the sleeping loft where Nonny fell upon me with great racking sobs, stroking my hair and crooning as though I were her favourite come back to life. I stared at her dry-eyed, numb and wordless inside, and she went scurrying off to get our wraps, for the trip to the Sacred Grove would be damp and cold, and we would need warm clothing.

While she was gone, I walked slowly over to the bed where Mama and the baby lay. They looked as though they were asleep, peaceful and serene, and I thought for a moment I could wake them with a touch. But my fingers found only a cold stillness, and I drew my hand back with a gasp as Nonny returned.

'Here, here, my pet. 'Tis something to keep you snug and dry, if we can find someone to carry you across the river.'

So I joined the rest of the court at the Gates, walking through the late afternoon as in a nightmare, powerless to change either the death behind or the fate ahead.

This time there was no gleeful splashing through the broad, shallow ford of the river, no light laughter and gay spirits to rejoice in summer's coming. The occasional words shared and greetings exchanged were glum and sullen at heart. Those who were sound enough carried friends or relatives too weak and sick to walk by themselves, and all concentrated on slogging up the muddy track to the top of the Sacred Hill.

The people formed a restless circle around the giant pyre that awaited the Gods' coming. The young men took turns twirling the sharpened point of the wimble against the ancient Beltane log and everyone watched intently for the eruption of flame that would prove the Gods attended us.

I huddled in Nonny's arms, safe under her cowhide wrap like a small child, listening to the rise and fall of the people's mood. Twice the tinder caught and a cry of hope sprang up from their throats, lifting cautiously as the torches were lit, and falling to an ominous growl when the flames guttered and went out.

The crowd began to mill about nervously, the faint tremble of hysteria nipping at its edges. When the torches died for the third time, someone shouted 'A sign! It's a sign! The Need-fire won't catch without a sacrifice!'

'Oh, Nonny,' I whimpered, 'what will they do if it won't light?'

'Shush, child! Of course it will light; it has to,' she muttered back, but I knew in my heart she was unsure. Without the Need-fire new-made and gladly leaping, the summer would be filled with pestilence and despair. The world would grow cold, and the warmth would go out of the sun, just as it had gone out of Mama.

I clung to my old nurse, thinking of Mama and my brother frozen in time, like the robin I had found frozen in flight outside the gates early in the winter. It seemed so poignant somehow, like a child's footprint captured forever in the snow, and the weight within my chest broke as a flood of tears sprang forth.

My sobs turned into howls, and I poured out my anguish over Mama's death even as the crowd screamed for my father's blood, our different agonies blending into one great supplication to heaven.

'Look, child, look at the King!'

Nonny shook me hard and pushed me upright until I was staring, wide-eyed and terrified, at the pyre.

The fire had caught at last, and there, silhouetted against the licking flames, the twisted form of my father capered and leapt about at the top of the roaring pyramid. He was dancing in the centre of the blaze, making himself a bridge between the Gods and his people. It was the fulfilment of his promise as their king, and I stared into the heart of the inferno with awe and horror as the whole world blurred into a wheel of sparks.

Years later Edwen the Bard would sing of how the King had taken up one of the burning torches and, in spite of his crippled legs and shaky step, clambered up the wood-pile to thrust the brand deep into the drier centre, where the flames had quickly caught. But at that moment I saw my father as half man, half sacrifice, and I screamed aloud as the sight burned into my memory.

The people cheered as their king climbed down, and rushing forward, they hoisted him on to their shoulders and paraded around the bonfire in gleeful triumph. The magic, the marvel of salvation surged through them and found voice in great shouts of praise for the King who had delivered us.

Too weak to rise from Nonny's arms, I threw back my head in terror and rapture, and found a cautious cluster of stars peeping through the tattered clouds. They were the first we had seen in months, and such a beautiful sight I tried desperately to tell Nonny about them, babbling and gesturing incoherently.

From far away I saw her struggling to calm me; then someone took my body from her, and I heard Vida clucking sadly, 'Poor little tyke, sick as her mother no doubt . . . just feel the fever she has!'

The crowd around us was parting as people faded into the shadows when we started down the track. And then there was Mama standing on the path ahead, waiting with the smile of the May Queen on her face.

'Come, Gwen, come help me gather flowers for the crown,' she called, laughing and skipping merrily ahead. She was as radiant as I had ever seen her, and her invitation was so full of joy and love, I smiled and reached out my arms to her.

It was the last thing I remembered for many days, and whether she was really there that night or just part of my delirium I'll never know, but she has never truly left me since.

8

Bedivere

I was so wrapped up in memories, I didn't realize Brigit
had spoken until she reached across and caught hold of
my arm. The misery of that long-ago spring gave way to
the rhythmic sound of hoofbeats and jingling bridles, and
the new green of the woods around us.

I looked over at my friend and found her watching me
intently.

'Are you all right, Gwen?' she asked, concern furrow-
ing her brow.

I nodded, slowly coming back to the present.

'Not moping or brooding? I don't want to be sitting up
all night keeping watch that you don't try to run away
again,' she said, only half in jest.

'Have no fear . . . I was remembering my childhood,
and there's no way to run back to that. And thinking
about Mama . . . I wish you'd known her.'

'What with the way Nonny used to carry on, and the
comments here and there among the women, I might just
as well have known her,' Brigit said gently. 'She seems to
have been a perfect saint, from what everyone always
said.'

I smiled at the notion of Mama's sudden inclusion in
the Christian Church. Loyal, considerate, laughing, regal,
playful, gentle, gracious . . . she had been all these and
more. But the mantle of self-denial and withdrawal from
the world that Christian holy people wear was definitely
not something my mother would have chosen. Her love
of people and good rich comradery was part of what had
made her a good queen, and I thought it unlikely she

could have changed that part of her nature. Perhaps it is impossible to be a devout Christian and a queen as well.

'Well' —I laughed— 'for all of that, Mama was about as pagan as they come.'

Arthur's lieutenant came trotting over with the news that we should stop at the roadhouse up ahead for our midday meal.

'Give the horses a chance to rest, as well,' he added.

The tavern was a comfortable old place. Extra rooms with dry-stone walls had been added on to a Roman way station, and the whole building huddled under a thick roof of thatch. The owners must have been expecting us, for the tables were laden with food and a room had been prepared in case I wanted privacy. Lavinia thought it would be more seemly to have our meal brought in to us there; but the room was small and oppressive and made me feel all the more a captive, so I joined the rest of the group in the courtyard where the trestles were laid.

I knew the innkeeper and his wife slightly, as they had come to the Councils at Watercrook whenever court was held there. The woman was a big, openhearted sort, eager to show off her culinary skills and somewhat flustered to be hosting so notable a party. Her husband was as trim and tidy as she was blowsy, and he set out quantities of good ale and mead, no doubt to make up for the lack of wine.

'Nothing but our best for Arthur's men,' he stated, thereby earning a round of applause from my escort.

After a meal of cold meat and cheese, barley cakes and pungent pickles, our hostess brought forth a pudding that was topped with a glaze of berry preserves.

Bedivere dished up two bowls of the dessert and, bringing one to me, sat down across the table.

On closer observation, Arthur's lieutenant was younger than I'd thought, with the kind of craggy face that loses

83

the roundness of youth early. His tawny hair had the look of hornbeam leaves in autumn, and though he spoke Latin among his men, he addressed me in the native tongue of the Cumbri. The badge of the Red Dragon which blazed forth on the shoulder of his cloak was the only indication that he came from Arthur's court.

He nodded politely. 'I hope the pace isn't too tiring for you.'

'Not at all,' I said, wondering what sort of woman he took me for. Perhaps the southern ladies really did do all their travelling by litter. 'In fact, I would be quite happy if we moved a little faster. Would that be possible?' I asked hopefully.

'I'm afraid not,' he replied between mouthfuls, 'what with Merlin not wanting to strain his old gelding, and the baggage train to look after. But I'll see what I can do when we reach the main Road.' His eyes crinkled in a smile as he added, 'I take it that you are not one of those women who are terrified if they have to manage as much as a trot?'

I grinned at the understatement, and nodded. 'Indeed, I suppose I was raised as much ahorse as afoot. And I can tell you, there is nothing I would like better than to be racing along the sands of Ravenglass this very minute.'

I realized after I'd said it that the remark could be taken amiss, but Bedivere seemed unperturbed. It was hard to tell whether he was very diplomatic or just insensitive, but I reminded myself to watch my tongue.

'It was an honour to hear your bard last night,' the lieutenant went on. 'And one I had been looking forward to for some time.'

'Edwen?' I was surprised that anyone beyond our borders should have heard of our family chronicler.

'Oh yes,' Bedivere assured me. 'He had a fine reputation in the south, and well earned. I used to think I'd like to become a bard myself, if I hadn't been chosen to be a warrior.'

He finished his dessert and put down the bowl. 'I hope the fact we could not wait for the Lady doesn't disappoint you too much. Surely the trip would be less tiresome for you if you had more familiar people among your companions.'

'Not at all,' I assured him, touched by his thoughtfulness. It dawned on me that being escort to a stranger who would soon be their queen might be an uneasy business for these men; they knew as little of me as I of them, and had no real idea what my needs and desires would be. So I tried to put Bedivere's mind at ease by telling him the Lady and I were not what you would call 'familiar,' for all that we'd known about each other for some time.

'I gather that she has much power and support here in the north,' he commented. 'At least, that is what we hear at Arthur's court.'

Bedivere had risen to his feet, and I hoped the subject was closed, but he turned to watch me and there was nothing for it but to respond.

'It's true that most of our people have returned to the Old Ways,' I said, carefully avoiding saying anything about the Priestess herself.

My companion cocked a quizzical eyebrow as I stood up, but our hostess came bustling forward with a bouquet of flowers before he could say anything further.

'For our Queen-to-be . . .' she announced, making a formal curtsy. Then suddenly she threw her arms around me in a big hug. 'Who would have thought our own little Gwen . . . that we broke bread with at Lammas so many times past . . .'

I hugged her back, thinking how typical she was of the warmhearted people I'd known all my life and how I'd miss them in the future.

We continued our journey, coming into Kendal where the river runs quick and clear.

As we approached the settlement, people turned to wave and cheer. They saw me as the kinswoman who would represent them at the High Court, and therefore smiled and blessed us with all the different signs that the different gods demand.

In the square the brokers paused beside the wool scales, turning from weighing out the fleeces to salute us as we went past. And from the spinning galleries the women and girls nodded and curtsied, their spindles put aside for a moment as they leaned upon balcony railings and smiled happily at our procession. In one place the Road passed so close to a spinner's house that a child on the gallery tossed flower petals down on me, then hid, giggling, behind her mother's skirts.

Along the stream bank, pieces of finished fabric were stretched on tenterhooks to dry. Freshly dyed, they made a patchwork of yellow and crimson, blue and warm brown, all interspersed with soft creams and the stiffer, harder greys from the Herdwick sheep. And of course there was the deep green for which the town is famous.

I remembered the cape I had made for Arthur; thick and dark and covered with embroidery and signs of the Goddess worked in my own hand. It was the best wedding gift I could think of, considering that we hardly knew each other. My memory of our one meeting, long ago, was dominated by others, and I had no sense at all of his personality, nor any emotions about him specifically. He was as much a cipher now as he had been when the betrothal was arranged.

Even his country was unknown to me, and I wondered again if there would be great open moors to go riding over, and Standing Stones that capture the cycles of the

Universe, and Beltane fires to rouse the earth and bless the people with fertility.

Or would it be, as Vinnie said, a place of proper laws and formal manners, where the only dancing to be found would be within the court and not wild and free, out in the starlit meadows? The very thought brought the lump back to my throat, and with an inward groan I turned my thoughts away from the subject.

Brigit was riding placidly beside me, and I looked over at her, wondering what she felt about leaving Rheged. We would be spending the night with her family, and it seemed odd to be going to visit strangers whose children had been so much a part of my life. The memory of her arrival floated to the surface of my mind, and I gave myself over to it gratefully.

9

The Hostages

We moved through the months following Mama's death in a kind of constant grief.

I had lain ill for weeks, and recovered to find a world irreparably changed. Not only Mama but Vida and Gladys' daughter had died, and many more besides. Even Llyn was gone, and no one, least of all me, felt like laughing and playing.

My father's decision that I should learn to ride Featherfoot did little to cheer me up, for the sorrel mare reminded me constantly of Mama. Then too, I was not allowed to take her out of the exercise yard by myself, and everyone else was too busy to accompany us beyond the gate.

So we struggled through the summer, weak in spirit and sad of heart, and when it was certain that the people of Appleby would be seeing enough of the harvest to tide them through the winter, my father moved the court to Ambleside.

Here the people were more cheerful, for they had had only the bad weather to contend with, and escaped the ravages of fever. Our household's spirits began to lift, and when the King announced that we would accompany him to the Standing Stones in Furness to witness an important ceremony, there was almost a feeling of festivity in the air.

It seemed we were going to meet a family of Irish refugees who were fleeing from the internal wars of their homeland. They had asked permission to settle among us, and planned to give us two of their children as hostages.

I was shocked and curious at the same time. My knowledge of the Irish had come strictly from hearsay; it was their pirates who raided our shores, and their warriors who had enslaved the Cumbri of Wales before my forefather Cunedda had ridden down from Lothian to free them.

Nonny's family had been among those forced into slavery, so according to her the Irish were fierce and arrogant, singers of grisly songs and drinkers of blood. Kaethi said they were gay and laughing, in love with the Gods and never conquered. I wondered who was right, or if they could be both at once.

The idea of new, and motherless, little children within our household was totally unexpected. I wondered what they would be like, if we would understand each other's speech and how they would fit into the life at court. I hoped they were old enough so they wouldn't need a nurse, for Nonny was not likely to welcome them wholeheartedly. She had still not recovered from the death of Mama and the little Prince, and went about her chores with the distracted air of someone who is listening for unseen voices. It might do her good to have a new bairn to look after . . . just not an Irish one.

On the day of the refugees' arrival I was sent to watch for them, and climbed into the branches of a huge oak where the track levels out and heads for the stone circle.

It is a point suspended midway between the windy moor and the peaceful shimmer of the estuary below. Behind me Black Combe Fell turned its heathery back to the shore, while gusts of cloud and mist whipped in over its flank, driven by a cutting wind. It was the west wind from across the Irish Sea, sending fish and wave before it and scouring the seaward side of the mountain until only the barest windwarped plants remained. Yet in the protection of the mountain's hunched shoulders summer lay lush and green along the stream bank and the wind barely stirred the banner by our tents. Below to the south, at the bottom of the brook's rocky course, the waters of the Duddon estuary glimmered among the mud flats, silver and gold and lit from an unknown source. It looked as though some god had thrown down a skein of molten treasure.

The strangers came into sight about midday, moving slowly up the hilly track. I ran to tell my father, and then to find Kaethi, who was making the guest tent ready.

'They don't seem to be so many,' I said, helping to spread out the sheepskin rugs between the pallets. 'Maybe only a dozen or so. And all on foot.'

'But of course, child. How would they get horses across in a curragh?' She stood back to survey our work, and handed me a pitcher. 'Now, you go fill that from the beck and we'll be all set.'

'Well, they brought some kind of animal with them,' I persisted. 'Not big enough to ride, but larger than sheep, walking along with them and not being herded.'

'Pigs, maybe?' Kaethi speculated. 'I've heard the Irish set great store by their pigs. Ah, we'll find out soon enough. Get on with that pitcher, Missy, or they'll be here before we're ready to make them welcome.'

So I trotted down to the stream, finding a bright pool amid the grey rocks where the water swirled clear and cool. Normally I would have dallied there, watching for the flash of a kingfisher or the antics of a dipper, but today I filled the pitcher and scampered back to the tents.

By the time the guest quarters met with Kaethi's approval, our company had arrived. We joined the rest of the household along the edge of the track, watching the band of strangers come into camp. My father had ridden out to meet them and he escorted them into our midst as graciously as if they had been emissaries of an allied king rather than refugees begging for shelter.

The grown-ups were tall and redheaded, with the same high colour and freckles as the people of Argyle. Both men and women were garbed in bright-coloured clothes with finely worked borders to their cloaks, and they wore an impressive array of golden jewellery.

They didn't seem to be such brutes, and I scanned the party, wondering which of the babes would be left with us. My attention was caught by a dark-haired boy who walked with a limp. He held fast to a stout leather leash at the end of which was an enormous grey dog, and my jaw dropped open at the sight.

The animal's huge rectangular head came almost to the boy's chest, and in its rough coat and leggy build it was unlike any other dog I'd ever seen, for the hounds in our kennel had lean muzzles and satin coats patched with brown and black and white. I wondered what these beasts were used for, and how they kept that tangle of hair from getting matted and torn.

All told, there were four such creatures and they walked along sedately, neither lunging at the leash nor paying attention to the mutterings of our curious greeting. I decided to ask the boy about his charge as soon as possible.

The company disappeared into their tent, dogs and all, and it wasn't until late afternoon that the men began to emerge, making their way to my father's lodging and joining him in the customary wine-sharing. The weather had lifted, and gave promise of bringing a fair summer evening, so we set up the pillows and wooden bowls near the roasting spits at the edge of the trees and prepared to break bread with our guests.

There was no chance to meet the boy with the dog before the ritual began at the Standing Stones, however, for all the children were kept under the careful supervision of the women.

At last, when the meal was over and the long twilight had settled in, we made our way along the moorland bench to the circle of stones.

Laid out by the Gods before the beginning of time, these sacred spots are scattered across the land like fairy rings from the days of giants. Always near an ancient track, always set by stars and sun or moon, they serve as universal meeting points for all people; a place apart, where man is stripped of war and pretence, pride and possessions, and meets his fellow with the honesty of his own integrity. This was not the first meeting within a stone circle I had attended, but it was certainly the most exciting.

My father came on horseback, but dismounted when we were all seated within the ancient arc and made his way slowly to the centre where the King's chair was already in place. Nidan and Rhufon accompanied him, each carrying one of the long pointed shafts that end in brackets holding torches. These they planted in the turf behind the King, then stood at attention as formal witness to the proceedings

After the Circle was called closed and the words to open the Council were spoken, my father looked around the gathering and inquired, 'Who has business with the King of Rheged?'

The leader of the Irish group stood up and came before my sire, walking slowly as though still weighing the wisdom of his action. At last he straightened his shoulders, bowed to the King and, turning, addressed the whole assemblage:

'I am Angus, a man of Ulster, come to Rheged with the wish to settle and abide peaceably by your laws.' He spoke clearly, without preamble or flourish, and his accent had a pleasant lilt to it.

'And why do you wish to leave Ireland?' asked my father.

'We were a family of high rank with our king, but he has been killed by his brother, and it is unsafe for us to stay.'

The answer was flat and straightforward, perhaps to cover whatever pain the man might be feeling.

'And what surety do you offer if I give you refuge?' My father's response was equally direct, and one would have thought it was a business deal for the purchase of a cow.

'My daughter Brigit, who is a good girl and will serve you well, and my nephew Kevin, son of Finn, my brother and co-leader in this venture. Both children are firstborn and have an inheritance of honour in their homeland.'

'Bring them forward,' the King said, and two of the women, who had obviously been crying, detached themselves from the group and escorted the hostages to the King's chair. The torches flickered in the soft twilight, and our people leaned forward to get a better view of the children.

One was a tall, angular girl with red hair, and the other was the dark boy who limped. They were both much older than any of us expected, and a murmur of surprise ran through our household.

'He was born with a dragging foot,' the Irishman explained hastily, 'but is very quick with words and thought, and was being trained by one of the best story-tellers in the whole of Ireland. Perhaps you can apprentice him to your own bard, or set him to help your scribe. It should not be difficult to teach him to write.'

My father had not laughed aloud in months, but I thought I could see an amused twinkle in his eyes at the man's assumption that we had a scribe. With no one in

Rheged needing to read, there was no reason to retain someone to write.

The King stared thoughtfully at the women and children for a bit, stroking his moustaches in an absent fashion. At last he nodded and turned his attention back to Angus.

'Where do you wish to settle?' he inquired, apparently satisfied with the nature of the hostages.

'That, M'lord, is up to you. We would prefer a steading of our own; we'll clear the land and till the soil, since we're not overfond of sheep-herding. We trust your judgement in giving us an area that will meet our needs.'

'Very well,' my father replied. 'If you go east along the edges of this Bay, you'll find promising land near the Roman Road that leads south. I will draw you a map and show you where to land. Or if you would prefer to go on foot, I can provide you with horses and some gear.'

The Irishman looked surprised, apparently not having expected such a helpful welcome.

My father's eyes were sparkling with good humour and he continued. 'Those are details we can take care of later. Now, as to the hostages, there are some things you should know.'

He motioned to the youngsters, who came to stand on either side of his chair. The girl simply stood there, wrapped in a shawl of many colours, staring at the ground with quiet dignity. But the boy gazed openly at the King, then at the people of the circle.

'It is a special trust you give to me in handing over the heirs to your line,' my father began, his voice reflecting the solemnness of the occasion. 'It shall be as a pledge between us. There will be no insurrection, no breaking of the peace or plotting of treason on your part. And for my part, I promise to hold you and yours as freemen of the land, and will guide and protect and include your children as members of my household. They shall be treated as

94

would any fosterling, with care and consideration for their welfare. I will not have you worry,' he added, turning to the mothers, 'that they might be mistreated or ill-used. It is a poor leader who does not recognize the respect and dignity due to children who have been placed in his care.'

The spaces between the Stones had filled with shadow, and above us the stars were beginning to dance in the darkening sky. One of the women sniffed loudly, and the King turned again to their leader. 'Do you agree to these terms?'

The man nodded silently and my father had the hostages join hands, after which their kinsman put his hand over the two smaller ones. Carefully the King laid his own palms over and under the intertwined knots of fingers, saying, 'Do you, Angus of Ulster, swear on the lives of your children to keep the peace of this kingdom and acknowledge freely that I, Leodegrance of Rheged, am your leader and king?'

The big redheaded Irishman bowed his head, but spoke out firmly: 'I do so swear.'

The hands were unclasped, and my father shifted to a more comfortable position in his chair. There was a collective stirring and sighing throughout the audience, and somewhere in the distance I caught the faint hoot of an owl.

Turning to the girl, my father smiled. 'How old are you, Brigit-with-the-flaming-hair?'

She had stared at the ground during the entire ceremony, but now raised her head and answered in the same firm manner as her parent: 'I shall be thirteen following the next Samhain.'

'And you, Kevin?'

The boy bowed solemnly. 'I turned twelve this spring, M'lord.' He already had the diction of a bard, and I suspected that when his voice changed it would be easy to forget his deformed foot and frail look.

'Both of an age to be company to my own Guinevere, and no doubt good for her spirits as well as mine,' my father said as he looked about the circle again, and slowly asked, 'Is there anyone who opposes this arrangement?'

When no one objected, he nodded, satisfied.

'It is as has been spoken,' he intoned, closing the matter and nodding to the Irishman. 'Would you and the ladies like to keep the children with you until you are ready to leave on the morrow? It is a hard enough parting without the pain of knowing they are in the same camp but already under someone else's wing.'

There was a flurry of appreciation from the guests, and then Brigit and Kevin were swallowed up by their guard of women and my father began to call the Council closed.

When he came to the final prayer, he paused and added a new thought of his own:

'And for this reminder that life flows on, that we must move beyond the time of mourning, we thank you, O Brigantia. The moiras of all humans change and flow, and only the most arrogant think they have seen Fate sealed. These children, who are well nigh young adults, will find the patterns of their lives entwined forever with ours. But they are not the only ones to be affected; their presence brings a new energy, a new colour to the court of Rheged, and surely we shall all be the richer, and happier, for it. So let us call this Council well met, Great Goddess, and pray our agreement finds favour in Your eyes.'

It rounded out the ceremony nicely, and I went off to bed with a new gladness of heart, eager to get to know the hostages even if they were Irish.

10

Brigit and Kevin

We were up early the next morning, breaking camp and preparing to say goodbye to the Irish clan. As he had promised, my father supplied them with horses and saddles, and in return Angus insisted that we accept one of the big dogs as a gift.

'To tell the truth,' the Irishman said gruffly, 'the boy is powerfully attached to the creature and quite good at handling him. It will make the parting less lonely if he has something to remember his childhood by.'

We were on our separate ways by the time the sun had gilded the estuary below, the Irish heading off to their new home and our household striking northward along the mountain dale to Lake Windermere and the fort at Ambleside. The boy Kevin stayed behind with Rhufon and the men who were bringing along the tents and trappings at a slower pace, while Brigit rode next to me in the retinue of the king.

It was a glorious morning, full of larks and high fleecy clouds and a gentle breeze.

'Is it so different from your homeland?' I asked, watching the new girl stare about her once we were under way.

'Perhaps, a little. Though the stone circle is very like the ones we have in Ireland. Tell me,' she asked carefully, 'is there a chapel near the King's palace?'

'Palace?' I responded, surprised. It had not occurred to me that she might expect to live in a building specifically made for a king.

'You know, your home. You do have a family home, do you not?'

'Well, yes . . . in fact, several,' I told her, explaining that when we followed my father we might stay in anything from a Roman bathhouse to a rich steading such as Patterdale or the Great Hall at Appleby with its sleeping lofts and tall wooden pillars that held up the high roof.

'But I don't think any is what you'd call a palace,' I concluded. Worried that she might be disappointed, I hastily pointed out that it meant we got to travel a lot. 'Didn't you travel with the Court when you were in Ulster?'

She shook her head slightly. 'Not often. We stayed at the King's palace, even when he wasn't there . . . There was a chapel, however. And here?'

'Well,' I temporized, 'there's the monastery Saint Ninian built—the White House, on the edge of the Solway. And occasionally one of the wandering Christians comes to court, or lives for a while in a cave by one of the rivers. There's the ruins of a church in Carlisle, I think, but it's deserted . . . Is your family Christian?'

'I am,' she answered proudly, 'I and my parents, though my cousin Kevin's branch is not. But then, they've never met a saint, so perhaps it will take them longer to find the Path.'

I looked at my new companion with even greater interest; at last I could hear at first hand about the faith these people followed.

The morning went by in talk of miracles and magic, of hermits and holy men and the great teachings that they espoused. As Brigit told it the saints sounded very like the druids, except that their sacrifices were different and they worshipped a god who had become human himself. She said the new god took a personal interest in what you did—unlike the Old Gods, who insist you come to them and may or may not listen to your prayers.

I already knew that when the Old Gods chose, they could sweep you up into the vastness of their embrace and carry you to the threshold of joy or terror. It didn't sound as though the followers of the White Christ had much experience with that, so I decided inwardly I'd stay with the Old Ways and hoped the Irish girl wouldn't seek to convert me to hers.

When we came to the shore of the first lake, my father called a halt to rest the horses and have a midday stretch. Brigit and I ran down to the pebbly shore, munching a handful of nuts and cheese and still chatting about all manner of things. I was enjoying her company immensely, for she was the first real friend I'd made since Llyn died, and I looked forward to showing her everything I could about our land.

She dipped her hand in the waters of the lake and drew it back with an exclamation of surprise.

'Coniston's always cold,' I told her, and then pointed to the island by the far shore. 'That's where the cormorants perch to dry their wings, and the crested grebes build floating nests and sometimes do their fishing in the moonlight. It's not my favourite lake, but it does have good fish.'

'You have other lakes?'

'Mm-hm. There's Windermere, where we're heading now, and Ullswater, with its great stags, and the Black Lake, where the Lady lives.' I made the sign and then wondered if it bothered my guest, but she seemed not to notice. Perhaps she was not one of those Christians who abhor all other beliefs.

'What lady is that?' she asked, pulling her bright shawl around her shoulders, for we had come to a spot where the trees grew close to the water and it was noticeably cooler.

'Why, the Priestess . . . the Lady of the Lake. Don't

99

your people know about the Goddess, and Her Lady, and all?'

'You mean the Morrigan?' She hastily made a sign of her own. 'Everyone knows about her. But who is this Lady?'

I explained how a small number of women are trained in the same arts as the druids, and when the old Priestess dies a new one is named to take her place and continue teaching others for the rest of her life.

'And she's known as the Lady of the Lake because the Sanctuary is at the Black Lake,' I concluded.

'Is she the leader of the druids?' Brigit asked cautiously.

'I don't think so, though they hold her in great respect. She's more a teacher than a governor, I guess . . . and a great healer. People go to the Sanctuary for all kinds of problems.'

'Is it like a monastery, then, only for women?'

'I don't know.' I shrugged. 'I've never been to either the Sanctuary or a monastery. But I think there must be both men and women at the Lake, while there's only men in Saint Ninian's house at Whithorn.'

Brigit thought about that for a minute, then smiled. 'At home, the Saint for whom I am named has started a holy house just for women. I didn't have a chance to meet her,' she added wistfully, 'but perhaps she will travel to Britain one day.'

We began to make our way back to the group of adults, walking carefully because the roots of the trees twined and looped out of the ground and threatened to trip the unobservant. One of them had grown round a stone and when the earth wore away, the rock was captured in a kind of living cage. I have always suspected there are a pair of gods at work here, the one of the stone and the other of the tree, and I silently saluted both as we moved past.

'How do you get to be a saint?' I asked.

'Oh, I guess mostly by living in accordance with the Holy Laws, and teaching them to others,' Brigit said.

'So, in a way, the Lady of the Lake is a saint?'

The Christian girl came to an abrupt halt, the look of shock plain on her freckled face. Then she burst out laughing. 'Well, it's the wrong god, but otherwise, maybe so. I'm sure the monks and priests wouldn't approve to hear her called so, however. They don't like the Old Ways, you know, and say it's unwise to consider them holy.'

I nodded and grinned, very much liking this new friend with the lilting voice and full laugh.

Getting to know the Irish boy was quite another matter. My days were full of work with Brigit, since Gladys found plenty for us to do in the kitchen, and Kevin was off doing things with the men. The only time I saw him was at dinner, when we joined the other youngsters in serving the adults. There was much carrying and fetching but precious little chance to chat. On top of that, he seemed shy and reticent whenever I spoke to him, and it was beginning to look as if we'd never have a chance to get acquainted.

Then I went loping down to the stables one morning, planning to curry Featherfoot. As I came round the corner of the barn, I found Rhufon by the stable door intently watching what was happening in the paddock.

Kevin was astride a young chestnut gelding, putting him through his paces. He circled the paddock twice, keeping the beast at a steady trot, then urged him into a canter along the far fence while the Stable Master looked on.

'Seems he's no stranger to horses,' Rhufon commented as I came up. 'I've had him riding every animal here—

101

except the King's, of course—and there isn't one he can't handle.'

'Then maybe he can go riding with me,' I suggested with elaborate casualness, trying to sound as if this were merely a practical observation instead of a whole, bright future that had leapt suddenly into my head. 'You know Featherfoot isn't getting enough exercise, and if I had an escort who's that good with horses, there'd be no danger in letting us go out on our own.'

Rhufon gave me a long, slow look of appraisal, the teasing in his eyes holding his mouth in a thoughtful non-grin as he nodded very, very slowly.

'Could be, Missy . . . could be,' he finally opined.

'I'll have her saddled in no time,' I promised, whisking into the stable before he could change his mind. Within minutes, Kevin and I were through the gates and over the causeway that crosses the double ditch.

'Do you always do things so fast?' he asked when we'd cleared the village and headed towards the little valley that opens up between the great fells.

'When I get a chance,' I answered happily. 'Don't you?'

'When I get a chance,' he mimicked, and we both burst out laughing. 'I just wish we'd brought Ailbe along; there wasn't time to go fetch him from the kennels.'

'He can come next time,' I promised.

So we rode along and I plied him with questions about his dog, and Ireland, and all the things he found here that were different. Unlike his gentle cousin, he was restless and curious and full of observations, assessing everything from the way the Romans had placed the fort to the best place for snaring ducks along the lakeshore.

I was immensely impressed. He was only two years older than I, but seemed to understand things I'd never even thought about.

'How do you know all those things?' I asked.

102

'All you have to do is look,' he replied. 'Just keep your eyes open, and pay attention to what you see.'

'Like what?'

'Like signs of the Ancient Ones, for instance. At home they leave messages for one another all over, clear as can be, and I've found one or two of them here already.'

'You have?'

The idea that Kevin could read the presence of the half-magical creatures usually met only in stories was intriguing, and I turned to stare directly at him. A shock of black hair fell forward across his forehead, almost obscuring the sparkling blue eyes, and it occurred to me that he could be one of the sidhe himself, so different was his look.

'Sure,' he confirmed. 'Whenever you find a flower with two petals missing on opposite sides of the centre, you know it's a sign of theirs. Or a notch in the bark of a tree about three feet up from the ground . . . they're not very tall, you know.'

'How do you know? Have you ever seen one?' I was sure he could talk to any of the spirits he might choose.

He looked away, the shyness suddenly coming back.

'Oh, do tell me, please. I promise I won't tell anyone, if you don't want,' I begged, terrified this new friend would withdraw from the easy mood of our conversation.

'I get teased enough about being a changeling, what with being the only dark child in a flock of redheads,' he said cautiously. 'And the grown-ups wouldn't like to know I'd had contact with the Little People.'

'Then you did meet one, once, didn't you?' I prompted.

He looked over at me and nodded, a sudden beautiful smile lighting his face.

'I'd gone fishing in a small stream, way off where no one else bothered to come. Because of my foot, I couldn't rough it up with the other boys, or practice with the sword, or run errands for the King, so I used to go off by myself and spend the whole day fishing or collecting seashells, or watching the birds nesting in the headlands.

'That afternoon I was sitting on a bank that hangs over the water, trying to coax the lord of the hole to take my bait, when a shadow fell across me, and I looked up to find a little man standing there, his hands on his hips and one eye sort of squinted up.

'He looked like a regular person, only smaller, and he had black hair and dark eyes, what I could see of them. I said something, and he said something back, and that's when I realized we didn't speak the same tongue. He came around to where I didn't have to look into the sun to see him, and squatted down in front of me. He was so close I could smell him, and he was pretty rank, I can tell you. The skins he wore were poorly tanned, I'm not sure he'd ever had a bath and the musky odour of peat smoke clung to his hair and pelts.'

Kevin paused and looked to make sure I believed him, then continued his story.

'Without a word he reached out and took hold of my foot, the bad one. I was sitting with it sort of tucked to one side, and he just took hold of it and straightened my leg so he could see the foot better. Then he took off my shoe, and tried to trace the bones through my skin.

He was very gentle. But no one, not even my mum, has ever been willing to look at it that closely, so it seemed very strange. After a bit he made some signs on the skin, and said some words while he held the foot between the palms of his hands. Then he nodded to me, put my shoe back on and sat back. I couldn't have spoken if I'd tried, but whether it was surprise or a spell he'd put on me, I don't know.'

Kevin made the sign against evil, and I nodded, waiting for him to go on. The path had come out into a meadow,

104

and we stopped, letting the reins go slack so the horses could browse.

'He reached out and taking hold of my fishing line, pulled it up out of the pool. The bait was still on it, and he stared and stared at the hook, turning it over with the same care he'd shown when he handled my foot. Finally he looked up at me and shook his head, very firmly, and pointed to the stream just in case I didn't understand. Taking a flint knife from his apron, he cut the fishing line and carefully pocketed the knife again. But he held on to the hook with one hand, and reached forward with the other as though to shield my eyes from something. I closed my eyes and jerked my head aside, but when I opened them again, he'd gone, as soundlessly as he'd come.'

'I've thought a lot about it,' Kevin concluded, 'and I don't know how much was curiosity on his part, and how much he actually meant to heal my foot in exchange for my leaving his fishing hole alone. He'd obviously watched me come up to the stream, or he wouldn't have known I was lame. Most people look away, and try to pretend it isn't so; he reached out and tried to fix it. And that's something special.'

I nodded silently. Somehow his story made the Little People seem less ominous than before.

'I heard, once, that they have a prophecy,' Kevin went on thoughtfully. 'They claim a great king will come, a man whose reign will be ushered in by a comet. Under his rule there will be no more wars; not Celt against Celt, or Roman against Briton, or Briton against Saxon. And that's something special, too.'

'Is it possible?' I asked. The very idea was so strange and grand, it must surely have originated in the Otherworld.

'Perhaps.' Kevin shrugged. 'But Edwen's been teaching

me some of your British songs, and the genealogies of kings and warriors for many generations back . . . none of them were very much interested in peace. It doesn't seem to have a high priority on heroes' lists,' he added with the same dryness of tone Brigit used.

So we laughed and spurred the horses into a race across the meadow, and by the time we were heading home we each knew we'd begun a special friendship.

11

The High King

Within a month, Brigit and Kevin had become as much a part of the household as though they had been born to it, and life took on a richer cast than I remembered even from before Mama's death. When I was not doing something with Brigit, Kevin and I were together. We took to running the horses several times a week, roaming about the countryside when the weather allowed, jumping streams or climbing trees in search of honey, and thinking up no end of adventures.

In the house my knowledge, if not my love, of domestic matters broadened under Brigit's watchful eye. Whatever antipathy Nonny may have felt towards the newcomers evaporated the first time Brigit scolded me for having torn my breeches.

'If you're going to be so handy at ripping the fabric, you can learn to be handy with the needle as well,' my companion announced, marching me to Nonny in order to get the sewing kit.

The old woman blinked in surprise, and unlocking the cupboard with Mama's keys, pawed through the basket until she found the polished bone splinter with a hole at one end.

'It's all right, Nonny; I'll make sure the bodkin gets put back properly,' Brigit assured her, and sat me down then and there for a lesson in mending. Nonny's eyes were too old to make out the awkwardness of my stitches, but she was so pleased to discover someone was taking me in hand, she wasn't overly critical.

As the autumn nights began to lengthen, my father

decided we should winter on the northern coast of the Solway; the weather was mild there and we could put the pain of last year's loss behind us.

So we headed north, stopping frequently along the way to learn what the harvest promised to be. It was not the best, of course, the spring having been so wet and cold, but it appeared that most people would have enough to squeak through the winter, and my father allowed it might have been much worse.

Leaving Carlisle behind, we threaded our way through the tangle of rivers and streams that flow into the firth where the Stones of Mabon stand. A gathering had been scheduled there, and people came from all along the Wall to share their news: barons and warriors, local men of power and a few who came for more personal reasons. Emerys the Miller arrived from Appleby to report that although Urien had mounted several raids along the Pennine border, he had made no gains in his claim to Rheged's territory.

There were various other reports and exchanges of gossip, and in the afternoon my father led the thanksgiving ceremony while the musicians played and Cathbad taught us a Greek dance in the young god's honour. He said that even though the Greeks call Mabon by the name Apollo, they understand the importance of the dance almost as well as we Celts do.

In general it was a cheerful meeting, though there were rumours of the High King's having fallen prey to a wasting illness.

I watched a long skein of geese winging in from the far north, their honking muted and soft as it drifted out of the silvery sky, and wondered what a 'wasting illness' was.

'Probably something the healers can't fix,' Kevin suggested the next day.

My father was pleased with the new boy's talent with

horses, and had made him a gift of the gelding, who was now named Gulldancer. We rode together, the big dog Ailbe trotting at our side, as the court headed for our winter quarters.

'Is it important?' I asked, wondering why it mattered who the High King was. We never saw him, after all, being in that shadow area between the heartland of Britain and the wild land of Caledonia. Indeed, I would have thought the health and temperament of the northern leaders was of more concern to us than the welfare of a figurehead off in Logres.

'As long as we're a client kingdom, it's important,' Kevin averred. 'Besides, not all High Kings are as limited in activity as Uther is. It's said that Ambrosius travelled widely through the land; probably as much as your father travels here.'

We were coming out of a rumple of hills, and I caught my breath as the broad valley beyond came into view. It's a sight I dearly love. The farmland sweeps gently down to the southern shore, and is bounded on the west by the first of the ridged peninsulas that stick into the Solway like fat, stubby fingers, each separated by the roiling waters of a firth.

This afternoon the fields wore the burnished bronze of autumn, and the blue mass of Criffel's ridge defined the edge of the world ahead. The wind laughed in the woods on the higher ground, while beyond the collar of marshland the Solway looked deceptively smooth and peaceful. When the tide is low you can walk far out across that silvery mud, suspended between the heaven above and the one reflected in the wet slickness underfoot. But when the tide turns round, it rushes hissing over everything in its path, and then a person can be lost between one step and another.

'According to Edwen, the unanswered question is who will be king after Uther.'

Kevin's voice cut across my thoughts, bringing me back so sharply that the roaring tide and the matter of the High King went down together in a torrent of confusion.

'After . . .?'

'After Uther dies, silly. Edwen says we are at a junction point, a crossing of past and future, and the strands are made as much of what has gone before as of what is ordained ahead.'

I smiled, for it was clear from the tone of his voice he was settling in to repeat one of the stories our bard had recently taught him. He was learning to endow the tales with majesty and mystery, and I loved to listen to him practice.

'As the days of the Empire were ending, the military commanders took their troops from Britain and sailed for Rome, hoping to defend her from the onslaught of the barbarians.

'Then began the Time of Troubles, with plague and famine everywhere, and because the Legions were gone, the enemies of Britain grew brave and bold. They swept in from north and east and west: Picts with painted bodies and fierce war cries, Saxons in their longboats and Irish from across the Little Sea. Britain was besieged, and cried out to Rome for help, but the Eternal City had fallen to the barbarians and could send neither troops nor encouragement.

'There was chaos everywhere, until one man arose to bind the wounds and seek to rally the Cumbri against the fearful foe. This man was Vortigern, a tough, proud warrior who killed and looted and fought his way to supremacy over all the others during the mad scramble for power when the Empire collapsed. He was a man who believed in the Old Ways, praising the history of the Celts and trying to wipe out anything that had a Roman taint; and those who opposed him fled for their lives and found refuge in Lesser Britain, which we call Brittany today.

'In his effort to stop the onslaught of the enemies who threatened to overrun the land, this tyrant Vortigern made a pact with the Saxon tribes, enemy though they were. He offered them both land and funds if they would take arms against the other invaders, and on that promise Hengest and Horsa, the Saxon leaders, brought three boatloads of warriors to Britain's aid.

'Then did the new allies fight at the Briton's side, routing the invaders from the north. But when the Picts had been driven back, the Saxons, discontented with their gift of land, began demanding more, and turned against their host, sweeping across the rich midlands of Britain like a wave of death.

'And then there came, from across the waters in Brittany, the sons of the men whom Vortigern had murdered in his rise to power. Well grown by now, and powerful, they brought armies and courage and hope to the land once more, and the people joined them in rising against the tyrant and driving him even from his mountain stronghold in the heart of Wales.

'These new leaders were Ambrosius, well trained in the arts of statesmanship, and his warrior brother Uther, who led the men in battle. Between them they restored order to the realm, and drove the Saxons back to the eastern shore.

'Ambrosius was proclaimed High King, and he called the young magician Merlin to his court, recognizing him as his own son, though born out of wedlock. Roman in training and thought, Ambrosius set out to reinstate the rule of law and order, travelling throughout the land to seek unity among the different tribes of Celts.

'Yet Ambrosius fell victim to a poisoner at court, and

as the warriors felt most at home with his brother Uther, they elected him to the High Kingship, to take his brother's place.

'That was sixteen years ago,' Kevin mused, resuming his normal tone. 'Uther has been without heir for all the years of his reign—except, of course, for the mysterious princeling Merlin is said to have created by magic and witchcraft. Neither the boy nor the Sorcerer has been seen for years; no one knows where the child is, or what his name might be . . . or even if he's still alive. Princelings always have enemies when there are proud contenders for the crown.'

'But who is there to contend for it?' I asked, still not seeing how this affected us in Rheged.

'Edwen says there are many who are not happy with this Roman line, and wish to see the High Crown returned to the old Celtic families who were in power before the Troubles began. Since the High King is chosen by consent, there's many who might compete for the honour, and power, that go with the title.'

His dark, piercing eyes were watching me intently.

'Tell me,' he said, 'how would you like it if the High Crown were to be given to Urien, for instance?'

'Oh . . .'

It was difficult enough with Urien as a neighbour; I certainly didn't fancy the idea of his having High Kingship over us as well. I nodded silently, staring out at the water again, thinking how tricky and unstable things could be when you looked beneath the surface.

A shiver ran across my back and I put the problem of the High King and his heir out of my mind. We were heading to the floating houses at faraway Loch Milton, and I told myself that even the High King wouldn't be able to find us there.

Older than anyone can recall, the houses rest on islands

of mud and brush and logs, much like the nests built by crested grebes. They're wonderful in summer, when the dugouts are tied up at the verandas that surround each house, and the wash of water on all sides keeps the mood cool and green. And even in the winter the polished wood floor and snug sleeping rooms radiating from the flagstone hearth are every bit as comfortable as any roundhouse on the fells.

The weather was mild and calm that year, perhaps to make up for the terrors the last winter had brought, and many mornings Kevin and I took the horses out at daybreak, riding through the muted, misty landscape as the sun came up. Standing black and ochre in the fog along the lakeshore, the winter reeds would part suddenly as a heron rose squawking into the day, and my heart would lift with it. Even the bare black skeletons of the alders became beautiful when the sun set the frost on their branches flashing like splintered jewels.

It was on one such morning that we stumbled across the wild man sleeping in a lean-to of branches and boughs. Any unknown person living in the forest bespoke strange and sinister forces, for only outlaws and madmen made their home in the woods. Beyond that, this ragged creature's clothes did little to hide the tattoos that marked him as a Pict, one of the strange, untamed people who lived on heather beer and rugged determination in the Northern Highlands. Kaethi said their fierceness and scorn were so terrible, the Romans had built the Wall in order to keep them out. I swallowed abruptly and reined Featherfoot away, and Kevin laughed.

'What kind of Celtic queen are you going to be if you turn and run at the first challenge?' he teased. 'Come on, let's find out who he is.'

I started to protest, but Kevin grabbed a pine branch and began tickling the sleeper's balding head.

Halted in the middle of their run, the horses sidled impatiently while the steam rose all around us in the frosty air. Gulldancer, always curious, put his head down and blew cautiously against the stranger's exposed foot.

'Dear God, defend me,' the raggedy stranger mumbled, trying to swat the pine twitch away even as he drew his legs up under his wolfskin wrap. 'All right, all right, I'm getting up,' he added with admirable good nature.

He sat up slowly and rubbed his eyes while we stared in astonishment. A wooden cross hung round his neck, and he made the Christian sign, though it was unclear whether it was a greeting for us or protection for himself. Kevin tossed aside the pine branch.

'Where are you heading, Father?' he asked, taking in the temporary nature of the shelter and the lack of fire site.

'Why, to Whithorn's monastery, of course,' came the reply.

'How long since you've had a full stomach?' my companion asked, and the Pict grinned ruefully.

'It's not a subject I think on often,' he answered, 'for I've learned to be satisfied with whatever the Lord provides.'

So we gave him directions to the lake and headed home at a full gallop. The arrival of any visitor is cause for excitement, and one so strange and unusual was bound to be even more interesting.

We left the horses in Rhufon's care and pelted across the causeway to the house, full of shouts and high spirits.

'Company's coming . . . a guest, Gladys, a guest!'

The cook looked up from the pot of porridge she was stirring, her stolid frame registering the barest hint of surprise.

'This time of year?' she questioned, and we told her all

114

we knew while she ladled out portions of the thick, hot oatmeal and put the bowls in front of us.

'Well, he'll just have to be satisfied with what we've got . . . good strong oats and a dipper of cream.' She shrugged.

'Oh, I'm sure he will be,' Brigit put in, obviously thrilled at the idea of such a visitor. 'Holy men don't look for much, you know.'

So Father Bridei arrived, his ragged clothes and dirty look belying the bright spirit that lit up his eyes. He spent the day with us, and people came from all the other houses, gathering round and asking questions. Even my father joined us that night at the fire to listen to the traveller's tales of life in the wilds and the monastery at Whithorn, which even boasted a library.

'There are scrolls and tablets and works of all kinds; some with pictures and beautiful covers, and others old and fragile, but all filled with the words of God.'

His face glowed with enthusiasm, and Kevin listened to him intently.

'I've a mind to go back there now,' Father Bridei went on, 'to live among my fellow monks; my years as a hermit are over for a while.'

'Weren't you scared,' Kevin asked, 'roaming around out there in the forest all alone, without food or fire or anyone to help?'

Our guest smiled, a wise and wonderful look crossing his face.

''Tis the love of God, and the knowledge that he will protect me from wolf and bear, starvation and the acts of wicked men which makes life beautiful no matter where I am. With the White Christ beside me, I need fear no evil, hoard no gold, desire no luxury. And always, always I return to the monastery with a full heart and praises for my Lord.'

Many in our circle nodded admiringly, impressed by the faith that made this man so brave.

The holy man spent the night with us, and my father gave him permission to say Mass the next morning in one of the outbuildings on the shore. Rhufon muttered about such goings-on, but Brigit and those among the local folk who were also Christian were deeply pleased.

Later, as the monk prepared to continue his journey, everyone crowded round to wish him well. A few asked for a blessing, and he made the sign of the cross over all of us, Pagan and Christian alike.

'Don't forget,' he called as he turned on to the lake-shore path, 'the monastery welcomes any who wish to find shelter in Christ. All you have to do is make your way there.'

Brigit and Kevin and I stood on the causeway, waving with the rest of the household and bathing in the comradery the Pictish monk had created. I slid my arms around my companions and gave them a squeeze of love and appreciation.

Surely, I thought, one could not ask for a dearer family, or a more pleasant way of life.

12
The Irish Family

'It's been a long day, M'lady,' Arthur's lieutenant said, nodding a greeting when he reined in beside us. He turned to Brigit. 'I figure we should be coming up on the track soon, since we passed the milestone a little while back.'

The Irish girl pointed to a spinney of trees ahead. 'That's the turnoff. And I, for one, will be very glad to get down off this animal and stand on firm ground again!'

We left the Road and after a bit of winding and turning came out on the side of a hill which overlooked Brigit's family's steading.

The roundhouses clustered within the protection of a bank and ditch, while beyond them spread fields and barnyards carved out of the wild. A pigsty stood off to one side, and a row of smaller thatched roofs covered the storage pits for grain and other winter provisions. A pair of horses stood prick-eared and curious about our arrival. I wondered if they were the animals my father had given Angus back when the family first came to Rheged.

The track dipped into the trees again and we passed a stand of birches, their 'lamb tail' catkins glowing gold in the afternoon light. Traces of sap tapping stained the trunks of several trees, indicating there might be fresh birch wine for our refreshment. Obviously Brigit's family were using their land well, and it pleased me to think my father had made it possible.

The entire clan was waiting to greet us as we approached the gate. The adults were much as I remembered them, big-boned and red-headed. There were more

117

children now, and one young woman was large with child.

When the greetings and introductions had been made, we all began to file off to the different roundhouses where we would be housed.

'We don't often have so many guests.' Aunt Oonagh, Kevin's mother, smiled at me shyly.

'Or such important ones,' put in Brigit's mother, showing me to the weaving house they had put aside for us. The building was so big that a second circle of posts held up the roof, and box beds had been placed between them and the wall. A half-finished piece waited in the loom beside the door.

'Will you be wanting a rest before dinner?' my hostess asked. 'There's still some little time before it will be ready.'

'Thank you, but I'd rather walk around for a bit. We've been in the saddle all day, and my legs could use a stretching,' I answered.

'Ah, sure'n I should have thought of that. Maybe you'd like to have Brigit show you about the place? It's not exactly a palace, but we've done it all ourselves, and it's home.' The woman fairly glowed with pride.

Lavinia was busy shaking out the dress she expected me to wear that evening, and she looked up now with a scowl. I knew there would be ruffled feathers to soothe where she was concerned, so I thanked Brigit's mother and told her I'd meet Brigit in the main house in a few minutes. Our hostess left, flushed and happy, and I turned round to face my chaperone.

The little Roman matron stood in the centre of the room, as out of place in this rough country house as a fresh-minted coin at the Carlisle fair. Indignation flushed her plump cheeks and crackled in her patrician voice.

'Who ever heard of such a thing? Inviting a girl who's

118

about to become queen of the whole of Britain to go poke about a farmstead!'

'Now, Vinnie, I think it was very sweet of her. She's just trying to be hospitable, after all. Why, look at all the trouble they've gone to to make us comfortable.'

It was clear the hampers of fleece and bundles of flax that would normally fill the space had been removed, and the house thoroughly aired. Baskets of linen thread and several wooden chests, no doubt filled with woven goods, were stacked under the eaves, and a fresh-filled water pitcher sat in its bowl on top of a cupboard.

'You know you'll get your pretty dress all splattered with mud and droppings,' Vinnie complained, smoothing the garment tenderly, as though protecting a child.

'Well, as a matter of fact,' I said as tactfully as possible, 'I was thinking that it would be better not to wear the dress, since it might get dirty, or even spoiled. In fact, I'd much rather just put on another set of breeches and a tunic, and you can brush these clean and hang them up to air for tomorrow.'

Vinnie was predictably aghast at my suggestion. The good matron still believed that women who rode horseback and wore breeches were an affront to the whole of civilized conduct. She would grudgingly concede that breeches were handy for outdoor activities, but once under a roof she expected me to 'remember my station.' Now her pink face registered aggravation and disappointment in equal measure.

'You mean you won't be wearing the dress either tonight or tomorrow?' she sputtered. 'But surely, if you're going to be riding in the litter a dress would be more fitting.'

We'd reached the nubbin of the problem, and I came over to her and took her hands in mine.

'Vinnie, I've been thinking about that too. I'm just not

119

comfortable in the litter: I can't see where we're going, or feel the breeze, and its motion makes me sick. It's a nice idea, and I appreciate your concern, but I'm much happier riding Featherfoot.'

'But the litter was built specially for the occasion,' she reminded me, 'copied from the one my grandmother brought from Rome, so that you could come to the High King in style, not straddling some animal in the rags of a barbarian.'

'And I appreciate the trouble you went to. If it will make you happier,' I said quickly, hoping to mollify my governess' hurt feelings, 'I promise to ride in it when we enter Winchester, but until we meet King Arthur, I'll be much more comfortable wearing my "barbarian rags" and riding with the rest of the party.'

Lavinia kept up a kind of half-scolding as I slipped out of the day's clothes and into a fresh set.

'And you needn't think you'll be getting by with this sort of thing at the High Court!' she concluded as I prepared to go through the door.

I was tempted to say 'I know, I know . . . why do you think I want it so much now?' But I held my tongue and thanked her when she handed me a short cloak with the admonition that it was still nippy out these nights, no matter what the calendar said.

Brigit took me around her family's farm, and the younger children tagged along, showing off the cows and pigs, and even the flock of greylag geese that came waddling towards us, heads extended and long necks swaying like snakes as they clucked and muttered and hissed their imprecations at us.

The wattle-and-daub buildings were well made, and a squabble of house sparrows filled the upper regions of the barn. The high point of the tour was the kennels, where a

120

litter of pups romped and played, growling and leaping at one another.

'My father's still proud of his dogs,' Brigit said over the swirl of children that circled round us. 'I think he sets more store by them than by his offspring. Certainly he boasts about them more,' she added with a wry smile.

Dusk had fallen by the time we trooped into the main house for dinner. The meal was a gay, noisy affair with members of our escort crowded in among the friends and relatives of Brigit's family. It was a veritable feast, with roast duck and fresh fish from Morecambe Bay, and a delicious spring pudding of young hawthorn shoots, as well as oat and barley cakes of all kinds.

Angus insisted that I sit in his place at the centre of the table, with Bedivere on one side and Brigit on the other. Brigit had offered to help her mother, of course, but had been shooed out of the kitchen with the admonition that this was as much a feast in honour of her as it was for me, so she laughed and plunked down on the bench beside me.

The rest of Arthur's men were seated randomly about the tables, and all seemed to be enjoying themselves. There was no sign of Merlin, however, and I finally asked Bedivere why the Magician wasn't with us.

'Do you always keep an eye on everything, M'lady?' His tone was serious, but I saw the same quizzical smile he had given me at lunch.

'Well, uh . . .' I faltered, not knowing what to say.

'Nay, now, I meant no offence. It's a good trait is what I'm saying. A queen who thinks only about herself is easy enough to find, but one who is concerned about the welfare and whereabouts of her party is much more to be admired.'

My face went scarlet and I looked hastily down at my plate. Public flattery and compliments for what seemed

121

common sense were not something I was used to, and I felt both foolish and awkward in my reaction.

'I did not mean to embarrass you, Your Highness,' Bedivere added hastily, leaning towards me in order to speak more privately.

When I glanced up, the consternation on his rugged face was so genuine I had to smile.

'Sir Bedivere, I am not used to such flattery. I'm not even used to being called "M'lady," and who knows how long it will be before I think of myself as a queen? Perhaps our northern ways are considered backward and uncouth by some, but at least they are direct and honest, and not full of . . . of . . .' I stumbled to a halt, unable to think of what to say without being insulting.

'What would you rather be called?' he asked, his pleasant manner covering my embarrassment.

'Gwen, I suppose, just I have been all my life.'

'All right,' he answered solemnly, but the twinkle had not left his eyes. 'From now on, in any private conversation, I shall call you Gwen until, or unless, you ask me to stop. Is that better?'

'Much,' I said with relief, feeling as though I had just put Featherfoot over a hazardous jump.

'Now, about the King's Enchanter . . .' My companion glanced around the gathering, then shrugged. 'Our worthy sage is not fond of crowded rooms and rich food, so he's probably taken a small repast and retired to a nearby hilltop to eat alone. He is a bit peculiar, you know, but given his age and his importance to The Cause, one can certainly honour his wishes.'

'Ahh,' I said, relieved. 'I was afraid that the day's long ride had overtaxed him. You are sure it is no more than personal preference?'

'Absolutely,' came the response. 'I have known him since I was a child, and he's as durable as they come, for all that he gets out of sorts when forced to travel. Don't forget, he's a master of disguise, and while it sometimes suits him to appear as the frail, seedy old man, the Sorcerer inside is still strong and vigorous.'

I laughed. 'So I suspected, after our encounter with the Lady's messenger.' One of Brigit's sisters was holding a bowl of fresh greens for me, and I took some and thanked her before turning back to Bedivere. 'How have you come to have such a long acquaintanceship?'

'Arthur and I were raised in the same household.' He helped himself to the salad and began to spear the tender leaves with enthusiasm. 'I was the decoy, I suppose, meant to draw attention away from the other child, should anyone be looking for him. Of course, neither of us knew that at the time. We were just fosterlings, growing up in a small court without any special fuss or attention. Sir Ector treated us the same as he did his own son, Cei, and we might have been three brothers from any Cumbrian kingdom.'

'And Merlin?'

'He was our tutor, more or less. We had no idea then who he was—just an eccentric scholar who found himself in our out-of-the-way corner of Wales. Sometimes a visitor would bring news of the doings at the High Court, and there might be talk of King Uther's son, hidden by the Magician in some secret place. But that was all so far removed from our own homespun life, it might as well have been one of the fabulous tales our teacher told about distant lands . . . it never occurred to any of us boys that we were part of the fable.'

I nodded, remembering Cathbad and his wonderful stories. 'Like the Trojan War: something mythical that took place in another world . . .'

Bedivere grinned. 'So your own education has not been

all that provincial!' he exclaimed. 'How did you learn about the *Iliad*?'

'From my own tutor, Cathbad the Druid. He introduced it early in our studies. I remember telling my nurse about it that night, while Mama braided my hair, and how astounded Nonny was at the idea that a queen would desert her people just to be with a lover. "It may be all right for some sloppy foreigner, but no Celtic queen would do such a thing!"' I mimicked Nonny's scorn, and Bedivere laughed. 'Up until that moment I suppose I had rather envied Helen, what with being beautiful and sought after by so many men, but from then on I was very glad I was a Celt and not a Greek.'

We ate for a bit in silence before I asked, 'How does it feel now, being part of the fable?'

'Well, it took some getting used to, as you can imagine.' I nodded emphatically, and he smiled again. 'Yes, perhaps you're going through the same sort of thing. But truly, Gwen, once the shock and the first confusion wear off, it's much the same as it was before. One still gets up in the morning and gets dressed; the day's plans have to be gone over and then put into action; the dinner is still served at dusk, and the harp still needs to be tuned before one can sing. There's nothing particularly magical about the things we are doing. But The Cause for which they are done is very splendid indeed. That part of it never ceases to amaze me.'

He paused and, taking up his goblet, turned it slowly between his fingers so that the birch wine swirled gently around the bowl, giving off the clean, pungent scent of wintergreen. His rugged face softened, and his voice was a mixture of reverence and enthusiasm.

'I don't know whether it started as Arthur's dream, or Merlin's, or perhaps was writ in the stars, but it's a wondrous thing to work for. And' —he raised the goblet to me— 'I would say we are lucky to have you as part of it.'

The compliment took me by surprise, and I fixed my eyes on my plate while the flush crept back into my face.

He lowered his voice and said firmly, 'Look at me, Gwen,' and when I did, he was all seriousness. 'I am not speaking as a flattering courtier, but as one friend to another. I was afraid Arthur would end up saddled with a simpering fool for a wife; one of the daughters of the courtiers who scramble about looking for favours, or a convent darling interested only in prayers and primping. There are too many important things to be done to have a leader such as Arthur troubled by the nagging of a spoiled, self-centred vixen who came to power just because she's beautiful. I, for one, was relieved when he announced he intended to take a northern girl to wife. He needed a Celtic wife from the Cumbri, and he'd already taken a liking to you and your family.'

I looked down again, for the disappointment of hearing what I already suspected was more painful than I had anticipated.

Bedivere must have read something in my face, for he went on gently: 'Shall I tell you what Arthur said to me? We were in his chambers following the announcement of his decision, and he was tired of arguing with those who would have him look elsewhere. "Bedivere, she is not only a logical choice, she comes from good stock as well, and there is no other woman I wish to consider. You can tell that to the pack of hopeful fathers down there, and maybe that will shut them up." I think he would have gone to war with them for you, he was that sure you are the woman he wants.'

I smiled, partly at Bedivere's diplomacy and partly at the idea there had been some personal preference involved.

'Now—that's better,' Bedivere affirmed, watching me carefully. 'But if I may be permitted a bit of advice . . . you must learn to accept compliments, and attention, and sometimes even flattery. It is disrespectful to the giver of a sincere compliment to dismiss it, and it is disconcerting to the flatterer to meet with a gracious acceptance of what he knows in his heart is an effort to mislead. I think you will find many among Arthur's people who will genuinely love and admire you, and it will hurt them if you do not receive their tributes in the spirit in which they are given. And as for the others, well, better to keep them off balance, I always say.'

I laughed at that, and this time when he raised his goblet to me I nodded slightly and smiled, remembering the many times I'd seen Mama do much the same. I couldn't help wondering how she'd learned to be a gracious, dignified queen, and if she had had as many qualms then as I did now.

After dinner the Irish family brought out gifts. Angus himself had carved a small wooden cross for Brigit so she would have the symbol of their faith wherever she lived, and there was also a necklace of the grey-green pearls found in the rivers to the west.

'To remind you of the Lakes, where your family is,' Brigit's mother said softly.

The women had made a wonderful shawl for me, bright and colourful as the one Brigit had brought from Ireland. But this one, they hastened to point out, had all six colours, in honour of my status as a queen. There was a pair of earrings, fine-worked and delicate, made of Irish gold, and I wondered which of the women was parting with these, her own reminders of a home long ago left behind. It was a gift to touch the heart, and mindful of Bedivere's recent words, I accepted them as graciously as I could and showed my gratitude most openly.

'For being so good to our child,' Angus said, as pleased as though he were giving up his own personal mementos.

Last of all, our host signalled to one of the boys who darted outside and was back in a moment with an angular bundle of wriggling grey fur.

'Wouldn't do to leave the bridegroom out of this celebration,' our host announced, holding up the puppy for everyone to see. 'Pure Irish stock, he is, and promises to grow into a fine, strong wolfhound.'

Bedivere looked puzzled, for to anyone unused to the breed it resembles nothing so much as a frame of sticks covered with rags that one puts up in a field to scare away the birds. I was laughing and clapping my hands and, reaching out, took the funny, awkward thing into my lap.

'Just ask M'lady here what kind of dogs they grow into.' Angus beamed, obviously enjoying his role of benefactor. 'Brought the original ones over when we came, some five years back, and they do as well in this country as in Ireland. You can tell the King there's more where this one comes from, if he'd care to start a kennel of his own.'

The puppy nuzzled into the crook of my arm, blinking sleepily and wagging his tail slightly. Suddenly I wondered how we were going to transport it over the next two hundred miles; graciously accepting a gift might be one thing, but knowing what to do with it was another.

Bedivere was speaking, thanking the family for their hospitality, their loyalty, and the puppy, all in the name of the King. 'Perhaps,' he added, 'we might purchase a crate from you in order to carry the dog?'

'Of course,' said Angus gustily. 'As a matter of fact, I made one up special, just in case you might need it. Strong and roomy. And the dog's already weaned, so there shouldn't be any trouble caring for him,' he added, proud to have thought of all these details.

Then the good man brought out a flask of his own and

poured us each a bit of strong brown liquor, which burned the throat but certainly warmed the heart. 'A wee secret like unto the Waters of Life,' he said when someone asked him what it was, and there was laughter and much merriment all around.

Brigit's brother Sean uncovered his harp, in which Bedivere showed much interest, and began to fill the room with Irish songs and the stories of great heroes. It was his young wife who was pregnant, and she sat in placid contentment, listening to him play. The soft shadows and comfortable curve of the roundhouse embraced us in the age-old way, while generations past and as yet unborn were captured by the music.

Later, when we were all tucked in and warm against the spring chill, I thought back over the evening. Brigit's family had been cordial and welcoming, and of all the gifts bestowed upon me, the sharing of the family hearth was the most touching. Perhaps they held no resentment over my taking their daughter so far away . . . or even for what had happened to Kevin. The old pain of that loss throbbed dully in my heart, and I turned away from it restlessly.

The day's journey had been more pleasurable than I expected. The High King's lieutenant was turning out to be friendly and personable and since he had known Arthur for so long, it was possible he would tell me more about the man who expected me to be his queen.

I yawned sleepily. There was no harm, after all, in finding out what he was like. It needn't change my determination to avoid entrapment, and it might help me find a way to change the direction in which my life seemed to be going.

13

King Uther

Morning came dazzling bright and clear, with neither trace of fog nor remnant of the clouds that had brought a shower in the night. Brigit was already up, sharing a time of prayer with her parents before the demands of getting our party under way took over. I was just heading for breakfast when she returned and swung into step beside me, shooing a clutch of chicks out of the way.

'It's nice to see your family again,' I commented, looking over at her. 'I've been wondering . . . wouldn't you rather stay here, with them, instead of going all the way to Logres with me?'

'What for?' Her question was so direct and forthright it startled me.

'Well, they are your bloodline, after all. They gave you life and brought you well through childhood . . . and they are Christians, which I can't promise you'll find a lot of in the south. I . . . I just want you to know you have the choice . . .' I finished lamely.

'Some choice,' she answered, tossing her head with a laugh. 'Here you are, riding into glory knows what sort of future, and you ask if I wouldn't rather stay behind!'

She strode through the cluster of children who were fetching water from the well.

'Don't forget, Gwen, I've only been back in touch with my parents since Kevin . . . left. And then just for occasional visits. Before that there was a good long while when you and the court were the only family I knew. I honour my clan; they are my parents and my kin—but you are my family. I know you far better than I know them now, and prefer to stay with you.'

As usual, she made everything sound simple, and I nodded gratefully.

'If only we didn't have to ride so far,' she added ruefully. 'I didn't know I had so many places to be sore in.'

I had forgotten that riding was not the Irish girl's favourite means of travel, and she took to a horse only when distance or time demanded it.

'Why don't you sit in the litter with Lavinia?' I suggested. 'The thing was made big enough for two, after all, and it would give you a chance to rest your sore muscles.'

It was her turn to grin with gratitude. 'I may just do that,' she responded.

We left the Irish family in a fine, cheerful mood. As I was preparing to mount Featherfoot, Sean's wife came over and shyly offered to let me touch her belly 'for good luck.' When I put my hand on the rounded mound and felt the life stirring within, she and I smiled at each other, and I offered a silent prayer that she be delivered safely.

Once on the Road, I began to study my escort, trying to see them as individuals instead of just 'Arthur's men.' They shared a comradery that had nothing to do with rank or age, and it extended from the unbearded youth who attended the litter to a grizzled veteran who oversaw the packhorses. It spoke well for the High King's future, since nothing is so corrosive as followers who are split into warring factions.

When we were well under way, Bedivere reined in beside me. White billowy clouds were scudding in out of the west, half-threatening to soak us with a springtime shower, and Featherfoot pranced and sidled excitedly, impatient for a chance to run. I glanced at Arthur's lieutenant, wondering if he'd be interested in a race, but decided against asking. It seemed a good time to find out more about Arthur, however, so we chatted amiably and soon came round to laughing over the complication of the puppy.

'Arthur's a man to appreciate a good dog,' Bedivere allowed, 'and if that bundle of bone and fur grows into the kind of animal promised, he'll be delighted. I think the thing he missed most about leaving Sir Ector's court was that he no longer had time enough for the kennels.'

'But what about the family? Didn't he regret leaving them?' It seemed to me that only a coldhearted person would miss dogs more than people.

'Oh, we went with him. I, of course, because I was his best friend. And Cei because he was our brother. Sir Ector and Drusilla stayed with us at court all through the first months, and Merlin is with him still, as you see. So it's not as if the people closest to him were forgotten along the way.'

I nodded, trying to imagine an entire Cumbrian family suddenly set down in the heart of a Roman court. It seemed a bit preposterous, and I smiled at the thought.

'When did you first discover who your foster brother was?'

'Same time as everyone else, including Arthur,' Bedivere replied with a grin. 'I don't think anyone, except Merlin, had any idea what changes Uther's last battle would bring. Certainly there was no hint that the hidden Princeling was about to be revealed. Like many people, we assumed that the boy was being raised in Brittany, just as Ambrosius and Uther had been. Remember, the idea of hiding a kinglet from his enemies till he's old enough to be fledged was not new in Arthur's case. But there was the added complication of how Arthur came to be at all, and that may have had something to do with Merlin's taking the infant away as soon as he was born.'

I wondered what Bedivere knew of the mystery surrounding Arthur's origins, but my companion continued with his story before I could find a tactful way to ask.

King Uther had been a proud man, apparently unwilling to consider his own mortality, and he'd put off naming his heir or even a regent to keep the kingdom until the Princeling came of age. When rumours spread that Uther was ailing, the client kings grew restless, fearing that the lack of a logical successor would lead to bloody internal struggles. Then word came that a new group of invaders had landed to the north and Urien needed help to contain them.

Even though it was too early in the spring, Uther had been determined to go to war. Perhaps he knew in his bones what he wasn't willing to admit with his mind . . . that he was dying.

Sir Ector announced that the High King would need every warrior possible and since all three boys were of age, they could join the troop as well.

'Drusilla was much against it,' Bedivere recalled, 'but Sir Ector said it didn't matter where a warrior was blooded, he could get killed as easily in a border skirmish as he could in a big offensive. And in the end we answered Uther's call, in spite of the weather.'

'The men of Rheged did too,' I broke in, wanting Bedivere to know we had responded loyally also. 'There were still patches of ice on the Stainmore, so my father chose to go by the southern route, through the Aire Gap. Also, with Urien being such a chancy neighbour, it seemed wiser not to march the main body of our troops down the length of his kingdom.'

'Your father is an astute man,' Bedivere said. 'But I had no idea he had shared his military thinking with you.' He gave me the same quizzical look I had seen before, half smile, half question.

'Perhaps because he had no son to pass it on to,' I replied. 'Anyhow, what was it like, when you went to meet the High King?'

Arthur's foster brother returned to the tale, his voice warming to the subject as we went along. I let his words wrap round me, conjuring up the pictures of those events.

They had come out of the steep green valleys of Wales, three children and a hermit-tutor, heading into manhood and history without so much as a pause for consideration. Merlin knew, of course, and Sir Ector surely suspected that his foster son would soon be the centre of all attention. But all the rest were unaware of what was about to happen, and for the boys it was adventure enough that they were discovering the world beyond the Marches, where the land smooths out into rolling hills and there are few waterfalls or crags to mark the horizon.

On a late afternoon their small contingent topped a ridge and looked down on the tents and picket lines, cooking fires and pavilions of Uther's camp. The wind was out of the east, cutting and chill, and on it they heard the ring of a smith's hammer and the crack and flapping of banners. These were everywhere, ranging from long skinny pennants to huge impressive flags, each carrying the device of its people, each providing a rallying point for the soldiers to gather round. The boys had never seen such a display before, and they gaped in amazement.

Coming into camp, Sir Ector sent the rest of the men to find a spot to pitch their gear. He seemed distracted, and later Bedivere asked what he had been feeling. 'Nervous, like a man on the eve of his son's wedding,' he answered. 'I kept wondering if I'd done the right things; if, after all these years, Uther would be satisfied with how the boy'd turned out . . . if he'd be harsh or happy with his newfound son . . . and most of all, how Arthur would react to discovering his royal heritage.'

133

Sir Ector called the boys to follow, and together with their teacher they made directly for Uther's tent. The Red Dragon floated over it like a tethered monster instead of a banner, and there were guards and messengers, pages and servants all clustered about the royal pavilion waiting to be of service to the High King.

The hermit rode right up to them, and they drew back in awe and deference as though he were himself of royal birth. Bedivere and Arthur exchanged glances at that, but it was obviously not a moment for asking questions.

When they reached the tent itself, someone ran forward to help Merlin down from his horse, and suddenly their tattered old tutor was standing in the midst of the King's own guard, drawing that immense presence into himself. It was the first time they had heard him use the Voice of Power.

'Tell the High King that I have arrived,' the Magician ordered, and within seconds the tent flap was drawn back and they were ushered inside.

Someone had been burning herbs in the brazier, so the space was hot and stuffy with the smell of medicine. Uther was sitting in his carved chair, dressed in the full regalia of his estate, with the jewels and gold gleaming from his crown. There was such splendour and richness about him, Bedivere hardly noticed he was propped up with pillows and a fur robe had been placed across his knees.

Yet ill or no, there was no doubt he was still the sovereign lord of Britain. He was so gaunt and thin, his face was like a death's head, and his hands were as bony as those of a man twice his age. But his dark eyes burned with an eager fire, and his gaze moved constantly between Arthur and Cei and Bedivere.

Merlin stepped foward and without so much as a greeting asked the High King, 'Why didn't you let me know how badly you're ailing?'

Uther looked him up and down before replying. 'You are not the only physician in Britain, Sir. But I think you've brought me a better tonic than any concoction the doctors could prescribe . . .' and he gestured the Enchanter out of the way. The great garnet ring, carved with the Royal Dragon, flashed in the lamplight, looking out of place on the wasted hand.

Merlin took a step back and, turning, began the formal introductions. 'M'lord, I am pleased to present Sir Ector and his family.'

Sir Ector moved forward and knelt before the King's chair, but Uther hardly noticed him, so intent was he on scanning the three youngsters.

'And these are my sons,' Sir Ector said. 'Cei, of my own blood, and Bedivere and Arthur, whom I have fostered until you should need them.'

The boys came forward, one at a time, and knelt before the High King. He dismissed Cei with a nod, but continued to scrutinize Arthur and Bedivere closely. And when Merlin called Bedivere forward, Uther's gaze was so intense, it was all the boy could do to keep from shaking.

'And what is your lineage?' the King inquired as Bedivere knelt before him, staring at the hand with the Dragon Ring.

'I am an orphan, M'lord, whose parents were killed by raiders when I was very young,' Bedivere said, bracing himself to meet the High King's eyes. 'Sir Ector took me in, to be company to his son, Cei, and the fosterling, Arthur.'

Somehow Uther divined that this was not the child he was seeking. Perhaps some slight shake of the head passed between him and Merlin. All Bedivere knew was that he felt the change of the High King's attention, like the sun going behind a cloud, even before Uther turned towards Arthur.

135

Merlin called the other foster brother forward, and there was a moment of utter silence when, after kissing the Dragon Ring, Arthur looked steadily into Uther's eyes and announced that he had no idea who his parents were.

'You have brightened this bleak day, and brought hope such as I never expected,' the High King said, leaning back among his cushions with a sigh. His face was flushed and bright, and one of his attendants came forward with a cup, but Uther shook his head and gestured the man away.

'It's not medicine I want now, only time. Only a little time.' He tore his gaze from Arthur's face and glanced at the rest of Ector's party as though wondering why they were still there. 'Leave the boy with me,' he ordered, and looking directly at Merlin added, 'You are to be much commended for your service, M'lord, and I will speak with you later. For now, I wish to get acquainted with the fosterling.'

So they had left the royal tent and made their way to their own encampment. Sir Ector was silent, and when Cei asked petulantly why Arthur had been singled out for royal favour, Ector shushed him with a reminder not to pry into the actions of his betters. Cei had withdrawn in a huff, sulking crossly as he chewed on a piece of dried meat. Bedivere was more curious as to why their tutor had been received so magnificently than he was about Arthur's being given special attention; he knew Arthur would tell him all about the audience with the King, but he wasn't sure the hermit would ever explain.

'I waited for Arthur's return all night long, sleeping lightly and waking to find his cot empty. Indeed, I didn't have a chance to talk with him again until both the battle and the Declaration were over.'

Bedivere paused, but the scene he had evoked lingered all around us.

'Did Arthur tell you what had happened during his stay with the High King?' I asked when I could no longer control my curiosity, and Bedivere nodded.

Uther had plied the boy with questions concerning his parentage, about which Arthur could say very little, not knowing himself. And the King wanted to hear about his swordsmanship and training, his education, his ideas about the future of Britain and the attainment of the King's goals. It seemed clear to Arthur that Uther might have been a solid military leader but he had little by way of vision about his country in a broader sense. Mostly he had been content to do battle with the Saxons and stay in his southern court when not out on the war trail.

The two of them supped together when night came, and Uther insisted that Arthur spend the night on a cot in the royal tent. So the bed was made up, and when the coals of the brazier had been banked and the last of the King's medicine brought to him, the servants were sent away and Uther began to reminisce about his own younger years.

He talked of the days when he and his brother Ambrosius had returned from Brittany and overthrown the Wolf, Vortigern. And how Ambrosius had called Merlin to him, acknowledging him as his son and giving him a place at court. Together they planned to make Britain strong and whole in her own right, an independent country instead of one tied to the fading fortunes of Rome. It reminded Arthur of the kind of thing his teacher used to talk about, but the fact that the tutor and Merlin might be one and the same did not occur to him.

'We never did get on well, Merlin and I, for all that he

is my nephew. I hope,' Uther said suddenly, 'that you aren't all that bookish?'

Arthur grinned and shook his head. Uther seemed satisfied and went on with his musings. 'I've sometimes wondered if I should have kept the Magician by my side, as Ambrosius did . . . if things would have gone better with his guidance. But the only venture Merlin and I made together turned out . . . oddly,' Uther said uneasily, and he stared at the fire for a long time.

'It is rumoured that you gave your son into Merlin's keeping,' Arthur reminded him, and the ailing King nodded.

'It was part of a bargain ill made . . . or so I have always thought,' Uther answered guardedly, then looked up at his guest. 'I'm coming to reconsider that judgement, however, and I no longer regret it. You see, you are that son, and your tutor is Merlin, and you have been brought back to me when I am most in need of help and aid.'

There it was, flat out and indisputable. Arthur stared at the older man, too shocked and surprised to know what to say.

Gradually a dozen questions came to mind, and the two of them talked far into the night, with the sick King showing no signs of weariness and Arthur too stunned and excited to put an end to the conversation, even for sleep. It wasn't until the messenger arrived with news of the Saxon approach that they realized it was almost dawn.

The scout reported the enemy had been moving through much of the night, no doubt planning to surprise them in camp at dawn. Uther sent him off with the message to rouse the troops and prepare to intercept the enemy in a spot of their own choosing.

'I had thought to present you to the army this morning,' Uther said, nodding to Arthur, 'but I suppose it can wait until after we take care of this band of barbarians. Just

138

stay beside me during the battle, boy, and we shall come through together. Oh, my dear son, there is nothing that is impossible for us, now that you are here!' the ailing King cried out, filled with renewed hope.

So Arthur rode into battle with the High King, mounted on one of the King's own horses and wearing the same plain white wool garments he had travelled in. Later he told Bedivere there'd been no time to change, and when he strapped on his old belt and sword, he was sure the whole thing was a dream, and any moment he'd wake up in his bed at home.

'I suppose,' Bedivere concluded in his wry way, 'that one could say it was the beginning of a dream none of us have wakened from yet.'

I smiled at that and was going to ask him what had happened next, but we were approaching the ford of a sizable stream, and he went off to oversee our crossing while I thought about the story he'd recounted.

Events I had known about only at a distance were taking on a dimension I'd never thought of before, and Bedivere was fleshing out figures I'd perceived only in shadow form. It was fascinating, and I waited eagerly for the lieutenant to return and continue his tale.

14

The Declaration

'What happened during the battle?' I asked Bedivere as soon as he had come back to my side. He looked at me blankly for a moment, then grinned.

'Uther's last battle? A whole lot, and depending on whom you listen to, it was either good or bad. The best I can do is tell you what I personally saw and let you decide from there.'

I nodded, eager for him to resume the story, and after a moment he did.

Urien knew his country thoroughly, and had advised King Uther well, for when the troops were drawn into position they could look down on a shallow valley that funnelled up to the small pass where the track ran. Trees provided cover to the right and left, and there were rumpled rocks on either side. The Saxons would have to cross the open valley below without protection on their flanks. It was a spot no army would want to fight in unless they held the high ground.

The Saxons came on at a loping trot, the kind that covers ground well. Each man bore a shield slung over his shoulder, which left him free for easier movement, but not quite ready for combat. Most likely they had heard that Uther was an ailing leader and so did not expect to find him waiting for them.

The enemy came to a straggling halt as soon as they saw the British forces in the little pass. Incredibly, the ravaged King was in the front ranks, leading his army from a chair specially built to be carried on the shoulders of four men. He held the Sword of State naked for all to see and was the very picture of an indomitable warrior defending his realm against an invading army.

The peaceful glen was suddenly filled with shouting and raging on both sides, and Uther had the war horns sounded while the Saxons scrambled to establish their wedge pattern. Those with swords and helmets were in the van, while the men with battle-axes formed the centre. Wave after wave of them bunched into a solid mass, round shields hastily brought into place as the central body of Uther's troops surged forward and down upon them.

Astride one of the royal horses, Arthur remained next to the High King throughout the encounter, using his body and weapons to shield Uther's sword side. 'Thank goodness,' he told Bedivere later, 'this group didn't use those wicked little throwing axes so popular among the Franks. The King would have been an easy target, lifted as he was above the press of battle.'

Being mounted, Arthur himself stood out in the midst of the screaming, grunting, surging wave of brutality. He shone in his white raiment like a ray of sunlight and became the rallying point for the warriors struggling in the muck of blood and filth below.

In the midst of the tumult few stopped to wonder who he was or where he came from. It was enough to see him, bright and quick as a young god, breaking the force of the Saxon foe. The men hearkened to his enthusiasm, taking up the war cry and rushing into the gaps that began to appear in the Saxon wedge.

Bedivere fought his way towards Arthur, slashing and parrying on all sides, too excited to see the arms and legs and spilt brains that were being trodden underfoot. He came up on Uther's shield side, adding his weight to the press of men that kept the howling mob away from the litter, and suddenly the man ahead of him went down, both legs severed below the knees. A long ash pole came free of the wounded man's grasp and began a slow, lethal pivot across Bedivere's line of vision.

Bedivere reached up to fend it off, not yet realizing it was the Banner. But as he felt the weight of the standard plunge earthward, a shock of recognition went through him and he fought against the pull until it was balanced again, risen from its dip towards the blood-soaked mud and offal. Dropping his sword, Bedivere continued to steady the Red Dragon for the rest of the battle.

Arthur had glanced over as the Banner started to fall, and in that moment he was set upon and only just brought his sword up in time to deflect the blow of an axe. The Saxon weapon caught the blade and sent it spinning from his grasp.

There was a moment of horror among the ranks when the Britons saw their young hero suddenly naked and vulnerable to the enemy.

The High King raised himself in his chair, calling out, 'Here, boy!' and handed over the Sword of State there in the sight of all.

A great cheer went up from the men when they saw Uther's action, and within minutes the Saxon force had been split in two, with Uther's men sweeping down from the forest cover to attack their flanks. The enemy milled about, trying to hack their way through to some path of escape, then began to thin as those to the rear turned tail when they saw clearly that the day had been lost. Within the half-hour the British had taken the valley and were turning the victory into a rout.

The men surrounding the High King were so intent on the battle, they saw and heard nothing else until a lieutenant rode up, requesting further orders, and drew back in consternation. Uther sat upright, propped or perhaps strapped in his chair, a grimace of amazement frozen on his face. The jaw had gone slack and the glazed eyes stared at nothing. In all the screaming, howling roar of carnage no one had noticed when Uther died.

The shock that swept through the knot of men surrounding the High King's chair threatened to send his troops into confusion and lose the victory they were so close to claiming.

'Have we enough fresh men to pursue the Saxon stragglers?' Arthur called across to the lieutenant, and when the man nodded, Arthur swept his arm up, brandishing the Sword of State. 'Then have the aurochs horns sound,' he cried. 'The Saxons must not learn the King has died.'

The lieutenant saluted, and Arthur thrust his way forward, spearheading a party that swept after the routed enemy while the rest of the men limped back to camp, sore and tired but full of the brimming excitement that follows victory.

Merlin, who never bears arms in battle but whose presence ensures success, appeared from nowhere to escort the High King's body to the royal tent. And when Arthur returned from the battlefield he strode to the front of the pavilion and took charge of the milling men.

Lieutenants came and went, asking directions of the young stranger as if he were their natural leader, which in a way was true. He responded to them all, asking quick questions and giving sure answers as though this were a campaign that he himself had planned. He had been slightly wounded, but bound the cut with a strip of cloth and refused to retire until all the details had been seen to. No one thought to challenge his right to do so, and it was only later that voices were raised in question.

The Magician called for the entire army to gather at the High King's tent come eventide, and when all were assembled the branched torches were brought out and lit.

They guttered slightly in the breeze that played with the smoke from the cooking fires and occasionally ruffled the edges of the Dragon Banner, which had been returned to its place of honour. Like an echo of the flickering shadows, murmurs and questions ran through the men, quieting only when the tent flap opened and Merlin led Arthur out for all to see.

'Warriors, heroes, survivors of this day's death, hear me,' the Enchanter cried, stirring the evening with his majestic voice. 'I bring you a report of sadness and much joy. Uther Pendragon, High King of Britain and leader of your armies, has died this day. Died in battle, surrounded by glory and defending his country. This was no man cut down by enemy swords, robbed of his life by the foes who wished to steal his realm. He suffered no wounds, lost no blood and met death in victory, not defeat. This was a man who gave even his last strength over to his people, and much honour shall attend his name.'

There was a pause as each paid silent tribute to the king who had so recently led them. Then Merlin looked out over the assemblage and began to speak.

'I would have you know that Uther died in joy, with the knowledge that a new hero had risen by his side. A hero of his own stock, his own son fighting beside him, protecting his father even as he will protect you, his people. Did you not see this boy always in the thickest part of the press, leading you bravely and surely to victory over the Saxons? And did you not follow him, inspired by his example and glad to have his youth and vigour at your command? I present you that young leader now: Arthur, son of Uther Pendragon and future High King of Britain.'

He turned with a gesture that directed all eyes to where Arthur stood solemnly before the torches. There was much shifting and murmuring as the crowd craned to get a better look.

Arthur was calm and composed, his hands clasped in front of him. Neither Celtic torque nor Roman laurels signified his leadership, yet there was no denying that he looked what he was, the uncrowned hero of the day.

'Proof!' someone cried. 'Where is the proof?'

'In your own eyes, man,' Merlin shot back. 'Did you not see Uther hand over the Sword of State to him today? Did you not see the young warrior assume the role that he was created for? Did you not follow him and his orders, both during battle and afterward?'

The crowd hummed its confirmation of these things, and Merlin raised his voice. 'And last of all, am I not proof? Have you not heard, through all these long years, that I was raising the young Prince, teaching and training him to be what we need most sorely, a High King to put the realm to rights and stop the Saxon advance across our land? I, Merlin, Seer of the Crystal Cave, Counsellor of Kings and Speaker for the Gods, tell you that this is your destiny made visible. He shall be known for all times as Britain's greatest king, warrior and champion, and his name is Arthur Pendragon!'

A cheer rose then, carried forward on the gusting wind, and the Red Dragon of the Banner stirred and stretched lazily against the night sky. The roar from the people subsided only when the wind died down and the dragon folded back upon itself, as though sinking into watchful slumber.

'Hold! I would speak!' came a voice from the shadows, and a stocky chieftain made his way through the crowd to stand before Merlin. 'Is this a true Council of Celts to choose a king, or the trick of a kingmaker who wants to establish a Roman-style dynasty?' he demanded.

Merlin's face was impassive, and he stared at the speaker with neither respect nor disdain. Then he looked out at the army and announced formally: 'King Lot of

145

Lothian and the Orkneys has requested your attention.'

'Fellow warriors, brave men and free,' Lot began, pacing slowly back and forth before the troops. 'I come before you to point out that we are in danger of being swept into the acceptance of a young man about whom we know nothing. A boy who has been among us for a bare day, at the most. A lad whose one feat seems to have been the taking of the Sword from the grasp of a sick king too weak and feeble to protest such thievery. A pretender to the throne whose claim is based on the flimsiest of reasons: his supposed bloodline. Have we not seen too well what happens when dynasties are founded? When kings inherit their power rather than earn it? Where is our Celtic freedom which allows us to follow a man well tried in battle, proven in Council, recognized in quality of leadership? I will not be robbed of the right to choose my king, will not be swayed by the spellbinding of a sorcerer and above all will not sit idly by to see the High Kingship go to one whose training and concepts are more Roman than Celtic!'

Murmurs of assent could be heard, and Merlin stepped forward.

'What is this "Celt versus Roman" nonsense?' he asked. 'We are all a mixture of both. Our grandfathers called themselves Roman citizens and were proud of it. The Empire has been split and shattered by the barbarians, it is true, but the knowledge of civil organization knows no geographic loyalty. To condemn a useful system of government because it comes from a certain source is as foolhardy as to refuse a good joint of meat because it comes from your neighbour's cow!'

A spate of laughter ran through the audience, beginning with Lot's own northern allies who still engaged in cattle raiding now and then.

Lot started to speak out again, but Merlin continued

146

blithely. 'I do not ask you to accept this young king because I have foisted him upon you, as Lot implies. I ask only that as freemen of the realm you follow your own conscience, your instinct to recognize a hero when he appears among you and your willingness to give your pledge to one trained and reared specifically for this job. Arthur owes no man here a favour, has no debt to any one of you, carries no vendetta or grudge to cloud his judgement. He can be just and fair precisely because of this fact. What more could you wish? What more can anyone give, as High King?'

Merlin paused to look carefully around the gathering, no doubt noting who nodded in agreement and who did not.

'Because of Uther's death this day,' he continued, 'we are a land without a leader. And yet the same fate that took the High King from you has also provided his replacement. Would you turn to internal bickering and petty politics when you have, this night, the chance to recognize a new star rising in the sky of Britain? He is here, now, before you, and awaits only your sign as to what you would have him do. What say you, freemen of Albion?'

Perhaps it was his use of the old name for Britain, or the wind tugging at the Banner again, that set the troops to chanting. Soft and low at first, then growing in pitch and volume, their chant carried as one voice until the whole camp rang with it: 'Arthur, Arthur, Arthur Pendragon.'

Lot still stood his ground, and Arthur remained unperturbed, as though the tumultuous cheering were but the crash of a wave on some distant shore and not the heralding of his own kingship.

At the moment when the energy of the crowd began to

147

wane, a tall broad man wearing the badge of the Boar rose and requested permission to speak.

'Your words are powerful, Great Merlin, and the future you spin is alluring. And of all men here,' he said slowly, 'I have the greatest reason to distrust you. But I, Cador of Cornwall, am here prepared to pledge my loyalty to Arthur, not on the basis of what you say, but on what I myself saw in the field this very day. This lad is a leader, born to the sword, such as comes rarely to any land, and I am willing to follow him from this night forth.'

Cador moved from his place in the front row of the assembly and striding up to Arthur, bent on one knee and raised his hands, palms together. Arthur looked down at him and carefully enclosed those two hands between the palms of his own, then freed them when Cador looked up at him.

'The smile that broke through Arthur's reserve was a joy to behold,' Bedivere said, his voice touched with wonder. 'And when he helped Cador to his feet the army roared and stamped its approval. I think,' he added, 'that it was the first time I had ever cried for happiness, and it had nothing to do with the fact that Arthur is my brother.'

'What happened then?' I blurted out, enthralled by the scene he had conveyed.

'I guess you could say Arthur was proclaimed by unanimous uproar, while Lot stood to one side, his fists tight-clenched and his eyes all but shooting sparks. One after another of the kings came forward, each bending the knee and offering his loyalty and receiving in return a smile, a nod or even a personal comment from Arthur.

'When he saw the majority would not listen to him, Lot turned on his heel and, gathering his followers and allies, left the camp. It was only later that we learned he and his troops departed that night for the north, choosing not to join the rest of us in taking Uther's body south, back to his court and his widow.

'I myself went to our tent, for the press around Arthur was too thick for me to get through, and by then the long time without sleep was beginning to tell on him; he looked too tightly drawn to have time for a childhood playmate. I didn't see him again until the next morning.'

'Was it very awkward, when you did meet?' I queried.

Bedivere laughed with full good humour and shook his head.

'Arthur sent a squire round at first light to roust out Ector and Cei and myself, and the next thing you know we were all seated at a table in the kitchen tent, eating oatmeal and each telling his own part of the battle as though we were back home again after an outing at the Fair. I tell you, Gwen, Arthur has a way of making people feel comfortably part of the grand adventure no matter what else is swirling around him. It's not just a trick of manners or a thing that can be learned. It's something native to his soul. You'll see . . . you'll see when you meet him.' And he smiled encouragingly at me.

I nodded, halfway admitting to myself that unless the Gods intervened, I might have good reason to care what sort of person King Arthur was.

A scout rode up, reporting that we would soon be coming to the community of Ribchester and our lodgings for the night.

So Bedivere went off to the front of the caravan, and I thought back to what Uther's last battle had meant to Rheged.

149

15
Gawain

Uther's call to battle had reached us just before the spring equinox, raising a flurry of conferences and grim arguments. Rhufon doggedly pointed out that it was much too early to take horses on the warpath, and he'd have to take fodder for the animals, since there wouldn't be enough grass for forage. Many of the roads weren't open yet, and between the ice and frost of winter in the higher elevations and the mud and melt of those places which had thawed, the idea of hauling a train of supplies across the breadth of Britain was, in his estimation, insane.

Nidan nodded in agreement, and my father suggested to the messenger that since King Uther himself was not well, perhaps it would be wiser to wait till later in the year, when both he and his allies might be stronger and more fit.

The royal messenger raised his head stiffly. 'King Uther is ready for battle,' he announced, 'even if he must go before the host in a litter! He is a strong, brave-hearted man, M'lord, and counts on your support in this matter. If he can face such a foe under these conditions, surely you can find a way to manage the problem of supplies.'

Kaethi says you can get the Celts to do most any foolhardy thing if you appeal to their pride, and sure enough, after a heated discussion of routes and transport, Rhufon suggested that if each horse carried additional nets of hay as well as a rider, it might be possible to make do with fewer wagons. And in the end it was agreed upon, as though some kind of logic had prevailed.

Word went out for the war bands to rendezvous at the

Aire Gap, and we began gathering and packing whatever would be necessary. In the evenings we sat together around the hearth, measuring and looping and tying the linen twine into fodder bags while Edwen recounted the glory of past victories. Within a week we were all on the Road together, the household accompanying the men as far as the path that would take us to the safety of The Mote while they were at war.

I could not remember my father going off to battle before, and was swept up in the excitement of the impending conflict. By the time our two parties separated I enthusiastically joined in the clapping and cheering and singing, as zealous a warrior's bairn as anyone could find.

My high spirits continued as we turned down the path, for The Mote is a spot both wild and primitive, as if untouched by time. The huge grey rock juts proudly out from the hillside, rising sharply above the turbulent waters where the Rough Firth joins the Solway. Softly thatched roundhouses cling like mushrooms round its base, creeping up the hillside from the pebbled beach to the upper rampart. And at the top the fort perches, neat and trim as a peregrine. It seemed a fittingly dramatic place to wait out a war.

Once the spring gales were past, the fine weather came quickly, and with it the freedom to explore both the coast and the woods close by. We collected the sea kale's tender stalks for Gladys and brought her the odd, hollow mushrooms known as morels that grow in the ashes of Beltane fires. In the high forest the red squirrels rained pine chips down on us, and once, when we first got there, we came on a husk of hares dashing madly about a clearing, occasionally rearing on their hind legs to box at each other like children. I burst out laughing and they leapt away, running crazily through the woodland.

Yet even while the high spirits of springtime ran free

around us, fear and worry for the men who were off fighting the Saxons hemmed us in. Nowhere was it more noticeable than around the evening hearth, where Kevin's voice, just now changing, provided the only deep male tones to be heard.

Then one wet, grey day a small party of travellers appeared on the shingle, moving slowly through the rain because of the stretcher. At that distance I couldn't clearly identify my father, but no one else would have been riding his stallion, and it was Nidan's steed that was being led home riderless.

White-faced and grim, the King's best warrior barely opened his eyes when they reached the fort. My father helped lift him on to a pallet by the hearth, and Kaethi set to work with her herbs. Wet and exhausted, the rest of the group silently ate the steaming nettle soup Gladys put before them, then went to bed. Rhufon stayed at the hearth a little longer, but refused to give any details about the battle.

With the warming of the next day's sun, the whole population of the settlement trooped up to the fort, bringing pillows or rugs and making themselves comfortable on the broad flat top of the rock.

I have always taken special delight in sitting there with the wind whipping round me while the black-headed gulls circle endlessly below and the waters of the Rough race and ripple towards the Otherworld realm of Annwn. Across the mouth of the narrow firth an ancient fort lies hidden in the forests atop the next ridge, and on nice days the fisherfolk leave their huts to venture forth upon the chancy tides. Today I found a spot on the edge of the gathering where I could look out across the water while Edwen reported the news of Uther's last battle.

He began with a recounting of Uther's background, just as Kevin had told it on our trip out to the Loch. Half-listening, I let my mind drift, dancing on the little waves that were sparkling along the firth. Even on misty days the currents are patterned with shimmer and shadow, and Nonny says they mark the passage of souls making their way to that strange land where a magic caldron graces the feasting hall. I wondered if the spirits this day were the recent dead going to join the festivities in Annwn, or those returning to the world to be born again as new humans.

There was a gasp at the news of Uther's death, and I sat up suddenly, remembering the question of his successor. But Edwen was telling of a new hero, unknown and unexpected: Uther's mysterious young son, long hidden by Merlin, had come to the fore and rallied the armies behind him.

'And that,' the bard concluded, with a run of the harp strings, 'is how Arthur Pendragon burst across the horizon, burning like a firedrake that appears out of nowhere and streaks in glory through the night sky.'

The audience smiled, and clapped their approval, though it was hard to tell whether their enthusiasm was for Arthur or for Edwen's presentation. All I could think of was that a bare boy, hardly older than Kevin, now stood between Rheged and the threat of Urien. I watched the tides shift in the firth and wondered what the young man's moira held for him.

'Perhaps,' Kevin said softly, leaning towards me so as not to be heard by others, 'this is the Great King the Ancient Ones tell of, whose reign will be like a comet.'

I had forgotten the prophecy, and nodded now with remembrance. I hoped it boded well for the lad, for in a way we owed him a debt of gratitude.

Gladys was calling me to come help prepare the feast, so I got up and ran off to the kitchen, the king-to-be already dismissed from my thoughts.

* * *

The warriors were not the only ones that suffered in Uther's last battle. Bad travelling conditions and short rations had left the horses thin and exhausted, so it was decided to put them out to pasture over the summer. I was glad for the horses but disappointed for myself, since it meant the household would have to stay in one place.

We took up residence near Lake Derwentwater, in a hill settlement that overlooks the broad vale leading from the Lakes to the Pennines. It is an ancient site, built up of stone slabs and hard work over many generations, and as far as I was concerned its greatest advantage was the proximity of the ancient tracks that run along the mountain ridges.

The valley floors and lower flanks of the mountains are so thickly forested that travel is confined to waterside trails and twisting footpaths. Only the high ground, with its stunted trees and tufts of grass and heather affords easy passage, and here the old tracks have been worn broad and smooth by centuries of use. The one that passes near Threlkeld Knotts not only leads west to the lake, and east to the Roman Road, it runs for miles along the fell tops and offered many a place for Kevin and me to race our horses.

Nothing is as cold as a stone house, for the walls harbour the chill of winter long after the flowers of summer dot the meadows, but during times of sultry heat their cool shadiness is most pleasant. This year the hot, dry days arrived in August, and it was a pleasure to take our late-evening meals in the central compound that is open to the long twilight and roofed only by the bright stars.

Early one evening a rider came to court with the message that King Lot of the Orkney Isles would be arriving within a day's time, come for a state visit and the chance to address our Council. My father grumbled to himself, then sent the messenger off to the kitchen, where Brigit began to confer with Kaethi as to how we would feed and house the guests.

I looked at Kevin and grinned; visiting royalty rarely came to the Lakes, and we could certainly use some excitement. At the age of eleven I thought not much past the present moment, and it never occurred to me that the events of the next few days might have repercussions for years to come.

The party was bigger than I had expected, for King Lot travelled with a full complement of warriors and personal retainers, and had brought along his oldest son as well.

The boy Gawain was short and stocky, not having caught up with his manhood yet, and his hair was every bit as red as his father's. Everything he did conveyed his quick energy, from the way he strutted behind his sire to the flash of his smile when something amused him. He was no more arrogant than other northern princes I had seen, but this was the first time I was expected to entertain one, and I wondered what he would enjoy doing over the next few days.

He turned out to be a good companion, eager to participate in anything I suggested, although I soon found that nothing we provided could compare to the wonders he was used to in the Orkneys. Even the wolfhound Ailbe only caused a momentary widening of Gawain's blue eyes before he allowed there were deerhounds of equal size at home.

'We have stone buildings too,' he informed me in a heavy northern accent as we went off towards the corrals with his horse. 'But ours are made of red rock worked into thick walls that are many storeys high and honeycombed with rooms. You can see them from a far distance, towers of strength and grandeur, and if you climb the stairs within the wall, you can look for miles in every direction.'

'Are they like the Roman forts?' I asked, trying to imagine walls thick enough to have rooms in them.

'Oh, no. The brochs are ancient places, often dark and crowded. They were used as forts when the Romans first threatened, but we made treaties with the Empire and never had to host their soldiers on our soil. I think the brochs frightened them away,' he added proudly.

'Where do you live now?' I asked, trying to ignore the implication that Britons who had become part of the Empire were somehow less brave or clever.

'Sometimes we stay at one of the wheel houses, where the structure doesn't go up so high, but on the inside of the wall there are wooden rooms built up that open on to a courtyard as big as yours here.'

He sketched a circle in the dirt and drew a series of lines across it, like the spokes of a wheel. The layout reminded me of the floating houses beyond the Solway, but before I could say so he went on with his bragging.

'They're much taller and airier than these,' he announced, gesturing towards our low houses and small doorways. 'Most of the rooms facing the courtyard are open, with hide curtains you can pull back so you can look down into the court, or up at the sky. My quarters at Midhowe are on the top tier, and it's like sleeping in a nest.'

I glanced around, seeing our settlement as dark and mean for the first time, and wished we had hosted our guests at Carlisle, where the house by the river is large and imposing. Kevin said nothing, but a small smile played around his mouth.

The call for a Council had gone out shortly after our guests arrived, but because people must come from so far away it would not be held until the third day. Lot and my

156

father were busy conferring on matters of state, and since there was no need for us to hang about the settlement, we spent the next day trying to avoid the heat by exploring the trails through the woods.

For a while my guest talked of the things he had seen on this, his first major trip through his own lands and those of his neighbours. His father's fortress on the massive rock of Edinburgh impressed him mightily, as did the inland reaches of the Firth of Forth and the great settlement at Dumbarton, on the Clyde. And he was looking forward to seeing Urien's capital, which had once been a powerful Roman city.

Yet his chauvinistic attitude towards his northern island home came through in everything he said. Nowhere else were the colours of the Great Crown so brilliant, the warriors so brave, the women so fine. His mother, though originally of Cornish stock, was now accepted as the Queen of Orkney, and was the most beautiful and powerful woman in the world.

'There are no arts known to man or god she is not versed in, and she can command even the secrets of the Goddess.' His voice was full of awe, and he carefully made the sign. 'Why, my Aunt Morgan says Mama could have become a priestess herself, if she'd studied with the Lady.'

I nodded silently, wondering what a queen would do with the powers normally reserved for a religious leader. It seemed an unholy combination of interests, and not one I was easy with.

In the late afternoon we turned towards home, making our way to the end of the lake and passing the tanner's holding that sits on the knoll overlooking the watercourse. One of the children in the yard looked up from the hide he was scraping and waved as we went past. At least Gawain would go home with the knowledge that our people are friendly and cordial, even to strangers.

The path followed the river, which was low because of the lateness of the year, but the water itself ran bright and clear, dancing over its rocky bed with a merry sound like the high gills after a spring storm. I told our guest how the salmon rush up it to spawn, fighting their way against the current and turning the water into seething silver. He shrugged, and said it was much the same in the Lothian rivers.

On a whim, I took the turn that leads to one of the finest spots in the Lakes, not telling Gawain where we were heading. Let him surpass this, I thought as we climbed amid green ferns and grey rocky ledges under a stand of fine old oaks. When we reached the top of the hill the trees thinned abruptly, and ahead of us stood that great circle of stones known as Castlerigg.

They rise proud and solemn on the greensward, crowning the hill which lifts above the junction of three mountain valleys. On every side the ground slopes away to the dales below, and the massive mountains ring the sky beyond, as though one were standing in the centre of a bowl.

The usual mists and fogs of late afternoon were nowhere to be seen, and the sun cast a bright, hard glint off rock and scree alike. Yet the presence of the Gods surrounded us, flickering in the thousand greens of the forests below and looming up on the steep sides of the fells.

We stood there in silence, as if on an island in time. Only the lack of wings kept me from soaring out across the wonderful moat of space that encircles the soft green knoll.

Kevin took his flask from his belt, and after pouring out an offering to the Gods, passed it among us. No one said anything until we had started home again, and Gawain let out a long whistle under his breath.

'Now, that's the most impressive thing I've seen in Rheged,' he announced, once we were safely on the trail again. 'Old as time, I would imagine. But the red stones of Stennes are taller by a good bit, and in that circle there is a carved timber that rises from a flagged hearth, and when the fire is lit beneath it, the faces on the post come to life.'

I glanced at Kevin, furious that I could not win unqualified admiration from this boy, but Kevin studiously avoided my gaze and I had to keep my frustration to myself.

After the evening meal Gawain arranged to sleep on the hillside with the soldiers, saying he found the stone rooms too dark and stuffy for comfort. I looked across the court at my father and wondered if King Lot was as difficult to please as his son was.

When I mentioned it to Nonny, she snorted with indignation.

'Proud as eagles, those two, but rude as well. The code of hospitality applies to guest as well as host, and someone should have taught them that when they were young!'

'Maybe he's just uneasy, being so far from home,' I said, surprised to find myself coming to Gawain's defence. I remembered his quick grin when we stopped to watch a marten chasing a squirrel noisily through the treetops.

'The little beggar got away,' he'd cried gleefully when the squirrel scampered to safety after the marten misjudged a branch and fell to the ground. I suspected there was a streak of rooting for the underdog in Gawain, and wondered what his father thought of it.

The next day dawned hot and brazen, with the sun a copper disc pounded flat against the sky. We spent the day down at the lake, trying to snare ducks while Kevin took the coracle out fishing. I caught two birds, but Gawain got none, for he lacked the patience necessary for snaring and tended to give himself away with his quick movements.

'I prefer hunting the beasts of the forest,' he said, eyeing my mallards disdainfully. 'The royal stags in our glens are as fine as any you'll find anywhere.' I didn't say that I'd rather eat solid duck than fill my stomach with imaginary venison, but I thought it.

When Kevin brought the coracle back to shore, I asked our guest if he wanted to row out to the island.

'There's ruins on it,' I noted, gesturing towards the rocky crags half-hidden by the trees. It shimmered in the afternoon heat like a fairy image, mysterious and strange. 'They say it was once the home of Bilis, Dwarf God of the Underworld who rides about on the back of a goat,' I added casually, hoping to reclaim our prestige.

'And you would trespass on his property?' Gawain asked, appalled at my effrontery.

'It's part of my kingdom,' I answered with a shrug, not bothering to add that all the lakeside children climb among the now harmless rocks and rubble on warm days.

'Nay, I'll not be party to such an act,' Gawain countered, making the sign. One of Kevin's eyebrows shot up quizzically, but he said nothing, and we both kept from smiling.

It dawned on me that while human ways and simple accomplishments might not inspire Gawain with awe, encounters with the Old Gods did, and I spent our homeward trek telling him about Rough Firth with its strange, frightening pathway to the Underworld.

'Annwn lies somewhere beyond The Mote,' I explained, the words inspiring a delicious shiver of fear and amazement within me. 'And many's the morning I've sat high up on the rock and wondered whose souls were being borne past on the rush of waters. Why, once,' I added breathlessly, carried to new heights by the very idea, 'I saw the shadow of the Gods as they trooped off to Arawn's Hall.'

Gawain's eyes had grown large with wonder, and he stared at me in respectful silence. I felt somewhat mollified; at least it showed he could admire something beyond the boundaries of his own kingdom.

Morning of the Council Day dawned bright and clear, with a promise of more heat by afternoon, so we decided to take the horses out early and give them a run along the track while it was still comparatively cool.

Gawain's mount was a good solid creature, hardy and trustworthy, though I suspected not as fiery as he would have liked. One doesn't use the best of animals for long treks unless there is need for them at your destination.

Kevin had rounded up the horses and Featherfoot was saddled and ready for the day's outing by the time we reached the stables.

Rhufon helped me into the saddle with the terse warning, 'Your mare's feeling plenty frisky this morning. Don't you be doing anything rash, now, Missy.' I laughed and nodded at him, knowing that when I wasn't around he liked to brag I could manage a horse better than most boys my age.

We headed off along the forest path, with Kevin riding ahead as usual. Up until now Gawain had ignored my dark companion, which was fine with Kevin, who generally preferred to watch and listen to what was happening around us, occasionally making a droll comment to me which no one else could hear.

As we neared the juncture with the track our guest turned to me and asked, 'Do you always have a servant with you?'

'Servant?' I gasped. 'Kevin's no servant. He's my foster

161

brother and the High Prince of a proud kingdom in Ireland!'

I knew I was exaggerating, but after days of putting up with Gawain's condescension, I didn't care.

'High Prince? But I thought no king could hold the throne of Tara if he was deformed.' The visitor's tone was one of flat statement rather than challenge, and I writhed inwardly, ashamed that I had lied and vexed that it brought embarrassment to Kevin.

'I didn't say Tara. He comes from a small northern realm, and his father is a client king of Tara's just as we're client kings of the young Arthur.'

'Your father's sworn fealty to Uther's bastard?' Gawain's shock was evident in both tone and expression, and he looked at me dumbfounded.

'Of course,' I answered, furious now for having brought up a subject I should have remembered would not sit well with our guests. I was as hemmed in by my runaway blunders as by the trees and undergrowth on either side of the trail.

The track lay just beyond the turn of the path, and I suddenly gave Featherfoot such a kick in the ribs she lunged past Kevin and out into the open space. It wasn't the most honourable way to end a difficult moment, but it did work.

We bolted down the broad track, the high, bare landscape flashing by in a blur. I crouched forward on the mare's neck, feeling the wind lifting my hair from my back. The boys were pounding behind us, but so far only the dog had been able to catch up, and he loped along now with the same grace of released energy that I felt. We kept our lead, flying into the morning sun as though our pursuers were the spirits of Samhain, and I saw Ailbe drop back to Kevin's side as Featherfoot held her pace.

The track dipped down to the rocky ford at the beck,

and I swerved away from it, so that we galloped across the rough ground towards a spot where the banks of the creek were high and firm. Featherfoot saw the drop ahead and gathered under me, taking the leap as though we had practised it every day. For a moment we were suspended free of the earth, flying over the small chasm and landing cleanly on the other side. A few strides more and I swung the mare's head around, turning in time to see Kevin's gelding barely complete the jump.

I brushed my hair back from my face triumphantly and watched as Gawain's horse came to the bank and plunged to one side, in spite of his rider's commands. The red-haired boy took his mount back up to the rise of the track and set him at the jump again, whipping him forward with the rein. The horse came on gamely at first, then swerved aside a second time, almost unseating his rider.

Kevin and I walked our horses down to the ford and came back up to our guest, who was roundly cursing his animal.

'It's all right,' I said, as tactfully as possible. 'Your horse probably isn't used to jumping.'

The Prince of Orkney glowered at me, red-faced and furious. 'He's only a travelling horse. I could take my stallion over it easily.'

I nodded and saw Gawain's blue glare flicker to Kevin. It was obvious he didn't want to be outdone by a boy he had assumed was a servant. 'I could take it on your horse,' he proposed, turning back to me.

'All right,' I answered, slipping from her back, 'but she's got a very gentle mouth, so be careful not to jerk the reins about.'

Together Gawain and I walked Featherfoot to a rocky ledge, letting the mare get accustomed to his smell and voice.

I used a light saddle, barely more than a leather pad,

and he scrambled from the rock on to the seat with more determination than grace. When he took the reins I had a moment's misgiving, wondering if he'd remember my warning about her mouth. But he handled her gently, if not well.

It was only when I stood there watching them trot back up to the track that I realized he was nowhere near the horseman I had supposed. Dear Epona, I prayed, don't let anything happen to him while he's my guest. I glanced at Kevin and saw him frowning with the same concern.

Featherfoot came down the track well, cutting off into the rough and heading for the stream more by her own volition than by Gawain's guidance. She reached the bank, leapt up into the air and sailed across the rocky chasm with all the grace in the world. Gawain clung to her mane, grinning from ear to ear, but as she landed he lost his grip and tumbled from her back.

He hit the ground with a horrible thud and rolled over on his back, still as death.

I scrambled over to him, terrified he'd split his head open on some half-hidden rock. I wondered what I could offer the Gods to bring him back to life if that was the case.

He lay amid the tufts of grass and bracken, gasping for breath and looking very surprised. His face was spattered with blood, and a steady stream of it ran from his nose.

'Are you hurt?' I asked, kneeling next to him and trying to staunch the nosebleed.

'I'm fine,' he wheezed finally. 'Landed on my shoulder and rolled some, I think.'

I was relieved to see his eyes tracking and his skin unbroken, and when we had got the nosebleed stopped he struggled to sit up. There was a red spot along one cheek which would probably turn to a bruise, but at least he was in one piece.

He grinned then—the fierce, bright smile I'd found so contagious before—and shook his head in admiration. 'You may live in dark little houses and eat birds and cabbage like a peasant, but you certainly have fine horses and great sport,' he said.

I was so surprised, I burst out laughing. The arrogant disdain and raging temper were all gone, and although he moved gingerly, he looked around with good cheer. 'That horse will be halfway to the Wall by now. Will she be hard to catch?'

'Featherfoot? No, she's too much part of the family to run away.'

I stood up and scanned the landscape, spotting my mare browsing among the grasses by a stunted tree.

'I'll get her,' Kevin said, handing me the reins of the other two horses.

'You're quite sure you're all right?' I asked again as Gawain got to his feet. The nearness of catastrophe caught up with me, and my knees started to shake. What if he'd been thrown into the streambed itself, crashing against the jumble of dry rocks and bringing grief to his family and dishonour to my own? I was appalled at what might have happened, and found it amazing that Gawain himself seemed unconcerned.

'Of course,' he was saying, 'just bruised a bit here and there. I've taken worse in sword practice at home.'

We rode more sedately after that, in part because of the morning's mishap, and in part because we began to encounter people on the track, all heading for the settlement and the afternoon's Council. When the trees around the settlement came into view, Gawain called a halt.

'I'd just as soon we not mention this to the grown-ups,' he ventured, smiling shyly.

'But what about your nose?' I asked, noting that it was red and swollen, and no longer truly straight.

'I'll say my own horse shied unexpectedly. He's a dull animal, and my father would rather hear that than know it was poor horsemanship on my part, particularly if I had not acquitted myself well in a challenge.'

I sighed with relief inwardly, and Kevin nodded in silence, but looked upon our guest with admiration and an almost-smile.

'So we'll leave it at that?' Gawain pursued hopefully.

'That's fine with me,' I said, grinning, and on that note we returned to the stables and the afternoon Council.

King Lot

Royal Councils that summon the citizens from more distant parts of the kingdom are not common, for Councils are usually local in nature and are held wherever the King happens to be staying. To have a special convocation at the request of a visiting monarch was most unusual, and the throng that gathered was full of cheerful curiosity. It was plain that those arriving were glad to have this unexpected break in the summer routine as they greeted old friends and exchanged family news and speculation on what the Council would be about.

The settlement was soon overflowing with people, and many set up camp outside the walls, having travelled so far they could not hope to return home by dark. There was even a travelling peddler who spread his wares on a rug beside the well.

The man's blond hair and blue eyes set him apart as a foreigner, and I watched curiously as he tried to sell his merchandise to one farm wife after another, without any luck.

On closer inspection the items on the peddler's rug were rich and various: plenty of the usual bronze and copper things such as one finds at any market, but also a silver brooch in a solid disc shape such as I had never seen before.

'Saxon work, Miss,' the man confided. 'Very popular around York. But dear, much too dear for any save a princess.'

I was tempted to tell him I was a princess, but since I

had nothing to trade for it anyway, decided to let the matter go.

He help up a small purse, richly coloured and decorated with intricate designs. 'Egyptian, as I recall. From Cairo, anyhow. Maybe the weaver was in Damascus.'

I wondered where Damascus was and who the artisan had been, and marvelled at the traders who carried the products of man's endeavours across the world. I wished we could sit and talk about the campfires he had joined, the forges he had seen and the stories he had heard in all his wanderings. But Gladys was calling me to come help decant the wine, so I grinned at the man and trotted back to the pantry.

The afternoon was hot and sultry, and when it was time to start the Council the people crowded into the central court. There were so many that some overflowed into the doorways of the houses, sitting or standing packed close together, trying to make room for everyone. The servants had to pass the flagons of wine among the guests, since there were nowhere near enough cups to serve everyone properly. Gradually the feeling of celebration began to fade, and by the time the King's chair was brought out to the centre of the compound, the mood of revelry had disappeared and all was serious business.

My father opened the Council with a formal invocation of the Gods in honour of the importance of the occasion, and when the libation had been poured he immediately introduced King Lot and sank wearily back into his chair.

The northern king's restless energy filled the space at the heart of the gathering, and captured every eye. He was a sturdy man with magnificent moustaches, their ends waxed and twisted so that they hung elegantly down to his chin. His high colouring and broad stature conveyed an abundance of health and vigour, and I stared at him with awe and admiration. Standing there with his green plaid sash held on one shoulder by a great jewelled brooch and his linen tunic coming barely to his knees, he looked like a timeless hero, proud and powerful.

It was easy to see how Gawain came by the kind of bluntness that is sometimes perceived as being rude. But whereas the son's actions were often hasty and brash, the father's were overlaid with the poise of a warrior who has learned always, above all else, to keep his balance.

He began with the ritual words of a guest, thanking the King for our hospitality and the people for their willingness to hear what he had to say. His voice was not particularly rich, but he had perfected its use as well as any bard might, and at first I was more interested in his delivery than in the content of his words. If there had been more room he would have prowled about the circle, but as it was he had to be content with standing in one spot and turning, with great sweeping gestures, to face the different parts of the audience in turn. They, of course, were fascinated by his display of confidence and power.

Somewhere along the line the compliments and flattery gave way to the death of King Uther and the point of Lot's visit.

'Now they are putting about the story that this Arthur is really Uther's child, conceived by magic and hidden away until suddenly he is proposed as heir to the High Kingship,' Lot declared, his voice rising with indignation. 'What claptrap! They're playing politics, mind you, trying to satisfy the Romanized south, who expect sons to inherit regardless of their capability!'

He spat out the word 'Romanized' with such contempt that I wondered what Kaethi was thinking, but the crowd was so thick I couldn't see her.

Lot bent to someone across the circle from me and took the flagon that was offered him.

'Oh, it's a very clever story, all right, making him half-Celt, and on his mother's side at that, in the hope that we northerners will be satisfied that the bloodline is direct and pure. But we'll not be fooled . . .'

He took a long draught, then gave back the flask and wiped his moustaches with the back of his hand. You could see the scars of past battles webbed palely across the darker wholeness of sound flesh up the whole length of his arm.

'This young Arthur's claim to Logres is one thing; it was Uther's realm, and if the people wish to accept this "son" of his on Merlin's word, that's their business. But we who never became Rome's servants, we northerners who are proud to remember we are Celts, choose our High Kings on merit and proven leadership. It has always been thus, and we won't change now. We'll not accept an untried boy, sprung on us after fifteen years of hiding. No matter what his blood, the Celts will not follow a leader who has not proved his worth. Why, he's barely a year older than my own boy here, and while Gawain has been in half a dozen battles already, this young Arthur has appeared in only one, and we all know that is not enough to test the mettle of a fighting man!'

He looked around at the warriors who stood at the back of the audience, and a few responded by clapping their hands or stamping their feet.

'Not only that: the boy appeared as if from nowhere, conjured up suddenly by the Magician. There was no question of his moving up through the ranks, his learning and military arts upon the field, his earning the privilege of fighting beside other kings. No background, no experience, no proof of fitness . . . no, I say, no, no, no!'

He had worked up to a controlled fury, and his whole body radiated indignation. I thought surely the son's wrath had been nothing compared with what his father must be capable of.

'If this Romanized stripling would aspire to be High King, let him earn the right in battle, on the bodies of his slain foes . . . on mine, if necessary!'

Quick as lightning Lot's hand was at his belt and his dagger flashed in an arc that left it embedded in the hard-packed earth at his feet. For the space of half a minute it vibrated there, the echoes of its silent challenge shivering through the people.

'To arms, to arms!' someone cried, and a roar of approval followed instantly. Lot's men were cheering now, and not a few of our own brave fighters joined in, joyful with the promise of released tension. I stole a look at my father, who sat hunched over his wine cup, watching the proceedings with a thoughtful frown. Compared with the splendid figure cut by the King of Orkney he looked old and frail, and my heart went out to him.

As the cheering died down, the King of Rheged raised his arm for silence.

'King Lot, you speak persuasively. And the points are well taken. But I wonder if we are forgetting the more important enemy. We have had reports that the Saxons are preparing another invasion from the Continent. Isn't it more prudent to unite against these, our known enemies, than to splinter our forces by internal squabbles? The Saxons, after all, are a threat to every British kingdom, and would be cruel masters if they succeeded in conquering us because we are too busy killing each other.'

'Do not lecture me about the Saxons, my man.' Lot's tone had changed to one of comradery, and he spoke as if the two kings were old friends. 'Or about the Picts and Irish, for that matter. Who knows better than I, a king of two countries that are separated by lands long held by the hostile Picts? It is no easy matter to rule in two places at once, particularly with unfriendly forces in between.'

He laughed proudly and after retrieving his knife, looked confidently around the gathering.

'Were it not for the sea wisdom of my Orkney sailors and the fine shipwrights – and good forests – of my Lothian people, I would not even be able to move between my two capitals. A kingdom divided is always in danger. And that comes back to what I was saying: we must have a leader who unites us, who can be trusted to look to the needs of the Celts, and take the field with our men in battles of a common cause.'

'Do you, by any chance, have such a man in mind?' My father's voice was mild, with only a slight hint of irony. 'Perhaps yourself?'

For a moment Lot hesitated, and I expected him to slide over into the fanciful bragging and bravura so dear to the warrior's heart. But he was playing a more important game and now turned deftly back to the Council.

'I cannot say I would not be honoured if the title were offered me. But in truth, I think there is another who not only is as experienced as I, but commands one of the largest armies in the whole of Britain. Not only that, he is a Celt by blood and by training, and is married to a Celtic princess of the south. There is no taint of bastardy there, no twist of Roman ambition or question of military aptitude. Of all the British leaders he is most qualified to be High King, and most strategically placed to counter the Saxon threat. I am proposing Urien of Northumbria as our next High King, and seek your support as allies in this matter.'

I caught my breath in surprise and dismay, and glanced quickly around the gathering to see what sort of reaction there would be. If Lot expected a spontaneous outburst of support, he was roundly disappointed. His rhetoric had been among the best I'd ever heard, and his arguments well presented, but there were few among my father's warriors who had not sustained some sort of wound from our neighbour, and they were not ready on such short notice to embrace Urien as their future overlord.

Our men shifted uneasily in their places, scratching their chins or adjusting belt buckles with averted eyes and sullen mouths. Lot's crew assessed the change in mood and left it to the leaders to bridge the awkward gap.

'Ah, yes, Urien,' my father said smoothly, moving in his chair so that he was leaning against the other arm. 'Your brother-in-law, as I recall.'

Lot shot him a quick look, then smiled broadly. 'Yes, indeed. Urien and I were each lucky enough to marry a daughter of Gorlois, Duke of Cornwall. These are the legitimate offspring of Queen Igraine's first marriage.' He stressed the word legitimate ever so slightly, for Igraine was also mother of the young Arthur by her union with Uther. 'Through our wives we are bound to the south, as well as the north, and one could argue that this is another point in favour of uniting behind Urien.'

'And these sisters, Morgan and Morgause, are they not also kin to Cador, present Duke of Cornwall?' my father asked.

'Half-siblings only,' came the quick reply. 'Cador is much older, being born of Gorlois's first marriage. No one disputes that he has a rightful place in Cornwall.'

Lot was growing irritated at this recitation of genealogy, for like most warriors he was interested only in those lines which were of use to himself, and found the reciting of other kinships cumbersome and unnecessary.

'But,' my father continued in a conversational tone, 'doesn't that suggest that an alliance between your wife and her half-brother in Cornwall would be most likely? And since Cador of Cornwall has backed the claim of the

173

young Arthur, isn't it reasonable to assume that the sisters might also honour his claim?'

'Absolutely not!' Lot's voice rose to its full pitch and he turned back to the Council, seeing his way on to firm ground. 'It is a matter of history that Uther, our recently dead High King, took Igraine by stealth, even at the cost of her rightful husband's life. And the first thing he did upon marrying Igraine was send her daughters away. Are they now bound to show allegiance to the son of a man who so roundly displaced them when they were but children? Uther tore apart a legitimate royal family, replacing a loving father with his own lust-driven self and casting aside the children of the man he'd killed.'

There was a growl of appreciation from the throng, who had been raised in the lore of blood ties and family pride, and knew full well that an insult from one generation will carry to another unless there is restitution made.

'I'm not sure that "cast aside" is the best way to describe his marrying Morgause to you,' my father interjected with a note of amusement. 'It appears to have been a good thing for both of you; she has a proud king for a husband, to take care of and protect her, and you are the father of, what is it . . . three sturdy young princes?' He nodded approvingly towards Gawain.

'Four it is now. Yes, four boys of fine mettle and proud spirit.'

I had never seen my father play with another man in the way he was playing with Lot, and I experienced the same sort of fascination that one finds in watching an adder approach a toad.

The King of the Orkney Islands moved from righteous indignation over his wife's lost patrimony to the glowing pride of a man who sees his sons as reflections of himself and so is well satisfied. He called off the names and virtues of each child: Gawain the brave, Gaheris the cunning, Agravain the proud and Gareth, whom he classified simply as the youngest. They were obviously the great joy of Lot's life, and he boasted about each in turn until the crowd began to lose interest and my father intervened.

'You are indeed a man to be envied,' he said pleasantly. 'And we appreciate hearing your news and listening to your ideas. But the day grows long, and many of my people will want to get back to their steadings by dark, so perhaps we should adjourn the Council.'

'And what of the question of Urien?' Lot asked, caught fully off balance. It was not a propitious time to request a vote on whether or not the people of Rheged would join him in challenging Arthur's claim to the throne, but he was loath to let the subject drop entirely.

So the matter was opened for discussion, with freemen asking questions or making points of their own. There was little interest in giving our neighbour more power, and when the vote was taken, the result came out strongly in Arthur's favour.

'I would hope,' my father said solemnly as he prepared to close the Council, 'that this question will be resolved soon, for internal bickering will not benefit anyone but the Saxons, and I have heard that Arthur is likely to be invested with the Sword of State next spring.'

'Not,' grumbled Lot, 'if I have anything to do with it.' But he swung back to his seat and took part in the formalities that ended the Council with a fair amount of grace.

It was only much later that night, when I took my father the mixture Kaethi made up to ease him into sleep, that I was able to ask about the Council, and whether or not it had pleased him.

'Pleased . . . No. I would rather there were no need for

such a Council. But considering the nature of King Lot, perhaps it came out well.'

He shrugged and turned from the small window where he had been looking out across the moonlit forest to the vale below. The people on the hillside had settled down for the night, and Lot's party had already retired since they would be leaving early the next day. The air was still, but the heat itself seemed to have lifted, and in the quiet of the night the world that lay before us was calm and peaceful.

'Remember, my dear,' he said, moving to his favourite chair and gesturing for me to be seated, 'every man, and woman too, has some vital flaw. Perhaps it is sad, or perhaps it is a blessing, but it is there in every human being.'

He sighed and rubbed his fingers along one temple as though to dispel some painful thought.

'Lot's flaw is pride. He has all the bravery of a hero, and the love of glory and honour that we Celts have always cherished. But he is too proud to see that times, and needs, are changing. I fear he will stop at nothing to deny Uther's son the High Kingship.'

'And you,' I asked: 'you think Arthur's claim is just?'

'As just, I suppose, as any other that could be made. At times like this, justness is not quite so important as the finding of a leader the men will rally to. There's been nigh on to threescore years of confusion and infighting, what with Vortigern discarding anything that wasn't Celtic, and Ambrosius coming back and trying to reinstate Roman ideas. Uther was a small blessing in our lifetime, if only because he didn't worry so much about internal affairs, and did concentrate on the Saxon threat.

'Uther caused a further split with his taking of Igraine, and now things are in danger of becoming polarized between north and south. Yet in spite of that heritage,

176

Arthur seems to have gained the support of many of Uther's followers. And he has the Enchanter with him, which bodes well. Merlin has shaped the events behind British history for more than a generation now, and while I cannot credit all the stories that I've heard of him, he seems to see some greater purpose than most of the rest of us can.'

My father sighed wearily and reached for the cup I had brought.

'I do not like sessions such as today's; they leave me tired and feeling very old. But I've spent three days with Lot, finding where his weaknesses lie because it was important that the people see them clearly. One must always take stock of the man you're dealing with, and if you give him plenty of time and courtesy, he'll usually show himself plain enough.'

He took a sip from the cup and then closed his eyes. 'I had hoped the people would see how much his wife Morgause is involved in all of this, but while he alluded to her loss because of Uther's marriage to her mother, there was no real substance to catch hold of. From what he told me privately, however, she's a real wildcat, full of black powers and terrible rages, and I imagine the two of them make a lively team. And she bears no love for her young brother Arthur, that much I'm sure of.' He sighed then, and opened his eyes. 'One must always be careful when pressing any man as closely as I pressed Lot, especially if it's on a matter as touchy as his wife. And if you're dealing with an Orkneyan, you can be sure his pride will get involved!

'Did you see,' he asked suddenly, 'how quick that dagger flew? It was embedded a good quarter of the way up the blade in a trice! Now, that is a man to respect, and be wary of. Even when he was younger Nidan could not have beaten that, and Nidan's the best man with a knife I've ever had.'

He shook his head in genuine admiration; then, glancing down at the cup, finished off the contents and gave it back to me.

'Stuffy business, politics,' he opined slowly. 'Always taking place in close quarters, with too many twists in the thinking. If I had my way, we'd hold all Councils on horseback, down there by the lake, or up where the river runs bright across the rocks. Only the sky for a roof, and a man's word direct and honest, as the Gods meant it to be.'

'Now who's sounding like a classic Celt?' I said, laughing, and it brought a smile to his eyes.

We chatted a bit more, before I took leave of him and walked slowly back to the house I was sharing with the other women. Politics, I had decided, was not my favourite pastime.

The memory of such innocence made me smile in spite of myself. What had I known then of politics, or expediency, or the fact that sometimes a pattern of events is simply bigger than oneself?

Well, I thought fiercely, let other royal women expect their lives to be defined according to the political tides of the time. This Cumbrian lass would not be among them. At least, not willingly.

17

The Coronation

Bedivere led us down out of Bowland's wood with the storm clouds roiling behind and the town that guards the Ribble valley just ahead. The checkered sign of an inn offered welcome refuge, and as we turned into the courtyard I noticed a group of horsemen in a field across the way. They appeared to be young men who charged back and forth on horseback in spite of the weather, and they made up for their lack of discipline with noisy shouts and great enthusiasm. They hardly looked up when we arrived, and it occurred to me how closely one's fame is linked to geography, for we had reached the outer edges of Rheged and I knew no one here.

The inn was large and well appointed, with a number of guests already seated at the tavern's tables. Merchant travellers and artisans from east of the Pennines mixed with the usual flow of market people from north and south. The texture of their dialects was as thick and warming as the mutton stew we ate, and I leaned back against the bolsters at my corner table and watched the people from the safety of my newfound anonymity.

The talk hummed through the room, with now and then a particular voice rising in good cheer or zealous rhetoric. There were several games of dice going, and the kitchen help were kept busy fetching an endless stream of orders. The need to band together for safety on the Road more often than not means overcrowding when a group stops at a hostelry, with everyone wanting to be fed at once. The mood here was one of good-natured banter, however, as people waited their turn for the stewpot or ale pitcher.

A sturdy Dalesman from the other side of the mountains lifted his voice in argument with a Lancashire lad, and for a moment there looked to be trouble, but his companion ordered another round of ale for all concerned and took his friend off into the night once the commotion had died down.

Someone took up a harp, and conversations quieted at the prospect of a song. I have heard it said that all Celts, whether Irish, Breton, Cumbri or Cornish, are so touched by music that it can heal their wounds and mend their broken bones, and perhaps that's not far from wrong.

Certainly it put me in a gentler mood. The longing for days past was less poignant, my resentment at leaving Rheged somehow less fierce. I let the music wash through me, and by the time the brisk fire of mealtime had dwindled into coals I was thoroughly drowsy and relaxed.

When the innkeeper's wife came over to escort us to our rooms, I got sleepily to my feet and followed her through the wickerwork door.

'It's not fancy, Ma'am,' our hostess said, 'but it's the best we have, and I'm sure you'll be warm and comfy.'

I smiled in gratitude, and looked about my quarters.

It was a large room, furnished with massive pieces and good rugs, and had the air of much regular use. It occurred to me that it might be the owners' own bedroom, and I inquired if that was the case.

'Yes'm. I hope you don't mind. The other rooms are much more . . . bare, and we couldn't give you just any old place,' she answered simply.

'But where will you and your husband sleep?' I asked, touched by such thoughtfulness. 'I don't want to turn you out of your own bed, after all.'

'Ah, there's plenty of room in the servants' quarters,' she assured me. 'We're already set up for it, and Grandma has spent the last two days sweeping and dusting and

180

airing everything here . . . it would be a great disappointment to her if you were to refuse it.'

Indeed, a glance about the room showed it to be spotless, with the wood fresh-waxed and gleaming, and the pillows plumped up to perfection. Even Lavinia seemed to approve as she laid out my nightclothes.

Our hostess was turning back the covers of the bed, smoothing the fabric of the quilt with gentle pride.

'It's stuffed with down,' she announced, 'and far better than woollen blankets or heavy fur throws. I'm sure you'll sleep well under it.'

I had been admiring the large bronze mirror that stood by the clothes cupboard.

'I've never seen a mirror so big. Is it very old?' I inquired.

The woman nodded and dimpled with pleasure. 'Our family's lived in this town for more generations than I know, first as soldiers of the Empire and now as tradespeople and hostelers. So we've collected all manner of interesting things. That,' she said, pointing to the picture of a solid man mounted on a sizable horse, 'is a portrait of the ancestor who came from Sarmatia, back when the town was new.'

I moved nearer to see the picture more clearly, and she brought over a lamp.

'A proud warrior he was, too. Sent here from his home far off in the east, and fought well, I have no doubt. There's many in the area who can trace their line back to the Sarmatians that retired here when their time was up in the Legions.'

'What's he holding?' I peered at the cavalryman closely, noting his fish-scale tunic and the pole he gripped firmly in one hand.

'His lance. They fought from horseback, our ancestors, and used those long lances as well as swords. Grandma

181

says that we kept his sword in the family for many years, but no one knows where it is now. Probably lost to some Irish raider,' she added pragmatically. 'But the boys hereabouts still play with wooden lances and like to boast of their long lineage as mounted warriors.'

That explained the scrimmaging youngsters on the field we'd seen on our way into town. No wonder they had paid our arrival little notice: if someone were coming at me with one of those weapons, I wouldn't want to be looking elsewhere!

I slept very well that night, too tired even to dream. The light, fluffy quilt was every bit as warm and comfortable as our hostess had predicted, and I resolved to ask her where it had come from.

At dawn the smell of bacon drifted in from the kitchen. There was already much bustling about, and rather than disturb our hosts, I went out to the stableyard in search of water. The sky was only lightly clouded, and I looked out across the broad river valley as the sunrise faded from peach to gold to pale blue. There was no ice on the trough, so I tied my hair back and splashed about with the pleasant realization that spring was really here.

The drum of hoofbeats caught my attention, and I glanced up to see a young man gallop into the enclosure and swing his horse towards the kitchen door. He controlled the animal only with his knees, for in his hands he held a basket of eggs packed in moss; I marvelled that he could transport so fragile a cargo at such a breakneck pace.

The horse came to a well-practised stop as the boy called me over. Handing down the basket, he swung off his mount and traded me the reins for the eggs before dashing into the kitchen. I took them, naturally, and led the animal around the yard in order to cool her down properly.

She was a young mare of good size, though not so tall as our Shire horses, and for all that she'd worked up a sweat on this early-morning errand, she showed no sign of being winded. I noted with interest the long loops of leather that hung down on either side of the saddle and wondered what Rhufon would make of them, for they were stretched and worn as though much used, but poorly placed for securing saddlebags or bundles.

The boy came running out of the house and took back the reins with a quick smile. 'Aunt Hulda said if I didn't get those eggs here in time to feed the guests, she'd have my hide!' Then he grinned impishly. His hair and eyes were black as jet, and there was a bronze cast about his skin such as I had never seen before. 'It seems you have some "pretty important people" in your party, eh?'

I laughed and allowed that that was a matter of opinion. 'What,' I asked, pointing to the leather straps, 'are those for?'

'This,' he announced, and drawing one leg up, he slid his foot into the loop and vaulted up into the saddle.

I stood there gaping while he wheeled the mare around and began to trot across the yard. When he'd wriggled the other foot into position, he braced his knees and stood upright straddling the animal, still balancing with the motion, and urged her into a canter. Then he performed a number of feats, crouching low over the mare's withers, lying back along her spine, hanging far over on one side and trailing his hand through the water trough as they galloped past.

At last he turned and rode back to me, his dark face shining with excitement, and I grinned up at him with admiration.

'Where ever did you learn to do all that?'

'Here. When I first got here I'd never even been astride

a pony, but after all these years I've got the hang of it, and can fight among the best of them.'

'The boys in the field.' I nodded. 'But what prompted you to build those straps into the saddle?'

'That's the way we do it here.' He shrugged. 'I've always wondered why others don't do it too. Sometimes it's very funny watching a guest who's all puffed up with self-importance balance on the rim of the trough in order to climb aboard his animal, when I know something as simple as two strips of leather would make mounting and dismounting so much easier.'

I laughed at the notion and took another, closer look at how the things were attached so that I could have my own tack modified in the future. It certainly didn't look difficult, and like the boy, I wondered why others didn't copy the idea.

I started to ask if I could try them out when a great commotion came tumbling through the kitchen door. Cook, servants, hostess and Lavinia all rushed to surround me, scolding that I was standing ankle deep in mud and insisting that I take my place at the breakfast board. So I waved farewell to the lad on horseback and went back inside.

My chaperone scowled fiercely as she recounted having looked everywhere for me, and added, without much resignation, 'I might have known you'd be out with the horses!'

Breakfast was hot and toothsome, with platters of fresh eggs flanked by slabs of bacon and solid oatcakes. When I had finished eating, I called the hostess over to our table and complimented her on the excellence of her hospitality.

'I must apologize for the boy, Ma'am,' she said quickly. 'He had no idea who you were.'

'I know,' I reassured her, 'and that made our conversation all the more enjoyable. I gather he's your nephew?' I thought of the picture of the Sarmatian warrior and assumed the child came by his talent with horses through that lineage.

'Adopted son, more like,' she answered, shaking her head fondly. 'Poor little tyke was born to slavery, I would guess; at least, he was slave to a Greek eye doctor when they arrived at my cousin's inn up at Corbridge. His owner claimed the child was an Arab, but who knows? He was barely more than a tad when he and his master came to town, but an eye doctor doesn't need a big, strapping servant. The master died soon after and the child was left homeless, so my cousin took him in and later on sent him down to me. She'd got four sons at home already, and knew how much I wanted a child of my own . . .'

The good woman paused, and I saw the pain of barrenness reflected briefly on her face.

'Palomides came to us the next spring, and he's been here ever since. He's really a fine boy, if a little high-strung at times, and so fond of horses he's like to forget himself with the guests.'

She smiled lovingly, and I thought how fitting that a child in need of a family should have been found by a woman equally needful of children.

'I do hope you'll overlook his rudeness this morning,' she concluded, her voice suddenly very earnest. 'He meant no offence.'

'And I took none,' I assured her, looking for some way to turn the conversation away from the matter of the horse yard. 'You certainly were right about the quilt; it's quite wonderful.'

A smile of appreciation crossed her face, and I asked how she had come by it.

'Oh, that same cousin sent it, a few years back. Seems

185

some travelling merchant had one in his stock, and when she saw how fine and warm and light the thing was, she set about making one for herself. Since then she's bred up quite a flock of geese, and has made a quilt for most everyone in the family. I'm sure,' she added sweetly, 'that she'd make one for Your Highness' bed, if you wish.'

I was so startled at her use of the title, it was all I could do to promise I'd let her know if I ever needed one. Bedivere strode up to the table, allowing that we were all packed and he was anxious to leave while the weather was still good. I hastily thanked our hostess and waved goodbye to the Arab boy in the horse yard. He waved back bashfully, then looked away in embarrassment.

And so we left Ribchester, with its sweeping view of the river dale, memories of ancient ancestors and a boy from the other side of the world who could work wonders on horseback.

Once the day's pace was established and our mounts had settled into the rhythm of it, Bedivere reined in by my side. After the usual morning greetings the talk drifted back to Arthur and I asked if Bedivere had been at the Coronation.

'Of course,' he said, grinning. 'There's been few times I haven't been at Arthur's side these last five years! It began as such a gay and festive time, I wish you could have been there, Gwen.'

Bedivere paused and I nodded, remembering the excitement of the occasion. When the invitation arrived I had begged Kaethi to let me go, for I wanted to see the pageantry and horses. But the crone only shook her head, saying that I must stay in the north a while longer.

'Lot had been unable to muster enough support for Urien's bid for the throne during the winter,' Bedivere continued, 'so Merlin declared the King Making would take place in the spring. He chose to hold it at Caerleon, a city without specific ties to either north or south. Two ceremonies were planned, one Pagan and the other Christian, each one binding to the followers of that faith.'

All the client kings came, including Lot, who swaggered about full of bravado, but never openly opposed the Magician. Merlin was everywhere, talking to this group and welcoming that. He kept stressing that Arthur was the destined leader of all the British, a king for everyone.

Arthur asked Bedivere to attend him in dressing for the ceremony, and the lieutenant, who had never seen clothes as rich as those which hung in the High King's closet, marvelled over the grandeur of them.

'You should try wearing them!' Arthur grinned as he pawed about in the cupboard for a pair of boots more comfortable than the fancy ones Ulfin had placed out for him. He pushed aside a cape that was edged with fur and lined with silk. 'Each one of them must weigh more than a full set of chain mail. Thank goodness it's only for a little while; as soon as the Lady bids me follow her to the Sacred Hill I can take off the royal cape, for she says it isn't necessary for the Investiture.'

'Are the two rites very different?' Bedivere queried.

'Some,' came the muffled response as Arthur dived into the back of the wardrobe to haul out the battered old boots he used to wear in the kennels at Sir Ector's. 'The Bishop will dedicate me to the Christian God, while the Lady will ask the Goddess to dedicate me to the people. And, of course, the Lady will give me the Sword, while the Archbishop only sets a crown on my head. At least *that* isn't as heavy as it looks. Here, now, enough of that—I can still pull on my own boots!' he said abruptly when his foster brother bent to serve him. 'You don't think I really need any help putting my clothes on, do you? I just wanted you here to talk to, and when they said I should have someone special attend me, it seemed the best way to get a little time together in private.'

He laughed and pushed Bedivere away, and began explaining some of the things he wanted to explore as soon as the crown rested firmly on his head; things relating to trade and taxes and treaties for the future.

It seemed, that morning, that one could do marvellous things just by thinking them up, and Arthur's enthusiasm was wonderfully contagious. When Ulfin came to tell them it was time to leave, Arthur was standing there with a scruffy old boot dangling forgotten in his hand, discoursing on the need to repair the roads so that trade between kingdoms could be encouraged. It sounded like the sort of thing Merlin used to talk about when they were boys, and Bedivere couldn't help thinking that Britain was about to enter a new era, and how exciting it was to be part of it all.

The Christian ritual was long and tedious, and the chapel small, with barely enough room for the various kings. They all stood for the entire ceremony, and at one point Bedivere realized that Arthur was balancing on one foot, trying to rest the other, though both were hidden by the long robes of state.

There was a lot of mumbled ritual and the northern leaders began to get restless, particularly those who didn't understand Latin. At least the Investiture that afternoon would give the northerns a ceremony in their own language, with a sacrifice they could see and understand. And once it was completed, there would be no disputing Arthur's kingship.

Finally the prayers were for Arthur himself, and Uther's crown was placed on his head. The jewels winked and glimmered in the candlelight, looking rich and regal, and Arthur was now truly High King of Britain, at least as far as the Christians were concerned.

The Cumbrian choir sang a final anthem as the royal

cape was put across his shoulders and the new King turned and walked out to meet the people who had not been able to find space in the church. The Companions fell in behind him: Cei and Bedivere, Baudwin and Brastias and all the other young men who had pledged themselves to him since Uther's death. The client nobles followed next, beginning with Cador of Cornwall, and then came the women, led by Arthur's mother, Igraine.

A cheer went up when Arthur appeared before the masses, and they pelted him with flowers and good wishes which echoed even inside the chapel itself. The townspeople had turned out in their best clothes, and they filled the square before the steps, joyful and noisy and full of excitement. Arthur was properly solemn, but the rest of his Companions were grinning from ear to ear.

The new High King raised his arms, making the cape spread out and up like an eagle's wings unfolding, and the throng became silent. Then he started down the steps and across the square to where the Lady of the Lake awaited him.

The people parted to let him through, quiet now and intent on this, the more public and popular of the two events. The High Priestess Vivian was very frail and old, but she stood proud and erect as she waited for him, holding the Sword of State flat in her outstretched hands. The entourage moved slowly towards her, and she seemed to grow in majesty as they came closer.

When Arthur was five paces from her he knelt, and the Companions filed around him to form a circle which joined the Lady on one side and the High King on the other. Some in the audience made the Christian sign, and one or two of the Companions as well. Cei and Bedivere were on either side of the Lady, and Bedivere noticed that the man next to him, Balin, was pale and nervous and crossed himself twice.

189

Balin was an odd person, terribly intense and nervous. He was a big burly lad, strong as an ox and still carrying the rough ways of the country, for he'd come to court only recently. He had a terrible temper; he was extremely sensitive and proud, and quick to take offence if he thought anyone was ridiculing his bumpkin ways. There were rumours of his having killed one of Urien's cousins, but as there was no proof, people did not pry into past matters that didn't concern them.

It was clear he wanted very much to please Arthur, however, and was always volunteering for tasks that would make use of his remarkable strength.

Bedivere knew that Balin had become a Christian, for he had once confided how sorry he was that neither his twin brother nor their mother had been willing to convert. His greatest fear was that either of them should die unbaptized and go to some form of perpetual torment in the next life. And when his mother did die, he grieved so deeply that he barely ate and refused to talk to anyone for more than a month. He had only recently returned to court, and this was the first time Bedivere had seen him.

The Lady began her invocation, greeting Arthur as the son of the Great Goddess. Her voice was less frail than her look, and it rose in strength and vibrance as she summoned the Three Part One to the ceremony. Bedivere glanced at Balin, whose face was now glistening with sweat as if he might be going to faint.

The Lady was looking only at Arthur, and the love and devotion that poured from her were rousing an equal response in the people as they heard the familiar words of benediction.

Suddenly Balin moved, striking so fast that no one could have stopped him. Grasping the pommel of the Sword, he lifted it from the Priestess' palms with the blade still flat, and with one great swing cut off her head.

A gasp of disbelief went up from the crowd as the Lady's body pitched forward in a fountain of blood while her head bounced and rolled on the pavement and came to rest at the feet of her murderer. He stood there shaking as if with the ague, his eyes turned back in his head and a terrible moan coming out of his mouth.

The crowd froze, too stunned even to move, while Arthur struggled to his feet and out of the way of the spurting blood. Only Merlin reacted, stepping forward and taking Balin firmly by the shoulders.

'Give me the Sword, son,' he commanded, and when Balin's eyes rolled back down, the Wizard gently took the weapon out of his grasp.

'She was a witch, a foul fiend, who sent my mother to burn,' Balin began to stammer, staring at the headless form crumpled grotesquely before him. The severed head, mouth agape and eyes wide, stared back at him.

Merlin turned to hand the Sword to Cei, and in that moment the crazed man grabbed up the head of the Priestess and, holding it high before him, raced through the crowd. The people drew back in horror, and within seconds Balin had reached one of the horses that were waiting for the procession to the Sacred Hill. With a leap he was on the animal's back and galloping away through the city.

'An awful string of screaming gibberish poured from his mouth, and then he rounded a corner and we were left in silence.' Bedivere became silent too, no doubt seeing again the twisted violence that had put an end to what should have been a day of great rejoicing. I shuddered and made the sign against evil.

'You undoubtedly know the rest,' my escort continued with a sigh. 'How the Investiture had to be postponed until a new Lady was chosen and a new Sword made. And word was sent out that the culprit must be caught and returned for justice in Arthur's court. I think Merlin hoped that that would mollify the militant Pagans somewhat, but the northern kings cried out that they would not follow a High King who had not been initiated by the Lady; the Christian ceremony was of import only to those who were servants of Rome.

'King Lot seized the chance to turn the tragedy to his own advantage. He announced it was a sign, a terrible ominous portent that Arthur's reign would mean a bloodbath for all the followers of the Lady. He played on the fear and suspicion of old enemies, and before the day was out had rallied most of the northern kings to his side. They left that evening for Urien's city of York to regroup their forces.

'So Arthur's first day as High King ended with Britain more divided than ever,' Bedivere concluded grimly.

'How did he take it?' I asked, wondering how anyone would deal with such a blow.

'At first he was terribly shaken. He even talked about stepping aside and letting someone else, like Cador, take the throne. And he told me later that for weeks afterwards he had nightmares of a great pool of blood spreading out in front of him, lapping at his knees and staining him forever with the Lady's life.

'But Merlin sat up with him all through the bad nights, letting him talk and talk, and brought him round to seeing that it was not an augury from the Gods, but the work of a man demented and crazed with grief and hysteria. So eventually Arthur was reassured, and began to make plans for handling the insurrection in the north.'

There was a long pause, then Bedivere sighed. 'It was not,' he said bitterly, 'what you would call an auspicious beginning.'

We rode in silence for a bit, Bedivere struggling with

his anger with the Gods while I tried to keep from conjuring up too clear an image of the Lady's death.

At last the grey-haired veteran in charge of the pack-horses drew abreast of us to report a problem with one of the animals, so Bedivere nodded courteously to me and turned away, and I went back in memory to the day when my father had returned from the Coronation.

18
Balin

'War,' the messenger cried as he hurtled past. 'Civil war!'

Kevin and I were returning from a ride by the river and were so busy arguing whether skill or size was more important in a smith, we'd not heard the man coming until he was upon us.

Now we looked at each other in astonishment, and at the same moment lashed our own mounts into a wild gallop. We had all but caught up with the rider by the time he reached the gates of the fort at Kendal, and the three of us pounded through together.

My father and his men rode in a bit later, only a little less breathless than the messenger. And when the Council had been called, Rheged's King sat before his people, grimy with road dirt and bone-weary, but determined to report what he knew.

'Merlin has promised,' he said slowly after the tale of Vivian's death had been told, 'that when the new Lady of the Lake is chosen she will have a special sword fashioned, a weapon more powerful than any Britain has seen before. Bright and pure, forged specially for this purpose, it shall be an emblem of Celtic faith, a mystic talisman specifically made for the High King. Thus the ancient rites will be satisfied, and the Lady herself will perform the ceremony for all to see.'

My father looked carefully around the circle. 'One of Arthur's gravest concerns is that this matter not be twisted into a religious war, and he has declared that he will not tolerate vengeance taken for religious beliefs. Whether or not that will keep each side from beginning a slaughter in the name of a holy cause, I don't know. What I do know is that the people of Rheged have lived peacefully among themselves, monk and druid, Christian and Pagan, for many years now. There has always been mutual respect, and I as your leader am proud and glad it is so. I want to make sure that all of you here understand that the Lady's death was the work of a fanatical madman, and does not reflect Arthur's attitude towards religion. We need to keep that fact in mind.'

My father stopped talking, and silence lay heavily on the group as each member tried to absorb the import of the news. We were all stunned by the flailing violence of the Lady's end, and as I looked about the gathering, my eye was caught by the movement of a tall, white-robed figure in the shadows. When Cathbad had arrived I had no idea, but I was very glad he had chosen to join us now.

'I am loath to bring up the subject of war again,' my father continued with a sigh. 'We have only just recovered from the effects of Uther's last battle. But there are matters of gravest consequence that must be decided upon. It's most probable the northern kings will choose Urien for their leader, and we can expect to see a gathering of military might within his borders. Urien might well use our past support of Arthur as an excuse to attack Rheged, whether or not we side with him now. So it seems we must prepare for war regardless of what position we take where the High King is concerned. At the least we need to defend our borders, and at the most we need to consider whether we should go to the aid of the Pendragon, if Arthur should call upon us.'

'When do you think such aid might be needed?' someone asked, and again my father sighed.

'I can only guess. It will be necessary for Urien and his allies to gather their forces. That's not something they can accomplish overnight, so I doubt they will make their move

195

until next spring. And there is much we need to do between now and then. We have a winter of preparation before us: weapons to be repaired or replaced, chain mail to make, drills to be held, extra stores to be laid aside, wagons to be prepared. If we agree to follow the Pendragon, there must be a full commitment on our part, for if we side with the High King and he loses, the victors will not overlook our participation.'

There was another silence, and then the murmur of friend consulting with friend. The restless noise grew until it became a babble, and as I looked about, Cathbad detached himself from the back of the crowd and stalked to the centre of the circle. He stood before the King and called the gathering together again.

'I have but one question, Your Highness,' he said formally, and all other voices stilled. 'What do you advise?'

My father raised himself fully upright in his chair, and answered with a voice more powerful than I had ever heard him use before:

'It is better to fight for something you believe in than to try to remain neutral and pray the forces of the Pendragon win.'

'The Pendragon!' someone cried. 'To the aid of the Pendragon!' and the chant was taken up like a hymn, sweeping all before it. Whatever other concerns our people had, it was clear they had no desire to back Urien.

There was much clapping and chanting, and a musician picked up his hand drum, rattling the bones against it and bringing the rumbling excitement of a war beat into play.

It reminded me of the high, proud days before the men had left for Uther's last battle; but this time I was less quick to respond, for I had seen the devastation of man and animal that war had brought about. Along with the thrilling songs I heard the groans of Nidan's near-death;

in the shadow of the flags of glory, I remembered the small grey figures trudging home in the rain.

Now, once more, the people of Rheged were being called to battle in the name of a High King. A shiver of fear and anger went through me. I fervently wished that young Arthur would get his kingship in hand, and go away and leave us in peace!

I threw myself into the summer as though there might never be another, finding every excuse I could to collect Kevin and go out into the countryside. Sometimes we went in search of honey trees, or tried new fishing holes, or visited the family of swineherds who followed their charges through the forests. Generally we brought back food for the larder, and sometimes reports of local news. No one at court mentioned our absence, and the freedom to come and go as I wished soon became second nature.

By mid-August there were reports of general unrest; now that the kings were busy elsewhere, outlaws were becoming bolder, and roving bands of warriors plundered farms and sheepfolds as they made their way south to join various leaders for the war effort.

Once the harvest was in, our household moved to Patterdale, which lies in the shadow of the fells at the foot of Ulswater. I have always been fond of that steading, with its thick thatched roofs and many outbuildings. The river that flows into the lake was lined with alders glowing pale gold in the chilly autumn air. During the fall the great red stags sent their booming challenge echoing from cove and cliff face, and in the spring I watched the does carefully bring their fawns down to the lake to drink. In such a haven one could almost forget the fever that was rising in the land beyond the fells.

Almost, but not quite. As the weather warmed, stories of strife and confusion trickled through to us. Rumours circulated about the massing of troops and of people taking to the forests in order to escape the impending conflict. Some of the tales reflected a world gone mad, and we listened in dread as the reports grew worse. It seemed as though a madness of fear and despair were tearing Britain apart before the royal opponents had even begun to fight.

My father had spent the winter moving from one fort to another, keeping the men busy at anvil and forge, training the warriors and readying the equipment. His military precautions proved to be well justified, for after the spring thaw the number of troops camped around York grew and grew, and our spies reported plans for a major offensive come summer.

Our own forces began to gather in Brocavum, where the Stainmore meets the Main Road, and when the horses arrived from Stanwix my father decided it was time to move.

He made a hurried trip to Patterdale to check on the small group of men he was leaving behind to protect us, and to say goodbye to me. He brought Brigit's brother Sean with him, for the boy had volunteered to be one of his messengers, and came now to exchange family news and say farewell to his sister.

It was a brief, tense visit. My father was so preoccupied he bade me a scant hello, and when he left there was no time for more than a hasty admonition that I keep out of mischief.

I stood beside Nidan and waved a frightened farewell. Made stiff and slow by his Saxon wounds, my father's lieutenant would never go to war again, and so had been left to guard the home. It was the first time ever that his king had ridden off to battle without him, and though he accepted it with Celtic courage, a sad, slow tear slid down his cheek. To judge by my father's expression, the poignancy of their parting was as powerful for the King as for the old warrior.

Where once I had hated the time we spent hiding in the valleys, now that I was old enough to understand the situation I welcomed the shelter of the mountains and was content to help Kaethi and Brigit with the daily running of the household.

Kevin stayed with us, for he would be more useful at home than on the field. During the first several weeks we received reports that our troops were mainly involved in holding actions against a few small war bands intent on border raids. It appeared that Urien was much less interested in us than in his bid for supremacy in the south, however, and my father was very much concerned for the young King's chances against so formidable an opponent.

Then a week went by with no messages at all, and Kevin decided to ride out along the Stainmore and see what he could learn.

He returned two days later, saying that he'd met a messenger who reported that Urien was moving the main body of his forces to the south, and it was doubtful he would expend any troops in an effort against Rheged at all.

'I heard something else that worries me, though,' Kevin told me privately, his dark brows meeting in a frown as he reached for an oiled rag.

We were in the shop where the whetstones were kept. Kevin was honing the blade of his dagger while I sat by the scrap box, searching for a piece of leather with which to repair a bellows. I looked up, startled by the Irish boy's tone.

He paused to check the keenness of the dagger's edge against the ball of his thumb, then shook his head with a scowl. Laying the tip of the dagger on a hand stone, he began moving it around in small, flat circles. 'Do you remember the stories about the man who ran amok through the kingdoms of Wales?'

'The one who attacked King Pellam when he was a guest in that king's court?' I asked, revulsion stirring somewhere deep inside. It had been a particularly gruesome tale, for the stranger had turned against his royal host and wounded the monarch with his own sword. Afterwards, the fiend had raged through the land burning everything in his path—barns and cottages, chapels and sacred groves alike—creating a wasteland as bad as any Saxon might.

Kevin nodded and paused to make the sign against evil.

I shuddered at the thought; a man's sword must be his friend as well as protector, and the sacred Swords of State were the power of the monarch made manifest. It was said that King Pellam's wound, delivered by his own weapon, would not heal. He hung between hope and despair, immobilized by the blow between his thighs, and his people didn't know whether to rejoice that he had not been killed outright or despair that he would never be whole again.

'The culprit got away,' Kevin went on, carefully drawing the knife out in larger and flatter circles on the stone. 'Now there are tales of a pair of madmen roaming our woods, screaming and howling as if tormented by spirits. Some say they are brothers who have fallen into a blood feud, and that each swears vengeance on the other for past atrocities. So far there hasn't been any thatch fired, but the people are frightened, remembering what happened in Pellam's land.'

'Does anyone know who these men are, or where they come from?' I asked.

'Not really. They say the one seen more often is very big and brawny, and the gibberish he spouts is mostly Celtic. But if they are twins, as has been suggested, it's not certain who has seen which. They've both been living wild for some time apparently, in tattered clothes and ugly, unkempt beards. I think,' he said soberly, 'I should find out where they're headed and if there seems any likelihood they'll come this way.'

Something shifted inside me as though the bottom had dropped out of my stomach, and I stared at Kevin. He tested the blade along the hair on his arm, turning it to the light to check the black hairs it had razored off so neatly. Apparently satisfied, he slid the dagger back into his belt and glanced over at me.

'The trail should be fairly easy to pick up.'

The sinking feeling hardened into a knot, and I looked at my foster brother with dismay.

'Surely you're not going to go after him by yourself, Kevin. At least take Nidan with you, in case there's trouble.'

'Can't,' he said flatly, looking down at where I sat, the bellows forgotten in my lap. 'We have a minimal guard here as it is. If Urien's troops decide to turn on us, we'll need every man possible to defend the passes and protect Patterdale. And if either of these wild men is coming west, I don't want to be worrying that while I'm out trying to find his trail he's slipped past me and found you too lightly guarded.'

He shrugged and grinned suddenly, the light of challenge shining in his blue eyes. 'Don't worry, Gwen, I'll not be doing anything foolish. I just want to find out what it's all about, and see for myself if there's any danger. It may be just another case of someone fleeing to the safety of the mountains, or touched by the sacred madness, off looking for the Old Gods in the wildwood.'

So early the next morning he saddled up Gulldancer. Brigit and I walked with him as far as Patrick's Well,

201

where the Saint of the Irish was said to have converted so many Pagans to his own faith.

Springs and wells of all kinds are sacred in the north, and even though this one now belonged to a Christian spirit, there were gifts and decorations from many generations past hanging in the tree that arched above it. Some were old and faded, while others were newer and brighter in colour. Several fresh crosses, clumsily made of twigs and tied with twine, indicated that the new religion was still holding its own against the return of the Old Gods.

Brigit dipped her hand into the cool water and sprinkled some on Kevin, who, to my surprise and hers, didn't protest.

'Aye, cousin, you can pray to whomever you want for me today, and I'll be that glad of it, as long as you don't promise I'll become a Christian when I come back,' Kevin cautioned, laughing lightly as Brigit shook her head.

Then he blew us a kiss and, turning the horse out on to the path that follows the lakeside, cantered away without looking back. We watched him cross the gentle meadow where the mountain wall that surrounds the lake opens a little to the west and the grasses grow sweet and green in pasturage.

At the foot of the grey cliff, where the rock soars up sheer from the water's edge, he entered a stand of trees and was swallowed from both sight and sound. Brigit was crushing my hand in her own.

'Will you say a prayer with me, to the Good Patrick?' she whispered, and I nodded, so we knelt in the trees above the little spring and each in our own way asked that Kevin return safely. And afterwards we walked back together, holding hands as sisters do.

Brigit and I never spoke of Kevin's mission, but went about the routine of domestic life as though time itself had stopped. I accompanied her to the Well every morning in a kind of silent alliance to keep our kinsman safe, and occasionally she would rest her hand on my shoulder if her duties took her past where I sat and spun or churned the butter or renewed the barley straw in the mattresses of our box beds. I think it was the only time I have ever enjoyed the thousand chores that are necessary to keep a household running, for it seemed as if by keeping busy at those hearthbound tasks I were weaving a kind of security for Kevin to return to.

We had another message from my father, who had moved south, saying that Arthur's forces were far greater than he had expected, and the upcoming battle might yet be won by the Pendragon.

I was glad and relieved to hear the rider's message, and sent him out to the kitchen for a well-earned meal. At least one of the threats to my family was looking a little less terrifying.

By the time Kevin had been gone for five days the strain on Brigit showed in great blue circles under her eyes, and I felt as though I would jump out of my skin whenever a horse came cantering down the path. Surely, I thought each night, he must return tomorrow.

He came home late one evening, leading Gulldancer, who had gone lame that afternoon. Taking the gelding to the paddock, he rubbed him down, then walked in through the kitchen door as though returning from milking the cows. I was so surprised, I almost knocked over the jar of honey I was filling and would have flown at him with a noisy welcome but for the expression on his face.

He was worn and haggard from the days on the road, and dirty from lack of bathing as well. But his eyes were haunted and wary, and the grim line of his mouth froze me where I stood.

He nodded to Gladys and asked if there was time to

bathe before the meal was ready, then headed for his own quarters.

As he passed by me he said softly, 'There'll be no more trouble,' then disappeared. Whether from exhaustion or the desire to avoid questions, he didn't appear at dinner, and it was the next day before I had a chance to speak with him.

I found him at the far pasture in the morning, carefully examining Gulldancer's legs.

'Are you all right?' I asked, taking hold of the halter and steadying the animal.

'Of course,' he said curtly.

The gelding dipped his head to see if I'd brought him anything interesting and began nuzzling my hair impatiently. He'd nipped me more than once in the past, and I cuffed him now and pulled his head away. Kevin began checking each hoof, cleaning the soles with great care. He frowned heavily as he worked.

'I'm sorry, Gwen, I didn't mean to be rude,' he said when the job was finished and Gulldancer moved away with a toss of his head. 'There never was much danger to me; I wasn't the one he was searching for.'

We walked back to the tack room in silence, and when the salves and hand tools were put away, he suggested we go to the stream near Patrick's Well.

Once we'd settled beside the bright and bubbling brook, Kevin stared into some nondistance for a bit, then swallowed heavily.

'No one between here and Penrith had seen or heard of the brothers,' he said at last, 'but once I got to the Main Road everyone was talking about them, and the trail wasn't hard to follow.'

Kevin spent the first night at an inn where one of the brothers had stopped the week before, asking if he could have a meal in return for chopping firewood. By the time he'd finished his job he'd worked himself into a frothing rage. He muttered and swore, crying that his twin had become a follower of the Christians, and had unaccountably begun slaughtering anyone who followed the Old Ways, including their mother. The tavern owner was relieved to see the fellow leave, as he seemed more crazy than sane.

The trail turned east along the Stainmore, and Kevin made his way slowly along it, for many people had seen or heard of the feuding brothers.

A young boy reported there'd been a stranger in the cave across the Eamont from his family's farm. It's one of the caverns the holy men sometimes stay in, so they're used to having hermits come and go. But this man ranted and mumbled constantly, and though he crossed himself and called out the name of Jesus often and loud, he acted more as if he were possessed of the Devil. He'd disappeared after a couple of days, but the boy and his mother kept their doors locked and barricaded in case the howling Christian returned.

By the end of the third day Kevin had reached Kirby Thor, where the trail turned cold, for though the people there had heard of the wild men, no one had seen them.

The next morning he began to follow the Eden, working his way along its banks. Here he met an old man fishing for trout who told of finding his dog dead—its throat cut—and the coop empty when he went to let the chickens out, three mornings back. It sounded as if at least one of the brothers were sticking close to the watercourse, so Kevin continued to head downstream.

By the afternoon of the fifth day the Irish boy had reached the waterfall we'd found last summer. It's a lovely cataract, set well back at the head of a deep ravine where a stream comes down to the river. Someone had built a sort of house at the edge of the waterfall's chasm,

205

leaving it open along the side that faces the plunging water. It's peaceful and secluded and long since deserted, and more than once we'd climbed the steep, slippery trail up the side of the ravine beside the cascade and spent the afternoon in the cool shelter at the top.

This day the forest was full of birdsong and light breezes, and since the wild man's trail seemed to be getting cold, Kevin decided to stay over in the summerhouse and start for home come morning. At least he was satisfied the brothers posed no threat to us at Patterdale.

He rode up the easy path under the trees, lulled by the beauty of the day and sound of the water falling into the pool below.

Suddenly the afternoon calm was torn by a racking scream. Gulldancer snorted sharply, and the hair on Kevin's nape stood up. There was something so terrible in the sound, he dismounted immediately and tied the horse, white-eyed and nervous, securely to a tree.

He crept cautiously up the path to the back of the deserted cabin. A jumble of accusations and scraps of argument came from inside; then someone began to sob and cried out loud enough to be understood.

'Balin,' the man moaned, 'you wretch, may the Goddess feast on your entrails! I will feed your eyes to the crows, and drink a toast to the Morrigan out of your skull. Slayer of priestesses, betrayer of kin, most vile blasphemer of all time, I'll make you pay!'

The speaker went on and on, spewing out his loathing for the man who had killed the Lady, and the things he threatened to do would have made even the Old Gods cringe.

After a bit he fell silent, and there was no further trace of word or movement from inside the structure. Finally Kevin crept to the end and very slowly peered around the corner.

The creature was alone, slumped on the edge of a makeshift bed, his chin resting on his chest and his hands hanging slack between his knees. He was filthy to look at, and pitiful too, with only rags and scraps of clothes for cover, and his hair was matted and hanging lank and unkempt over his face. There was a dirty bandage tied around one leg, and the wound had gone foul, so that a wretched yellow stain oozed through the fabric. The stench of decaying flesh was awful, and it was a wonder that he was still alive at all.

From time to time he twitched and jerked in his sleep, and once he thrashed out his arms, which were covered with slash marks far worse than any brambles could have made.

The Irish boy crouched there for a long while, trying to think what to do, and wondering where the other twin might be. At last his knees grew stiff and he slowly stood upright. He'd decided to ride for Carlisle, even in the dusk, and see if enough men had been left at the fort for him to lead a few back here and capture the poor lunatic.

Suddenly a jay began scolding and the madman came awake with a start, his head swinging from side to side like a snake's trying to find where the danger lies. He grabbed up the dagger that had slipped from his fingers when he fell asleep and, with a terrible wide gaze, looked carefully along the open side of the shelter until he was staring right at Kevin.

The twisted mouth let out a shriek, then growled: 'Aha, Balan, Pagan swine, defiler of souls, tormentor of Christians . . . so you have dared to show yourself at last!'

The sound of his voice was barely human, and he stared at Kevin fixedly. Making the Christian sign with the hilt of his dagger, the wild man began to pray.

'Sweet Jesus, behold the fiend of Hell before you! There . . . there, see the head of his victim hanging from his belt? A holy one, no doubt, who rests with You in heaven this day. O Great Lord,' he pleaded, 'send down Your angels to take vengeance on the infidel!'

He sprang to his feet and coiled in the half-crouch of one about to do battle, and for the first time Kevin saw a hideous mass of putrid flesh and hair hanging from his belt.

The realization made the Irish boy's gorge rise in his throat, for even though it was rotted beyond recognition he was sure it was Vivian's head. It was horribly clear this was the man who had beheaded the Lady.

Balin leapt forward, and Kevin scrambled for the trees along the edge of the waterfall's chasm. Twilight was fading, and the crippled boy prayed desperately that the shadows would hide him.

Balin raged anew, challenging his tormentor to come out and fight. Kevin managed to get behind the tangle of brambles and undergrowth, crouching to stay out of sight as he fled from tree to tree in an effort to keep ahead of his pursuer.

The wild man had turned cunning and began working his way along the path by occasionally darting forward, then stopping, crouched and silent, intent on listening. Every time he stopped, Kevin had to freeze as well, for any sound would give him away, and sometimes it seemed they spent hours in silent concentration. Kevin's heart was pounding so hard, he wondered that his pursuer couldn't hear it.

The moon was just past full that night, and soon flooded the path, so Kevin remained in his cover, hoping he could reach the stairs that lead down into the rocky cavern of the waterfall before the madman discovered where he lurked.

An owl glided by on noiseless wings, and as the shadow

brushed across Balin he whirled and slashed at it, screaming out, 'Pagan bastard!'

Gulldancer, hearing the cry, whinnied suddenly, and Balin's head whipped towards the sound.

'Taunt me, will you, Christian scum?' he challenged, and Kevin went sick with the sure knowledge that Balin would attack and kill the gelding.

'It's me you're looking for,' the boy cried, desperate to distract Balin from the horse. Scrambling out from behind the brambles, he made his way into the moonlight so the crazed one could see him plainly.

Balin leapt forward with dagger raised and hair flying. Panting, Kevin dodged behind the nearest tree, but the brambles were too thick to cross and he was forced to hobble from shadow to shadow along the edge of the path.

Balin stumbled and crashed to his knees, arms flailing wildly. When he regained his feet there was a fresh gash across his thigh where he had wounded himself in falling.

'Come out and fight in fair combat!' he screamed, brandishing the dagger before him. Then he began to dance, lunging and parrying in the moonlight, all the while howling the names of Balin and Balan. Occasionally he swung wide and, throwing himself off balance, would open a new gash on arm or leg. But each time he did so he renewed his attack with greater fury, until in the end he must have been bleeding from a dozen wounds.

Kevin had reached the place where the steps are cut into the side of the ravine, and moving down them so that he was hidden from view, he peered across the lip of the chasm.

The revilements continued, accusations and insults that rent the night and hurt the soul. The Irish boy crouched there through the night, with the roar of the waterfall behind him and the madman hacking himself to pieces before him.

By the time the moon had reached mid-heaven, Balin was on his knees, swaying with fatigue and loss of blood. As the hours wore on, the hate and venom drained from him, until at the end he was sobbing, 'My brother, my brother, how could you do such a thing?'

When first light came, Kevin stole out on to the path and approached the silent lump of humanity cautiously, half-expecting him to rise, ranting, from that dark stain of blood-soaked earth.

'He was much younger than I had thought, Gwen,' Kevin said sadly, 'and perhaps had once been fair to look at. But now his eyes stared at a sunlit sky he'd never see, and the throat that had voiced so much anguish was forever silent. I had no idea what sort of honour should be paid him; to bury him with either Pagan or Christian rites would seem a mockery, and I finally left him, counting on the crows and scavengers to do their job. I hope,' he finished slowly, 'that I never see another human so torn by conflicting loyalties again.'

I shuddered and laid my hand on top of his.

'Do you think he was the only one, and there was no twin?'

'I'm sure of it, Gwen. He was both brothers, trapped in the one body, the proud Celt and devout Christian unable to reconcile their differences.'

I drew my knees up under my chin and sat there hugging them, chilled and scared by the idea that man's nature could wage such war with itself.

'Here, now, you've gone white as a sheet!' Kevin exclaimed, peering anxiously at me and scrambling to his feet. 'I didn't mean to tell you so much about it! Look here, I'm back, whole and safe within my own skin.' He pounded his chest triumphantly. 'And I'll not have you spoiling my welcome by getting sick on me. Hear me?'

He caught hold of my chin and made me look up at him. 'Come on, it's a lovely summer day, and not to be wasted with brooding over some poor creature the Gods chose to make a pincushion out of.'

I smiled more at his efforts to cheer me than because my mood had changed, and getting slowly to my feet, challenged him to a race back to the barn. It lifted both our spirits considerably, but the memory of that story stayed with me for a long time.

19

King Ban

News of Arthur's victory over the northern kings was received with cries of joy and much relief. With the help of the King of Brittany he had prevailed in a Great Battle in which a number of people, including King Lot, had been killed. Urien had surrendered and offered to swear fealty to him, and Arthur had accepted it. The men would be returning to their homelands and with any luck we could put the civil strife behind us. My father intended to come back to Rheged once Urien had disbanded his army, so we could look for him in a fortnight. In the meantime Nidan was to take the household to Carlisle and await his return there.

The grain stood knee-high, and the weight of the thickening buds made the stalks bend before the breeze. We could expect a good crop if nothing untoward happened, and with the men coming home in plenty of time for harvest, there was double reason to celebrate. People began to come from farm and steading, sheepfold and township, flocking to the walled city that lies at the heart of Rheged in order to give our troops a triumphal welcome.

Carlisle has been a centre of trade and travel since the time of the Empire, for not only does it command the western end of the Wall, it also straddles the Main Road which leads both north and south. In the days of the Legions it must have been a lively place, playing host to a steady stream of soldiers and supply shipments, military commanders and visiting bureaucrats.

Nowadays the King is the government, and the centre

of the state is wherever he happens to be. With no more need for office space and administrators, the buildings of the Empire stand empty and decaying except where the local people have appropriated the space for purposes of their own.

Carlisle always makes me uneasy, for though the ways of Rome are fading from current custom, the structures remain like old skeletons that cannot be avoided. The walls that surround the city are as stern and precise as they were when the engineers first laid them out, and the ghosts of Legionaires haunt the shadows. The people have softened and modified the town much as mosses blur the edge of a rock by a stream; now it is the travelling peddler and the local farmer who set up shop in the half-ruined colonnades, and when the Great Fair is held in August the people who laugh and sing and dance in the streets think of themselves as Cumbri, not Romans. But in spite of that, I tended to avoid the big house on the bank of the Eden and spent as much time as possible at the cavalry fort of Stanwix on the hill across the river.

Stanwix commands an excellent view, and when a watchman in the tower called out that the army was in sight, Kevin and I scrambled up to the battlements to see for ourselves.

Already people were running towards the Road, shouting the news to neighbour and stranger alike. They were all converging on the east gate, chanting joyfully: 'Hail, the warriors!'

Flag bearers were approaching from the south, riding with the arrogance that victorious men always wear. Rheged's banner rippled high and proud above the rest, and below it a harper, no doubt one of Edwen's students, rode with them and sang the praises of the returning heroes in fine Celtic style. As official bard, Edwen himself would be riding with my father.

The King's contingent was still some way off, so Kevin and I clambered down from the rampart and ran to join the exuberant welcome.

My heart swelled with pride when my father rode through the gates behind his honour guard. Looking as fit and hardy as ever I could remember, he radiated, if not joy, at least a kind of full satisfaction. I pushed through the crowd, and when he saw me running along beside his stallion, he reached down and helped me scramble up before him in the saddle. It wasn't quite the same as being a triumphant warrior myself, but close . . . close enough to satisfy me.

We had a simple family dinner that night, for the public feast would follow in two days' time. Gathered cheerfully along the trestle tables, we listened to the details that would soon be immortalized in Edwen's lay: how Ban had brought his forces across the Channel in order to help the son of his childhood friend Uther; how Merlin had shown Arthur the need for tactics rather than bravura and finally how the rebel kings had sued for peace and, gathering their defeated forces together, had followed Arthur to York, where the formalities of surrender were observed.

It was there, in Urien's capital, that Merlin announced a new Lady had been chosen by the druids: Morgan le Fey, wife of King Urien, would be High Priestess at the Sanctuary.

'What's she like, this highborn lady who will take the place of our own Vivian?' someone asked, and my father pursed his lips thoughtfully before responding.

'She has a notable presence,' he said at last, picking his words carefully, 'very dark and intense. And I gather that she will be much more active than her predecessor. We talked at the feast, where I assured her we would protect the Sanctuary now as in the past. I found she has many strong opinions and a kind of driving energy that will not be gainsaid. It's possible she expects to play a major role in her brother's reign, and she certainly seemed to take him in hand at York. She could be very useful to him. And Cathbad tells me she is well thought of among the druids,' he added.

Something in my father's voice gave me the distinct impression she would not be an easy person to have dealings with.

Later, when only Kevin and Brigit and I remained at the board, Kevin told my father the story of Balin's death. The adventure had been kept a secret until the King's return, but now that I saw his expression go from concern to admiration for Kevin's courage, I wished the whole household could know how much the Irish boy should be admired.

'What a tragic ending to a grotesque story,' my father mused, when the tale was finished. 'Perhaps,' he suggested softly, glancing round at us, 'it's kinder not to mention this to anyone else. The war he inadvertently started is over; a new and vigorous Priestess has now succeeded the old one, and there's no point in sullying either memory further.'

I nodded my assent grudgingly, wishing there were some way to keep it secret and still see Kevin receive the honour due to him.

The Victory Feast was held in the City Square, with cooking fires set up in each corner and the casks of wine and ale arrayed next to the fountain. Edwen told The Triumph of Arthur, binding even the rowdy swineherd's children into silence with his powerful ballad, and afterwards there were many 'Well come home' toasts and much singing and dancing.

The general opinion was that Arthur had won not only the battle, but the admiration of his subjects as well, for his acceptance of Urien as an ally was said to show a

215

gracious heart as well as a good head for political realism.

There were reports that Lot's widow, Queen Morgause of the Orkney Isles, had presented her children to the young High King at York, where everyone had gathered once the Great Battle was over. She had thrown herself and her sons on Arthur's mercy, and asked him to accept the older boys at his court. She reminded him that they were his nephews and, by Celtic law, his heirs. Arthur took the boys into his household, promising to train them as warriors and Companions. I wondered how Gawain felt about serving the man his father had died fighting.

There was much speculation about Morgan le Fey. That she could command such power when she was not yet past thirty was impressive, and those who had mocked the last Priestess as being old and feeble suddenly ceased to make fun of the Lady's presence. Cathbad was very well pleased with her appointment, for she was a fine healer, and gave promise of becoming a strong spiritual leader as well.

After the food and dancing, the druid announced his plans to go to the Sanctuary in order to welcome the new Lady. With the summer ripening there was more than enough work to keep us children occupied, so my father allowed we could do without him until autumn, but would hope to see him back among us when the bracken turned to copper on the fells. We wished him on his way and thought no more about it; it never occurred to me that he would never be my teacher again.

During the next week the country began to return to the routine of peace, and we made plans for our sojourn in the autumn. It had been some time since we had sojourned in the north so it was decided we should return to The Mote and then make our way westward to the various settlements beyond Wigtown Bay.

The day before we were to leave, my father and I headed out to Stanwix together, for Featherfoot's foal would be staying here in the horse fields and I wanted to say goodbye.

It was a fresh, clean morning following a night's rain and the city was full of summertime bustle when we came out of the big house on the river's edge. The farmers' wives had put up their awnings in the Square, where they brought eggs and vegetables, new cheeses and bundles of fleece to trade with the people who live within the confines of the city and must rely on others to grow their supplies for them. The sound and colour of the market swirled around us.

As we passed the fountain, a courier wearing the badge of the Red Dragon came riding through the gates and hauled his horse to a clattering stop when he recognized my father.

'I have a message for Your Highness,' he said, saluting hastily. 'The High King wishes to meet with you to discuss a very important matter. He will arrive the day after tomorrow, and he brings with him King Ban of Benwick as well.'

'Bother,' grumbled my parent.

Never one to enjoy the sociable aspects of court life, he was clearly piqued at the inconvenience this sudden intrusion would cause, and I could see him mentally juggling this change of events with our plans to go north.

'Did he say what this is all about? Or how many retainers we shall have to put up? Or when he plans to leave?'

'I don't have the details, M'lord, but they're travelling light, with not more than half a score of men total, and I gather they won't be staying long, as King Arthur plans to head for Strathclyde from here.'

My father sighed and turned to me. 'Better tell Brigit we're to expect company, and remind her we must look to the wine,' he announced, then added in an undertone,

217

'Tell her not to unpack everything just yet, however.'

By now Brigit was as accomplished at running the domestic side of our life as Mama had been, and my father left all such details in her capable hands.

Preparing for a visit from the High King was no small matter. It seemed impossible that we would be able to get everything organized in time, what with Nonny muttering about no proper notice while Brigit and Kaethi, Gladys and I frantically tried to decide just what would be needed for whom.

Kevin went off to fire up the old baths, making sure there was plenty of charcoal to heat the water and checking for any major leaks in the plumbing from the aqueduct. Gladys and Brigit took charge of the menu, while Kaethi and I poked about in the storage rooms trying to find enough chairs and tables, good bedding and bolsters to make our guests comfortable. We were able to outfit the guest bedrooms, and even provide oil and towelling for the baths, but there simply were not enough chairs to accommodate all the visiting dignitaries.

'Are those couches I see, over there in the cobwebs?' Kaethi asked, peering through the dim light at a collection of discarded furniture.

I clambered through the jumble of stuff left over from who knows how long ago and managed to pick out a number of couches and several low tables. They were covered with dust and showed the years of neglect, but turned out to be sturdy nonetheless. After a quick conference with my father, it was decided that if the visiting kings were as Romanized as everyone said, they would feel right at home eating in the Latin fashion.

I eyed the couches dubiously when they were set up in the main hall. Kaethi laughed and said it just proved how much a daughter of the Cumbri I was; if I were a true Roman citizen I would appreciate learning to eat while

218

propped up on one elbow. Nonny announced that she would not be in attendance at all that night, as she preferred to take a plate to her room rather than dine with people too lazy to sit upright. My father made a few attempts at getting up and down from one of the couches and, groaning, concluded that perhaps he could simply sit on the end of it.

'Why don't you use your carved chair?' I asked, thinking that the host's comfort should certainly be more important than the question of fashion.

'And find myself looking down on the High King? No, no, my dear, that would not do. Perhaps with enough cushions under me, my bones won't rebel too much,' he sighed.

The next day I was returning from the fountain where I'd gone to fetch a bucket of water for Gladys, when I heard a sound like nothing I'd ever encountered before. A pair of riders had come through the gates and were blowing on battered metal horns which must have been left behind by some Legion commander.

The noise was so unusual, it took me a minute to realize that the kings had arrived earlier than we'd expected.

The people who rushed out of shop and shed to throng the Square were a far cry from a gala reception, and I was carried forward in a wave of turnip vendors and butcher's apprentices all eager to get a glimpse of the new High King. When I tried to hang back, my bucket was jostled so badly it spilled half its contents, so I stood there, barefooted in a pool of water, looking like any scullery maid as the entourage bore down upon us.

The horses were so close I could have touched them; gleaming like satin, they were well fed and powerful, though I noticed that none were as big as my father's stallion. When the trumpeters had passed, I found myself staring into the ruddy face of a young man, and for a moment I wondered if this was the High King of Britain. But he wore the wool of a common labourer, and while I'd never seen a High King before, it didn't seem reasonable he'd go about in workman's clothes.

Next to him rode a Celtic chieftain bedecked with armbands and a gold torque. Proud as Lot but much leaner, he was a fine tower of a man, with fair hair and deep blue eyes that crinkled when he smiled down at me. His face was clean-shaven, except for a great sweeping moustache that curved down around his mouth and extended past his chin, and both his bearing and his jewellery made plain his royal status.

Behind them came a figure so thoroughly wrapped in a great cloak that one couldn't see more than his eyes, and I looked down involuntarily when he turned their flintlike stare in my direction.

A handful of guards rode at the rear and then they were gone, sweeping into the courtyard of the big house and leaving the rest of us to wonder and puzzle as to who was which. Either the High King was not as young as everyone had said, or he'd decided not to come at all.

Our guests paid their respects to my father immediately, then went off to soak in the bath. Kevin attended them from the time they arrived, and only later joined me in the kitchen.

'The Sorcerer is with them,' he reported, helping to fill the wine pitchers. 'He never said a word, but he watches everything like a hawk.'

'I know; I saw him in the Square as they rode in. No wonder he's called Merlin,' I answered, thinking of the beautiful but deadly bird that nests on our fells. I wondered if the Archdruid made a practice of swooping down on his prey in midair as those birds do.

'More likely he should have been named for the owl,'

Kevin responded, 'wise and silent and wrapped in the shadows of night.'

I had just time to skip upstairs and change my clothes before dinner, and sat as patiently as possible while Nonny tried to make my hair do something halfway civilized. She wanted me to wear Mama's armband, but Kaethi pointed out that it wasn't really fitting, as I was not old enough to be presented and so would only be serving tonight. I ran back down to the kitchen in time to pick up a platter of venison liver for my father's table.

This was a visit of state, not a Council meeting, so the banquet hall was less crowded than might be expected. The people around my father and those nobles of Carlisle who were mindful of their Roman heritage happily made use of the couches, but the rest of our people sat on their rugs here and there between the tables, their wool and deerskin clothing in odd contrast to the linen finery of the guests. It made for a very peculiar mix indeed.

I balanced the tray as carefully as possible and knelt to put it on the table around which my father's party lounged. A sudden wave of shyness kept me from looking up at our guests, lest they recognize me from this morning in the Square.

'Ah,' my father was saying, 'here is my daughter, Guinevere.'

Drat! I thought, biting my lower lip and knowing there was nothing for it but to raise my gaze.

It was the merry blue eyes of the chieftain that swam into focus in front of me, and they danced and sparkled most wickedly as he nodded solemnly at me. There was absolutely no doubt that he knew we had met before, and I felt my breath catch in my throat as I prayed he wouldn't mention it.

'And may I present Arthur, High King of Britain,' the Celtic king said, his rich voice making a royal gesture of the words. He turned, smiling at the youth next to him, and I blinked in consternation; it was the ruddy-faced boy, no longer garbed in rough wool but still looking like any young man of the land.

'Oh . . .' I said stupidly, not knowing what else to do.

'You have beautiful hair, child,' the King from Brittany went on, the amusement clear in his cordial tone. 'It has the red gold of the hawthorn in autumn, and is a fitting crown for the Princess of Rheged.'

I blushed in spite of myself and wondered how on earth I was going to get to my feet when my knees seemed to have turned to honey.

Somehow I managed it, and I fled back to the kitchen to help Gladys, determined to avoid returning to the Hall. I hadn't the slightest idea what to say to any of them, and all I wanted to do was stare in fascination at the Breton leader.

As the meal was coming to an end, Brigit thrust a pitcher of wine into my hands with the firm admonishment that the Kings would expect me to pour for them after dinner.

King Ban is just another warrior, I told myself, covertly watching the three heads of state before I crossed the room to them. Yet in spite of that, I was immobilized when he smiled at me, and forgetful of the wine I was pouring, found myself unable to look away from those laughing eyes.

'That's a handsome flagon,' Arthur broke in, rudely raising his goblet until the rim pushed against the spout of the pitcher, forcing the flagon up. Glancing down, I saw how close I had come to disaster, for the goblet was in danger of overflowing. I glanced at the High King and smiled gratefully.

'Mama told me it came from Egypt,' I responded, somehow finding my voice. 'The blue on it is enamel.'

He reached out to take hold of it, leaning forward to study the decoration on its lid. Compared with King Ban, Arthur was but a boy; pleasant enough, but not very memorable. Only the gold-and-garnet Dragon Ring marked him as a powerful king. It was possible that when he matured he would be more impressive, and I suddenly wondered whether he would adopt the Roman habit of going clean-shaven or attempt to grow his own long moustaches when his beard came in more fully.

A strange feeling began to crawl along my neck, gradually becoming a chill as I turned to find Merlin staring at me. Reclining on the far side of Arthur, the King's Wizard appeared to be taking note of everything that went on although he neither moved nor spoke. The pressure of his implacable look made me shiver, and I hastily retrieved the flagon and finished filling the goblets.

Edwen brought out his harp and began the songs. At first he played the simple melodies the common folk enjoy, then later retold The Triumph of Arthur in the High King's honour.

I found Kevin seated in the shadows and settled down next to him, glad of a chance to watch the gorgeous chieftain with impunity.

King Ban lounged on his couch with a kind of feline grace, and it struck me as odd that a man so obviously Celtic in blood and background was comfortable following the ways of the effete Romans. Perhaps his family had originally come from Britain and fled to the Continent with all those others who deserted the villas and towns when the Saxons first brought slaughter and devastation to the south.

Later that night I picked up Mama's mirror from among the things on the dresser top. For years Nonny had kept the paints and perfumes carefully laid out as though she expected Mama to return momentarily; it never occurred to me she was waiting for the time when I myself would take an interest in such things.

The mirror came to life as I lifted it, but I couldn't find anything special in its reflection; just a thirteen-year-old face with freckles, grey eyes and a childish grin. There was none of my mother's beauty, no waving copper hair, no sign of gracious tranquillity, and even when I made my face serious it had neither the firm resolve nor the cool poise a queen should possess.

Someday, I temporized, someday I'll look in the mirror and see the face of a woman and be willing to take up the duties that will be demanded of me . . . but not yet. There's still too much to do and see before I give up my freedom!

With that I put down the mirror and promptly forgot King Ban's compliment.

The High King and his councillors spent the next day closeted with my father, and left that afternoon with little fuss and no fanfare. When they were gone, I asked my father why had they come.

He pushed away from his big worktable with a slight frown, then gestured towards a roll of parchment. The ribbon that held it closed was fastened with a small lead device such as I had never seen before, and I stared at it curiously.

'Our fledgling King has all the earmarks of a remarkable statesman,' he said. 'It seems that while he was about securing his throne and putting Urien in his proper place, he also devised a treaty of peace he wants both Urien and me to sign.'

'How can he do that?' I asked, bridling at the arrogance implied by such a demand.

'Oh, he quite understands it will have to be approved by the Councils. But he says he does not have time to run about settling domestic squabbles when the Saxons pose a far greater threat to all of us. It's a point well taken, and I agree with him in principle. What I didn't foresee was Arthur's using our realm as the proving ground for his power over the rest of us, now that he's High King.'

'What does the treaty say?' I eyed the thing suspiciously.

'It promises a complete end to border warfare, the recognition of Rheged's sovereignty and Arthur's right to enforce the peace if either Urien or I should break it.'

'And what does it give Urien?' I knew enough of treaties to understand that they must work to both parties' advantage, and I wondered what we were being asked to promise away.

My father picked up the scroll and carefully slid the lead glide down the tails of the ribbons, then began unrolling the sheepskin.

'That's the rub, my dear. If both you and I die without an heir, Urien can rightfully claim Rheged as part of his own kingdom, and rule it as such—with, of course, the consent of the people.'

'The people will never accept him!' I spoke quickly and without real thought, remembering the response when Lot had tried to enlist our alliance with Urien. They hadn't thought much of that notion then, and I didn't think they would accept this new idea now.

'I'm not so sure, Gwen. If Urien honours this agreement, by the time the question of who is to be the next ruler of Rheged comes up, the freemen may be more inclined to accept him; when it comes to politics, the people have remarkably short memories. Urien knows it's the only way for him to get a foothold here without massive bloodshed, and may just decide to wait us out, so to speak.'

My father ran his fingers along the edge of the vellum, absently staring at the words written on it. I moved over

225

to his side and peered down at the thing. The writing was just so many squiggles to me then, but the Great Seal of Britain stood out clear and very impressive. The dragon curled and writhed in the splatter of red wax as though emerging from a drop of the Goddess' blood.

'But what about my own children? Surely the people would not accept an off-comer in preference to a child born in Rheged?'

'Ah,' answered my father, 'it appears that Arthur has already considered that argument. If you stay here and become queen yourself when my reign is over, then your offspring will be protected, and can stand for the kingship without fear of rival claims from our neighbours. The treaty is very firm on that.' He tapped his finger slowly against the document. 'It's a very tempting offer, Gwen, and I have agreed to present it to the people. If they will accept it, we could look forward to an end to the cattle raids and such. That would be a popular idea, I think, particularly among those who live in the Pennines and bear the brunt of our neighbour's ambition.'

My father slowly rolled the treaty up again and then handed it to me to refasten.

'How do you feel about it?' I asked, trying to thread the tail of the ribbon through the lead glide.

He cocked an eyebrow and snorted. 'I can't help wondering how much of this is Arthur's idea, and how much comes from Merlin. I don't suppose it matters much who thought it up, but if it was the young King himself, I'm very much impressed; it bears the mark of an excellent mind. In either event, I shall be calling Councils throughout the summer, and will put this before the freemen everywhere we go. I can't see that it does us any harm, and the ending of border feuds would be good. So we'll see what the people say, eh?

226

'Don't forget,' he added, stretching slowly and looking as though he might break into a smile, 'in the end the people always have their way, no matter what the Royalists like to think.'

20
The Investiture

After Arthur's visit to Carlisle our plans for a leisurely trip to the north had to be changed. As many Councils as possible needed to be held during the next year, and my father outlined a schedule that was going to keep him on the move for many months.

'If we can cover the area south of the Wall while the weather holds, and be up on the north shore of the Solway by Samhain, I think I can report the people's will to King Arthur come next Beltane. But it means moving quickly now. I'll take a light, fast-moving party out to the smaller places while the household makes its way through the main settlements.' My father smoothed out the faded map which both he and I knew by heart, and traced his finger along the Roads. 'My men and I will catch up with you every few days to hold Council in the towns as well.'

He stared off into space considering weather, length of day, the condition of the Roads and presence of trouble as he calculated the best route. 'We can rendezvous at Carvoran and Whitby Castle,' he speculated, 'but even so my party will probably reach Kirkby Thor before you. Ah well, if that happens I'll just pop on over to Appleby and see how things are going there.'

Rheged's King was never so happy as when he was laying out a campaign of some sort, and although he complained of the pace that this schedule would mean, I could see that he relished the activity.

The next two days were filled with talk of the towns and forts that lay in the shadow of the Wall. Their names evoked the mysterious gods and places Kaethi had brought to my childhood: Castle Nick and Haltwhistle Burn, Camboglanna and Vindolanda, the temple of Mithra and Coventina's holy well. The household generally stayed in the safer, central areas of Rheged, and since the Wall was still prey to raiding marauders from both north and east, I had never travelled along it.

In my head descriptions of wonderful bathhouses and giant, soaring bridges mixed with stories of powerful deities. It was there that goddesses from distant lands, with names like Hamia and Viradexthis, Cybelle and Isis had once been worshipped by Legionaires transplanted from the Middle East. It was even said that our own Great Goddess Brigantia, winged in victory and vengeance, sometimes paced the walk that topped the Wall, and the very idea of seeing these places filled me with excitement.

But when I asked Rhufon if he would ask my father to let me accompany him, my old friend stared at me in disbelief.

'It's one thing to let you learn to ride when you're little,' the Horse Master growled, 'to teach you how to care for the animals, and the equipment, and even a bit about breeding and such. But if you think I'm going to encourage your father to take you along into border country on a man's errand, you're very wrong, Missy, very wrong!'

Rhufon finished checking a new goatskin water bag and sent a severe scowl in my direction. Whatever argument I might have made would be futile in the face of such logic, and I turned away, disappointed. Probably my father would say the same thing, so I dropped the subject and in the morning began the slow trek with the household caravan.

The next month was a jumble of people and places as we moved ponderously from settlement to settlement.

Everywhere the people listened thoughtfully to Arthur's proposal, and most agreed that it would be of benefit to all. And at each place Edwen recounted The Triumph of Arthur and included a special lay for the men who had not returned from the civil war, immortalizing the brave hearts and fiery spirits of the fallen warriors. I noticed that he never mentioned Urien as the enemy, but instead stressed our loyalty to the new High King.

We were at Ambleside when a messenger from the Lady arrived, and after a brief conference my father rode off with him, taking Edwen and Nidan as well. He told no one what it was about, but left Rhufon to help us on the journey over Hardknott Pass, as it is one of the most dangerous in the whole kingdom.

The rarely used Road runs up to the top of the fells, looking like a ribbon flung carelessly across the steep sides of the mountains. It's necessary to ride single file in places where the paving has washed away, and the pack animals must be led carefully along the ledges, while the land falls off in wild splendour.

Once on the high moors you can look across the roof of the world in all directions, with only the bare peaks and the flight of eagles above. Gills run bright and bubbling between rock and heather, and even the smallest of pools is dark blue, reflecting the northern sky. Far to the east the Pennine ridges lie like purple smoke, while in the west the green cleft of Eskdale leads down to Ravenglass and the sea.

In the late afternoon we followed the Road along the spur of the mountain, heading for the shepherd's outpost in the ruins of Hardknott Fort. Great clouds of mist and rain rolled in from the coast, and a bitter wind drove spitting storms across the sky. The fells are notoriously unpredictable where weather is concerned, and we bundled up as much as possible and hurried for shelter.

That night was spent huddled in our cloaks around the shepherd's fire, snuggled in against each other as the sharp wind whistled past the broken stone walls.

I woke at dawn, sure someone had called my name. No one else was stirring, yet I could not rid myself of the sense that I was being summoned. Crawling out from between Nonny and Brigit, I pulled the hood of my cloak up over my head and went outside.

The fort is perched on the shoulder of the world, in a place of power, terrible and awesome in its solitude. The shepherd's dog, wary of so many strangers in the area he guarded, followed me cautiously as I made my way slowly to the rim of the sheer, dizzying slopes that drop away to the north.

The rain had left the world newly made and full of beauty, with wisps of mist rising in the dark, wooded valleys below. It is easy to feel the presence of the Gods at such a time, and I perched on a fallen lintel stone, staring across the upper end of Eskdale to Scafell Pikes. Beyond the craggy edge of those mountains lay the Sanctuary.

Gently at first, I was lifted from myself till it seemed I floated on the edge of a void where time and space had no meaning. Distant thunder rolled past and strange shapes gathered and dispersed within the crystal abyss; bright lightning glimmered along the blade of a sword raised high against the sky; a swirl of smoke enveloped it, and flames came leaping upward, roaring and crackling like the fires of Beltane; a figure loomed, pale and proud, and for a moment I thought it was my father, still caught in the burning heart of the royal promise. But instead of dancing, this person was standing quietly in that blaze of destiny, and I tried in vain to see who it was. Tears of fear and awe blinded me, and I was carried, breathless, to a crest of emotion so strong it had no name.

Slowly the vision faded and I began to breathe again, drained and shaken. Turning from the dark force of the mountains, I stared at the Isle of Man floating out to the west, almost on the horizon of the silver sea. It is said to be the home of spirits awaiting another call to the human life, and I knew suddenly that Mama must be there, carried on the ebb to that place of laughter and song. Surely she could protect me in this world gone strange and unaccountable. I reached out to her, laughing and crying at the same time.

The sheepdog whined and licked my fingers, as scared and eager for reassurance as I was. It brought me back to myself, and I looked down to find him staring nervously into my face. His uneasiness touched me, for no doubt he too had felt the presence of a god.

The dog came closer, and I scratched him behind the ears as he pressed against the folds of my cloak. Together we stared out to sea and let the magic wash over us.

'Goodness, child, you'll catch your death of cold,' the shepherd's wife cautioned, peering at me in dismay. 'Are you all right?'

I nodded, only then aware of the tears that continued to course down my cheeks. How could I tell her it was neither sorrow nor joy that filled me, but something greater than both? She appeared satisfied when I managed a small smile, and turning, made her way back to a storage shed with the dog bounding along beside her.

When the breeze had dried my face I rejoined the household, feeling light and calm but somehow changed. I didn't mention my encounter to anyone, but the sureness of Mama's presence stayed with me all through the day's trek down to the shore.

Ravenglass is a lovely spot, with soft red embankments rising above a pooled estuary where the three rivers join in the face of the sea.

The walls of the fort are kept in full repair, of course, for Irish raiders still sometimes visit our coast. But whenever my father held court here, the household stayed in the bathhouse, set in lovely woods overlooking the dunes between the sea and the lagoon. I much preferred the bathhouse to the military buildings, for in my room I could listen to the doves murmuring in the woods and watch the shimmer of the strand through the dappled shadows of the trees.

That afternoon my father and his men returned from their visit to the Sanctuary and called for a Council to be held that evening.

The news spread throughout the dale, and by the time the tables were cleared and the circle formed, farmers and fishers and freemen of all kinds had come to join us. When the circle was complete, Edwen brought out his harp and recounted a strange and wonderful tale.

Arthur had gone north when he left Carlisle, stopping first at the great fortress of Dumbarton, where the King of Strathclyde entertained him royally. From there he travelled through the glens proposing treaties and alliances among all the client kings. It was a time of truce, if not peace, and after visiting all those leaders, large and small, he came back to the Sanctuary, where he stayed in vigil with the new Priestess, Morgan le Fey.

When she deemed he was ready, the Lady sent messengers throughout the lands, gathering the Celtic kings to her Lake. They came from all quarters, each, as she had requested, bringing only one warrior and a bard. And each asked of all the others, 'Why are we here?' but no one knew.

The meadow on the western shore of that forbidding water filled with tents and banners, and some of the finest horses in Britain were hobbled nearly. There were games and competitions, and after dinner the different bards

233

took turns singing for the group, recounting the ancient stories we all love, though each was careful to avoid the tales of recent battles for fear of opening wounds barely healed. And still there was no word as to what the Lady wanted of them.

Finally, when the long twilight of the third day deepened and everyone had arrived, the Lady had the torches lit and called a Council on the rock-strewn shore of the Black Lake. She wore the white robe of a druid, and her black hair swung free and loose down to her hips. When she raised her arms in invocation the gleam of gold armbands caught the light, and with slow majesty she opened the Council and summoned the Great One to that dark and magical spot.

'Men of Albion,' the Priestess cried, 'Celts of long lineage and great fame, Cumbri and Scot and Pict, I call upon you to bear witness to a special ceremony. To you is the honour of participating in this great moment of history, that you may return to your people and tell them what the Goddess has done.'

The Lady stood in the centre of the northern kings and her eyes gleamed with green fire when she spoke again.

'Now, at last, the time has come round to the Gods' bidding, and I can present to you not only the new Sword of Britain, but also the one for whom it was made.'

A murmur of surprise rumbled through the monarchs, and the Lady turned and walked out into the Lake, majestic and silent, to a flat rock that rises above the surface of the Goddess' home. This she mounted, and bending down, lifted from a ledge at the back of the stone a magnificent weapon.

She held it up for all to see. The scabbard glowed with embroidered work, and both chape and pommel were set with gems.

'Behold the sword Excalibur, fashioned in the secret

ways of the Smith God Gofynion at his forge in the heart of Furness!'

She drew the sword, and as the point of its blade cleared the scabbard mouth it rang with the voice of a bell.

Slowly the Lady lifted the sword high over the water while the red light of the torches rippled like fire along the shiny blade, making the snake pattern run down the metal before it steadied to a silver gleam.

A gasp of awe and admiration came from warrior and royalty alike as they looked on the mystery of Excalibur. Morgan le Fey's voice rang out in triumph.

'Forged in the fires of a windy night, it is invincible.

'Worked by the dark of the moon, it is invincible.

'Tempered in waters sacred to the Gods, it is invincible.

'Risen now from the heart of the Lake, it is invincible.

'No other blade will withstand its stroke.'

Speechless, the men gaped as the Priestess lifted the scabbard in her other hand.

'Behold also the sheath, enriched by my own hands with the spells of healing, that it may staunch the flow of blood for the man who wears it on his belt. Mark well this weapon's magic; from this day forth it shall be the sign of Celtic destiny, shall give witness to the integrity of its owner, shall be the symbol by which all men know the choice of the Goddess. For there is only one man for whom Excalibur was made . . . the next High King of Britain.'

The mountains round the dark water echoed with the applause of the monarchs, and only as it crested and began to die away did she lower the sword. Slowly and reverently she sheathed the weapon and cradled it in her arms as though it were her child.

'Be it known that I have prayed, and sacrificed, and tested the auguries of bird and star, to be sure I understood what She has decreed. There is no taint of politics, no whisper of family favourites, nothing that could cast doubt upon the desire of the Morrigan Herself. In every trial that I have put before the candidate there has been only victory; She has made her choice unquestionably clear. Having served the Goddess faithfully, I present you now with the one She wishes to be High King.'

The crowd grew silent, waiting for her to announce the Goddess' choice. Without a word, the Lady gestured to a youth near the edge of the water. The boy came forward, dressed in plain homespun unadorned with any jewel save for the shining copper of his hair.

'It's Gawain; she's giving the magic sword to Lot's son,' the Kings whispered, staring in amazement as the lad walked through the cold black whisper of water to stand before her.

'He who draws forth this sword shall be the rightful king of Britain,' the Lady cried, laying the weapon across the boy's outstretched palms.

Gawain turned and, wading back to the shore, marched slowly towards a large outcrop of rock that thrusted upward along one side of the little vale.

A flame burst suddenly from the pile of dry bracken at the base of the boulder, sheeting up in bright array and filling the glade with light. And when the smoke of the first blaze cleared, it could be seen that Gawain had climbed with Excalibur to the topmost ledge.

The Priestess stood to one side, arms raised in blessing as her words carried through the dusk:

'I present to you the High King of the Celts, monarch of Logres and Emperor of the whole of Britain . . . Arthur Pendragon!'

A figure in simple white tunic and breeches stood revealed in the bonfire's blaze, proud against the shadows of oncoming night. Gawain knelt before him and with profound humility offered up Excalibur.

Arthur's hand went round the gc 'en hilt and slowly drew forth the shining blade. Then, v h a great sweep of his arm, he brandished the Protector f the Realm above his head, saluting the royalty below who had gathered for this, his Investiture as their sovereign.

'Arthur!' roared the crowd, 'Arthur, King of the Celts!' while the fire flickered upward and the new king bent to Gawain and helped him to his feet.

And so the ancient rites were held and the vows made between Celt and King. The very leaders who had most grudgingly surrendered on the field now gave him their hearts and fealty. With the presentation of Excalibur, Arthur became, at last, the legitimate leader of both Christian and Pagan Britain.

'We who were there bring back this tale of great power and magical weapons that you may know a new era has begun. There is a new Sword of State, sanctioned by the Goddess Herself, raised from the black waters by the Lady and placed in the hands of the Chosen One by the son of his vanquished foe. May his reign be as spectacular as his beginning . . . Long live King Arthur!'

Edwen finished on a rousing note, and the people picked up the cry and echoed it around the room.

'Long live King Arthur!'

I sat there stunned, knowing I was in my own Hall yet surrounded by the memory of the morning's vision at Hardknott. Had it been so important, so great and powerful a moment in Britain's destiny that the echo of it had lingered in the air, engulfing even the bystander on the mountaintop who had nothing to do with it?

A rush of surprise and relief swept through me as the explanation hit home, and I joined in the accolade, clapping and cheering along with the rest. I was sitting next to Kaethi, and the old woman put her arm around my shoulder and gave me a warm hug—for no reason at all that I could see, but the comradery was infectious, and the singing and drinking lasted well into the night.

Remnants of that festive mood mingled with the pleasant sounds of our progress, and I surveyed the present with bemusement. Travel had grown safer, with fewer bandits and less fear for wayfarers; the people seemed to be prospering and trade was flourishing; Rheged no longer suffered the raids of Urien's men, and so far the truces between the various kingdoms were holding.

It seemed the young King had indeed got his realm in hand, and was apparently doing something right.

21
Merlin

'I hope,' Bedivere said quizzically, 'that you have no objection to sleeping in a meadow tonight . . .'

I looked over at him sharply, wondering if he still thought me one of those fragile flowers of the south. His grin was spread from ear to ear, however, and I laughed in return.

'I think I can manage,' I answered, glad of the chance to sleep in the fresh air.

We made camp that evening in an open woodland where the hazel undergrowth had been newly coppiced. The cluster of tall straight poles that sprouted from each stump looked like columns of fluttering leaves, so dense was the growth. In the cleared areas around the base of each column a carpet of violets, primroses and cinquefoil had sprung up. It lay in colourful abundance between the green pillars and gave the woods a cheerful, cared-for air, reflecting the fact that the people hereabouts had both the time and the energy to husband the forests well.

The women's tent was pitched on the high ground of a meadow, and the men were making themselves comfortable around the edges of the cooking fire. Everyone was busy preparing for dinner and the coming night, and when Lavinia complained about having to walk down to the stream for water, I took a pitcher and headed for the bank myself. I wasn't more than twenty paces beyond the camp when the boy who had charge of the litter caught up with me.

'I'll get the water, M'lady,' he said, reaching for the pitcher, 'and you can go back to the tent.'

'Oh, I don't mind,' I answered, and seeing the consternation on his face, added, 'I need the exercise, and it feels good to be doing something useful.'

'No, you don't understand. There's strict orders that you're not to go anywhere without an escort.'

'Whose orders?' I asked suspiciously, wondering if they had guessed I might want to run away.

'Why, the King's, I suppose, though it was Merlin who sent me after you just now.'

So much for the Magician's pose as a sleepy old man! I stifled the quick retort that popped to mind as the boy fell into stride beside me.

'What's your name, lad?' I inquired.

'Griflet, son of Ulfin,' he responded.

'Have you been in the King's service long?'

'Well, in a way,' he hedged, his bright eyes twinkling. 'My father was Master of the Wardrobe for King Uther, so I grew up helping him at court. I volunteered for this journey; it's my first official job.'

'How do you like it?' I asked, curious if he was really as open and frank as he seemed.

'Oh, very much, Your Highness.'

The formal title still sounded odd to my ear, and I suspected he was trying to ingratiate himself with me.

'Oh, come now, Griflet,' I chided, 'riding along beside two packhorses that are carrying an old lady in a litter can't be that interesting!'

He shrugged and grinned at me. 'It beats polishing shoes.'

It was my turn to grin then, amused as much by my own obtuseness as by the boy's honesty.

The brook ran fresh and clean, with rocky shallows and small pools. I began gathering handfuls of the cress which grew in the shallows while Griflet stooped to fill the pitcher.

'Besides,' he went on cheerfully, 'Bedivere put me in charge of the dog, so in the evenings I have him to play with.'

'Oh, my word! I forgot all about the pup. How's he holding up?'

'Much better now. The first evening he was pretty scared and lonely, what with being away from his family and all. He whimpered a lot until I got up and took him into my bedroll, and then he calmed right down and slept all through the night. Since then he's been just fine.'

The boy was so obviously pleased with his own resourcefulness, I laughed. It was a good practical solution, though I wondered if he wasn't finding himself being eaten by fleas.

'He's even got used to his name,' my companion went on, then stopped abruptly, perhaps remembering that the dog was not really his to name.

'What do you call him?' I prompted, curious as to whether it would be a descriptive name or that of a hero.

'Caesar,' he announced, and I flinched at a choice so obviously Roman in origin.

'When I was a child we had a hound named Caesar, and it seemed right to call this dog after one I had loved,' the boy explained, and I ruefully reminded myself not to look for political goblins everywhere. 'He'd be with us, still, the first Caesar that is, but for a boar hunt two years back. Boars are nasty things, M'lady, for all they provide good meat.'

We'd returned to the crest of the meadow, and Griflet handed back the pitcher. On impulse I suggested that he bring the dog around for me to see after dinner, and we parted company.

I took the cress to the cook, thinking how much like any other lad his age Griflet was. The fact that he'd been

241

raised in a High King's court didn't seem to have affected him at all.

The evening meal was simple and casual. Since there was no formal seating arrangement, I took my plate and went in search of Merlin, wanting to ascertain just how long I would be kept under guard. The Enchanter looked up sharply when I planted myself in front of him, and mumbled a reply to my greeting before going back to his meal. For some time he concentrated on his food, seemingly oblivious of the fact that my eyes never left his face. I prayed that he would acknowledge my presence pretty soon, for the longer I stared at his craggy countenance, the more of my courage evaporated.

After finishing the last crumb of bread, he sighed elaborately and glanced up from under his brows. Finding me still watching him, he looked hastily back at his plate and began to hum a little song absently under his breath.

Why, you old fraud, I thought suddenly. You're every bit as frightened of me as I am of you!

The idea was so surprising I smiled, wondering what sort of power he thought I, a young woman, would have compared with the scope of his; I could barely control my tongue, much less command my shape to change. Yet I could swear he was desperately wishing I would go away and leave him alone, and had no idea how to make that happen.

'Well, uhm . . .' he said, putting his empty plate on the ground and pressing both hands against his knees in preparation for standing up. 'It's been a good trip so far, eh?'

I nodded in assent, then gathered my courage and blurted out, 'Why do you feel it necessary to keep me under guard, M'lord?'

'Guard, child? What are you talking about?' He relaxed

his arms, cautiously resigning himself to a conversation with me.

'I understand I am not to be allowed to go anywhere without someone with me.'

Merlin looked puzzled for a moment, then nodded slowly.

'Ah, you mean on the Road, or when we're exposed in the open, such as now. That's just good common sense. You are the chosen bride of the High King, and it is our responsibility to get you to him safe and sound. It's not as though you were under arrest, or anything like that. But you are in need of protection, whether you realize it or not. There are some among the Cumbri who would not scruple at using you to wound the new King. Now,' he added hastily, seeing the indignation on my face, 'I don't mean that as any reflection on you or your people. Rheged has always been loyal to Arthur, and most of the other kings have learned that Arthur is just and fair and not one to carry a grudge. Why, look at Urien! Opposed Arthur in outright war, and yet when the battle was over and treaties were being signed, Arthur took no vengeance on his opponent. He even supported Urien's wife's becoming the new High Priestess after Vivian was killed. No ruler who was mean or petty would dare give so much power to the King of Northumberland and Morgan le Fey together.

'But there are always those few who are so fanatic in their beliefs they place themselves outside the law. It is from these that we wish to protect you.'

I nodded, willing to concede that he meant the guards to be protectors, not jailers.

'Have you known the Lady long?' I asked abruptly.

'Dear girl, a man of my years has known practically everyone since they were children,' he opined, then looked back into the past. His voice, while not filled with the Power, had taken on the full, rich timber of a man in his prime. It seemed more fitting than the reedy tones of his old-man disguise, and I suspected he was speaking from a place closer to his own heart.

'When I was a child there was a centre of learning for those who wished to study with the Lady, only in those days it was located on the Tor at Ynys Witrin. Nowadays the Christians call the place Glastonbury and claim it as their own holy spot, and the Lady and her druids have moved up north, as you know.

'I was sent to the Tor to study for the priesthood as a druid, and the one who was the Lady then took several of us as initiates into the Inner Secrets. Vivian and I were both chosen, so in a way you could say we grew up together. Full of mischief, she was then, and a bonnie lass as well.'

He paused as if bemused by some fond memory, and I tried to picture any priestess of the Goddess as a young and playful girl. It was hard to imagine, so I waited patiently for him to come back from his reverie and focus on the present again.

'What about the one who is Lady now?' I prompted.

'Morgan? I think she'll handle the power well enough, though she comes to it late. She was sent into a Christian convent when Uther married Igraine, and I think they expected her to stay there after she grew up. But she left to marry Urien.

'Urien's not much of a homebody, preferring the life of a warrior, so Morgan has had the freedom to explore all manner of things, including the Old Ways.'

'M'lord,' I asked, curiosity making me bold, 'would it be improper to inquire what it was that the Lady sent you in the packet, that made you laugh so heartily?'

'Eh?' He had slipped back into the old man's voice as though the conversation were over. My question must have touched some nerve, however, for he turned and looked at me sharply.

'You were there, girl. What did you see?'

'Nothing.'

'Just so. The good Lady made me a present of the elusive fern seed, which is essential for one who wishes to become invisible.'

He looked at me expectantly, and not knowing what else to do, I nodded and murmured, 'Oh,' as though the whole mystery were explained.

And on that note the Sorcerer rose to his feet, this time succeeding in putting an end to our chat.

Griflet arrived with Caesar bounding along on a leash. Both of them were in rollicking high spirits, so we went off to find Brigit and give her a chance to play with the pup as well.

The dog responded to the Irish girl as though she were his lifelong friend instead of a new acquaintance, and his joyous enthusiasm was contagious. We took him out across the meadow, away from the temptations of the cooking area, and let him off the lead. With fierce growls and happy yips of triumph he gamboled about us, charging clumsily after a butterfly one moment and stopping to investigate a nodding yellow poppy the next.

We romped along with him, glad for the chance to run and laugh, and when he dropped, tongue lolling and energy spent, we plopped down beside him in the grass.

After we had caught our breath I asked Brigit how she was getting along with Lavinia in the litter. She grinned broadly and allowed that Vinnie seemed to view all Celts as heathen, even if they'd been Christians their whole lives long.

'You can always come back and ride next to me if it gets too bad,' I reminded her, and she shook her head.

'Thanks, but I'll stay in the litter. I just hope that next

245

time we have to travel so far we can go by boat.'

Griflet had looked round when Brigit mentioned her religion, and on a hunch I asked him if his family was Christian.

'Yes, M'lady. That is, my mother and I are. My father was initiated as one of Mithra's followers, back when he was a lad.'

'Doesn't that make for problems, having two different gods under one roof?' I asked curiously, fending off Caesar, who was tugging on the cuff of my sleeve.

'Not really. It's mostly the bishops who make a fuss about it. The people at court follow lots of different beliefs. King Uther and his warriors favoured the soldiers' god, Mithra, but there's some that keep the Old Ways, and both Celtic and Roman Christians gather to hear Mass together.'

That was reassuring, for with so much diversity perhaps I would not be out of place after all.

It was coming on to twilight and I knew Brigit would be wanting to find a quiet spot to say her evening prayers. Thinking that Griflet might wish to join her, I suggested that they go off together while Caesar and I waited until they returned.

'I'll be well within sight and sound of both you and the camp,' I added, mindful of Griflet's responsibility. So the two of them went down to the willows by the stream while the pup snuggled up next to me and went to sleep.

It was a sweet, peaceful evening and before long the full-throated song of a thrush filled the gloaming. Other songs may be more delicate, or more finely made, but I know of none that is richer or more joyous. It swelled and glided in the soft dusk, lilting and happy and triumphant in its free beauty. It was as close as I needed to come to the Goddess, and I smiled and stretched contentedly, thinking it a kind of prayer in itself.

Later, as I lay waiting for sleep in the darkness of the tent, it was the cuckoo's call that kept me company. I wondered suddenly where Kevin was, and if somewhere he too was listening to the first sounds of spring. Even now I would not admit he had been sung into Eternal Sleep by the Birds of Rhiannon, and if memory could keep him tethered to this earth, then I would not let him go unremembered.

22
The Black Lake

On the day after we learned of the King Making, Kevin and I went riding over the dunes at Ravenglass, racing along the shore and laughing as the flocks of black-headed gulls surrounded us with screeching disapproval when we thundered past their nesting sites. Afterwards we headed for the trail along the far edge of the estuary and fell to arguing over whether it was fair that I couldn't take part in the important things, such as riding to the outlying areas with my father, or attending the King Making at the Sanctuary.

'It's just common sense, Gwen. You haven't been trained in sword-play; you can't defend yourself in case of attack, and there's too much danger involved in those situations to ask our warriors to look out for you as well as themselves.'

'Well, then, I should have been taught! Look at Boudicca. She defended her territory with the sword, and all but drove the Romans out when she led her armies against them. Or Vennolandua, the Warrior Queen of Cornwall who donned her armour and went against her husband in single combat rather than have their two armies slaughter each other. She won; in a fair battle, she won!'

'And killed the High King,' Kevin said with a grin. 'Maybe that's when they decided to quit teaching women to be warriors.'

'Nonsense! No Celt would argue that. After all, he had it coming to him; he had betrayed her publicly, and she had the right to call him down on it. No, I'll bet it was the

Romans who turned the women into tabbies-by-the-fire. For all their superior attitudes, I'll bet they were afraid to face an armed woman.'

'I don't blame them,' Kevin answered good-naturedly, and I wondered if the Irish women still fought beside their men. Before I could ask, Featherfoot shied to one side, startled by an adder that slithered away from the path. Kevin had his dagger to hand immediately, but the snake disappeared, and since it didn't coil for an attack, we let it be.

'It's still not fair,' I continued with righteous indignation. 'When I'm queen, I'll come and go with the warriors as I please.'

'Unless your husband forbids it,' Kevin teased.

'No husband's going to forbid me to do anything,' I flared. 'Maybe I won't bother to get married . . . Why should I, anyway, except for children? But if I did decide to marry, I'd choose someone here in Rheged, who would travel at my side and not expect me to stay behind while he goes off and does the interesting things. If Gawain was there, I should have been there,' I persisted, refusing to be sidetracked.

'Gawain, my dear, is the eldest male of his house's line,' my companion said reasonably. 'And even though his mother is the reigning monarch of the Orkneys, she wasn't present at the King Making.'

'Well, she should have been,' I fumed, pausing to watch a heron try to swallow a frog. It was no easy matter, for the frog struggled against the grip of the bird's bill, its legs jerking wildly. It had no intention of becoming a nice tidy meal without a struggle.

By the same token, the women's exclusion from the King Making refused to slide comfortably into my craw. I found it puzzling that Morgause had not attended the ceremony. Not only was she a leading monarch, she was half-sister to the new King and full sister to the Lady of the Lake. Had I had her rank, nothing short of childbed would have kept me away. I doubted Morgause was pregnant at the time of her husband's death or she would have declared it, for it was now up to Arthur to look after all of Lot's children. Whatever the reason for her absence, I was sure it was based on her own decision rather than the fact she was a woman.

The heron finally got his catch in a more favourable position and swallowed it, then haughtily stalked away.

'What do you suppose the Sanctuary is like?' I asked as the bird disappeared in the rushes beyond a rotting log. 'Have you ever been there?'

'How should I have got there without your knowing?' Kevin shrugged. 'I did hear King Ban speak of it, when he and Arthur were at Carlisle. It seems his son Lancelot is being educated by the Lady, in the ways of both the scholar and the warrior.'

'I think Ban's son was one of the princes Cathbad mentioned when he first told us about the school,' I mused. I watched a dragonfly hovering over the water and wondered how the druids' wisdom and a warrior's heart would blend in one person. It seemed an odd combination, as chancy and unpredictable as the blue-green-purple colouring of the insect in front of us.

There was a sudden flash of iridescence, and Gulldancer tossed his head in wide-eyed surprise as the dragonfly flitted past his ear. Laughing, we resumed our leisurely pace down the path.

'Are you sorry you didn't go study with the Lady?' Kevin inquired.

'A little. I've always been curious about it. Don't you sometimes wonder about her? What she knows? What she can do?'

I glanced over at my companion, but he was squinting

250

at something moving through the water. I followed his gaze and caught a glimpse of the sleek dark head and supple spine of an otter. It slipped into and out of sight, holding its tail upright instead of floating out behind, so that it looked like a miniature dragon coursing through the ripples. The creature played about in the water for the sheer joy of it, and I watched it roll and circle, dive and surface, for all the world like a rook tumbling about in the currents of the sky. Oh, I thought, to have such freedom!

When we came to the crossing of the track and path, I turned Featherfoot to the east and stared at the long valley which led into the mountains. Somewhere beyond that shield of rocky fells lay the Black Lake and the school I could have been part of.

'Let's go see for ourselves what it's like.' The suggestion leapt out before I thought, and from Kevin's expression I knew it didn't surprise him. But he frowned and shook his head.

'I don't think it's a good idea,' he said uneasily.

'Oh, come on,' I urged, alight with the desire of adventure. 'What harm could it do, just to go and see the Lake? We don't have to enter the Sanctuary, you know— just see where it is. And it's not even midday,' I went on, taking a quick reading of the sun. 'We'll be back in time for dinner, and no one will even know we've been gone.'

'But we don't have Ailbe with us,' Kevin pointed out. 'We'll have to ride home and get him, and tell Brigit where we're going.'

'Oh, bother telling people where we are all the time! I'm tired of never doing anything without getting someone else's permission,' I flared.

He was silent for a minute, duty and curiosity each struggling for the upper hand. I knew which one would

251

win if I left him to work it out, so I turned Featherfoot on to the track. 'Well, I guess I'll just have to go by myself,' I announced.

'You can't do that!' he exploded, catching up with me.

'It's better than having to order you to come with me,' I retorted, knowing I was straining the delicate balance of our relationship but too irritable to care. 'You can do whatever you want, but I'm going to the Lake.'

I set a smart pace along the river way, keeping enough in the lead so he couldn't try to talk me out of it. Ahead, the rolling landscape funnelled towards the feet of the crags, and the track turned to a narrow pathway alongside the riverbank.

Before long the trail roughened and we moved into a rock-strewn, hummocky land of open woods. The river meandered in endless curves and double-backs, and gradually the gaunt grey peaks ahead of us loomed closer.

At one point we passed a fox's earth, its pungent odour hanging heavy on the balmy air. A few minutes later Featherfoot pricked her ears and I heard the sharp yip of a fox kit.

We were riding below an embankment, and when I looked over its crest I could just make out a pair of kits rolling about in mock battle. The vixen was busy burying the remains of a bird, while another of her offspring stalked a stray feather. We paused for a moment to watch the pouncing, growling youngsters go charging after shadows, their mother's tail or each other.

Suddenly one of them tumbled away from the rest and half-ran, half-rolled across the open space. It came to its feet at the edge of the drop-off, exactly on eye level with me. Featherfoot snorted and tossed her head, the kit froze in amazement and the vixen let out a sharp bark of warning at which the baby fox turned and streaked for cover. It all happened in the space of a breath, but not before I had seen the quick, sharp look of surprise followed by immediate assessment in the eyes of the small, wild animal. There was a cunning behind its momentary stare that was well worthy of respect, and I grinned at Kevin.

'Pity one can't make pets of them,' he said. 'They seem to have the best qualities of both dogs and cats.'

I nodded, trying to remember if I had ever heard of anyone's taming a fox. 'Perhaps they need to stay free in order to go on being themselves,' I suggested.

'More likely they have no desire to change. You can't tame something that doesn't want to be tamed.'

The dale was narrowing abruptly where the mountains form a curtain that shields the secrets of the Sanctuary from the bright openness of the coastal plain. Night-shrouded yews, their rough-barked trunks hidden in dense shadow, intermingled with the lighter, happier trees. The light was growing dimmer and I wondered if the afternoon had passed already, but decided it was only the shade of the heavier woods that caused the twilight gloom.

Whereas the rising slopes of Eden's vale lap upward to the Pennine crest, here there seemed to be no foothills, no gradual lifting of the land, no casual approach to the mountains themselves. They rise with sheer power directly from the dale floor, dwarfing all the creatures below. If Hardknott is perched on the shoulder of the world, the Black Lake is hidden in its navel.

We came to a wide, beaten path that had been much travelled of late.

'It's probably the route most of the nobles left by, after the Ceremony was over,' Kevin suggested, so we followed it away from the river and headed over a small rise.

The track brought us round the base of the mountains, and the woods thinned out to an open meadow lying along the Lake. We paused at the crest of the curve to

253

look out over the scene, too awestruck to say anything.

The place was aptly named, for the water before us was black and silent, a wedge of mystery under the high, steep wall of the opposite shore. The cliff face across from us glowed rust and grey in the late afternoon light, its long screes fanning down from the knife-edge ridge high above. It is a solid wall, stretching the length of the Lake, without peak or canyon, fold or spur, and no tree or bush softens its outline. The towering barrier of rock and loose stone was reflected in the water below, adding a bronze cast to its already metallic look.

I stared about, unnerved by the austere majesty of the place. Off to the right was an outcropping of rock, high and prominent by the shore of the Lake, and at its base lay a scatter of ashes. Kevin pointed wordlessly to the remains of the bonfire. The echo of affirmation still whispered from rock and forest: 'Arthur! Arthur! King of the Celts!'

I nodded silently, unable to break the spell that hung over us. Farther to the right, beyond the rock, a dark forest hugged the shore, while far to the left, where the Lake's head nestles under a cluster of triangular mountains, the smoke of evening fires rose above a steading. Probably that was where the students lived.

Suddenly I was very glad I hadn't spent my childhood in this place, with its eerie silence and frightening Lake. I turned and grinned at Kevin, fully satisfied that we had come.

'Thirsty?' my companion asked, eyeing the water along the pebbly shore.

'Not for this,' I managed to say, grimacing at the dark liquid.

'Let's see if there's a spring in the woods,' he suggested, turning Gulldancer towards the shadowy trees beyond the King Making Rock.

Featherfoot followed, ears twitching and the whites of her eyes showing. Somewhere ahead a crow let out a rasping cry, and a cold chill ran over me. I didn't need the bird to remind me we were in the Morrigan's territory, and I would have turned back to leave by the way we'd come, but Kevin was already disappearing into the gloom of the forest and I didn't want to be left alone.

Inside the woods we found a spring, complete with a traveller's cup set in a rock niche above the trickling water. We dismounted and were careful to pour out a libation for the Goddess before drinking, then let the horses have their fill from the pool.

I stared about curiously while the horses drank, noting the votive offerings that hung near the water source. They were few and simple, probably set out by the pupils, for it seemed unlikely that many travellers came to such a secluded spot.

It felt good to stretch my legs, so I handed the reins to Kevin and looked around. Beyond the immediate trees a path appeared to lead through the shadows to a clearing of some sort. Perhaps it was one of the Sacred Groves from the old days such as Kaethi had described. Curious, I started off to explore it.

I must have misjudged the distance, for it seemed to take a long time to reach the trail itself. When I finally came near the clearing a sound of chanting drifted towards me, so I moved carefully to a spot behind a large yew, and peeped through its branches.

The trees formed a wall around that open space and the clearing itself was filled with grim darkness. Ancient shadows flickered across it, while in the centre a giant wooden pillar stood, thick as two men's bodies and bleached a sickly white, like bones left unburied. Odd niches had been cut into it here and there, perhaps to hold some form of sacrifice, and a ghastly face was hewn high up towards the top of it. It made my blood run cold just to look at it, as though the memory of unspeakable rites had soaked into it over centuries of secret use.

A dark-haired woman bent over something on a stone altar at the totem's base. Absorbed in what she was doing, she had no idea I was near, and as I watched she began to weave from side to side, crooning as though to a child. She stretched upright, eyes closed, and slowly raised her arms in supplication. The sleeves of her robe fell back, and a pair of golden armbands glimmered in the gloom. In her hands she held a chalice rimmed with silver as in the olden tales. With a shiver I saw the cup had been fashioned from a skull.

She stood motionless, burning like a pale ghost in the dark shadows, and I realized with terrifying certainty that this was Morgan le Fey. Shaking, I drew back from the sight lest my presence profane her ritual.

The singing continued, sweet and melodious at first, then rising to a harsher note, and ending finally with a high-pitched shriek, after which there was total silence. I wished fervently I had not come this far, but were riding back along the river with Kevin.

There was nothing to tell me what the Priestess was doing, and after a bit I decided I had best try to get back to the spring without her knowing. I moved cautiously out from behind the tree, hoping to regain the path unobserved.

We almost collided as she glided silently down the trail, and she froze as quickly as I did. For a moment we confronted each other eye to eye, and I saw the same quick, wild look on her face I had seen on the kit's: surprise, assessment and indignation. The green eyes narrowed to slits and probed my very soul.

'You!' she exclaimed in a whisper. 'What are you doing here?'

I gulped, unable to speak, as she scanned the woods behind me. I was too scared even to glance towards Kevin. There was such a primeval intensity in her face I dared not look away.

'You have no right to be here, girl,' she said scathingly, satisfied that I had not come with a large party. 'The Goddess' secrets are not to be spied upon by those who have not taken part in Her training.'

Now fully in control of the situation, the Priestess looked me up and down, then dismissed me with an abrupt, scornful motion of her hand.

'The time is not yet,' she hissed. 'Go now, if you can find your way.' And suddenly a dense mist swirled around us, hiding her completely from sight. I turned and stumbled towards Kevin, my ears ringing with peals of eerie laughter.

The horses were nervous and prancing, and Kevin boosted me up to Featherfoot's back in one fluid motion. I held her on a tight rein while he mounted Gulldancer, though I wanted nothing so much as to bolt from the darkness that filled the forest.

'Did you see those eyes?' I asked shakily as he came alongside and we turned towards the sound of the river.

'What eyes?' he asked.

'The Lady's. You did see the Lady, didn't you?' I half-whispered, my throat dry as sand.

'Nay, girl, I saw nothing but you, hiding behind that tree.'

'But she was standing there in the path, before she called the Druid's Mist upon us,' I said, starting to tremble now that the confrontation was past.

Kevin shook his head, looking back cautiously.

'Didn't you hear her singing? Or her words to me?'

Again he shook his head. 'Only the laugh of a woodpecker skimming through the trees,' he answered, watching me closely, 'What did she say to you?'

'That I shouldn't come here spying, and something about time . . .' My teeth were chattering uncontrollably and it seemed as though the dark of night had descended on us.

'Well, she was right on both counts,' my companion pointed out, reining in by the side of the river where the trees thinned out a bit. 'It's well past sunset, and even the twilight is starting to fade.'

I looked about then, appalled to realize that the moon had set already, and the late glow of the summer sky was giving way to night and stars.

'There'll be a real ruckus going on at home, I expect.' Kevin's voice had gone deep with concern, and I groaned inwardly at the thought of what we could expect ahead. 'We'd better find the path, and make the best time we can,' he added, urging Gulldancer forward.

So we left the Black Lake, with Kevin in the lead and me clinging to Featherfoot with a rising dread. I expected the Priestess to appear before us at any moment, barring our way and laughing at our distress. The hatred and suspicion that had crossed her face when we met was more frightening than anything I had ever seen before, as though somehow I had looked upon the very heart of darkness, and I fled from it, terrified.

As we made our way out of the Sanctuary the night spirits floated about us, gliding past in the form of an owl and rattling through the trees with the sound of the nightjar. Kevin set a reasonable pace, but it seemed unbearably slow, for I wanted to get safely back as fast as possible.

Once we were beyond the mountain base and the forest opened up, I drew abreast of him and pushed Featherfoot into a canter. Within a few strides she stumbled, and I careened forward, landing with a crunch on the ground below.

Kevin was kneeling beside me immediately, muttering dire warnings to the Gods and begging me to say something.

'Is Featherfoot . . .?' was the best I could manage, for my stomach was heaving and I couldn't get my breath.

'She didn't go down,' he answered, sliding an arm under my shoulders and raising me slightly.

'Yooww!' I howled as a flash of pain twisted through my shoulder. Kevin carefully ran his hand along the bones of my arm, then up over the shoulder, and paused at the base of my throat.

'No more racing through the dark for you tonight,' he said grimly as I cursed the web of bad luck enmeshing us.

'We'll be in for it now,' I gulped, furious that I had ever set out upon this mission.

Kevin went to check Featherfoot, and as he led her back to me I could see, even in the starlight, that she was limping noticeably. The fact that I had caused her injury made me feel worse than my own wrenched shoulder or the lecture I was bound to get at home.

'We'll both ride Gulldancer,' Kevin announced, bringing the gelding over. 'Featherfoot can walk, but slowly. We'll have to lead her.'

He lifted me on to the gelding's withers, then handed over Featherfoot's reins. It took a bit of scrambling for him to take his place behind me, but at last we were settled and making our slow way home.

This is all the Lady's doing, I thought, wondering what further disaster she might contrive for us. I sat rigid with misery and fright, seeing the gold eyes of wolves in every shadow and starting at the faintest sound.

'Now, now,' Kevin said softly, one arm around my waist, 'it won't do any good to spook the horses further.'

259

He began to talk, his voice gentle and reassuring as much for our mounts' sake as for mine.

''Tis a sky studded with diamonds, my lass, now that we're clear of the heavy woods. Look there—the Bear shines bright, and the mists are all gone. I'm thinking the Gods are with us in that, at least. Here now,' he added, pulling me back against him, 'you just relax and we'll be home in no time. I'll take you back safe and sound, with no more wild moments and fearful encounters.'

He continued to croon in a singsong fashion, lulling my racing heart and the throbbing of my shoulder. I nestled into the shelter of his arm, not even aware when I started to cry. There was something unutterably sweet about being enfolded within the protective circle of his care, and I gradually relaxed and let the tears of pain and anger and relief wash from me.

I could feel his cheek resting against my hair, and he suited his singing to the rhythmic motion of the horses.

'And if I had my way, sweet girl, I'd be taking you straight to the palace at Tara, with its great hall and carved pillars and fine rich trappings. And there I'd set you on the throne, and give you a golden crown as my queen, and together we'd rule the whole of Ireland.'

He spun the dream out slowly and beautifully, and I followed it softly in my heart. Tara it might not be, but surely the Great Hall of Appleby would do, and together we would reign in Rheged. The idea was so splendid, and such a surprise, it fluttered through me like butterflies. I wanted to laugh and sing and cover him with kisses all at once, and at the same time was loath to disturb the sweetness of our contact.

He lapsed into a song Brigit sometimes sang, and once I caught a snatch of a lullaby Mama used to croon before I went to sleep. I smiled silently, and turning in his arms, snuggled my head into the angle between his neck and his shoulder. I slid my good arm around him, and we rode for some time in that half-embrace.

When we reached the ford of the river a night bird awakened, sending a sleepy trill of song questing through the dark.

'Do you know what he says?' I murmured, and Kevin shook his head. 'He says I love you.'

Kevin was silent for so long I pulled away from my snuggled position. 'Did you hear?' I asked.

His eyes were hidden in the starlight, but the white flash of his smile was unmistakable. Still holding me in the circle of his arm, he planted the softest of kisses on my forehead.

'This is not the time to explore the matter,' he said gruffly, and I giggled. 'Now you just settle back and get some rest, lass, for we've still another hour or more to go.'

Leaning back against him, I was so happy I silently thanked the Lady for bringing us together this way, and drifted in a half-sleep where dreams and reality blended so that afterwards it was never exactly clear what had been said and what not.

I came slowly to wakefulness when we turned on to the flat road that leads to the bathhouse. The windows were dark and silent, but the light of a hooded lantern glowed by the gate, and a sleepy voice called out softly, 'Kevin?'

'Is that you, Brigit?' he answered, equally low. He pushed me upright as the horses turned into the yard.

'Aye, it's me. Where on earth have you two been?' she scolded. Then, seeing the empty horse behind us, she caught her breath. 'Where's Gwen?'

'I'm right here,' I whispered quickly. 'I fell from Featherfoot after we left the Lady . . .'

My voice trailed off, for I was now fully awake, and I turned to look at Kevin, wanting to make sure it wasn't

261

all a dream. But my companion was already sliding to the ground, and when he reached up to help me his face was hidden in shadow so I didn't see his expression.

The pain in my shoulder had awakened as well, and I bit my lip as I dismounted, half sliding, half helped by Kevin. He held me briefly while I steadied on my feet, then let go of me and turned to lead the animals off to the barn. I watched him limp away, dazzled by the love that welled up within me at that moment.

Brigit was looking at me intently, and now she unpinned her mantle and threw it across my shoulders.

'I suppose there's an explanation for this whole escapade, but morning will be soon enough to hear it. You have no idea how much trouble I had keeping the rest of the household from worrying. Your father is suspicious yet, though I said I'd sent you to the farm on the river and expected you to stay over with that family.'

I gazed contritely at the paving stones underfoot, wretched that our adventure had led to Brigit's having to lie. It had not occurred to me that my rebelliousness might lead to difficulties for her too. At least no one had been sent out looking for us.

'Are you badly hurt?' she asked when we reached the kitchen and she'd lit a rushlight from the flame of the lantern.

'Something happened to my shoulder when I fell. I think it's the shoulder, and not the collarbone,' I added hopefully. She ran her fingers along the bone, just as Kevin had, then nodded absently and turned to the cupboard.

'Do you want something to eat?' We were still whispering so as not to wake the household, and I shook my head.

'Well, best you sleep in my room for the rest of the

262

night, what there is of it,' she said. 'No point in waking Nonny by going upstairs.'

'What about you?' I asked as she pushed me towards her pallet.

'I'm going down to the barn to talk with Kevin. I'll be back later.'

'Don't be angry with him, Brigit,' I implored. 'I made him come with me, and it was the Lady who beset us with mists and darkness. It wasn't his fault,' I added, seeing the firm, set lines of her face.

'Maybe not,' she answered, her voice more gentle than her look. 'At least you're back in one piece, more or less, and that's what matters.'

And with that she was gone. I lay down on her bed, pulling the wool blanket over me, and fell asleep without even taking my boots off.

It was well past dawn when I awoke to find her leaning over me, stroking the hair back from my face. She looked tired beyond measure, and I guessed that she hadn't returned to her room during the night. I started to rise up on my elbow, but the shoulder rebelled violently and I grimaced and settled back down.

'Do you want to tell me about it?' she asked, sitting on the bed beside me. Her expression was weary, but there was no anger in her face, so I began at the beginning and told her everything up to the point of our return . . . the terrible magnificence of the Lake, and the echoes that lingered from Arthur's Investiture, and how the Lady had made me think of a wild, primitive animal, like the fox. For some unknown reason, however, I didn't want to tell her about my newfound dream.

'And that's all? You and Kevin didn't . . . stop any-where, for anything?'

The pause in her voice made me laugh. 'Of course not, silly. Why should we stop? We didn't have any food to cook, and we didn't meet anyone along the way. Something strange just happened to the time, for I'd swear it was only early afternoon when we entered the woods.'

I thought of the Lady's powers and hastily made the sign against evil.

Brigit sighed and grinned lopsidedly. 'Well, that, at least, is a relief,' she said cryptically. Then she stood up and began to strip out of her clothes, going to the basin to wash before donning new things.

'There's much that's happened while you were off cavorting with the Lady of the Fairies,' she said slowly. 'It seems the news that King Leodegrance has a daughter coming up on marriageable age has got out, and an emissary from your first suitor arrived last evening. That's the reason I had to cover so fast for you, for your father wanted to present you at dinner.'

'Instead of a third course?' I inquired, not really taking in the import of her news.

'They were put off until this morning,' she said, ignoring my attempt at humour. 'But you're to hurry upstairs and make yourself as fit for scrutiny as you can. Nonny will know what you should wear, and we'll have Kaethi check your shoulder at the same time.'

'Wait a minute,' I said, sitting fully upright. 'You mean I really am going to be looked over like some milk cow on Market Day? And just who are these suitors? Where did they come from?'

'They're from the court of King Mark, in Cornwall. I gather he heard about you at the King Making. It seems the old fool is looking for a young—very young—wife and since his party was in the area, decided to send a delegation to meet you and report back to him.'

She slid a long dress over her head, and when it was settled on her shoulders she turned and glanced at me.

'Good heavens, Gwen, why are you looking like that?'

'I don't want to be married, at least not to any old King Mark!' I sputtered. It was appalling that anyone would even consider the subject without asking me first. 'Besides, I'm not nearly old enough. I haven't become a woman yet, and no girl has to marry before she starts her cycles.'

'Some do,' Brigit said with a sigh, 'though I agree you shouldn't be forced to. I'm sure your father won't make you accept if you tell him you don't want it, but it is quite an honour to be considered. And you must be polite to them; they are our guests, after all, and due the best of Celtic hospitality.'

I went off to my chambers to be examined for broken bones by Kaethi and fussed over and scolded by Nonny. The shoulder was badly wrenched and bruised, but would not require more than poultices and general rest to let it heal. According to Nonny my hair was another matter entirely, so I sat while she combed and coaxed, braided and waved it into what she felt was a suitable coiffure.

And all the time I mulled over this new turn of events. Not only was there this unexpected talk about marriage, they also seemed to be quite matter-of-fact about the notion of packing me off to the other end of Britain. The very idea of leaving Rheged for such a reason was stupid and barbaric, and I vowed inwardly I'd never let them do it. Like the goddess Rhiannon, I'd run away first.

Nonny took the enamelled barrette out of Mama's jewel box, and I started to tell her there was no point in going to so much trouble, as I intended to get rid of these guests as soon as possible. But she seemed so pleased to be decking out a royal lady again, I held my tongue and concentrated on what I was going to do about the question of marriage in general.

There was really no reason why I couldn't marry Kevin. He could never be king because of his foot, of course, but other queens have had consorts while they ruled. Cartimandua, for instance, who was Queen of the Brigantes here in Rheged when the Legions arrived. Yes, it was possible that if I could fend off these suitors now, all I'd have to do was wait another two years until I came of age and then announce that I wanted Kevin to be my mate. That way, I would be able to stay in Rheged, and Kevin and I could continue to explore the tenderness that had begun to awaken last night.

The idea was so simple and so exciting, I was quite giddy by the time I went to meet my first suitors.

23

Tristan

The chamber that was used for State meetings was broad and comfortable, with tiled floors and walls of soft pink plaster. As I approached the archway I could hear our guests already in conversation with my father. Ailbe was lying by the door, head extended on his long shaggy paws, and he rose to his feet and came to stand beside me as I waited to be called forward.

The three men were so engrossed in what they were saying, I had a chance to appraise our guests unobserved.

The older one was trim and muscular, with a knowing look and mischievous smile, and he moved with the easy assurance of a man long used to being a courtier. He also appeared to be the spokesman for the two. The other was a tall heron of a fellow, angular of frame and hand, who spent most of the time scratching his dark head or stroking the cover of a small harp which lay in his lap.

Both guests rose to their feet when my father gestured for me to join them. As I started forward the wolfhound moved too, pacing beside me when I crossed the room. I let my hand rest on the top of his head as a reminder of my love for Kevin.

'Guinevere, this is Tristan, nephew of King Mark,' my father announced, gesturing towards the youth. 'And Dinadan, his companion.'

Once they were standing the true height of the young man became evident, and I thought it no wonder he seemed all knees and elbows when he was seated. I curtsied to both of them and Tristan stepped forward as though to take my hand. The moment he moved the dog came between us, hackles rising and a deep and continuous growl emerging from his throat.

'Ailbe!' I cried, 'stop that! This is a person come in friendship.'

The hound paid no attention but kept eyes, ears and nose all focused intently on the stranger. When I tried to step around him, Ailbe moved with me, always keeping that massive body sideways in front of me and always between me and the threat he perceived.

'I beg your pardon, M'lord,' I said hastily. 'I don't know what's got into him; he doesn't normally behave this way.'

I smiled brightly even as I realized how poorly I had phrased the comment, but Tristan was oblivious to its implication. Glancing hastily at Dinadan I caught a look of quiet amusement, and at that point Edwen managed to get a lead on the dog's collar and drag him, stiff-legged and unwilling, from the room.

So I took my place in the small circle of conversation, full of chatter and pleasantries. At first I wished someone like Kaethi had been included, so that it was not entirely up to me to fill the awkward spots, but as the visit progressed I found my father quick to fill in any gaps that arose.

At one point the visitors made some reference to having hoped to meet me yesterday, and I started to answer only to find my parent interrupting with a question about the harvest in Mark's country this year. I glanced at him quickly, wondering how much Brigit had told him. The subject didn't come up again, however, and I was relieved when we adjourned for the midday meal.

The trestles had been set up on the sands by the edge of the lagoon, and the food was served with all the splendour Brigit and Gladys could create. There were silver salvers and glass goblets, fine bowls of red Samian ware and even an enamelled wine pitcher like the one Arthur had admired in Carlisle. Having once been a rich Roman port, Ravenglass had one of the most complete treasure chests in the country, and this afternoon it was all on display.

The scene was lovely, for the tide was out, leaving a broad swath of ivory sand glowing against the soft blue of the water, and a gentle breeze tempered the sun's heat.

Tristan talked exuberantly about the wrestling matches he had won at the King Making games, his loud, booming voice making him sound even bigger than he looked. I found him boring and dull to talk with, but his obvious concern about where to put his feet and how to confine his gestures so as not to knock things off the table was touching in a way. It was clear that he took his position as emissary of his king very seriously, and wished to make a good impression on us.

This was the first time I was seated in the hostess' place next to my father at the main table. He asked me to lead the prayer before we ate, so I offered up the small, general grace that includes all deities and offends none.

It seemed odd not to be helping with the serving, and I kept looking for Kevin, hoping to exchange a conspiratorial glance, but I couldn't find him. Tristan was talking earnestly at me, so I turned my attention back to our guest.

'I notice that you began your feast with a pagan prayer,' he said, picking up a whole loaf of bread from the tray on the other side of the table. 'Can it be that Rheged is not a Christian country?'

'We have some followers of the new god,' I answered, 'but there are also those who prefer Mithra, or the Goddess, or the various local gods. I like this grace because it calls on the Spirit of the Place, and that can be whatever one wishes.'

Tristan frowned slightly and gnawed on the heel of the loaf.

'Your father has done nothing to stop the Old Ways, then?' he inquired, his mouth full.

'Of course not,' I said, surprised at the idea that a king might insist all of his people follow the same religion. 'My father has always felt that each man should be free to choose his gods or goddesses. Isn't it the same in King Mark's realm?'

'Oh, no, our king is a Christian, and all the people who can trace their lines back to the great Roman families are Christian too. Why, no one would think of performing the Goddess' rites at King Mark's court.'

The sanctimonious tone of his voice irritated me, and before I knew it I heard myself saying, 'What a pity. I was at Her Sanctuary just yesterday and found it very powerful and moving. Perhaps if your king would take the time to explore the matter, he would have a different attitude. It's possible we could arrange an introduction to the Lady, if you wish.'

The young man's shock was written all over his face, and I thought for a moment he was going to inch his chair away from me lest I contaminate him further.

My father was looking at me with consternation and I tossed my head back in high good spirits. I had managed to put an end to King Mark's interest in this child-bride without saying a word that wasn't true or making a decision that was insulting. The ease of it all amused me, and I had trouble stifling a grin.

Later, when the lack of sleep and the constant ache of my shoulder began to deflate my buoyant good humour, I asked to be excused and made my way back to the bathhouse for a nap. Brigit was in the courtyard, supervising the washing of dirty platters, and I paused to speak with her.

'I didn't see Kevin,' I began. 'Was he too worn out to get up today?'

She glanced up, the deep-set lines of the morning returning to her mouth and her eyes red with weeping.

'What is it? What's happened?' I stammered as she grabbed me roughly by the arm and pushed me towards the stairs.

When we were in my room, she sat down on the bed and gestured for me to sit beside her. Then she took both my hands in hers and without looking at me, said simply, 'Kevin's gone.'

'What do you mean, "gone"?' My voice came out as a whisper.

'Just that, Gwen. He's gone. Left. Run away. I . . . I can't say it was a total surprise when Rhufon told me, but . . . but I wish it hadn't happened.' A tear began to make its way slowly down her cheek and she made no effort to brush it away.

'I don't understand. Why . . . why should he leave?'

'For a lot of reasons, I think. He . . . he said he had become more fond of you than was reasonable. And he got very upset when I told him about the suitors and such. He also felt terribly guilty about your not getting home until almost dawn last night. He had not met his responsibilities in looking after you, and your father would have every right to have him flogged if he chose.'

Brigit paused, and shook her head sadly. 'Kevin felt it brought shame on our family, and that last night might bring shame on you if your suitors are Christian. You know that virginity is important to us . . . and what with all of his own feelings for you . . .' Brigit's voice trailed off, and she squeezed my hands tightly, but still didn't look at me.

271

'Well all that nonsense about virginity is just that, nonsense!' I said hotly. 'I'm just as much virgin now as I was two days ago, and anyone who thinks otherwise just because we couldn't get home before nightfall is looking for that famous Christian obsession, "sin."'

I had forgotten that Brigit was a Christian, so galling was the idea that someone else's religious beliefs should impinge on the fate of the people closest to me.

'Well,' I said with a sigh, 'where did he go? And when will he be back?'

Brigit didn't say a word, but finally turned and looked directly at me, and my heart stopped.

'He's not coming back,' she whispered finally.

'We'll ask him to,' I declared, unwilling to hear what she was telling me.

'How? He told no one when he left, or where he was going. He can't go back to our family, for he was given over as a hostage and has now broken the trust of that pledge. Even if he contacted them, they wouldn't help him, a fact he understands well enough. And he dare not go to any of the steadings where we hold court, for the people would recognize him and turn him over to your father . . . and he'd be right back in the very position he ran away from to begin with. No, there's no way to reach him; by his own actions he's made himself an outlaw.'

I had not thought of that, and now I sat in stunned silence as Brigit broke into sobs. Tears fell down her cheeks as she continued.

'Rhufon offered to ride out looking for him, but since he's on foot he needn't stay with the paths, so that seems futile.'

'He didn't take Gulldancer?' I asked dully, wondering what sort of chance a crippled boy without a horse had of surviving in the forest.

'No' —Brigit shook her head— 'nor Ailbe either. He

took nothing except for the clothes on his back and his dagger. I think he felt it was a matter of pride to leave with no debts owed.'

'Did you know he was going to do this?' I recalled how haggard she had looked this morning and thought it possible she had spent the night trying to dissuade her kinsman from such folly.

'No, not exactly.' Her sobs had quieted, and she let go of my hands to brush away the last of the tears. 'I knew he was quite upset, even when you first got home, but when he discovered the strange horses stabled in the barn, and heard that they belonged to men come to court you in their king's name . . . that's when he really became distraught. He cried when he talked about you, and how he wished things could have been different, but before I left him he was calm and seemed more at peace with his moira.' Her voice went husky again. 'I should have guessed what he intended when he asked me to remember him in my prayers.'

I lay back across the bed, suddenly too depleted to say anything. The thought of Kevin running, alone and outlawed, away from the future I had just begun to think about seemed unbelievably cruel. I stared, dry-eyed and aching, at the roof above and wondered if this was a further punishment from the Lady.

Brigit got up and began to unlace my shoes, and when I sat up she undid the girdle at my waist.

'Things will be better tomorrow,' she murmured, helping me out of my dress, 'after we both get some sleep.'

'Maybe he'll change his mind and come back,' I whispered, clinging to the idea that it was a giant misunderstanding. I was too weary to think about it further, and with a whimper crawled under the covers and let Brigit tuck me in. She sat beside me for a bit, until I fell asleep.

I must have been exhausted, for I slept all that afternoon and through the night; but it was a fitful time, for I was searching in my dreams for some thing or place which I could never find. And always there was the Lady, rising with her strange, cold laugh to block my passage.

At first light I awoke, aware with a sinking misery that something terrible had happened even before I remembered what it was.

I got up and made my way to the pasture to see Featherfoot, for I had not had time to check on her since our night's ride.

Rhufon was already out with the horses, changing the poultice on my mare's foreleg.

'How's she doing?' I asked, running my hand along her jaw. She bobbed her head and snuffled into my shoulder affectionately.

'Nothing that won't mend, Missy,' the Horse Master said. He crouched next to her foreleg with a warm herb pot nearby. I watched as he carefully applied handfuls of the limp, dripping leaves to her leg, then carefully covered the area with a strip of clean fleece. 'I hear you got a bit bruised yourself,' he added without looking up.

'Some,' I admitted. 'How's Gulldancer?' It was as close as I could come to asking about Kevin.

'Fine, nothing wrong with him. I think we'll take him up to Stanwix and put him out to pasture there, now the young man is gone.'

I nodded, feeling the lump rise in my throat, and blinking hastily, leaned against Featherfoot's neck and watched Rhufon work. With long-practised skill he drew the linen bandage around the fleece and began to braid the fabric tails into a neat, flexible seam. I knew from experience that it was a more delicate job than it looked, for the tension needs to be enough to keep the poultice from slipping, but not so much as to hinder the blood flow. Kevin and I had spent hours practising on each other's wrists in order to get the hang of it.

'Do you know where he went?' I ventured at last, when I thought my voice would be steady.

'No, Missy, except that he was most determined no one should go looking for him.' Rhufon sat back on his heels and surveyed his work, then glanced up at me. 'Your father is very concerned about the boy's welfare, but we had a long talk, Brigit and the King and I, and agreed this is how Kevin wanted it.'

I nodded again, and my old friend continued to watch me from under his scruffy eyebrows.

'I tell you, child, all things heal with time,' he said, 'even a young person's rage against the Fates.'

And so the matter was dropped. I wandered down to the kennels, where Ailbe was still chained, and sat down beside the big dog. He looked up briefly, doleful eyes scanning my face with reproach, as though asking why I did nothing in the face of this calamity. At last he sighed and lowered his head to his paws again. I stroked him and talked to him for a bit, but could not rouse any kind of response. Perhaps he too thought it was a bad dream and if he waited long enough he'd wake up.

Later in the day, when our guests had departed, I sought out Rhufon and asked how the dog was doing.

'He's pining, Missy. Pining for the young man. He didn't eat last night, or this morning, and even when I let him off the chain I can't get him to take an interest in anything.'

'Would he be able to catch up with Kevin, if we turned him loose?' I asked.

Rhufon looked at me very thoughtfully for a long time, then shrugged one shoulder. 'I expect so, if the dog knows he's got permission to go.'

'How do you give him permission?'

'Well,' my mentor said, rubbing his stubbly chin and frowning, 'I suppose I could take something of the boy's, something with his scent on it, and give it to the dog to smell. And then I could take him to the gate, and try telling him to go find Kevin . . .'

Rhufon's voice trailed off, and he glanced towards the kennels.

'Good,' I said firmly. 'You do that. Do that when the rest of the household is gathered for the main meal, so that the dog doesn't get distracted.'

The Master of the Horse had dropped his gaze while I was talking, but now he studied me carefully.

'Is that an order, Missy? You know the dog's valuable, and he was a gift to the King from the Irish family themselves. I don't want to go losing something of the King's, you know.'

I had never thought about giving anyone an order before, but now I looked directly at my old friend and said urgently, 'Yes, Rhufon, it's what I want you to do, and I will take the responsibility for it if there is any difficulty. Besides,' I added, 'how much good is a dog who starves to death in mourning for his lost master?'

So that afternoon, when the rest of us were eating around the tables, Rhufon took the big, shaggy beast out beyond the gate and turned him loose. Later he told me Ailbe just sat next to him for a bit, staring at nothing with a hopeless, patient misery. But after Rhufon held one of Kevin's shoes under his nose and then dragged it along the path, bringing it back for him to smell and then placing it down on the path again, the dog's ears suddenly lifted and he got to his feet.

'At first he seemed to be casting about randomly, but last I saw of him he was well on some trail, Missy,' Rhufon said, the hint of a smile crinkling his eyes. 'In summer the scent lasts quite a spell, so I think the young man may have company before nightfall.'

It was a thought I clung to through all the day, and after going to bed that night, I begged the Gods to protect the two of them together.

24

Lavinia

I entered my father's chamber with apprehension lying heavy in my stomach. There was no indication why he had summoned me, but whether it was because of Kevin's leaving or our escapade at the Lake or the loss of Ailbe, he had a right to be angry, and I approached the confrontation with dread.

The western windows were open, and the soft sound of the doves' cooing drifted in on the summer breeze. Rheged's King was staring intently at a schedule of breeding that was spread out on the table and seemed unaware of my presence when I came to stand beside him. When he didn't look up, I too began to scan the schedule, mentally tracing Featherfoot's line, until I realized my parent had shifted his attention and was studying me.

'What ever got into you the other day, child?' he asked, his tone more puzzled than accusatory. 'Surely you knew those men were Christian and would take affront at your suggestion they should meet the Lady?'

I shrugged and looked down at my hands, unable to frame an answer. With my mind full of other, more important things, I had forgotten my exchange with King Mark's nephew as soon as it had achieved its purpose.

'And since when have you become a champion of the Lady?' my father went on, sinking down into his chair and gesturing for me to be seated. 'I never thought you were that keen on her yourself . . .'

'I know, Father.' I nodded, wondering where to begin. 'And I'm sorry if I was rude to our guests. Really I am. I was so scared at the thought you were going to send me away to become a stranger's wife. It's . . . it's not what I want to do, Sire.'

The royal response was quick and indignant.

'Not want? What ever does "want" have to do with it? There's many things that monarchs, whether they be kings or queens, must do that aren't what they personally want. And sometimes marriage is one of them.' He paused for a moment, and seemed to change course. 'Kaethi tells me you set much store by the Irish boy, and that you're upset over his running away . . .'

I sat very still, not knowing where this new thought was going. If my father connected Kevin with my dismissal of the suitors, he could well put a price on the Irish boy's head.

'Well, you can rest easy on that account, child. I'll not send out a death warrant for him, nor is he to be banned from human contact. It's unfortunate, of course, and I'm sorry that it's happened, but you can't let something like that distract you from your duty. Life does go on,' he added, looking down at the ring Mama had given him.

Apparently my parent thought of Kevin's and my relationship as no more than a childhood friendship. This certainly was not the time to suggest that it could be more, much more, and I let out a sigh of relief, glad the King was not going to pursue the matter.

'Now that you're coming up to marriageable age,' he went on, 'there are bound to be more men come round to take a look at you, and some, I'll warrant, will offer their hands and crowns as well. Such matters involve tact, and duty, and you can't just go driving them away for the sport of it.' He paused again. 'If only your mother were here, I'm sure she could explain it better . . .'

'Hah,' I snorted, 'she would understand better than anyone else! Don't forget, she was being sent off to marry

279

someone she'd never met when she agreed to run away with you. She knew well enough what it is to be traded off like a piece of cheese for political advantage . . .'

My father shot me a quick, hard look, and one eyebrow went up.

There was a long minute when I held his gaze, refusing to back down, and he finally sighed audibly and looked away.

'Will it help if I promise not to make any commitments for you without consulting you first? We will go over all the pros and cons together when the time comes. But the present problem is how to keep you from alienating half the kingdoms of Britain with your quick tongue; I can't have you dishing out bright, spritely chatter that's full of toads and adders where company is concerned. And,' he said very slowly and firmly, 'while they might think you don't realize what you're saying, I know perfectly well you do.'

I bent my head in the hope that he would not read the expression on my face, for I was at odds not so much with him as with the Fates who had made things so complicated all of a sudden. If only Kevin hadn't run away, it would all have been so simple!

'Let's make an agreement,' my father suggested finally. 'I won't force you to accept anyone's hand if you truly and deeply dislike him, and you won't play fast-and-loose with our reputation for hospitality and good manners. That should ease some of the burden where you're concerned, and would be a vast relief for me as well.'

I nodded my assent without looking up.

'Is it agreed?' he asked, unwilling to accept the mute response of a child.

I raised my head proudly and tried to answer as an adult: 'Yes, Sire, it is agreed.' All I was promising was

280

that I would be polite to future company, and that was a long way from agreeing to marry someone.

But if I thought the question of my future could be put aside and forgotten, that hope was washed away with the first blood of menarche which came flowing from me the next day.

Thick and dark and unmistakable, it clearly branded me as a woman. Other girls, such as Gladys' daughter, might find promise in the transition from child to adult, but as far as I could see it only meant my days of freedom were numbered. Even the ancient rites, held in the shadow of the sacred Stones and full of chants and whispers and glad anthems to womanhood, didn't cheer me up. I took my anger to bed with me and cried myself to sleep like a baby.

My father and I rarely saw each other during the next few months; he continued travelling through the countryside holding Councils on Arthur's treaty, and I wandered about the court, unable or unwilling to think of anything else but the fact that Kevin was missing.

I worked in the kitchen with Gladys or tagged about after Brigit, but the only outings I went on were occasional berry-picking excursions with the younger children. I told myself that I didn't go riding because Featherfoot's leg needed to heal, but in reality there was nowhere I wanted to go, nor anyone I wished to be with.

The only solace I found was in the belief that Kevin would return when the winter had passed. I lived and relived our last ride together, endowing every comment, every action, every nuance with worlds of meaning that only he and I could understand. In my mind, we had sworn our love and promised our devotion; I had no doubt but that he knew how miserable I was without him, and that his love for me would bring him back. I could not believe we would not be united come spring.

As the leaves began to fall, the court moved up the coast to Carlisle and the final plans were made for who was to stay there and who was to come with us to the north. I watched the activity as one in a trance, forgetting how recently I had looked forward to returning to The Mote.

The morning before we were to leave, Brigit and I were summoned by my father to the State Chamber. I was shocked at how tired he looked; gaunt and greying, he seemed to me to have aged a decade since the beginning of summer.

'Ah yes, Gwen . . .' he said with a small start, as though surprised to see me there. 'How have you been?'

'Well enough,' I answered noncommittally.

'Good, good,' he said, shifting in his chair and looking directly at me. 'Goodness, you're turning into quite the young woman.'

When I didn't say anything, he glanced hopefully at Brigit.

'Your father and I have been talking recently, Gwen,' my friend began, 'about a portion of your education that's been overlooked. Oh, you know the basics of spinning and weaving and such, and you're good in the kitchen. But, well . . . now that it's time to think about your future, there's all sorts of things about court life you should be taught.'

There was an uncomfortable silence, and I wondered why this sudden interest in further education. There was something here that involved more than spending additional time with Cathbad.

'I've met a widow from York, a very proper lady with a good Roman background,' Brigit went on, 'and we've discussed it with her already. Your father and I agree she'll make a good chaperone for you. I can't run the

282

household and be your governess too, and there's all manner of things she can teach you that I can't.'

Brigit was looking at me earnestly, and I bit my tongue, determined not to say anything until I understood what was actually happening. It was beginning to smell like a trap, and I wished fervently there were some way to get up and back out of the room without their noticing.

'She's willing to come live at court,' my father put in hastily, 'so it isn't as though you'd be sent away somewhere. And there's probably much we can all learn from her.'

'But what about Cathbad?' I asked, wondering how an old Roman matron and a young Celtic druid would get on together.

'Cathbad's been very helpful these last few years,' my father responded, frowning slightly. 'And I hope he'll stay on with us at court. But you need a different kind of instruction now.' He was slowly turning Mama's ring as he searched for words to phrase his thoughts. 'You need a woman now, a lady who can give you the background for taking your place as queen at a court of your own. Someone who can teach you Latin, and etiquette, and how to read and write . . .'

His voice trailed off and he looked at Brigit for confirmation.

'There's a great many things you'll need to know in a large court, Gwen,' she said gently. 'Things we haven't even thought about here.'

'But I don't want to live in a large court,' I said, slowly getting to my feet. 'I don't ever want to leave Rheged. Rheged is my home, my own, my world. It's where I belong, where I want to be.' I had begun walking round the room, gathering energy from the sheer physical activity. It helped to ward off the feeling of being tangled in something I couldn't even see.

'These are my people, just as I'm their Someday Queen,' I flared, fiercely laying claim to the title Kevin had given me when we were children. 'And I don't need to learn Latin to talk to them. Why, most of our subjects don't know Latin at all.'

No one said anything, and as the silence pressed in on me I turned and flung myself back on to the bench. 'Besides, I'll never, never learn to eat lying down!'

My father's eyebrow lifted at that, and leaning forward, he promised solemnly that we would never become *that* Roman.

There was more discussion then, about monarchs' needing to know Latin for reasons of state and diplomacy, and how Rheged must be prepared to take her place in the High King's plans, and it became very clear that the whole thing had already been set in motion. I felt like the fox kit: angry, indignant and quite unwilling to be tamed. At least he had a burrow to run to.

Finally, seeing no way to avoid this new development, I retreated into silence. Surely, I told myself, when Kevin returns we'll get matters straightened out.

So Lavinia came to court. Small and plump, she wore her hair carefully curled and smelled of a perfume that she regularly sent for from a merchant in Marseille. She was neat to the point of distraction, and took over the management of my life like a mother hen trying to keep a duckling out of water, and with about as much success.

The first morning after her arrival I woke to find my tunic and breeches gone, and a simple long dress hung carefully on the peg where my clothes should have been.

'Tunics, particularly tunics of bright colours,' she told me firmly, 'are for ladies of ill repute. And no decent woman ever wears breeches. I can't imagine what your nurse was thinking of, letting you run about here like a barbarian, or worse.'

I wondered what the 'worse' was, but she was busy opening Mama's chest and sorting through the dresses that were stored there.

'We'll use those things which are appropriate, and make over the rest,' she said cheerfully. 'Of course, the really fine things will be saved for later. You'll be a grown-up one of these days, and then you'll need some fancy garments.'

I stared at the beautiful things edged with lace and encrusted with embroidery, and vowed I wouldn't be needing them soon.

The idea of sleeping in a room with unglazed windows was almost as much of a shock to Vinnie as my wardrobe had been, and it became a matter to be attended to at once. She moved to the smaller room that had been Brigit's, where at least the windows were intact, and Brigit took her place in the bed across the room from my own.

Nonny was still officially my nurse, but she had become more and more muddled, confusing me with Mama all of the time now and reminding me of scrapes and adventures that happened long before I was born. Occasionally she peered intently at Lavinia and blurted out strange comments, such as 'What's the matter with that woman's hair?'

Vinnie took it in stride, treating the old Cumbrian nursemaid like the childish crone she had become. At least she didn't seem to take offence.

My days suddenly filled with household lessons of all kinds. Vinnie took charge of the keys to all the cupboards and insisted I make the rounds of every closet with her.

'A really fine court has linen sheets,' she announced, looking sceptically at the plain but adequate woollen blankets we used.

'Hasn't anyone here ever heard of Samian ware?' she

285

asked, staring incredulously at the contents of the dish cupboard.

I tried to point out that we did have a few red bowls, but she just shook her head sadly.

'Ah, it's not like the old days, child,' she sighed. 'Why, even after my mother's family came to Britain, they used nothing but the finest ceramics from the Continent. Of course, it's much harder to get anything of quality since The Troubles began.'

I heard a lot about the days before The Troubles, when trade with Rome had flourished and one found libraries and jewellery shops and glass emporiums throughout the Empire. Vinnie's own grandmother had been born in Rome, and used to recount stories about that city's magnificence. Rome was still the arbiter of sophistication and civilized behaviour in Vinnie's mind, and compared with it, our northern part of 'The British Province' was very backward indeed.

By the time Cathbad returned, our routine was well established, and while the druid was made welcome at court, he was also informed that my education had been given over to the widow from York.

I was not present when he was told, but was in the Hall when he strode out of my father's chambers, his fair countenance dark with anger.

''Tis a poor thing when a daughter of the Cumbri is taught only Roman ways,' he commented curtly, glaring first at Lavinia, then at me. 'And the day will come when you'll regret it, Missy, mark me well.'

He continued through the room and out the doors, never stopping to bid farewell to anyone. I was sorry not to have a chance to tell him this hadn't been my idea.

After Vinnie's arrival the bulk of the household stayed in Carlisle while my father travelled through the north, still intent on being able to give King Arthur some final word on the proposed treaty come spring. I suspected he was using that as an excuse to escape the changes in our home life, for while Lavinia didn't insist on couches, she did introduce both finger bowls and hand towels at meals within the first week of her arrival.

Once she was established, my governess broached the subject of my learning to read and write. I rebelled openly at that, and we reached a compromise only when it was agreed that Brigit should learn with me, both for companionship and because she herself wished to have those skills.

I longed for the freedom of my former life, looking back not only to the adventures with Kevin but also to Cathbad's lessons. I missed his explanation of things, the long walks in the woods when the weather was good and the tales of other countries and times. They all became part of a dream I returned to over and over in my fantasy.

By now I had convinced myself that Kevin would come back at Beltane, when the general amnesty held and he need not fear reprisals for our misadventure with the Lady or his running away. It was the one thing that made the rest of life bearable.

Slowly the months went by. Winter came, and the Market Square stood empty and quiet for weeks at a time. The cold was bitter that year, and more than one night I awoke shivering, not because I was cold but because Kevin was out there in the darkness somewhere, without family or home or warmth.

Travellers stopped off at court occasionally, and now and then word came from my father, but compared with the years of travel and festivals, of close interaction with the people and great evenings of feasting and singing, life had become dull and dreary. I waited patiently, watching the sun come back after the Midwinter passed and clinging to the idea that Beltane would mean the return of all that

I longed for: freedom and laughter, and most of all, Kevin.

Vinnie was determined that I learn needlework of every kind, and before long a stack of embroidered pieces began to accumulate. Yet I noticed they were never made use of, but carefully folded and placed in the cedar chest Vinnie's grandmother had brought from Rome. Finally I asked why these things were stored away instead of being used.

'But child, they are for your wedding. They'll be part of your trousseau.'

I stared at her blankly, wondering why she thought I'd need a trousseau. When my father and mother had run away, there hadn't been a trousseau; it had all happened much too fast for planning. Depending on who told the story, it was as much a matter of abduction as elopement. When Kevin came for me I wouldn't bother with a trousseau either, so all this time and effort was to be for naught. It seemed ridiculous to spend my days putting bits of embroidery on cloth I would never use, and I whiled away the long hours imagining what the Beltane meeting would be like.

Sometimes I thought he would ride up suddenly on Featherfoot and, sweeping through the startled crowd, pause long enough to help me on to her back; then together we'd be off before anyone realized what was happening.

Or perhaps he would take his place among the farmers and craftsmen waiting for darkness and the circle dance, when we'd come together with only a small exchange of secret smiles. With everyone whirling about in the flicker of the bonfire light, we could slip off into the shadows like any other couple, and be gone before anyone else noticed.

Obviously, no matter how we met again, it would not be part of the orderly routine of Lavinia's 'proper' court.

As the days lengthened, I noted the increase of travellers on the road with a secret excitement, sure that each day brought my love closer.

The weather turned beautiful at last: balmy and mild, with a haze of alder blossoms swaying above the river. I looked forward to this Beltane with more enthusiasm than I had known in my life before, and even agreed with Vinnie that I should wear a long dress for the occasion, complete with the bright girdle of woven silk and the enamelled barrette from Mama's jewel box. This was, after all, a very special occasion.

Once I was dressed Brigit brought me the mirror, and I looked at my own reflection with surprise. The hair wasn't copper, nor the face serene, but I saw a young woman, not a girl, looking back at me. Somehow I'd grown up enough to take my life into my own hands, and while I'd never be a queen, I would be spending the rest of my life with someone I loved. That more than made up for any loss of royal status.

The bells on the ends of the girdle gave off a sweet tinkling sound as I moved, and I laughed with the realization that this might well be considered my bridal dress.

On the Sacred Hill the Need-fire sprang to life almost immediately, and the night of dancing commenced.

The joy and promise of the new season swept away all trace of winter's pall as we spun around and around the miniature sun that flamed in the centre of the circle. The heat of the fire and fertility pulsed through the universe, roused and rousing to a long, sustained fever. Couples came together, twined with longing and release from winter's oppression, and one by one they vanished into the night. I followed them with my eyes, longing, begging, willing Kevin to come to me now. Occasionally other men held out their arms to me, but they weren't the Irish boy so I smiled and shook my head.

Too soon the bonfire ebbed; the dark skeleton of charred logs collapsed, sending forth fountains of sparks against the night as it fell into piles of glowing coals. The livestock was brought forward; cows and pigs, all the horses, sheep and geese, even the randy goats and stupid chickens, all carefully driven through the embers while the husbanders called down the blessing of the Gods as protection against illness in the months to come. I watched each dark figure, poised to throw myself into his arms, yet none of the men was the one I sought, and a faint, fine rasp of panic began to draw across my nerves.

I waited, trembling, until the very last group of revelers began to return to town. Afraid to stay there by myself, I joined them, chanting and singing as the new-lit torches were carried back to our various hearths.

Now, I thought wildly: now is the time, Kevin. You must step forward before we reach the fastness of the stone buildings, where I could never escape without a fuss!

I searched urgently among the faces of every group we came upon, yet all I found was the high spirits and good-natured jesting of everyday people who had the freedom to live their lives as they chose, without the constraints of royal obligations hemming them in.

When the final celebrants retired, I made my way slowly up to bed in a state of shock and disbelief. Kevin had not come, and some part of me knew, now, that he would never return. The knowledge numbed my heart and made my eyes blur, and I trudged down the passageway without hope or desire or any interest in the future.

Brigit was turning back the covers, and she began to help me undress, commenting sleepily about the May-dance to be held on the morrow. As she folded the silk girdle the bells jingled one last time; all the dreams of what could have been lay broken in that light, silvery sound, and the dam of my sorrow burst in a rushing sob.

'Why, Gwen, what is it?'

Without waiting for an answer she gathered me in her arms, while the whole of my misery poured out in a torrent of tears and gusting gulps. She listened carefully, rocking me as a mother rocks her child, while I put words to my fears, my guilt and remorse over Kevin's departure and the whole of the hopes I had built in the months since then.

'He'll never come for me, will he, Brigit?' I whispered, wrung out with weeping and despair.

'Not likely, Gwen, not likely,' my friend answered, still holding me close. 'You must put aside the belief that he's alive, for he is gone as surely as if he had died, and you have to go on and create a separate life for yourself.'

I thought wearily of days full of perfect little stitches and fancy linens, and years spent dutifully sitting by the hearth; I could not believe I was expected to accept such dullness as a substitute for living.

But Brigit was right, of course, and by the time autumn came again I had put aside all but the memory of my dreams. Lavinia kept me too busy to chafe about lost freedoms, and I dared not think about either the past or the future. Only, sometimes, on a clear summer night when the stars were flung in a web across the northern sky, I remembered the ride home from the Sanctuary and the love that should have been.

25

The Betrothal

During the next year life at Rheged's court was placid and slow and dull. I stayed with the household at the big house in Carlisle, diligently studying Latin, turning out pieces of neat embroidery and occasionally doing mathematical problems. This last activity was based on the concepts Cathbad had taught, and it confused Vinnie considerably. That may be one reason I enjoyed it.

There did seem to be an increase in visiting royalty, particularly after Arthur's treaty with Urien was signed. Mostly our guests were kings looking for a wife for themselves, their sons or, sometimes, their grandsons. Once in a while women came too: protective mothers or sisters whose eyes assessed everything about me and my surroundings even as they babbled on about inanities. In general, however, the men came alone.

Occasionally my father took me on state visits if the weather was good, the atmosphere right and he felt I could learn something of value. I appreciated the chance to get away from Carlisle and found the interplay of personalities and politics among our northern neighbours fascinating. It was certainly more challenging than needlework, and I made an effort to learn the various dialects in order to understand the nuances of diplomatic discussions.

When Vinnie began to feel I was well in hand, she attacked the problem of the Church. At one time there had been a notable congregation in Carlisle, and the building they had constructed specifically for holy use still stood, half-roofed and mouldy, but a church nonetheless.

My governess set about trying to revive interest, not only among the local people but with the leaders of the Church itself. She sent off wooden tablets with letters inscribed inside, begging, pleading and cajoling any clergyman she had ever heard of, and was eventually rewarded with a letter from London saying that a man from Saint Ninian's monastery would be sent to Carlisle to act as pastor for the flock. I had never thought of Christians as sheep, or holy men as tenders thereof, but Vinnie assured me that in Rome that was how things were done.

I agreed to accompany her to the festivities surrounding the bishop's arrival after she promised me that it wouldn't commit me to anything in the future.

I was hoping the new leader would be Father Bridei, the Pictish monk we had hosted at Loch Milton, but he turned out to be a narrow, crabbed man who scowled at the world in principle and looked through women as though they didn't exist. I couldn't help wondering why some Christians were loving and caring towards their fellowmen while others were constantly judgemental and difficult. There didn't seem to be an answer, and in the end I thanked Vinnie for her concern over my soul and kept a fair distance between myself and her religion.

It was Vinnie's contention that women must live and work in their own separate world, and more and more I found myself sequestered in what she called 'the women's quarters.' It was so far from the mainstream of activity that I often didn't know who was visiting or when they arrived. So it was without any warning that I came into the Hall for dinner one night and found Merlin seated in the guest position next to my father.

Making a hasty curtsy, I took my place on the other side of the King, and wondered what had brought Arthur's Magician to Rheged. At least it was too late in the year to be war plans.

Watching the Archdruid, I remembered Kevin's comment that he should have been named for the owl; silent, unblinking and all-knowing, he even cast a shadow akin to those of the deadly predators of the night. I was glad my father was seated between us, as I hadn't the slightest idea what to say to our guest, and from his distant attitude, I suspected there was nothing he cared to say to me.

And I was even more surprised to find him in the State Chamber when I answered my father's request to join him after dinner. I tried to suggest that I would return later, but my father stopped me.

'No, no, child, I . . . that is, we called you here specifically. Merlin would like to speak with you.'

My father gestured towards a chair, and I sank into it, looking slowly back and forth between him and the Enchanter.

'There, now, girl,' Merlin said gruffly, 'you needn't fidget so. I just wanted to know how old you are.'

I would have been less astonished if he'd asked me about dragon eggs, and I stared at him like a dolt. Surely he could have got that information from my father.

'I'll be turning fifteen this December,' I answered, wondering why he began nodding.

'Early December?' he inquired, and when I nodded in return, he muttered something about archers and lack of tact.

Finally, however, he turned to my father and solemnly thanking him for our hospitality, declared that he thought he'd go to bed. I stood respectfully as he swept out of the room and then looked to my father in total bewilderment.

'Whewww . . .' My parent took in a deep breath and brought his shoulders up around his ears, then slowly lowered them as he exhaled and nodded for me to come closer. 'I think, Gwen, that you've just been chosen to become King Arthur's wife.'

'What?' The word ricocheted off table and wine flagon, map chest and tile floor.

'That's what Merlin was here to ask about . . . whether or not I would consider such a match. I told him I'd have to talk with you.' He was looking at his hands, and the silence between us sagged of its own weight.

'Well?' he finally asked.

'Well, what?' The wind was starting to return to my lungs, and with it a raging torrent of half-formed words and actions. 'Are you asking how I would feel about it? Are you seriously thinking I would consider it? Are you going to send me away from Rheged whether I want to go or not? I thought we had an agreement . . .'

'Indeed,' he said drily, 'that's why this is a conversation rather than my simply telling you what you will do. So let's begin at the beginning. Just what are your objections to marrying the High King?'

'Objections? I don't even know him. I'd have to go all the way to Logres to marry him, and live among strangers. I don't want to be High Queen . . . I just want to stay here in Rheged, with my own people. And most important . . .' I paused, giving the next point extra emphasis. 'According to the treaty, if I leave Rheged, Urien can stand for king after you're gone . . . and I don't want that.'

'All right,' my father conceded, 'let's pour the wine and go over these points more closely. It's time to decide whom you would prefer.'

'Prefer?' I squeaked, feeling the future close in on me.

'Yes, prefer. I will not tell Merlin that you refuse his offer without telling him that you have voiced a preference for someone else. Matters are awkward enough as it is, without our turning down the High King out of hand.

295

Now, you've met most everyone who's sent word saying he is interested . . . so let's go over the list and see what is the best we can do for you, girl. Preferably,' he added, 'over that glass of wine.'

So I filled the goblets, and we spent the rest of the evening considering the merits and drawbacks of every marriage alliance possible to me. I had no idea that so many men were interested, and the range of age was so broad as to be comical. Even after we ruled out those who were more than five years younger than I and any who were already approaching the half-century mark there was still a list far longer than I had expected.

Foremost among them was Urien's bid that I marry his son, Uwain.

'This,' my father pointed out, 'would bring our two kingdoms together, and put an end to the tension along the borders. But I cannot imagine that such a match would be a happy one for you. The boy is still young, and although Urien is a good leader, he's overbearing in nature, and he places blood and kinship ties above all else. He's a better man to have as an ally than an enemy . . . but he would want to run everything, and when the time comes, would simply shoulder you aside and name himself regent until your children are grown. No,' he concluded, 'far better to see you married to the High King, who is powerful enough to keep Urien in line, than to have you under the thumb of the smaller, pettier ruler.'

I nodded, thinking that a marriage to Uwain would also make me daughter-in-law to Morgan le Fey—a fate I wasn't sure I could handle.

'Then too,' my father went on, draining his glass, 'King Caw has always wanted to see you bound to one of his brood. He's recently suggested his youngest as consort for you.'

'Gildas?' I snorted indignantly, remembering all too

well the whining boy who had pestered me unmercifully on a state visit the previous spring. Narrow-minded and priggish, he was the last person I would have expected to be interested in marriage.

'I think he's more talk than action,' I suggested. 'Besides, his eyes are set too close together. He'll probably sire ugly children.'

My father nodded, and a bit of humour crept into his voice. 'I always thought he was too scholarly for you, somehow.'

We went through several more families, mostly from the north, and then Gawain's name came up.

'Not,' my father added hastily, 'that he's asked for you. But if you fancy him over Arthur, we might make inquiries . . .'

I burst out laughing, remembering that whirlwind of redheaded determination that had stormed through the summer at Threlkeld Knotts.

'Surely you're not serious?' I asked, and for a moment my father actually laughed aloud.

'It would be rather like tethering a pair of Soay sheep together,' he said. Then he sighed and made a face.

'Maelgwn of North Wales would like to gain this kingdom someday; because of his kinship to your mother he expects to claim the regency when I die, particularly if you're reigning in some distant kingdom. He has even suggested that he would put aside his present wife if you would consent to marry him and consolidate our countries now.'

I gaped at my parent in disgust, and he reached over and laid a hand over mine.

'Now, now, girl, I told him it was not to be considered; that I wouldn't bother you with such an unseemly request. Watch him carefully in the years to come, though. He's a greedy devil who sees his kingship as a right rather than a trust, and people as things to use and manipulate instead of individuals worthy of respect. I fear that his fame will be as a tyrant, and his legacy a bitter one for any land he rules.'

I filed the thought away for future reference, and we moved to the next name on the list of suitors.

By the time the wine flagon was empty and the oil lamps were beginning to smoke, my father and I had agreed on one thing: of all the marriages possible to me, the proposal from Arthur was the least fraught with difficulties. Not only that, it solved the problem of how to turn down Urien's son without hurting his pride, and it meant that Rheged would have the additional protection of the High King's special interest.

'But why,' I asked wearily, 'does the High King even want to ask for my hand? What possible advantage is there for him?'

My father sighed and looked into his empty glass.

'You're a Cumbri, and what better way to put an end to any northern resentment than by marrying a northern girl? Of course, Merlin also says Arthur was quite taken with you when he came to visit after the Great Battle, so it isn't an offer made entirely for political reasons . . .'

'Maybe not for him,' I grumbled, 'but I have no other reason than politics to accept him. It is not what one would call a love match; not at all like the relationship between you and Mama, for instance . . .'

There was a long pause, and my father stared disconsolately at his hands.

'Believe me, child, if there were one among the prospective suitors you preferred, one you really wanted to wed, I would not hesitate to tell Merlin no. But we have considered every one of them and from what you say, there is none for whom you have any particular fondness. It is a hard thing to ask you to marry for duty when I myself know how special a love marriage can be . . .'

His voice trailed off and he looked up at me helplessly, his face full of compassion and concern.

'There is another factor, Gwen, that must be taken into account. I am not . . . not as young as I used to be. There are days when I can hardly stand, and I tire far more quickly than is natural. The Medicine Woman does the best she can, but the potions no longer kill the pain, and I would feel more comfortable about your future if you were wedded to a strong young man who I knew would take care of you. It may not be the same as finding a "love match" for you, but it's the next best thing I can provide . . .'

And so, in the end, I agreed that come spring I would go south to become High Queen of Britain.

That was six months ago, and now, in the woods beyond my tent, the cuckoo was riotously announcing that spring had truly arrived.

Too wakeful to stay abed, I got up and slipping on my cape, went to the door of the tent.

The sky was spangled with an abundance of stars. The men of my escort lay sleeping round the campfire, except for the sentry who sat near the horses.

The night was calm, and not too chill, so I leaned against the ropes and stared up into the sky. Behind, in both time and space, were my childhood in Rheged and the love I had once so longed for. Ahead lay the conflicting strands of my moira . . . queen in a court I didn't want, wife to a husband I didn't know.

But here I wafted free of both worlds, touched by each but confined to neither. There was a promise of adventure I'd not appreciated before, for I was going into lands I had never seen, towards places I had heard of only in song. My future with Arthur might be circumscribed by formal Roman manners, but that was still a fortnight away, and it would be foolish to waste these precious days so involved with either past or future that I missed the present. Besides, I needed to be alert and responsive in case something remarkable occurred to change my destiny.

At the outskirts of camp a man appeared, exchanged a word with the sentry, then made his way towards the tent. Even before he spoke, I knew it was Bedivere.

'You are up late, M'lady,' he said, pausing when he saw me.

'It's a lovely night,' I answered quietly.

'Aye, and it will be an early dawn. We have a long day tomorrow, so you'd best get your sleep.'

I nodded, wishing there were some way to share with him the elation that was growing inside me.

Going back to bed, I smiled drowsily as Kaethi's voice echoed softly in my ears: '. . .a vast panorama, wherever you happen to be.'

26
Arthur

The light mood of adventure carried into the next day. With my farewells behind and the excitement of new horizons ahead, I rode with high heart and quickened interest.

A ramshackle settlement was strung out along the riverbank, and we wound through it with little comment from the townsfolk, though a few who recognized the badge of the Red Dragon called out a greeting, and the smith by the river ford hailed Bedivere by name.

Next time Arthur's lieutenant came to ride beside me, I asked him how the man knew who he was.

'I spent some time here last year.' Bedivere gestured round the circle of hills on the horizon. 'Manchester's at a natural crossroads, and now that Arthur plans to establish a Royal Messenger network, this could be the northern hub. Getting news from one end of the realm to the other is very important; during the Time of Troubles the Imperial Post died out, so we have to start all over again on our own. I came up to see what could be done.'

Bedivere's enthusiasm was contagious.

'Does it look possible?' I asked hopefully.

'Of course. Arthur likes to say anything is possible. But in this case it also seems likely. I think we'll have it fairly well established by next year.'

I had never thought about the need for a network of communication, and the full implication of such a system gradually dawned on me.

'He really does intend to be King of all Britain, doesn't he?' I said with some astonishment.

301

'Provided we can stop the Saxon advance,' Bedivere affirmed with a nod. 'He worked hard to establish the British truces so we could put our energies into fighting the Sea Wolves. Your father's treaty with Urien was instrumental in getting the rest of the Celtic kings to work together. Hopefully now the Britons will fight Saxons and not each other.'

The mood of the day was so peaceful and calm, it was hard to imagine we were threatened by enemies who slaughtered for the seeming pleasure of it and sometimes flayed their foes alive.

'Are the Saxons really as terrible as they say?' I asked, realizing I'd never even seen one.

'It depends,' he answered, urging his horse to a more rapid pace as the Road opened out to the west. 'There are some who have been living on the Saxon Shore for generations, ever since Vortigern invited them in as mercenaries. Those are the Federates; well-settled farmers who are loyal to Britain. And there've been peaceful Saxon settlements around York since before the Legions left.'

I remembered Vinnie's comment: 'People no better than pigs, living in scooped-out hollows in the ground.' Naturally, with her family's Roman heritage she took a condescending attitude towards the squatters who gathered in clusters outside the walls of her native city. But she'd never mentioned any trouble with the local Saxons, only the invaders.

'Why do they keep coming in?' I wondered.

Bedivere thought a minute. 'I suppose the land is better than what they have on the Continent. They're good farmers, once they put down their weapons, and they prefer the lowlands—the water meadows by the rivers—instead of the hillsides and highlands our own people like.'

302

That seemed odd, for I couldn't imagine anyone intentionally settling in the mire and marsh most lowlands offered. And sheep, of course, are not fond of wet feet. Maybe they didn't have sheep.

'The real problem lies with the pirates, the Saxon raiders who slip along the coast in their longboats and devastate any steading they come to.' Bedivere cast me a quizzical glance. 'Are you really interested in this, or just being polite?'

'Of course I'm interested, or I wouldn't ask,' I countered, piqued at the notion that he thought I was just making small talk. 'I don't know what your southern queens are like, but a Celtic queen is a working queen.'

He laughed then, tossing back his head and roundly enjoying himself. 'I'll remember to tell Arthur,' he said, and I wondered whether that was good or bad.

The morning was full of good-natured bantering, with Bedivere dropping back occasionally to check that the wagons were keeping up with our new pace. He even encouraged the Magician to move a little faster, and once I caught him watching me with that half-amused way of his, as though we shared some fine secret. Perhaps he too was waiting for an adventure.

In the early afternoon a rider came pounding down the road towards us, so Bedivere excused himself and went to meet the man. I noticed that Merlin suddenly grew more alert and joined in a hasty conference among the front riders of our party, after which Bedivere rode off the way the messenger had come while Merlin ambled over to my side.

'It seems we are about to be joined,' the Wizard commented laconically. 'The High King's party is on its way out from Chester.'

'Arthur?' It was so unexpected, the name popped out like a hiccup.

303

'Of course Arthur. He's the only High King Britain has, M'Lady,' Merlin noted drily.

'Oh . . .' The imminent arrival of the man who from here on would control my life filled me with confusion and consternation; now even the days of freedom on the Road must give over to protocol and royal trappings. A slow panic began to push against my heart as the horses carried us relentlessly forward.

'If you wish, we can stop and pitch the tent so you can receive him in proper style,' the Enchanter suggested, his reedy voice barely carrying over the sound of our hoofbeats.

I stared at him, wondering what was expected of me. 'And if we don't stop?' I asked, half hopeful of averting the impending rendezvous. Perhaps the King would turn around and ride away.

For a moment I caught a gleam of laughter in those shrewd old eyes. 'Then I suppose we shall meet him on the road.' He shrugged, still watching me slyly. 'Certainly it would save everyone a good bit of trouble, not having to bother with making camp and all that.'

I thought of the fuss entailed, and smiled pleasantly. 'There's no need for that, M'lord,' I said. 'I'd as soon meet him on horseback as not.'

Merlin nodded without comment and we continued on our way.

Vinnie, I knew, would be furious. I could hear her already, decrying that I had gone to my prospective bridegroom dressed more like a stable hand than a fancy queen. But, I told myself, it's me he's coming to fetch, not my wardrobe, and he may as well know what he's getting from the start.

There was a commotion up ahead, and a band of horsemen came bearing down on us. The front riders hailed each other as our two parties drew together with much milling and jostling. After a moment a young fellow on a large chestnut horse broke out of the rest and came to a stop in front of Merlin.

He had the fair colouring I remembered, with the tanned skin of one who spends a great deal of time outdoors. His hair was tied back with a leather thong, and in the two years since he had come to Rheged he had indeed grown a moustache, though it was neither as thick nor as impressive as King Ban's had been. His eyes were set wide and seemed to sweep across the scene as if to memorize it in one glance, and my first impression was of tremendous confidence coupled with a keen and energetic nature.

He scarcely looked at me, but smiled fully at Merlin.

'Arthur,' the Sorcerer said without preamble, 'I believe you have met Guinevere before.'

The High King gave me a polite nod, swung his horse into line next to mine and motioned for the caravan to continue.

'Is there any news that won't wait until this evening?' he asked the Wizard as we all moved forward again.

'Not that I can think of,' the Magician replied, 'except that your sister Morgan is several days behind us. I told her she was welcome to join us if she could catch up.'

Arthur grinned at that, and nodded. 'Then, if you don't mind, I'd like to get acquainted with my bride.' For the first time he turned his attention to me with a quick and merry smile.

The Enchanter nodded silently, and giving me a last amused look, dropped back to his plodding pace.

Arthur glanced at the press of men and horses around us, and grabbing Featherfoot's bridle, pushed forward in a trot, forcing our way through the foremost riders.

When we were clear of the pack the horses moved out

smartly on their own and my groom turned to me with a grin.

'A bit hard to talk privately in all that bunch of people,' he said amiably.

I nodded and inquired how he knew where we were.

'Bedivere sent a messenger to Chester, so I held over an extra day on the chance you would be coming along soon.'

'You planned it this way?' The idea intrigued me; perhaps Arthur wasn't as much concerned about protocol as I had expected.

'Let's say I hoped it would work out like this. Waiting for a formal meeting just before the wedding wouldn't give us much chance to get acquainted. And since I wanted to make arrangements for copper from Great Orme's Head, I stopped off here while Merlin and Bedivere went on to Rheged for you. Merlin didn't expect you'd be ready to travel so promptly, so I had to promise to return to Winchester when I was finished here unless I got word you were on the road within three days of his arrival at Ambleside.'

I smiled inwardly, thinking how disconcerted the Enchanter must have been to find me all packed and ready to leave the next morning.

There was a pause and Arthur looked quickly at me. 'I hope I haven't offended you. That is, I realize it's not exactly the usual way for people in our situation to meet.'

I laughed and shook my head. 'No, not at all. I'm just a little surprised.'

'Good,' he announced with an air of satisfaction.

We rode a bit in silence, the shyness settling between us. Now that we were free of the crowd Featherfoot pranced excitedly and I had to keep her on a short rein.

Suddenly Arthur blurted out, 'I understand that you are fond of horse racing.'

306

I nodded, hearing a good-natured challenge in his voice.

'Well, what are we waiting for? There's a solitary oak at the top of the next hill. Are you game?'

'Of course,' I shot back, and then his chestnut was bounding ahead and Featherfoot was scrambling to catch up. I was glad Arthur hadn't made me a patronizing offer of a head start, and I gave my mare her head and kicked her vigorously with both heels as she lengthened from canter to gallop.

The road carried us over a hillock, then dipped down to a copse of holly and ash. Beyond, I could see a long even stretch that gradually rose to the crest of the hill where a gnarled oak stood in silhouette. Arthur glanced back and gestured towards the tree, and I nodded briefly. His animal was big and powerful, with the wide chest and good wind of a proven hunter, and I knew if I was going to catch him it had to be here, where the slope of the Road would work to my favour.

I crouched low over Featherfoot's neck, urging her forward with voice and heel, and drew level with the hunter's rump as the shade of the holly trees flashed by.

Arthur had the advantage of a more powerful steed, but I was lighter, both in body weight and in the fact that I carried neither shield nor sword. He glanced around, and for a moment I was afraid he might pull back and give me the race just because I'd caught up with him. I was on the inside as we approached a gentle curve and skinned past him and headed up the long, gradual incline towards our goal without waiting to see what his reaction was.

Both animals were running flat out, ears back and necks extended, and I looked back once to see that Arthur was as intent on overtaking me as I was on keeping ahead of him.

The staying power of the hunter began to tell, and I could feel the ground shake under the pounding of his hooves as we thundered up the incline to the hilltop. I hadn't raced like this since Kevin left, and the blood was roaring in my ears as we headed for the finish.

As always, Featherfoot was full of heart, but inch by inch Arthur was drawing even with us.

When we reached the shade of the oak I looked across at my adversary and realized we were neck and neck, without so much as a nose's difference between us. I also saw the flush of excitement on Arthur's face that matched my own, and when he threw up one arm and pulled up on his reins, I did the same.

The horses slowed, then came to a halt at the edge of an elm grove. My heart still pounded and the day spun bright and glistening around us as we sat and stared at each other, panting for breath and grinning.

'My compliments, M'lady,' he said at last, 'you're every bit as fine a horsewoman as Gawain said.'

'Gawain?' I queried, then laughed as I remembered our escapade along the Old Track in Rheged.

'Of course,' Arthur said. 'You don't think I'd send off for a wife without asking around about her first, do you? And you certainly left a lasting impression on my best young warrior. I thought he must have been exaggerating some, but after what I've just seen, I'd say he was right.'

We began ambling down the Road again, now well ahead of the caravan.

'What else have you heard, M'lord?' I asked, wondering if he knew I was not overly keen to become his wife.

'Well,' he drawled, 'Bedivere just gave me one of his cryptic looks and allowed that I wouldn't be disappointed.'

I smiled at that, both relieved and amused at Bedivere's diplomacy.

'He'd make a good ambassador,' I mused.

Arthur nodded in agreement. 'I've often thought how lucky I am to have the people I need so close at hand.' His voice had deepened now, and I stole a quick look at him. The laughter and playfulness lay not far under the surface, but his expression told me we had touched a subject of far greater import to him than any light banter would ever be.

'There are so many things that need to be done, and sometimes I get impatient with people who want to quibble about this or that. Bedivere is tremendously helpful in getting others to see the importance of a new idea without ruffling anyone's feathers. It's a skill I'm afraid I'm not blessed with,' he added ruefully, 'but he's always been good at it.'

'He told me you were raised as fosterlings together,' I said, and Arthur nodded.

'In and out of scrapes, like any boys,' he answered with a grin. 'But it's in the years since then that I've really come to rely on him. When you're surrounded by all manner of people wanting all sorts of things, it's nice to know there's one person you can count on for an honest and impartial reaction. Someone to sort of steady things when the boat seems to be rocking overmuch. And he does a wonderful job of keeping court life in perspective for me.'

I thought of Brigit and nodded.

A sizable troop of travellers came into sight, merchants and businessmen and a farmer or two drawn together in the comradery of the Road. We turned out to let the larger party go by, though by 'proper' protocol the High King had the right of way. I looked at Arthur again, curious as to what sort of ceremony he did stand on.

He was watching the people trail past, smiling and nodding to those who greeted us with the good spirits of the day. In the centre of the group was a dark-haired man astride a big, sturdy horse, followed by attendants and packhorses in good order. The man himself was richly dressed and his cloak was fastened with a solid round pin very like those the Saxons favour. I wondered if he was a trader from the Continent; clean-shaven and well manicured, he could have come from Constantinople or even Rome itself.

'What is the court like?' I asked Arthur cautiously when the Road was free and open again. 'Is it very Roman?'

He shook his head impatiently, but when he spoke it was with bemusement, not anger. 'I don't know why that term keeps coming up. I get so tired of people saying we're too Roman, when in fact we're not Roman at all. The Empire began to fall apart a century ago, and Britain has had to look out for herself whether she wanted to or not since the barbarians took over Rome. That way of life, that system of government, even that way of thinking is part of the past. We can't go back and resurrect something that no longer exists, even if we wanted to. It just won't work. We need new ideas, new directions, a new system . . .'

He turned in the saddle to address me directly.

'We're a separate land. We have to look to our own people, our own defences, our own talents. The barbarians are moving in from east and north, and the Irish are always a threat to the west. If we don't use all our resources to keep them at bay, we'll be swept into oblivion.'

The intensity of his conviction shone on his face like a fever, and I could see how he had been able to rally men to his side right from the start.

'So,' he said earnestly, 'that means using everything that might help, whether its source is Roman or Celtic or even Saxon. If an idea, or a system, or a weapon is useful in this struggle, we should take it up and use it. To criticize and refuse to consider something simply because it's Roman in origin is stupid and shortsighted. And it's blind prejudice to assume that all Roman ways are corrupt or bigoted or effete, or worse, that they are somehow sacred and must be followed even if they don't meet our needs.'

He paused, and a sheepish little smile crossed his face. 'Merlin says I get so carried away by the meat of a subject, I forget someone has simply asked me to pass the salt. I guess I haven't really answered your question, have I?'

I'd been holding my breath while Arthur was describing what Bedivere called The Cause, and now I let out a soft whistle.

'Well, you didn't exactly address the question I thought I asked,' I said, beginning to smile. 'But you sure told me a lot about the more important things. If I'm going to be your queen, it helps to know what we're working for.'

The term 'we' had slid in without thought, and I realized too late how presumptuous it might be. But Arthur was looking at me long and fully, his eyes searching my face. A slow, rich smile welled up from some inner relief of his own. We stared at each other in silence, and he reached over and laid his hand briefly on top of mine. I looked down and saw the Dragon Ring winking in the spring sunshine.

'All right,' he said affably, turning his attention back to the Road. 'Let's back up a bit. What do you want to know about court?'

'Oohh . . . everything. Lots of little things,' I amended. 'Will I be allowed to ride horseback or do the women all have to travel in litters? Is there lots of entertaining to do? And must I learn to eat lying down?'

The last question brought a chuckle from my companion. 'The only time I've ever had to dine that way was when I visited a northern kingdom some years ago and my host had nothing but couches to sit on,' he said with a droll, sidelong glance in my direction. 'Abominable habit! One I hope my queen would never try to force on the people. Besides, we're generally too busy to lounge around like that. As often as not, unless it's a special feast, I eat with the men around a communal fire, and the fellows who have families go off to eat with them.

'We are not what you would call a "fancy" household, Gwen. I'm not sure that anyone, except Queen Igraine, even owns a litter. I hope you aren't expecting a lot of fine trappings and leisure. Some of the kingdoms in Wales still maintain that style of living, but we in the south and midlands are a much more ragged lot.

'One day, perhaps, when we've got peace in the land and aren't always on call to stop some fracas somewhere, then it would be nice to have the luxury of a fine proud palace and some of the comforts the southerners still remember from before The Troubles. But until then, we have to make do with what's available.

'Of course,' he added hastily, 'it isn't always roughing it in a soldiers' camp. The Christian centres are well organized and pleasant, and some of the cities are trying to repair the damage of war and plague and famine. With any luck, the whole country will prosper once we get the squabbles under control and re-establish our borders. Everywhere I go, I look around and think about what could be developed in the future.'

We had reached a rise where the road overlooked a dark and formidable wildwood to the west, while to the south and east lay the gentler hills of farming country. We paused and looked out over the scene, and Arthur asked, 'Have you travelled much?'

'Only in Rheged,' I answered.

'I've been all over in the last three years,' he mused.

312

'And Britain is an amazing land, with more variety than I ever dreamed while I was growing up at Sir Ector's. Why, just over there is a forest that leads to the Wirral; a strange, dark place full of ancient spirits and haunts. And in the south there's soft green downs that roll like endless breakers towards the sea, and the great plain of Salisbury with the Giants' Dance they call Stonehenge. We have rugged cliffs and broad river valleys and sunny shores and unbelievable marshes that stretch for miles in all directions. There's the highlands in the north, and your own lakes and mountains in Lakeland. And in Gwynedd I've found a hill fort on the coast that's one of the most magical spots in the realm.'

He was spinning out a kingdom of wonder, and now that he was focusing on North Wales, I felt a tingle of anticipation. 'What's it called?' I asked, hopefully.

'Dinas Dinlle. It's a bit beyond Caernarvon. On a clear day the waters are blue and green, and the cliffs rise up proud from the surf . . . I'm sure Bedivere could describe it better than I can.' He paused and then grinned. 'It's in your cousin Maelgwn's land, so perhaps you already know it.'

'No, I've never been there. But it was one of my mother's childhood homes, and my nurse used to tell how beautiful it is.'

'Someday I'll take you there and you will see it yourself,' he said happily. 'That's my first promise to you.'

We laughed together then, awkward and pleased at the same time, and I was suddenly sure Mama was listening and smiling.

'Where to now?' I asked as we reached the crossing of two main Roads.

'It's out of the way to take the whole caravan into Chester,' he commented, glancing at the sun. 'I think the baggage train should keep to the route, and we'll head on

313

to the city with a light guard. That is, if you can make do with just one pack animal?'

'Of course,' I answered, wondering how Vinnie would take the idea of giving up the litter. It was too big and bulky to be moved quickly, and while I knew she wouldn't be willing to let me go off without her, neither would she like the idea of changing to horseback.

'Didn't you just come from Chester?' I asked, curious as to why he wished to return.

'I finished up my business there yesterday,' Arthur said, nodding as he scanned the verge for a comfortable spot to rest in while we waited for the procession to catch up with us. 'It seems they have a great fancy for horse racing in Chester, and Maelgwn arrived last night with a group of his best animals, so I agreed to stay over tomorrow to see the races. I understand he has excellent stock,' he added thoughtfully as he dismounted.

'He should have!' I exclaimed, sliding off my mare and following him back to a small meadow that overlooked the road. 'We of Cunedda's line have horse breeding in our blood.'

'Wonderful!' He beamed. 'We can spend a couple of days at Chester and catch up with the caravan farther down the line. It's as fine a city as we have these days, and I'm sure you and your ladies will be comfortable. Besides, it will give you a chance to visit with your cousin.'

I flinched inwardly at that, remembering my father's assessment of Maelgwn's nature. But the idea of watching a good day of racing and exploring a 'fine' city overcame whatever apprehension I felt. And it would be interesting to see how Chester compared with Carlisle, which was the only real city I had known till now.

We hobbled the horses so they could graze, then made ourselves comfortable in the shade of a large linden tree and settled down to wait for the rest of the party.

The afternoon was warm and the hum of bees above us denoted a wild hive. Our talk turned to all manner of things: Sir Ector's steading in the hidden heart of Wales, my family's holdings on both sides of the Solway, the songs and stories we both knew, the importance of the friends of childhood. When I told him about Brigit's relatives and the present they had sent for him, Arthur was delighted and insisted that we be sure to bring the dog to Chester with us.

'Do him good to have a few days back on his feet,' he opined, 'after spending each day in a crate.'

By the time the rest of our party caught up with us, we were past the first shy uncertainties and growing comfortable in each other's company.

Once the new destinations got sorted out and our smaller party was under way again, Arthur rode with Bedivere and Merlin, exchanging news and information each had gathered in the last week. I moved into place behind them, glad to have a chance to collect my thoughts.

Arthur was so different from the 'proper' king I had imagined. There was no doubt about his commitment to The Cause, or his love of the land, but it was the memory of our race to the hilltop that brought a smile.

27

Chester

The Legionary fortress of Chester crowns a massive outcrop of sandstone that stands guard at the edge of the Cheshire plain. It is an impressive location, and the red walls loomed proud and imposing as we approached the eastern gate.

Near the wall a strange, sharp shape rose against the afternoon sky, and I studied it nervously as we came closer. It looked something like the henges the Gods gave us, those circular banks inside which the ceremonies of the moon are held. But this one was different, with sheer rock walls rising out of the bank and the entry full of broken stones. It shocked me to think a god's project might be left incomplete and I made the sign against evil.

A guard on the parapet above the gate saluted smartly and called down a greeting which Arthur returned with a wave.

As we rode into the heart of Chester, I caught my breath. Here, as in Carlisle, there was a tumble of cottages and crooked alleys in the shadow of the rampart. But along the street that took us to the heart of the citadel, the rubble of steeply terraced ruins had been turned into shops that climbed one above the other.

On the ground floor stores and stalls fronted the paved street, and above, behind the colonnaded walk of the second storey, the shopkeepers' families lived. It must have been market day, for gold workers and weavers, leather craftsmen and potters, bronze smiths and herbalists all displayed their goods. Here the sign of an eye doctor hung out over the street, and there a profusion of

316

ribbons graced the balustrade, no doubt to advertise the seamstress' shop within. Farther down the line an enterprising housewife had strung her laundry between the columns, and the day's washing flapped merrily in the breeze.

The people were busy, popping into and out of shops at the end of the day, collecting parcels or folding up awnings, and like the sentries, they paused to smile and wave as the High King rode by. It pleased me that the common folk in this distant outpost held him in such regard; I would have expected it from his immediate subjects in Logres, but this was far from his seat of power and spoke well of the people's trust in him.

Arthur dropped back to my side, obviously amused by my gawking interest in the city.

'Must have been very impressive at one time,' he suggested.

'Oh, it still is,' I answered, thinking it felt like a fair.

'I'll be staying here tonight and would like you to join us for dinner,' he went on, gesturing towards the Praetorium where the Legion's commandants once held sway. 'I made arrangements for you and your women at the nunnery by the west wall. It's well appointed, and has room for occasional guests.'

'I didn't realize the Christians in Britain had special houses for women,' I mused, thinking Brigit would be delighted.

'There are a number of them in the south, and more are being founded all the time. It started just after The Troubles,' he added thoughtfully, 'when so many women and children had nowhere to go, what with farms and families being destroyed.'

We turned into a quiet tree-lined street. The lindens grew in a straight row along the equally straight avenue, shading a long wall broken by a single heavy gate. Inside, the little stone buildings of the convent were strung out in

317

a line, joined by a covered walk that was as austere as the empty courtyard we stood in. With the ramparts of the city looming above on one side and the convent wall on the other, I found the place grim and unfriendly. At home, the houses clustered in a circle or spilled every which way within the confines of a protective stockade, and I could not help thinking the people who lived here must feel lonely and cut off from each other.

After we had unpacked Brigit went off to find the chapel and I was left to face Vinnie's considerable pique. Surprisingly, she was less upset by having to forgo the litter than by my initial meeting with Arthur.

'Of all the unheard-of, uncivilized, common things to do,' she fumed, 'running off like a coarse country girl with a man you've not even been presented to yet.'

'He is the High King, Vinnie,' I reminded her. 'Would you have had me refuse him out of hand?'

'Well,' she sputtered, 'he should have had better manners himself. But you didn't help any, child! Don't forget, it is a woman's duty to keep a man's behaviour civil. You could have reminded him of how unfitting it was to whisk you away like that, without proper respect for your status or your family's standing. Why, think how shocked your mother would have been if she were alive to see it!'

Apparently Vinnie'd never heard the story of my mother's elopement, and I decided this was not the time to introduce it.

'Now, Vinnie, there's no harm been done, and tonight I promise to act the lady at dinner,' I said gaily. 'What dress do you think I should wear?'

The good matron's indignation was appeased by my willingness to discuss dresses, and the news that we would be staying over for a day or two and she could use the time to explore this obviously Roman city.

'Arthur says there's an amphitheatre, and Brigit has

already gone to locate the chapel. Maybe,' I added, 'there's even a working bath.'

By the time Bedivere arrived to escort us to dinner, I was garbed in the best of my travelling clothes. Mama's amber necklace glowed against the creamy wool of my dress, and Brigit had braided and waved and piled my hair on my head, catching it up with the enamelled barrette. I looked at the embroidery that had taken weeks to do, and for the first time saw the beauty of the product, not just the hours of frustration that had gone into making it.

The Praetorium was in surprisingly good repair, and I stared about the long hall with interest and curiosity. A fire pit had been dug in the middle of the tile floor, and a pair of young pages kept the spits turning. Along the walls the trestle tables were filled with noisy, boisterous people from both court and township. There were warriors of several different badges, smiths and jewellers and other men of the arts, and I noted both white-robed druid and black-garbed priest as well.

The women were equally diverse in nature: elegant, rowdy, beautiful or plain, some of haughty, aloof bearing and others spilling over with good spirits. They laughed and talked with the men casually, and didn't seem to be the product of a special 'women's quarter' at all.

At one end, on a raised dais, a table stretched almost the width of the room. Arthur was seated in the centre, with an empty chair next to him and as our little party paused by the doorway a young man raised a trumpet and played out a cascade of notes.

The room quieted and Arthur turned and smiled when he saw us in the door, every eye following his glance. We made our way slowly through the milling servants and scrambling dogs.

By the time we reached the steps that led up to the

dais, Arthur had come around from behind the table.

Bedivere stopped, and moving to one side, called out in his rich voice, 'Arthur Pendragon, I wish to present M'lady Guinevere, daughter of King Leodegrance and heir to the throne of Rheged.'

Arthur looked down at me as solemnly as if I were a stranger, but when I dropped a long, slow curtsy and looked back up at him, I found the twinkle of a conspiratorial smile crinkling the corners of his eyes.

'May you be welcome in my court,' the young King said gravely, helping me to my feet. The hand he offered trembled ever so slightly when I took it, and I shot him a quick glance, wondering if he was less sure of himself than he seemed.

Once I stood next to him on the dais, he turned his attention to the people of the hall.

'Be it known to all men here assembled that this is the woman I intend to marry, and I present her to you now, the future High Queen of Britain.'

I looked out over the crowd, surprised to find that the guests had all risen to their feet. As my eye travelled from table to table, a smile spread across my face in spite of myself, and a great roar of approval went up from the crowd.

'Guinevere! Long live Guinevere,' someone cried, and then they all took up the chant and I heard my name swell and gather and come rolling towards me like thunder. It was a sound I had never known before, and I must have flushed, for Arthur broke into a broad grin, and the cheering redoubled for both of us.

We stood there, side by side, while the accolade of the people washed over us. There is a headiness that comes of being the centre of all that attention, and by the time the crowd had quieted down and Arthur led me round the table, I was light-headed and giddy with excitement.

A lavishly dressed nobleman was blocking our progress. He had the same tawny hair, neither blond nor red, as I have, and it dawned on me he must be my cousin Maelgwn. His mouth was smiling, but his eyes were cold as he reached out to give me a kinsman's embrace.

'Arthur is a very lucky man,' he said unctuously, and it was hard not to physically push him away.

I smiled faintly and inquired, 'Where is your queen this evening, cousin?'

'Ah, she was not feeling well. She's having another one of her bad spells, I fear, and it's uncertain if she can join us for the races tomorrow.'

I murmured some kind of condolence and wondered if she had any notion of the obscene proposal her husband had made to my father. Or perhaps she had been in favour of it, wishing to escape from the oily grasp of this officious man.

After we had taken our seats, a fellow with the body of a warrior and the habit of a monk rose and offered a prayer to the Christian god. He had a compelling manner, and I asked Arthur who he was.

'Abbot of the local monastery' came the answer. 'Maelgwn says he was one of the finest warriors, but gave up his career as a soldier to start the monastery here. I've seen men like that before, who make their mark in the world and then renounce it all for a life devoted to their god. In this case I'm more than a little sorry,' he added in an undertone. 'I'd rather have his military help for The Cause than his prayers for my soul.'

Maelgwn was seated on the other side of me and he proved to be a clumsy neighbour, prone to bumping my leg with his or brushing his arm against mine. When I drew away from him the contact persisted, so as soon as our initial hunger was appeased, I turned my back on my cousin and faced Arthur directly.

We chatted about the plans for the next day, and Arthur said that I was welcome to accompany him to the amphitheatre if I didn't think I would be bored.

'The troops have agreed to put on a display for us, and I want to see what's being done with the cavalry,' he explained. 'But if you'd rather spend the time shopping among the merchants, I'm sure that news of your arrival will have brought out every craftsman and jeweller in the area.'

'I'd much rather watch the horsemen than bargain for baubles,' I quipped. 'After all, the fate of the kingdom depends on the state of our troops, not the condition of my jewel box.'

Arthur chuckled at that, then leaning closer to me, whispered confidentially, 'Who knows?—the gems you buy now may pay the cavalry in the future, if times get tight.'

His cheerful attitude and conspiratorial air delighted me, and I was impressed by him all over again.

The rest of the meal passed in the same fashion, being a combination of public comment and private asides meant only for me. It added a dimension of excitement that I wasn't accustomed to, and I watched and listened to Arthur as intently as a kitten watches a flickering shadow. I hardly even noticed when Maelgwn leaned around me to participate in the conversation.

Fortunately Arthur was looking the other way when Maelgwn slid his hand between my thighs, for I jumped like a roe deer flushed from its covert, shocked and startled beyond words. Instinctively I brought my arm forward, but before I could turn and jab the point of my elbow into Maelgwn's midsection, Arthur had turned back to me.

My face must have mirrored my outrage, for the High King frowned and asked if everything was all right.

I nodded hastily and mumbled some reply between clenched teeth, pushing Maelgwn's hand away under the guise of smoothing the crumbs off my lap. Turning, I glared at my cousin, who stared back impassively as though nothing had occurred. From now on, I thought, I'll make sure someone sits between us.

Once the tables were taken down Arthur called for Griflet, and the boy came bounding forward with Caesar in tow.

'He's a fine young pup with lots of heart,' Arthur said, taking the leash from the lad and reaching down to pet the dog. 'I had a chance to get acquainted with him before dinner.'

Caesar wriggled happily, ears folded back and baby teeth showing in a wide grin.

'I would guess he'll be larger than any other dog I've ever seen,' Arthur mused. 'Probably heavier than the Scottish deerhounds. And if he's as feisty in the field as he is in the kennel, he promises to have a lot of courage as well. I understand there are others available in the north, and I think we should get a bitch to go with him.'

'Angus will be delighted,' I assured him, 'though I wonder how it will be sent. You have no idea how hard it is to transport a puppy!'

'We'll find a way,' Arthur replied, with a certainty that made me glance at Bedivere.

I could see Arthur's lieutenant mentally filing the problem away for future consideration, ready to do whatever was necessary to see Arthur's dream become a reality. He and the High King had a remarkable partnership, the kind which is of such long standing it is no longer consciously thought of.

For a fleeting moment I wondered if there would be room for me in such an arrangement; then Bedivere was telling about Griflet's adventures with the pup and laughter erased all other thoughts. By the time we left for the convent uncertainty was the farthest thing from my mind, and I had even forgotten the nuisance of my cousin's unwanted attention.

28
Maelgwn

The comradery of the night before was still evident as we went off to the amphitheatre next morning.

Arthur and Bedivere put me between them and teased me mightily when I tried to match them stride for stride. With Caesar romping along joyfully and all the laughter that was going on, I didn't realize we were heading towards the badly made henge until we were within its shadow. For a moment I hung back, unwilling to enter so bizarre a place, until the firm echo of Kevin's litany began to ring in my head: 'What kind of Celtic daughter are you . . .'

When the men paused to see why I faltered, I lifted my chin and with a gulp, linked my arms through theirs. If they could chance it, I could too.

Inside the stone shell steep tiers of seats rose out of the weed and turf, and we climbed about halfway to the top before Arthur sat down and settled the pup at our feet.

'Merlin says the Legionaires built this for holding military exercises,' Arthur said, gesturing around the stadium.

I stared at it uncertainly, wondering if humans could really make something so gigantic.

'Why is it so big?' I asked, feeling like a grain of cereal stuck on the side of an empty bowl.

'Because Chester was Legionary headquarters,' Bedivere chimed in. 'And they probably held entertainments for the townspeople as well.'

'What kind of entertainment?'

'Most likely combat games: gladiators and bears and

325

sometimes even lions. Merlin thinks that's where the spotted cats came from.'

'Lions?' My attention had been snagged by the improbable thought. Cathbad had told the story of the Greek Hero God who killed a lion and wore its pelt for a cloak, but he had never mentioned there were lions in Britain.

I looked from Bedivere to Arthur, unsure if this was more teasing. Arthur saw my puzzlement and grinned.

'Well, no one's seen a lion, but maybe a leopard. There are tales of a large cat somewhere on Anglesey. So far it hasn't been tracked down, and the stories have grown bigger with each sighting. If there's any truth to it, it may be a descendant of escapees from this very arena.'

The horsemen had gathered below us and our attention shifted to them, so I put aside the notion of the big cat and concentrated for the next hour on the manoeuvres down below.

'What do you think?' Arthur asked Bedivere when it was over.

'The horses are fine, but if these are the troops Maelgwn's been repulsing the Irish with, I think his victories come simply because the men are mounted, not because they're well trained.'

'I'm sure that more can be done on horseback than we've seen here,' Arthur agreed. 'Ever since I rode beside King Uther in my first battle I've been convinced that a crack cavalry force could hold off an entire army if necessary.'

'What you need,' I suggested, 'is those long loops so the rider can get a foothold on the saddle.'

Arthur turned and looked at me so abruptly I wondered if I had just consigned myself to whatever passed for 'the women's quarters' in his court. Perhaps it was one thing to be an equal in social situations, and quite another to speak up about those areas which were the King's own interest. There was neither scorn nor impatience in his expression, however, so I hurried on.

'I've seen how that can be done. Do you remember the boys we passed in Ribchester, Bedivere? The ones charging back and forth across the parade field?'

'Vaguely.' The lieutenant nodded.

'Well, I met one of them the next morning, and he showed me things that he could do on horseback that I'd never even thought of. They sew a long strip of leather across the saddle so that it hangs down on each side, and then make loops to slide their feet into. It not only helps to mount the horse, it also allows for all kinds of leverage once the rider's seated. The boy was able to stand upright and put his whole weight on his feet. Or crouch down low over the horse's withers and lean out and snatch things from the trough as he went by. I tell you, I've never seen such riding before . . .'

My voice trailed off as Arthur studied my face.

'Who is this boy?' he asked slowly.

'The innkeeper's adopted son; I think his name was Palomides.'

The level gaze of his eyes never left mine, and I stared back at him with outer calm, refusing to look away in shyness or admit the confusion that was making me wish I'd kept my mouth shut.

'And you saw this yourself? He wasn't just bragging up some tall tale to impress his new queen?'

'Oh, no, I saw it,' I assured him. 'He thought I was a page and showed me what he could do when we were alone. I was planning on having those loops sewn on my own gear after we got south, but I hadn't thought about using them in battle.'

Arthur exchanged a glance with Bedivere above my head, and suddenly let out a whoop of glee.

'Gwen, you may have just given us the solution that

327

will make my cavalry a real military force! If it works, that is. Certainly it's worth checking on. Bedivere, how is it that you missed such a thing?'

'Probably because I don't get mistaken for a page boy,' his foster brother answered, and they both laughed heartily. I joined in then, relief enhancing my own high spirits.

When the exercises were over, Arthur suggested we take Caesar for a walk around the walls while Bedivere and Griflet went off to discuss horseflesh with Maelgwn. So the High King and I climbed the stairs by the gatehouse and strolled slowly along the parapet.

The fort's walls are broadly built, with plenty of room for soldiers to fight along their tops, and the view over the surrounding country was spectacular. We stood looking out to the east, in a corner where the remains of a large machine lay in a heap.

'I think it was a catapult,' Arthur said, scowling at the debris. 'I've asked Merlin to take a look at it and decide if we can restore it. Maelgwn's line has kept the whole of North Wales stable since your ancestors drove the Irish out, but now that the Cumbri have given me the use of this fort, I want to make sure it can protect the vulnerable Cheshire area.'

He gestured out over the pastoral landscape. The farmers' clearings had a peaceful, well-kept look all the way to the north where the dark shadow of Wirral's woods lay.

'I'm counting on Maelgwn's loyalty, as much through kinship with you as through his own honour,' Arthur went on. 'Certainly the last thing I want is a rear action here when the Saxons are threatening in the south and east.'

I thought about my father's warning that Maelgwn would make an unsteady ally, and started to mention it to Arthur, but he and Caesar were already striding along the wall, so I hurried after them.

'Beyond there,' he called over his shoulder as he pointed towards a tower of clouds, 'are the peaks of Snowdon. All those giant mountains, filled with green valleys and bright streams! The people here are a wonderful lot, proud and independent and willing to fight to stay that way. Merlin says they never gave in to Rome. I have no fear as to their loyalty; the men of the mountains are always able allies when they see you don't intend to yoke them.'

I turned and looked towards the heart of Wales, remembering Nonny's tales of caves and dragons and the great gods who lived with eagles amid the craggy peaks.

'It's crucial that the Cumbri realize I have no interest in imposing my will over them; without their cooperation I can achieve nothing,' Arthur was saying. 'And with them, we shall do wonders. As long as they can keep the Irish from my flank, I'll be able to concentrate on the Saxons.'

He paused then and waited for me, a full grin erasing the serious tone of kingship. 'Come—there's a lovely spot up ahead.'

We stood together in silence at the next corner, looking down on the island of Roodee. It is a sweet, flat meadow cradled in the arms of the river, and the racetrack around its edge is hard-packed from generations of use. There are clumps of willows along the far side and it seemed an ideal spot for a sporting event.

Already the horsemen were gathering, comparing notes and eyeing one anothers' stock with appreciation and competitive interest. The nobles were decked out in their brightest colours, and here and there a pennant waved in the breeze. It made a wonderfully festive sight.

Arthur and I lingered on the ramparts, playing with the pup and discussing the best points of the animals we could see down below. There were Welsh Mountain Ponies, very like Featherfoot, and I was pointing out the similari-

329

ties between her and a white mare who had an undeniable grace.

'How is it that you come to know so much about horses?' Arthur inquired as we leaned against the parapet wall.

'Luck, in part. Our Master of the Horse had no family of his own, so I guess he became my second father. I spent lots of my childhood with him, anyhow. And then, of course, my mother was a fine horsewoman, raised in North Wales and proud of being Cunedda's great-granddaughter.'

'Ah, yes, the women of Cunedda's line,' Arthur said softly. 'The Queen Mother, Igraine, is a descendant of Cunedda too, although from the southern branch.'

He was silent for a bit, and I wondered what he felt about the lady who had birthed him but never raised him. As tactfully as possible, I inquired as to what she was like.

'She seems to be a proud, honourable woman, and the people must think well of her or they would not have accepted me as her son.' His voice had gone stiff and remote, and for a moment there was a look of uncertainty about him. 'I know her very little, and doubt that will change in the future. She's not well, and lives apart from the court.

'Now, my foster mother, Drusilla, is another matter entirely,' he added, enthusiasm making his voice lively again. 'She was as warm and hearty and Celtic as they come, for all her Roman name. She died about two years back, taken by the stone. But at least she lived long enough to see her fosterling crowned King of Britain.'

It was the first time Arthur had personally referred to his kingship and there was no arrogance in his tone, only the pleasure of having brought honour to his foster mother.

When the sun reached mid-heaven we left our perch

and ambled slowly towards the Bridge gate.

Here the Road known as Watling Street led through a ford of the river, then headed out to the south. A wooden bridge spanned the broad water just below the weir which glimmered silver with salmon, and a score of fishermen's huts clung to the willow bank on the far shore. Beyond the trees lay the scar of a quarry, and I thought I could make out a figure carved in the rock.

'Minerva's shrine,' Arthur said. 'Whenever the soldiers marched out of here, they saluted the War Goddess in a kind of farewell. It's said she is looking not just at the fort, but at the highest point the tide reaches. Have you ever noticed,' he asked, 'that the Romans placed their river cities just above the tide's turning, so they could use it for shipping without quite risking regular floods? Remarkable engineers . . .'

I stared down on the river view and wondered if Arthur ever just relaxed and enjoyed the moment. It would have been nice to stand and watch the fishermen netting salmon in the water below while their wives filleted the catch and hung the meat on racks to dry. But Arthur and the pup had started down the stairs already, intent on the horse-races at Roodee, so I sighed and ran after them.

Dinner that night was a fine festive occasion, without the ceremony of the previous night's presentation but full of good nature and much banter. Arthur and Bedivere were well pleased with the arrangements they'd made among the horse owners that afternoon, and on the other side of Vinnie, Maelgwn was boasting about the fine tableware he'd recently purchased. His court at Degann-wyn was famous for its elegance, and though the man himself was known to be a boor, his wealth was recognized in all the Mediterranean trade centres.

'You must encourage your lady to visit the ancestral

home,' he purred. 'I'll make sure we spread a fine table for you both.'

My governess' cherubic face radiated pure pleasure at the prospect of so much luxury. Maelgwn caught my eye now and smiled pleasantly, so I gave him a civil nod in return. I noted that his wife was still absent, however.

Merlin joined us when the meal was over and Arthur and Bedivere drew the Sorcerer into reminiscences of their days together in Sir Ector's court. The Magician's visage brightened with affection as he looked back and forth between the two fosterlings, and occasionally Bedivere would fill me in on some reference I had no way of knowing. It was fascinating to see the Wizard's cold and haughty reserve put aside in the presence of his two protégés.

'Did Bedivere tell you about the horsemen in Ribchester?' Arthur asked suddenly, and when Merlin shook his head, the High King reached over and put an arm around my shoulder, including me physically as well as mentally in the circle of attention.

'Gwen says there are lads up there who have developed a new form of tack,' he said, and then went on to describe the change in gear.

Merlin nodded thoughtfully and suggested that Palomides should be invited to give a demonstration of his skill.

'I'd been thinking the same thing,' Arthur agreed, 'for I'd like to start training my cavalry as fast as possible.'

Arthur's hand still rested casually around my shoulder, and as I leaned forward to follow the conversation on the other side of him, I found myself moving closer within the crook of his arm. It seemed such a natural place to be, I was surprised that my heart was beating so fast.

Bedivere volunteered to go back north and invite

Palomides to join us, and at the same time swing by Angus' steading to get a mate for Caesar.

'But we'll have to find a Celtic name for the bitch,' Arthur said blithely, 'lest we be accused of being "too Roman."' A quick roguish smile tugged at one corner of his mouth, and his sidewise glance touched me just briefly. I caught my breath, struck by a soft buffet of surprise. Somehow he'd turned my fears into a kind of intimate jest just between the two of us.

I blushed and looked down at my lap, very much aware of the shivers that ran down my spine. I wanted nothing so much as to close that half-embrace, but instead sat staring at the table, caught in the tension of desire and immobility. Arthur gave me a gentle, good-natured squeeze and dropped his hand.

Bedivere was saying he'd like to take Griflet with him, to help transport the mate for Caesar. 'After all,' he commented wryly, 'it's one thing to invite this young horseman to join the High King, and it's quite another to ask him to play nursemaid to a barely weaned puppy.'

So Griflet was called to our table, and on hearing the plan announced he would be delighted to accompany Bedivere on a mission to procure a second wolfhound for the court.

The excitement within me refused to subside, and though I listened to the details being worked out, all I could think of was Arthur's walking me home later in the evening. I watched him softly, wondering if he felt the same desire I did; from his outward behaviour there was no way of knowing, and I thought how practised royalty become at covering their own emotions.

'May I see the ladies home, M'lord?' Maelgwn's voice sliced between us at the end of the evening. 'In a short time you will spend every night in my cousin's company,

333

but on this eve of her departure I would like to bid her farewell from the family.'

I looked quickly at Arthur, hoping he would assert his right to escort me to the convent himself, but he was smiling politely at the client king.

'That sounds fair enough,' he said pleasantly, and turned to me with some comment about an early departure. There was no sign that he was as disappointed as I, and I had no way to tell him now how little I relished my cousin's companionship, so I bade him a formal good night and slipped into my cloak.

Maelgwn took my arm as we made our way through the dark streets, and I set a pretty pace in order to get the encounter over with as soon as possible. Brigit and Lavinia scrambled to keep up, and by the time we reached the nunnery everyone was out of breath.

A young novice answered our knock, no doubt relieved that the guests were finally home and she could go to bed.

'Your lady will be joining you in a minute,' Maelgwn said, turning to Lavinia. 'It's been a pleasure meeting you, Madame. My cousin is lucky to have so wise a matron to guide her in the first difficult days at a new court.'

Vinnie simpered at the obvious flattery, her plump face dimpling. Then the girl was guiding my companions across the courtyard, taking the torch with her, and Maelgwn tightened his grip on my arm and pulled me back into the shadow of the gate's arch.

'Well, young lady,' he said sharply, 'you seem to have netted yourself a fine fancy husband after all. I can't say I wouldn't rather have you here.'

He had me cornered against the wall and was leaning so close I could feel his breath on my skin.

'Such a pity to see a ripe young creature fall unknowing into the arms of a hot-blooded young man. Surely he won't initiate you as carefully as a seasoned lover would. I could meet you in half an hour by the little gate that's hidden in the corner of the back wall,' he added, running the back of his hand along my jaw.

'Get your hands off me,' I hissed, not wanting to cause a disturbance but unwilling to tolerate his touch.

'Is that any way to treat a cousin?' he asked, sliding his other arm around my waist and trying to pull me to him.

I struck him without thinking, as hard and fast as I could, the flat of my palm crashing against the bones of his cheek.

For a moment I thought he would strike me back, and I glared at him in fury and revulsion as the force of the blow began to register in my hand.

'Let go of me,' I ordered, 'or I shall tell Arthur of your behaviour!'

He dropped his arms to his sides and took a step back.

'You'll not always be protected by your new station, M'lady,' he rasped, his voice cold with anger.

A hot retort rose to my tongue, but I bit my lip and kept it to myself. I had faced him down for the moment, and wanted to make my escape while the opportunity was still at hand. So I turned away from him and swept through the gate with all the dignity I could muster just as the novice returned with her torch.

Once within her sight I paused and, extending my hand to Maelgwn, said flatly, 'It's been an interesting visit, cousin, and one that will be long remembered.'

'I hope so,' he answered in the careful tones of a public figure under scrutiny. He barely touched my hand. 'Good night, M'lady, and may your sleep be untroubled.'

I nodded and turned away, hoping the girl had not seen the bruise forming on his cheek. She trotted sleepily along beside me and gave no indication of having observed anything but the formal behaviour of two nobles, so I

335

composed myself and pretended nothing was wrong.

Once inside my quarters I looked about, sorry that they were too small to allow Brigit to share them with me. It would have been a relief to tell her what had happened, but each cell was separate from the rest, connected only by the colonnade, and I was loathe to go padding about in the middle of the night looking for her. So I undressed by myself, and going to the pitcher, filled the bowl with water and scrubbed my face in an effort to wash away Maelgwn's touch.

It infuriated me that my cousin should have felt free to make such a suggestion, and I was as angered by his lack of respect for the High King as I was for myself. Surely Arthur would have the man punished when he heard of it.

If he heard of it.

The first blaze of rage was subsiding and the voice of reason began asserting itself. This was not the sort of thing one wants to bring up about a necessary ally, and I was all too aware of Arthur's need to rely on Maelgwn while we got the Saxon matter under control. Making a fuss about this purely personal incident could jeopardize the whole alliance.

Then too, Arthur and I were still so new to each other, this might add an unpleasant tension to our relationship. I didn't want him thinking I was some silly young girl who couldn't keep a randy courtier in his place. And in fact my words to Maelgwn had implied that I would not tell Arthur if he backed down.

I lay awake for some time debating the situation, at last concluding that if it bothered me this much, it was likely to upset Arthur a good deal too.

As the convent bells began to ring for the midnight prayers I decided not to mention the matter. Arthur and I would be leaving in the morning while Maelgwn remained here; there was no reason to see him again for some time, and perhaps by then I would have been able to discuss the problem with Arthur. For the present it seemed best to ignore it.

29

The Temple

Having been so wakeful during the night, I slept later than usual and woke only when Vinnie brought me a bowl of porridge.

My governess was full of chatter and I listened sleepily while she extolled the virtues of Chester. Not only did the baths function well, the merchants were amiable and the jewellers eager to bring out antique pieces for her inspection.

'Isn't it a handsome signet?' she exclaimed, proudly extending a pudgy hand so that I could admire her new ring.

'Very nice, Vinnie,' I said, studying the carved jet in its gold mounting. 'Where did it come from?'

'They say the jet is from Whitby, but I'm sure the workmanship is Roman,' she confided, turning her hand this way and that in order to admire the thing.

'Be careful not to lose it,' I cautioned, for though she had slipped it on to her thumb, it was still obviously too big.

'Oh, I'll put it in my purse once we're under way,' she responded. 'But after all, what are jewels for if not to be displayed?'

I remembered Arthur's comment about subsidizing the cavalry and smiled to myself.

Later, while Vinnie checked to see if I'd left anything in the cupboard of my room, Brigit helped me get dressed, and I asked how her visit to the hospital had gone.

'Ah,' she sighed, 'Kaethi would have loved it. I've

never seen so many vials and bottles for salves and unguents and potions, and special little jars to hold herbs, each with its own name on it. It must have been a fine pharmacia at one time. The nuns do their best at keeping it up, and care for the local people as well as the soldiers. If there isn't one now,' she added wistfully, 'I'd like to see a healing centre like that at Arthur's court.'

Bedivere arrived and the packhorse was loaded with our luggage, while Vinnie ran about the courtyard urging the young men to be careful with this bundle or watch out for that. One would have thought the dresses they contained were the most precious in the world, but perhaps to Vinnie they were. At least she had not fussed when I returned to wearing my tunic and breeches.

As we set out for the Praetorium I made a point of riding next to Bedivere, for I had a specific favour to ask.

'Is there any chance you could tell Palomides' aunt that I want to order one of the down quilts for the High King's bed? Her cousin makes them, and she thought it would be possible to get one. But I'm not sure how to pay for it . . .'

I faltered, suddenly realizing such an act assumed I was willing to become Arthur's bride. I flushed, startled by the thought. Perhaps ascribing my confusion to maidenly modesty, Bedivere gave me an amused look and allowed that something could be arranged.

Arthur was waiting for us at the Commandant's quarters, cheerful and happy to be on the road so early. I was glad to see he was not one of those people who are sour and cross during the first hours of the day.

Caesar frisked playfully beside him until Arthur spoke firmly to him, at which point the pup sat down, tail wagging and eyes bright.

'Well, that's certainly progress,' I said, preparing to slip down from Featherfoot's back.

Arthur grinned and put up a restraining hand. 'No point in dismounting, I've already said goodbye to the men who will be staying here, and Maelgwn sends his apologies for not seeing us off.'

I raised my eyebrows, both relieved and surprised. 'Is his wife worse?'

'No, I don't think so. But he showed up this morning with a black eye that would do credit to a warrior. Said some whore gave it to him in a dispute over payment.'

Arthur laughed and turned to Bedivere. My face went scarlet, and I pulled my mare's head around and leaned forward to inspect the reins and bridle, letting my hair screen my face and the bulk of the horse's neck hide my shame. The virtues of charity, which Vinnie had listed for me more than once, were not uppermost in my mind, and I prayed roundly that the Goddess would change my cousin into a toad.

There was a bit of commotion as Griflet and Bedivere left for the easterly gate, and by the time our farewells had been made I had forgotten the insult.

Bridge Street was lined with crowds waiting to wish us well. They packed the colonnades and filled the steps leading down to the bridge, waving and cheering and pelting us with field flowers. One group even threw a handful of nuts at us, which I knew would make Vinnie happy.

'What on earth . . .' Arthur exclaimed, catching one of the hard round things and trying to identify it.

'I think they're walnuts'—I laughed—'from some old garden nearby. Vinnie told me it's a Roman custom to wish a couple fertility.'

'Great, if they don't leave me with a bruise as big as Maelgwn's,' Arthur said with a chuckle.

I couldn't suppress a giggle, thinking it wasn't likely I'd be dealing with him as I had with my cousin, and joined his laughter with my own.

So we left Chester, in a flurry of hearty gaiety. Even Caesar seemed to enjoy it, for he barked now and then from his position across the front of Arthur's saddle. Arthur rode with one hand on the pup's back, steadying him and keeping him secure.

We had come into Chester with a handful of men but we left with almost a score of Maelgwn's nobles travelling with us. It made for a bright and lively entourage, and we set off at a quick pace down Watling Street.

When we came abreast of Minerva's shrine I looked across the quarry, noting a scatter of flowers strewn below the statue. Stern and proud in battle, quick of mind and very wise, this Roman deity was only another face of the Goddess and I asked Her now to bless the journey Arthur and I were beginning.

The afternoon at the races had proved most useful for Arthur, and we were soon in a discussion of the horses he had bought and breeding arrangements he'd made. His most immediate concern was to develop an animal that could make his plan for a fast-moving cavalry unit a reality.

'The Saxons have the advantage of slipping in and out in their long-boats, striking without warning and disappearing before help can arrive. And they seem to have more chain mail than we do. But they can't bring horses with them, and if I can train the men to fight from horseback, we'll even the odds considerably. We need mounts with the speed to catch the raiders before they can get away, and the size to overwhelm massed groups. Between the Shires of Rheged and the animals from Chester, I hope to develop a line which serves both purposes.'

'Won't that take some time?' I asked, thinking of the years of breeding ahead.

'Time,' he sighed: 'that's my greatest fear. Ambrosius

341

beat back the main Saxon advance, and Uther more or less held the borders, so there hasn't been a major revolt among the Federates since The Troubles. But it appears there's a new wave of invaders massing on the Continent; people who have been pushed out of their own lands by other invaders from the east. It's these men who pose the greatest threat. If I can just get our forces whipped into shape before the Saxon wave crests, we'll be able to survive even a major assault.'

He grimaced. 'If . . . if the British kings will follow me, if the alliances among the northern kings hold, if the cavalry can be developed, if the Irish stay quiet to the west, if we don't have any more famines or plagues . . . sometimes it all seems like a pile of leaves that could blow apart at the first puff of wind.' He frowned deeply, as though trying to fulfil The Cause by the sheer strength of his own will.

'And if it does hold?' I prompted.

'Ah, that's the thought to keep,' he responded with a sigh. 'If we can work fast enough, and time doesn't run out, we'll create a whole nation and a lasting peace. I'd like to see trade increased with the Continent, as well as with the Mediterranean cities. They have much more to offer than just wine and glass, and if we can redevelop the tin mines in the south, and the grain production to the north . . .' He paused then and stoutly patted Caesar's back. 'Who knows?—maybe even the dogs will be in demand.'

The pup, who lay draped like a bedroll across the horse's withers, wagged his tail feebly and raised his head. Arthur looked down at him and smiled gently.

'Poor tyke, for all your bounce and fierceness, this can't be much of a way to travel for you. I wonder,' he asked, turning to me, 'if he'd do better in the crate with the pack train after all?'

'I don't know.' I hesitated. 'Maybe we should ask Brigit about it.'

'If he were bigger, he could trot along beside us,' Arthur mused. 'But I'm afraid he'll get under the horse's hooves, or kicked, or frightened and run away. Ah well, friend,' he added, giving Caesar a further pat, 'in the end it will be worth it. I promise.'

Arthur's face was full of tenderness and concern, and I marvelled that the depth of the man's compassion was equal to the height of his dreams.

About midday we came to a clearing in the woods where an old track runs down from the hills to the west. It is a spot of ancient beauty, where a sacred spring gushes on the greensward, sparkling in the sun like a dewdrop amid green ferns.

Behind the spring a ruined temple sat near the edge of the dark forest. It was in better repair than many I'd seen in the north, and while there were tiles missing from the roof and some of the colonnade of columns had collapsed, it did not have the forlorn look of an abandoned building.

The men took their horses to the edge of the stream formed by the spring's runoff while Arthur and I walked to the well. A traveller's cup stood in its niche in the rockwork, and after making an oblation to the local gods we each drank. Arthur cupped some water in his hands and gave it to the grateful pup.

One of the lieutenants approached, gesturing towards the rear of our cavalcade. I turned to discover the Road was full of people. Farmers, woodsmen, fisherfolk from riverside settlements along the way, they trudged into the green and gathered in knots of cheerful conversation at the edge of the stream. There were well over twoscore of them, all seemingly in the best of spirits. It made our travelling group one of the largest I'd ever seen, and I wondered how we'd manage at the inns.

343

Merlin went past us and walked slowly up the steps of the half-ruined building. A white-haired hermit had come from inside, standing between the columns by the door and blinking in the sun as he looked to see what gift the Road had brought to his shrine.

I watched, fascinated, as the two men greeted each other solemnly. Next to the wraithlike guardian of this ancient spot, the Enchanter appeared hale and vigorous, and hardly more than middle-aged. I wondered if it was simply the comparison, or if each had put aside his worldly image in favour of a form closer to the heart of his matter. With a respectful nod Merlin accepted the elder's invitation to enter the temple.

'There's no man Merlin is not willing to learn from,' Arthur said when I mentioned it. 'Always in my childhood he stressed that every person has his own story, his own wisdom . . . and it is a foolish leader, or scholar, who doesn't remember that.'

A butterfly had caught Caesar's attention and we followed him towards the trees as he bounded after it.

'What do you suppose they are talking about?' I asked.

'Probably the ways of the Gods.' Arthur shrugged lightly, calling Caesar to his heel and bidding him sit.

'But the hermit wears a cross.'

'Merlin won't mind,' Arthur answered, praising the dog for coming but having to bend down and push him into a sitting position. 'It's possible that the Christian is learning as much from our Sage as Merlin is from him. Out in the country the Christians care more for wisdom than for dogma and aren't as concerned with power as they are in the towns. Haven't you noticed that?'

I recalled Brigit's acceptance of other ways besides her own. Perhaps he was right, and it was only the city priests who scorned all other gods.

'How do you feel about the Christians?' I asked,

thinking this was as good a time to find out as any.

Caesar was now sitting placidly and Arthur smiled down on him, then gestured towards the trees, and the dog went running ahead as we moved into the shade.

'Christians?' he repeated. 'Their teachings seem about the same as any other. They beg their god's help for themselves, and call for curses on their enemies. I'm sure every god can be helpful at one time or another. But I can't say that I would follow their White Christ alone, and I don't condone their meddling in politics. The people need to follow those teachings they feel most comfortable with, and as long as I'm king, I'll not favour one religion above another. I can't afford to risk losing the people's trust, and the leader who tries to impose one set of beliefs on all his people deserves to be viewed as a tyrant.'

We stopped at an old log where Caesar was investigating a woodmouse burrow, and Arthur's brows knit with concern.

'I will not have the people divided by holy quarrels, and what or whom I choose to pray to in the little privacy I have is strictly up to me.' He glanced briefly at me. 'I understood your father raised you with much the same philosophy.'

'Yes, yes, I couldn't agree with you more,' I said, nodding vigorously. It was apparent that the subject was important enough for him to have considered my background before asking for my hand. I should have guessed that Arthur's determination to unify his realm would override all else, and any religion that tended to be exclusionary would definitely not be encouraged.

Suddenly all my fears of Roman courts and dogmatic restraints vanished. There seemed a wholeness of spirit between Arthur and me that filled me with the sheer exuberance of joy and I wanted to run and sing and dance in the April sunshine. The beauty of it flowed through me and I threw my hands up and laughed with pure delight.

Caesar leapt up, hopeful of a game. I made a lunge for him and he dodged away, dashing about in a circle and coming back to charge at Arthur. Of a sudden we were all three running and laughing in ever-widening circles across the green, chasing the wonder and lightness of springtime itself.

Brigit joined in the game, then several of the younger guard and the people from Chester, until everyone became part of the whirling circle, laughing and capering about as if we were a troop of sidhe. It was like the dance on Beltane morn, a celebration of pure pleasure in living. The Many-Named Spirit of this place was blessing us in the ancient way.

The gaiety and good nature continued even after we stopped for breath and the men brought the horses up. Now, instead of separate parties come together by chance on the Road, there was a bond of kinship that ran through the people like a heady wine.

On Brigit's advice Arthur returned the pup to his crate, promising to let him out the moment we next stopped. When he returned to my side the High King gestured towards the noisy crowd who were preparing to fall in behind us.

'It seems,' he said wryly, 'that the people have heard there's a wedding to take place at Winchester, and nothing will do but that they escort us thither.'

I looked at him blankly for a moment, but the grin that broke across his face was so contagious I smiled too. It was, after all, a wonderful compliment, for what better homage could a people pay their king?

'They feel it, Gwen. They know something new and exciting is happening, and they want to be part of it.'

His face shone radiant with hope and enthusiasm, and as I looked at him I realized that though he might not

346

have been raised at the Sanctuary, he was certainly the stuff of which heroes are made.

The festive mood carried well through the afternoon, and we caught up with the baggage train where they had made camp on the outskirts of Whitchurch. Arthur and his men stayed there, and the new people who had joined our party set up an informal camp of their own in the nearby woods while Brigit and Vinnie and I were escorted to a hostelry in the settlement.

My ladies and I were given a large room set well back from the noisy courtyard and after two nights in a nun's cell I was glad of the companionship. But I noticed that my chaperone went about unpacking with red eyes and an uncharacteristic silence.

'What ever is the matter, Vinnie?' I inquired as she took out Mama's comb and mirror.

'I should have known,' she said, sniffing. 'My mother always said no good would come of riding horses.' A large tear hovered on the rounded apple of her cheek, then slid over the curve and ran down to her chin.

'Did you get hurt?' I asked, looking anxiously at Brigit.

'She lost her new ring,' Brigit explained.

'It would never have happened if I'd been in the litter,' the matron whispered tremulously. 'And now it's gone forever.'

'Oh, Vinnie, I'm so sorry. Now, now . . . don't cry,' I added, putting my arms around her.

'But it was real Roman work,' she wailed, her dumpling face collapsing with woe.

'Shh . . . we'll find you a new one when we get down south; there's bound to be other "real Roman" jewellery in Winchester.'

I had said the first thing I could think of to comfort her, and it seemed to work. She drew back, a wan smile showing through the stream of tears.

'Would you really do that for me?' she asked. Standing there with her face all wet and her lower lip trembling, she looked amazingly like an overgrown child.

'If we can find one, Vinnie, it shall be yours,' I promised.

For a moment I thought she was going to start weeping all over again, but her sobs turned to hiccups, and she reached up to pat her hair into place.

'That's very sweet of you, Missy,' she said primly. Then, suddenly, she dimpled. 'I suppose I shall have to start calling you M'lady, now that marriage to the young King is assured.'

The idea was so absurd that I laughed, and began to say that wouldn't be necessary when Brigit cut in sharply:

'We all will, and we should be getting used to it now, on the road.'

Brigit's tone was completely serious and I looked over at her, startled. It seemed preposterous that members of my family should start calling me by a title instead of my name. I wanted to protest, but Brigit was nodding her head emphatically.

'We'll be less likely to have slipups at court if we've been doing it for a while,' she said firmly while Vinnie daubed at her eyes.

It occurred to me that perhaps Brigit was right; certainly it would be a good idea not to go into the strange court unprepared. So I agreed, reluctantly.

Later, when we were alone, I whispered to Brigit that I didn't want any of this 'M'lady' nonsense when we were in private. She just smiled, and gave my hand a squeeze.

It was midday when Arthur swung round to pick us up. The baggage train had been on the road since barely sunup, and when we caught up with them I was amazed to see how many people now walked along behind. As we came down the Road they parted to let us through, cheering and laughing when they recognized Arthur and sometimes even calling out my name. We waved and smiled and saluted them in turn, and later, when we were riding sedately at the head of the party, I asked Arthur if this was the reception he usually received along the Road.

'No, never!' he said with a chuckle. 'Most of the time I can come and go with a small party of men and no one notices. Or those who do don't pay much mind to us. I think,' he added, glancing across at me, 'that it's your presence which brings them out this time.'

'Me?' It seemed an unlikely notion.

'Of course. News that I would take a Cumbri wife was bound to spread through Wales like wildfire, and now they want to see for themselves what you're like. For people to whom the blood tie is more important than anything else, there's much prestige in knowing one of their own has been chosen High Queen.'

'Is that why you chose me?' I asked calmly. The question was neither impulsive nor premeditated, but something that came naturally in the conversation. Yet as soon as the words were spoken I regretted it.

He turned and looked at me with the level gaze we had shared at the end of the race when we first met.

'I asked you for the same reasons you accepted me,' he said simply. 'Britain needs a queen, and you need a husband. What we do with the future is up to us.'

I stared back at him, looking hopefully for an indication of love or tenderness, but he only grinned and added gruffly, 'Whatever else may be involved, we've made a good start. And neither of us will lack for a riding companion.'

The tension in me relaxed and I smiled, glad at least he

thought it a good beginning. Perhaps, as my father had said, the loving would follow.

Traffic on the Road was growing heavier. Sometimes an hour went by without our meeting anyone, and then a whole series of travellers would appear, spread out in clumps for the next mile or so. Most people stopped to stare at our cavalcade, moving off to the verge and occasionally saluting politely if they recognized the badge of the Red Dragon.

A beekeeper, his precious hives carefully wrapped in linen and straw for the journey, hailed us with great good cheer. Bees are always a good omen, and I was sure he would sit down next to his charges this evening and carefully describe all that he had seen and heard on the Road this day, for the little golden honey gatherers have to be kept advised of everything that affects their owner. I wondered how he would describe us, and what the bees would think.

As the afternoon lengthened we came within sight of Wroxeter, a city whose foundries and forges had once been famous throughout the Empire. Yet now the city gates hung open, and neither guard nor curious civilian watched us from the walls.

'It's deserted,' Arthur explained. 'Abandoned. Since the Time of Troubles, there's not enough people to man the walls, nor enough trade to keep them fed, so they return to the land. You'll find more such places in the south; wastelands that are slowly rotting into oblivion.'

'But why?' I shook my head, trying to understand.

'That depends on who you ask. The Christians say it's God's punishment for the sins of the people. The druids say it's because the Old Ways went ignored. The soldiers who follow Mithra say it's for lack of sanitation . . . and I,' he added with the lift of an eyebrow, 'say it matters less why it has happened than what we do about it. We

350

need to rebuild the communities, and salvage what we can. It's the same throughout Logres; where the cities have died the people have scattered, gathering around leaders who have gone to live in hill-forts such as that one.'

He gestured towards one of the strange islandlike hills that rose out of the landscape around us.

'The man who's claimed the Wrekin for his own observes the Old Ways and sees no reason to return his people to a city that has been deserted for twoscore years now. He's a friend of mine, by the way,' Arthur added, 'and I promised to spend the night up there with his family. Do you want to come too?'

'Of course,' I responded. 'Wouldn't he be insulted if I didn't?'

'Hard to say.' Arthur shrugged. 'The leaders of the Welsh Marches are an eccentric bunch; each local king is master of his own hill, and may or may not care whether we grace his hall. Knowing Pellinore, he'll be delighted to meet you; I've never seen such a man for the ladies. Or for spawning sons. And if they grow up to be like their father, I'd be pleased to have them fighting for me in the south.'

I eyed the Wrekin. It looked to be a natural stronghold, set well apart and difficult to scale.

'Will this be considered a State Visit?' I asked, wondering how we'd manage with the litter.

'In a way,' he said with a chuckle, 'but we'll take just a light guard with us. I don't fancy hauling our whole party up that trail.'

I nodded, wondering how Lavinia would react to that.

When we made camp Arthur saw to the evening's plans and took Caesar out for a run while I talked with Vinnie and Brigit. My governess balked at the idea of letting me go off unchaperoned, but she also had no intention of riding anywhere on horseback, so she dithered about in a flurry of conflicted concerns.

In the end Arthur himself convinced her I would be safe both from outside enemies and from himself. And as the day began to fade, our small party of riders left the camp and headed for the ancient hill-fort.

30
Pellinore

'Halt!'

The command echoed through the evening like the croak of a hoodie crow. We paused atop the Wrekin's trail and were immediately engulfed by a flock of noisy, curious children who swarmed out to challenge us before we reached the outer walls.

There must have been a dozen of them, ranging in age from early teens on down, and they were dressed in a ragbag of warm but mismatched clothes such as get passed from one youngster to another. I couldn't tell if there were any girls among them, but it was easy to see that there were at least two pairs of twins.

Arthur patiently reined to a stop and identified us, extending his hand with the Dragon Ring for verification. After a moment's consideration the troop gave way and allowed us to continue.

'Are you really the High King?' the oldest one asked, running beside Arthur's horse and looking up at him sceptically. 'I thought you would be older.'

Arthur made a grave face. 'Does this suit you better, son?' he inquired, pitching his voice low and looking sternly down at the lad.

'Maybe . . .' the youth said, unconvinced.

When we reached the gate I turned to stare out over the land below. A tumble of hills and ridges floated in the evening mist, shading from slate and charcoal to palest black against a salmon sky. It was a silent sunset, and still, as though the earth were holding her breath. Nothing moved, and one could well imagine sleeping giants waking and coming to stalk the land.

The stone wall of the fort loomed before us, offering warmth and protection to anyone bold enough to call it home, and as we filed through the sturdy gate I made a little prayer of thanks to the Spirit of the Place.

The children surged around us in the courtyard.

'Here, boys, make way for our guests!' a young woman cried, hurrying from the doorway of the main house and attempting to shepherd the troop out of the way. She carried a plump youngster on her hip, and it was plain to see from the swelling of her dress that she expected another very soon.

'Is he really King Arthur?' piped up one of the smallest.

'He certainly is!' answered a great booming voice from the barn. Our host ploughed his way through the gaggle of youngsters. 'And mighty good to see you,' he declared, beaming.

Arthur slid from his horse and the two men embraced in a jovial hug. Arthur himself was not a small man, but this giant engulfed him like a friendly bear.

'Well come, comrade,' Pellinore said, pounding the High King on the back. 'We only just got your message this morning, so didn't have time to plan anything. There is venison on the spit, however.'

The older man turned and scanned the rest of our party as Arthur stepped forward to help me from my horse.

'Thought you were going to bring the Cumbri girl with you,' Pellinore rumbled, glancing back in our direction. Arthur had just set me on the ground, and Pellinore's eyebrows went up in surprise. 'By the Goddess,' he swore lustily, 'I mistook you for a page!'

'It's not the first time that's happened,' I answered with a grin as Arthur slid his arm around my waist.

'Guinevere, may I present our ally and battle comrade,

Pellinore,' he announced formally, then added, 'and his band of future warriors.'

The boys were suddenly all shyness and silence, the older ones fumbling through their bows and the youngest staring at me in open awe.

'And this is my wife, Tallia,' Pellinore offered, extending a hand to the woman around whom the children clustered. She looked hardly old enough to have borne so many offspring, and as though to answer my thought, Pellinore said, 'We were married after the Great Battle . . . be three years come harvest time . . . and she's already given me one strapping infant and there's another due any day.'

The young woman blushed and dropped me a deep curtsy, her homespun skirt dragging in the dirt of the unpaved court. That, I thought, is real dignity, and I liked her immediately.

Once inside the Hall, Pellinore called for ale, and after we were seated next to him, proceeded to introduce his tribe individually.

The oldest, his scepticism now mollified, stepped forward proudly. At fourteen he gave every indication of becoming the same sort of giant as his father. Pellinore informed us his name was Lamorak, and the boy bowed formally to Arthur.

There followed an assortment of others, ranging from thirteen down to toddlers, and from the look of them they had had several different mothers.

Probably, I thought with a glance towards Tallia, this man sires enormous offspring and the poor women don't survive bearing them. It made me glad Arthur was not Pellinore's size.

After the children had been presented there were warriors and companions to meet, and freemen as well, for our host had invited those who lived close by to join the festivities. Then, as the meat was carved and the trenchers passed around, talk turned to the boy Lamorak.

'Naturally I'd like to keep him here by my side,' Pellinore boomed, 'but he has dreams of coming to your court one of these days.'

The lad blushed shyly, but held his head high and proud.

'If the son is like the father, I'd better look out,' Arthur replied with a grin. He went on to tell how Pellinore had bested him severely the first time they met, back before the Coronation. 'Knocked me clean off my horse, and broke my sword as well,' he concluded.

'I had both weight and experience on my side,' Pellinore allowed gruffly. 'Probably wouldn't be able to do it again.'

'Not if what I hear is true,' Arthur answered, and proceeded to tell him about the riders up around Ribchester and the change they had made in their tack. 'That should give even the lightest warrior an edge in combat,' he concluded.

'Sounds interesting,' Pellinore agreed, ripping one last shred of meat from the joint he was holding and tossing the remains to the pile of dogs that scuffled for scraps by the fire.

'Bedivere's bringing one of the boys down to Winchester in time for the wedding,' Arthur continued. 'I want to see the system for myself as soon as possible. Why don't you join us for the festivities, and get a look at it too?'

Pellinore nodded thoughtfully, and glanced about the circle of his men.

'Any reason why I shouldn't go south for a month or so?' he called to one of his lieutenants, and after scowling over the question for a moment the man shook his head.

Pellinore's big face broke into a broad grin and he turned to his wife. It was obvious she couldn't accompany him this far along in the pregnancy, but neither did he want to stay home when adventure called. So he looked at her fondly and inquired, 'What shall I be bringing you back from the city, my love?'

'Yourself – alone,' the young woman answered with a knowing laugh which caused all the older men in the circle to roar with pleasure. It was clear she was aware of her husband's roving ways, and the success of their partnership seemed to be based on her acceptance of them.

Talk turned then to reminiscences of the Great Battle, and how Pellinore had taken on King Lot single-handed after the rebel kings had fought Arthur's troop to a standstill.

'It was a brave thing to do, my friend,' Arthur said. 'And it may well be I owe that battle and my crown to you.'

''Twas only common sense.' Pellinore shrugged. 'Everyone else tired and stalemated, and here comes Lot, late as usual and riding in fresh to the fray. I was not only the one closest to him, I was also about the only one equal to his size, and I wasn't going to risk having him cut you to pieces just because I'd already done my share of skirmishing.'

He proceeded to tell of the encounter, stroke by bloody stroke, and I watched the boys' eyes grow round with admiration and the warriors nod and suck their teeth as they heard the tale retold. Strategy I could appreciate, or logistics, but I found it hard to understand the allure of recounting each batter and blow. I glanced at Arthur, who was listening intently, and made a note to ask him about it later.

'Perhaps, my dear,' he answered as we walked back from the midden in the moonlight when the feast was over and it was time for bed, 'you don't understand it because you don't have to live by the sword. If your very

357

survival depended on that split-second move, the instant response, the ability to tip the balance of leverage in your own favour, I wager you'd be fascinated . . . or at least respectful . . . of anyone else's prowess. If Pellinore were a richer man, he'd have a bard to tell his tale for him, but as it is we all relive it because he relives it.'

'Do you live by the sword?' I asked.

'Sometimes. I won't rule by it, that much Merlin has already told me. And learning to use military power wisely was the first lesson of the Civil War. I would have gone against anyone, anywhere, in my eagerness to put down the rebellion, if Merlin hadn't pointed out I would only waste valuable lives and time that way. One must live by the law of the situation, and if our enemies attack with the sword, I shall defend Logres and Britain with it, whether I wish to or not.'

His voice was quiet, but very serious, and looking at him in the flat light of the full moon, for a moment I saw the face of a craggy old man, grey and weary beyond measure. His kingship lay like a blessing and a curse upon him, and his brow was furrowed with sorrow. Those deepset eyes, sad as they were, still gleamed with his dream, and a rush of love and tenderness rose up in me.

Something crowded my mind . . . something I should tell him . . . something that would help. I reached out to touch his cheek, my eyes filling with tears and my throat aching to say the words that would heal his anguish.

'What's this? A bit of moon madness struck you?' he teased, catching my hand and turning towards me. 'What ever would your governess say?'

'I don't know,' I whispered, as much to the Goddess as to my companion, for the aura of the Other still clung round us. I had never felt anything so powerful before, and while I didn't understand what it meant, it was clear our moiras were intertwined for a lifetime.

He pulled me to him and kissed me soundly. My arms went around his young, strong body, reaffirming the youth and vigour of him. Cupping my buttocks firmly, he half-lifted me to him, and my mouth opened willingly to the insistence of his tongue. Bright tingles of desire erupted in my throat, plunging in delicate showers through my body to my loins. We were wrapped together like a couple at Beltane, and I held both present and future in my arms, aware of the ardent young man of the moment and the great sustaining force of Britain's resurrection in the years to come.

'Good heavens, girl, you're shivering,' he said suddenly, pulling away from me and unfastening the pin that held his cape. 'I'll not have it said I kept my bride out freezing just to enjoy the Goddess' blessing.'

He slung the cape around my shoulders and swept me forward into the light that poured through the Hall door.

Tallia was spreading two pallets with fur and fleeces for our comfort beside the hearth. The children were bundled off to other areas, and our hosts had their own quarters, but for propriety's sake it was to be clearly seen that Arthur and I slept in separate beds, well chaperoned by all our own men.

I smiled ruefully to myself, knowing I had already experienced a far greater and deeper union with this man than that which propriety was so busy guarding against. I had seen and accepted our fate here, tonight, on the crest of this ancient hill, and all the other ceremonies would be just that: rituals to please the people and make public the commitment that had been made in the privacy of my own heart.

As sleep claimed me, I wondered if Arthur himself had any idea what had happened.

* * *

Next morning Pellinore bade a noisy farewell to his family, expressly designating Lamorak to act in his stead while he was gone.

'Poor boy needs something to cover his disappointment at not being able to come with me,' he said as we clattered down the steep side of the hill, followed by our escort and the men Pellinore was bringing as well. 'Besides, do him good to have a taste of responsibility while I'm gone. Gives him experience along that line and frees me up for a little questing on my own.'

'Still chasing the ladies?' Arthur teased.

'Ah, M'lord, I cannot tell you how hard it is to cope with an appetite such as mine. It's a ravening beast, howling and bellowing like a pack of hounds. I must follow wherever the Goddess leads, no matter what. Infernally hard to make a wife understand that,' he added soberly. 'Oh, I try not to get lured away . . . can't run a tribe and be always out following the scent, you know. But when She beckons, the chase is on and I have no choice but to pursue. One of these days I'll catch Her, and then I'll hold the very Goddess in my arms.'

Arthur nodded. 'The dream of every man,' he said softly.

'Ah, but it's a curse, too,' Pellinore averred. 'You think you're master of the whole of the Universe, ploughing the stars and casting your thunderbolts into the heart of Creation, and you give yourself over to Her completely. But when its over, you discover you've embraced some poxy beast with mismatched limbs and a cast in one eye. You have no idea how much trouble it can lead to, lad, and it's not a Quest I would wish on anyone else.' He hastily made the sign against blasphemy, just in case the Goddess took offence.

Arthur did likewise, and we rode for a while in silence. I thought about the Goddess and Her many faces, realizing I'd never considered how She appeared to a man. Maiden, mother, hag of wisdom and old age, for me She was the embodiment of life and death, of fertility and ancient strength and power. Cathbad had described Her as land and seasons, stars and tides, implacable in war and glorious in the bearing of new life. That Her very nature could also drive men mad was understandable, but that men saw it as a curse as well as a challenge had not occurred to me.

I wondered if Arthur had ever experienced Her thus, and if he had, would he ever tell me. Perhaps, I decided, it was a question best left for the future.

The sun was gilding the tops of the grasses, and little eddies of steam rose from the meadows below. The lambs of spring gamboled in the pastures, staring at us in sudden amazement and dashing back to the ewes, where they fell to their knees, butting into the comforting udder even as their tails wagged frantically. The older animals simply raised their heads, small chins moving sideways in a constant chewing motion as they watched us pass. The shepherd lifted his hat in greeting, and his dog smiled with lolling tongue, but kept a careful eye on us nonetheless.

This was the face of the Goddess I liked most, and I thanked Her for the gifts of husbandry and plenty with which She had graced this year, and vowed to make a personal sacrifice to Her when we reached Winchester.

31
Morgause

When we caught up with the cavalcade we were met with rowdy cheering by the Cumbrian leaders who had joined our caravan overnight.

These were men who had fought beside Arthur in the Great Battle and, like Pellinore, had a special loyalty to the young man they had helped make High King. They swallowed him up in a chorus of current news and the happy recounting of past glories, so I dropped back beside Merlin and contented myself with watching Arthur at work.

He moved among them easily, responding to them as eagerly as they did to him. For those who called out in the native tongue he had a Cumbrian answer, slipping into Latin only when someone specifically addressed him in that language. It felt like a family reunion, and I thought of the bond I had so often seen between my father and our men at home. Perhaps that is the first quality a leader must have, that he be able to meet his warriors on an equal footing, neither arrogantly superior nor coldly aloof, but as one of them.

Merlin remained as silent and withdrawn as Arthur was outgoing and vocal, so I gave myself over to the mood of the journey. Here in the Marches the sense of the Other engulfed the thrusting hills and crumpled ridges. The land was alive with mists and secret winds, and I understood now why the Welsh kingdoms had never been conquered by Rome. Obviously this was a border guarded by the fey as well as men.

Wherever a hilltop overlooked the Road there was

evidence of a fort or ancient steading. Sometimes there were the familiar outlines of walls and ditches leading like giant steps up to sentinel towers by the gates. And sometimes all you could see was a plume of smoke rising from some fire in a courtyard that was hidden behind a screen of trees. Always there was the feeling that our progress was being observed, and I was glad that the Road was in the hands of our allies, not our enemies.

We made camp that night in a lovely dale sheltered between two softly folded hills, and Arthur suggested that after dinner I should meet the local nobility.

Lavinia helped me change into a dress while Brigit tried to get the snarls out of my hair and we had a chance to catch up on our own news. Their day had been as quiet as mine, though Brigit grinned and said she'd had a terrible time with Caesar the night before, as he seemed to be looking all over the camp for Griflet or Arthur or me.

'He wouldn't settle down until I finally tethered him to the tent pole and he curled up at the foot of my bed and went to sleep,' she concluded while Vinnie grimaced at the memory of having to share her quarters with a dog.

'I'll go find him and take him for a walk as soon as you're finished,' I told Brigit, and she allowed that he would no doubt be delighted to see me.

The baggage animals were quartered near the stream and as I picked my way across a marshy patch the pup made a mad dash towards me, muddy paws flying and shaggy face full of gleeful welcome.

'Heel, Caesar!' Arthur bellowed.

The command came too late, for the young animal had already launched himself full force against me. The impact sent us both tumbling into the wet grasses, though the pup scrambled into a sitting position immediately and sat, eyes laughing, while Arthur came up to us.

'I think he's glad to see you,' my bridegroom suggested,

snapping his fingers and ordering the dog to heel once again. Caesar whipped around to Arthur's side as fast as he could, looking up at his master and then back to me with eager expectancy.

'Are you okay?' Arthur asked, helping me up and surveying my mud-spattered dress with dismay.

I hastened to reassure him that neither my garment nor my disposition was damaged beyond repair, and we headed for higher, drier ground.

We found a soft spot on a small rise near a clump of elders. The bark at the base of the larger trees was shredded where a badger had scratched its claws clean and sharp, and Caesar's interest was immediately piqued.

'Too bad he's not old enough for the field yet,' Arthur said, dropping to the ground and stretching his legs out while he leaned back on his elbows. 'I could have used him as a hunter today, believe me. Do you realize we have over a hundred people to feed now that the local leaders have joined us?'

I found a scatter of wildflowers and picked a few, along with several strands of young ivy, then sat down nearby and began to plait a garland for the dog.

'That many?' I asked.

Arthur nodded thoughtfully. 'Goodness knows how we'll handle it when we get to Winchester, what with the westland lords from Cornwall and Devon and Somerset, as well as the men from Wales and the northern lairds down from the glens. Winchester has only a limited amount of space, and I don't want to see regional factions falling out over who uses which facilities. I think I'll send Merlin ahead to discuss it with Cei; Cei's particularly good at handling this sort of thing, and I'm sure he'll find a way to make everyone comfortable.'

'What's he like, your foster brother?' I asked, and Arthur laughed. Caesar came lolloping over and threw himself down between us, and the High King put a steadying hand on his back.

'Arrogant, difficult, with a sharp tongue and the eye of a hawk. Not much for diplomacy, I'm afraid, but he's great with details. That's why I've asked him to be my Seneschal. Bedivere gets people to agree; Cei makes sure they comply with their agreements. I asked Merlin once if he'd foreseen all this when he brought the three of us together as children, but he just smiled and said my closest companions would each bring a special skill to the aid of Britain, and I mustn't think it would be limited to just the family I was raised with.'

'How much does the Enchanter know of the future?' I asked, sliding the finished circlet of greenery over Caesar's head.

'Much more than he tells, of that I'm sure. He sees his glimpses of Sight as guideposts, not as a substitute for hard work and dedication, and says that no matter what the Fates have spun, we have the free choice to weave it as we will. It's important to make our own decisions, instead of leaving them up to someone else, or blaming what happens on the Gods. But sometimes it's a real tangle, trying to take every faction into account!

'Take the wedding, for instance. Everyone agreed it should be on Pentecost because this year that feast falls on the last day of April, and when the sun goes down, Beltane begins. That way the spring festivals of both Pagans and Christians are recognized. But deciding where to have the actual ceremony was quite another matter.'

He sat up and began to tickle Caesar's nose with a grass stalk.

'I suggested that it be held at Glastonbury because the Tor has been sacred to the Lady since time began, and with the Christian chapel nearby it seemed a reasonable way to satisfy everyone. But the Archbishop of London had a fit; he thought we should have the wedding in London, because he claims that's the most important Christian centre in Britain!'

Arthur snorted and tossed away the grass stalk. 'What a foolhardy idea! It took all of Merlin's wisdom and Bedivere's persuasion to get the fellow to realize how impossible that would be. London's as much Saxon as Celt these days, and even though we have a truce with the Federates, it would be sheer stupidity to assemble so large a party of our best leaders in such a place. We ended up promising the Archbishop he could help officiate no matter where the wedding was held, and that's when he finally agreed to Winchester. Merlin says he sees no danger in it, so I went along with it.'

Arthur was silent for a minute, fuming over such shortsightedness. It was obvious that he considered the meddlesome bishops a problem and I wondered what sort of alliance could be forged between this free-spirited monarch and the ambitious, dogmatic churchmen.

'Do you mind having a Christian wedding as well as one that follows the Old Ways?' he asked, turning his fine level gaze directly on me. It was the first time he'd inquired about my own preference on anything.

'No, not really,' I said carefully. 'Ceremonies must be structured to meet the needs of the people. You and I both know that public rituals are for bards to sing of later; vows of the heart are made much more privately. Or at least, that's what we do in Rheged . . .' I added softly.

There was an awkward silence, and suddenly Arthur got to his feet and indicated we should head back towards the camp.

'I understand your sister will be leading the rite of the Old Ways,' I said, standing up and trying to smooth out my dress. 'Are you very close to her?'

'Morgan?' We turned and started down the hill. 'Yes,

and no. I got to know her when I made the retreat at the Lake after the Great Battle. I had beaten the northern kings on the field, but I wasn't certain they would accept me as High King. She helped allay the last of my own doubts, and was instrumental in convincing them I was the Goddess' choice for High King as well. She's truly dedicated to what's good for the people, and I trust her implicitly on that level. But as a person, I know her almost less than I know the Queen Mother. Morgan was sent away to a convent before I was born, and I didn't meet her until after I had bested her husband in the Great Battle. Believe me, it was a relief to have Urien sue for peace, as I was loath to make both my sisters widows in one day. I don't need two women versed in the black arts plotting against me; one is quite sufficient.'

'Which is that?' I queried, unsure what he referred to.

Arthur kicked a clod out of the way and the viciousness of the action made me glance over at him. He was stamping stubbornly along, glaring at the ground as though it were a living adversary. His eyes had narrowed and I could see the muscles of his jaw clench as he struggled with the words.

The change in mood was appalling, and I wondered if he resented my asking about his kin.

'There is no love lost between Morgause and myself,' he said at last. 'And I prefer not to speak of her. Although I did not wield the weapon, she blames me for Lot's death, and perhaps a good deal more. I have taken in Gawain and his younger brother Gaheris because they are my cousins, and are proud, honest young warriors. And I will welcome Agravain and Gareth at court as well, when they are old enough. But their mother must never presume to call upon me as kin. I will not allow it.'

His voice was strained and tense, and unexpectedly cold for a man who generally radiated life and energy. It was clear that whatever trouble lay between brother and sister was not likely to be mended soon.

As we came to the clearing he went down on one knee and put the lead on Caesar's collar, pausing for a moment with his hand on the circlet of flowers that graced the pup's neck. Suddenly Arthur took hold of my hand and looked up at me.

'I didn't mean to speak so harshly, Gwen. I . . . I just can't talk about my sister, that's all. It's not that I want to exclude you . . . but I have no way to explain about Morgause. And I'd appreciate it if the subject did not come up again.'

I stared down at his face and found misery laid across it like the stripes of a whip. Instinctively I reached out to him, running my free hand over his hair as though he were a child frightened at Samhain.

'Of course, love,' I reassured him. 'It's all right. Whatever it is, it will be all right.'

He turned his head to one side and I could not see his expression, but after a long minute he sighed deeply and looked up. The bitter rage was gone and his eyes once more held the sparkle of enthusiasm I found so dear.

'I almost believe you could make it all right,' he said, only half in jest.

'Well, I can try,' I bantered, still wondering what we were talking about.

He pressed my hand to his cheek, then smiled softly. Caesar had been watching us uncertainly and now began to cavort happily as we headed back to camp and the promise of fresh, hot food.

I could not see what this strange interchange had to do with the realities of our present lives. As with the grey wraith of Arthur's old age that had come to me on the Wrekin, his anger had appeared like a half-hidden world that emerges on a misty night and then is gone when the warmth of the day arrives, so that you do not know what is real and what is fey. No matter what its source, I decided, I shall not trouble that well of poison in the future, and perhaps time will draw the pain from him. And in the meanwhile there are new kings to meet and another night to spend under the stars.

After dinner people began moving between tents and firesides, forming little knots for conversation or games of chance. The various leaders of small Cumbrian kingdoms drifted by, stopping to meet me and pay their respects to Arthur. The High King was pleasant but aloof, with a tension beneath his graciousness, and I noticed that he let others do the talking.

Pellinore sat with us for part of the time, his boisterous good nature filling the firelit circle.

'Wonderful way to catch up with what's going on elsewhere,' he said after a young man from one of the coastal valleys had come and gone. The news most frequently exchanged had to do with King Pellam, the king struck down by his own sword, whose wound had still not healed.

'Nothing much one can do to come to his aid, either.' Pellinore's big voice dropped in awe. 'Hideous idea, born of a hideous act. What ever happened to the fellow who dealt that dolorous stroke?'

'Balin?' Arthur sighed, and the flame in the fire hissed suddenly. 'I understand he and his brother killed each other in combat without knowing who the other was until it was too late. Kin killing kin . . . it's a tragedy to burst the heavens, to drive the sea away, to open the earth with anguish.'

Arthur had fallen into the Old Way with words, using the terms so familiar from days of past glory. No doubt he too had heard them in childhood.

We sat in silence, awed by the power of one's moira to

twist the threads of life into heartbreaking irony. I was glad they did not know the truth about Balin, for every Celtic warrior dreams of living on in glorious memory, even if his ending is tragic, and who was I to steal a dead man's reputation?

After the fires had died down Arthur rose and we walked back to my tent together. In the dark, the scattered campfires glowed among the clearings of the woods like fairy lanterns casting golden shadows amid the trunks of ancient trees. Each glimmering pool of light had its gathering of people, like moths around a rushlight and occasionally a short laugh or sleepy exclamation floated through the night.

'They do us honour, M'lady.' Arthur said formally, gesturing across the whole of the camp.

'May we so live as to deserve it,' I answered, and my bridegroom nodded stiffly as he pulled the flap of the tent open for me.

'It will be a long day tomorrow.' His voice was firm but distant, and I felt like a hen being shooed into the roost for the night.

What ever is the matter with him? I wondered when he dropped the tent flap abruptly behind me.

I told Brigit about Arthur's sudden anger when I spoke of his sister and his aloofness and formality during the rest of the evening.

'Ah well,' she said, taking the barrette from my hair once I was wrapped in a sleeping robe. 'He seems a man more used to armies and bivouacs than courtship and young women. And it's understandable for him to be concentrating on those things which are both more familiar and, in a way, more important to him. It can't be easy, after all, to suddenly find your wedding journey turned into a kind of continuous Council, with everyone tagging along for the joy of it. He's probably just got his mind on concerns of the realm, and doesn't realize he's being brusque.'

As usual, Brigit made the problem seem simple and easily explained. Perhaps the depth of disquiet I had seen in him was exaggerated in my own mind. I smiled at her gratefully, hoping that she was right and Arthur would regain his good spirits come morning.

32

Agricola

Arthur's good nature did indeed return, but we had very little time together during the next few days, as the problems of feeding the masses that followed behind us took most of his attention. Hunting parties went out each day, and lieutenants were sent into towns to pick up whatever other provisions might be available.

As we moved farther south, we met more travellers on the Road, many of whom, like the beekeeper we had passed earlier, turned in their tracks and joined the procession. Often people who were already going south put aside their original plans for the excitement of taking part in the wedding march.

Arthur kept us away from cities, though frequently the nobles of the area congregated there and hastened forth to greet us. A particularly large contingent was waiting at Gloucester, having come from the coastal kingdoms of South Wales.

The southern Cumbri were very different from the hardy men of the north. Many of them had Irish names, for the men of Demetia were proud that their ancestors had come from over the Irish Sea. Clean-shaven and elegant, they generally wore bright-coloured linen rather than wool, and preferred to speak Latin instead of the Cumbrian tongue.

There were several who rode about in special conveyances called carriages, which seemed a cross between a wicker war chariot and a farm wagon. I stared at the odd looking contraptions, light enough to be pulled by horses instead of oxen but too heavy to manoeuvre over rough ground, and wondered what they'd be like to ride in.

One nobleman was accompanied everywhere by a scribe. I couldn't imagine what he needed to have written down, but Arthur said there was regular trading between these kingdoms and what was left of the Empire, and many of the wealthier still sent their children abroad for schooling.

In spite of their odd ways I thought of them as exotic neighbours, not as foreigners, for like their northern brothers they brought an unswerving devotion to their High King.

It had been a particularly warm and sticky day, and as we moved between a pair of fortified hills the ridge ahead began to show itself as a towering escarpment. Arthur reined in beside me.

'We'll have a hard climb tomorrow,' he noted, wiping the sweat off his forehead with the back of his hand. 'How'd you like to stay at a villa tonight? There's a fine one up ahead where we'd be most welcome. The owner's a good man, and I'd like to get away from the crowd for a while; maybe even have a bath.'

I'd never seen a Roman farm, though of course it was something Vinnie talked about, and the idea of staying in one of the fabled houses of luxury and elegance certainly appealed. Arthur laughed when I asked if there would be room for my women to come too.

'Of course,' he answered. 'Do you really think we could go to a villa without taking Lavinia?'

So as soon as the plans were made for the main campsite the royal party headed off on its own.

'There used to be a great number of villas in this area,' Arthur commented, 'though most have fallen into disrepair since The Troubles. Agricola says this one was abandoned but never raided, and when he moved here after his wife's death he was able to gather enough people to make it a working farm again.'

'Did he originally come from the south?' I asked, wondering about the Roman name.

'Agricola? His full name is Agricola Longhand,' my future mate responded, rolling the Celtic surname richly on his tongue. 'You'll find many southerners bear a mixture of Celtic and Latin names. It's said to be a lively combination,' he added with a sly smile and sidewise glance.

I blushed and ducked my head, amused at his innuendo and ashamed at being so transparent in my suspicions. I might have accepted the man, but that didn't mean I'd blindly accept his court.

'Whatever his ancestry, Agricola fights like a Celt,' Arthur went on. 'He was one of the most helpful of Uther's lieutenants during the Great Battle. I think you'll find him a pleasant change from the roughshod company of these last few days, and I for one will enjoy talking about something other than past wars.'

We turned into the entrance of a fine, formal drive which was well paved and lined with tall, taperlike trees. They stood slim and regal and black against the spring twilight, and I marvelled at the neatness of them; our northern trees are bushy and billowy by comparison.

Just as marvellous was the man who came to greet us, driving one of those carriages which skim over the land like a coracle over water. He gave us a most courteous welcome and as he led us to the house I caught a glimpse of Vinnie peeping, wide-eyed, from between the curtains of the litter.

Arthur made the formal introductions when we all gathered in the foyer and Agricola bowed graciously. He had the firm and stocky build of a farmer, but his hands bore no calluses, and his thick grey hair was well dressed.

His tunic was caught at the waist by an ornately worked belt that had been the symbol of high civilian rank in the Empire. My governess carefully patted her curls into place before being presented.

My women and I were escorted to a suite of rooms that overlooked the central garden, where a working fountain splashed gently in the dusk.

Vinnie examined the flowers on the table near my bed, lightly touching the curved petals that were spotted with brilliant colour.

'I haven't seen lilies like this since I was a child,' she murmured. 'Our host must have a very talented gardener.'

I stared at the strange blossom in disbelief; its riot of colour and convoluted form were so bizarre I was certain it wasn't native to Britain's shores.

The cupboards and chests had been freshly aired, and in each drawer and closet were small packets of sweet, pungent herbs. I asked our host about the sachets when we gathered in the courtyard before dinner, and he smiled pleasantly, evidently pleased I had noticed them.

'They're filled with lavender blossoms, which dry well and retain their scent for some time. Lavender makes a happy addition to any garden, for all that it's more used to a warmer climate.'

I looked at the plants growing in formal beds around the edges of the walks, recognizing comfrey and foxglove and dock for the medicine cupboard, as well as potherbs for the kitchen. But there were many more I had no name for, and I asked how he came to have such an extensive selection.

'It was my wife who first got me interested in gardening. She came from Cornwall, where the climate allows you to grow almost anything. After I moved up here I found working in a garden to be very soothing,' he added. 'And this is a good area for experimenting. Fortunately the original owners of this place had the good sense to plant it well to begin with. Did you notice the cypresses along the drive?'

'The slim black trees?' I nodded.

'They are real treasures' – he beamed – 'as are the figs at the end of the guest wing. Wonderful trees, really! Great shady giants in the summer, with broad, flat leaves and silver-grey bark, and the sweetest fruit in the fall. Perhaps you've had dried figs? They keep very well and travel easily.'

I told him no, regretfully, but Vinnie allowed that she'd had them when she was a child in York.

'That's been some time back,' she said primly, suddenly shy when all attention was focused on her.

'And you've had none since?' Agricola inquired, to which she gave a mute shake of her head and looked bashfully at her plate. 'Well, that's easily taken care of,' our host went on, though he didn't elaborate any further.

Over dinner the conversation moved to our journey and the multitude of people following along behind. I sat back in my chair, secretly relieved there were no couches, and surveyed the room.

It was a handsome chamber, airy and light. The plaster was terracotta in colour, and someone had painted a picture of a young woman feeding doves on the far wall. I wondered if it was a portrait of Agricola's wife; whoever she was, she was very pretty. The oil lamps that sat on the tabletops and hung from tall stands by the doorways were made of something translucent, for they glowed slightly below the bright flame of the wick.

But what delighted me most was a cluster of large pots arranged just inside the courtyard door, for each one held a living tree. The idea of having a forest under one's roof

376

had never occurred to me, and I vowed to remember it for the future.

Dinner was an excellent meal of tender young lamb that was flavoured with an herb Agricola called rosemary. There were vegetables in fish sauce as well as mincemeats and a clear, pale wine our host said came from a place known as the Pfalz in Germany.

Vinnie's eyes fairly brimmed with joy as one course followed another, all served on the red Samian ware she so much admired. As a final touch, each person's wine was served in a separate glass goblet. Surely nothing could have made her happier.

The conversation ranged over a number of topics, none of which had to do with specific battles or relived glories. Agricola talked of crops, which had been good for two years in a row now, and of the chance of building up trade with the Continent again, particularly if the ports along the Saxon Shore could be used.

'I wouldn't mind entering into treaties with the Federates,' Arthur said. 'I'm willing to consider trusting them that far – if there were only some way to put a halt to the invasions!'

Agricola nodded in agreement. 'A great deal will depend on what happens in Gaul,' he suggested as another round of wine was poured. 'I hear that the Franks are driving the Visigoths out of the coast areas, and forcing many of them across the mountains into Spain. It's these Franks, under the king named Clovis, who keep harassing Ban and his brother in Brittany, and I hate to think what will happen if they overrun the Saxon territory to the north; it would mean a whole new flood of Saxons wanting to come here to live!'

'I have no recent news of Ban's situation,' Arthur said soberly as he watched the wine splash into the bowl of his goblet. 'If he can hold the Franks at bay until we have

Britain better organized, I'd be happy to send whatever men I can spare to defend his eastern front. He was, after all, instrumental in helping me during the Great Battle.'

'Well,' sighed Agricola, making a strange sign I had never seen before, 'with a little luck and a lot of work, perhaps the Gods will smile on both Greater and Lesser Britain.'

We all drank to that as a servant arrived bearing a grand silver platter. It was worked with ornate designs of all sorts, and in the centre was a mound of preserved fruit. Each person received a pair of the golden orange globes swimming in a thick, clear syrup, and I eyed them with the same mixture of curiosity and apprehension the lilies had provoked.

'What is it?' I asked when the strange flavour burst in my mouth.

'The fruit are peaches and the spice is a kind of root called ginger,' Agricola answered. 'They were my wife's favourite, and I grew quite fond of them. But ginger is becoming very hard to get, what with trade turning so chancy.

'That's something to consider, now that the Visigoths have fled into Spain,' our host went on, turning back to Arthur. 'Spain used to supply the Mediterranean with tin, but with the barbarian disruption, we might be able to re-establish ourselves in the market. Cornwall once did a thriving trade in that, you know, and bronze workers are always looking for a good source of tin.'

Arthur nodded thoughtfully, and Agricola went on to discuss the possibilities of trade with Constantinople. I found the man's range of knowledge to be amazing, and when there was a lull in the conversation I asked how he had learned about so many different things.

'My father knew the value of a good education,' he replied with a smile, 'so I was sent to places which are, perhaps, not so readily accessible nowadays. I've seen the Pillars of Hercules, and the harbour at Alexandria, and the temple of Apollo at Delphi.'

I was delighted to be talking with a man who had actually seen the things Cathbad used to tell of, and promptly asked, 'What's the most exciting place in the world?'

'Britain,' came the instant reply, and he smiled fondly. 'Grey and cloudy, full of mists and green forests, riotous spring days and golden rich autumns. She may be a bit bedraggled at the moment, but everyone struggles with the barbarians now; even Rome isn't what she once was. But don't forget, cities are only man-made, while the wonders of the Gods are gifts that survive every generation. There's nothing else to compare with the mystery of Cheddar Gorge, or the white cliffs along the Saxon Shore, or the peaceful majesty of a moonrise reflected on the waters around Glastonbury.' And once more our host made the strange hand sign.

'Is that the sign of a British god?' I asked, not stopping to think that my question might be rude.

The villa owner nodded and explained that he was a follower of Hercules, whose cult was very, very old.

'Merlin occasionally told me about the Hero God,' Arthur said.

'I wouldn't be surprised,' Agricola said with a chuckle. 'The Magician and I first got acquainted at a May Day rite on the hill above the Giant, back when I was a young man. Merlin was a simple druid then, helping attach the ribbons and set up the tree trunk before the dancing began. My wife and I had spent the night there, for in those days we had hopes of having children.'

'Under a Maypole?' I asked, thinking it an awfully public spot for such an endeavour.

'No, M'lady, we slept on the Giant himself,' Agricola

explained. 'The outline of the Hero, with his club raised and his member erect, has been cut out of the turf on the side of a hill in the chalk downs. It stands out clear and white against the grasses and can be seen for miles around. They say it was a gift of the Gods, to celebrate Hercules as well as the local gods of fertility. Have you no similar custom in Rheged?'

'We don't even have chalk to cut pictures in,' I answered, trying to imagine such a thing. 'Ours are the gods of misted vales and shimmering water, and occasionally the Great Crown of the North.'

'Ah, Britain,' Agricola said with a loving sigh as he raised his goblet in a toast. 'You see, every corner has its own enchantments; even its own gods. I keep telling Arthur this is the most mystical of lands, and I can't imagine why anyone would wish to live elsewhere.'

With that we lifted our goblets in a salute, feeling doubly blessed to have such a splendid homeland.

After dinner Arthur and I took a quiet stroll through the grounds, admiring the dark cave of shadow the fig trees cast against the star-strewn sky. It was the first time we had been alone for some days, and I revelled in the luxury of it.

'Are the rest of the nobles at court like him?' I asked hopefully.

'A few, but only a few. I wanted him to stay with me as a councillor, but when his wife died he decided to come live in a place less haunted by memories. He's a fine administrator as well as a scholar.'

'And he has no interest in remarrying? It seems a pity a man of so many sensibilities should live alone,' I commented. The soft splash of the fountain played quietly behind us.

Arthur chuckled. 'According to Bedivere there was more than one lady who would have been glad to catch his attention. But as you may have guessed, he loved his wife dearly. Perhaps if one has known that sort of union, it is not easy to put one's grief aside.'

I stole a quick look at him, wondering if he too had lost an earlier love, but found he was busy scanning the sky.

'There – there it is,' he said suddenly, pointing to a constellation of stars. 'Uther's courtiers assume I was named for the Roman family of Artorius, but when I was a child Merlin used to show me the constellation which the Celts call Artoris the Bear, and tell me that's where my name came from. In fact, he often called me Bear in those days.'

I was scanning the skies myself, thinking I had not seen such beauty since the night with Kevin. A bird began to sing, sweet and clear, from the nearby trees and we were surrounded by a shower of song.

'What is it?' I whispered when the music ended.

'A nightingale. Have you never heard one before?'

I shook my head, hoping it would begin again.

'Oh, we have lots of them in the south, where they'll sing you to sleep on any spring night. I'll ask Merlin to guarantee it for you,' Arthur added as we turned to walk back towards the house. My skirt brushed against the border plants, filling the air with the fragrance of mint.

'Does Merlin work that sort of magic?' I asked, thinking it a good bit below his normal activity.

'Well, not usually.' Arthur's tone had a light, whimsical note to it. 'But he has a terrible soft spot for young ladies, so perhaps he'd make an exception for you.'

'The King's Sorcerer?' I exclaimed, incredulous. It was impossible to imagine that sombre and majestic sage being vulnerable to a young girl. I looked at Arthur in amazement, still thinking he must be joking.

'Shhh . . . it's a State Secret. He mentioned it only once, and I couldn't tell if it was a prophecy about his own death or an ironic comment on human nature.' Arthur's voice slipped from banter to more serious matters. 'Merlin's been the one man who has always been there when Britain needed him, and he dedicated his life to The Cause long before either you or I were born. There isn't a skill, an art, an idea he wouldn't learn or pursue if it would help. Druid, military strategist, diplomat, engineer, doctor . . . and sometimes Wizard . . . he's woven it all together and kept the notion of civilization alive. Without him we would have been lost long ago. He's closer to me than a father, Gwen, and I think it would be nice if he could find a little human loving somewhere along the line. No one should grow old alone.'

There was something deeply touching about Arthur's comment, and I slid my arm through his as we went in to join the rest of the party.

But later I remembered Merlin's discomfort on the evening I came and sat by him for dinner, and it seemed possible that Arthur was right. I just hoped that whatever woman recognized it would be worthy of him.

33
The Reunion

Revived and refreshed, we left the villa next morning for the last stage of our journey. Arthur rode at the head of the entourage while Vinnie and Brigit were in the litter. I sat next to Agricola in his carriage and was sure that even in the days of the Empire there had never been a stranger or more elegant procession.

The expression on Pellinore's face when we came into sight was one of startled amusement, but he managed to greet us without bursting into gales of laughter. The rest of the people's reaction varied, depending on where they came from; the sturdy northerners guffawed outright, while the more elegant folk of the south nodded and curtsied and made room for us to pass. In the end I found myself of two minds about the contraption, since the thing was comfortable, for all that it was outrageous. I had no intention of giving up horseback riding permanently, however.

In typical Roman fashion the Road Builders had sought to scale the Cotswold escarpment with as few concessions to nature as possible. We struggled up three steep segments of Road devoid of switchbacks, and anyone in a carriage or litter dismounted, for the poor animals couldn't be expected to haul the extra weight up so steep an incline. Even Vinnie got out and walked. And when we paused near the top, panting for breath and sweating in the morning heat, it was to look back at a view that took my breath away.

The dramatic, rocky outcrops of the scarp thrust out above its forested flanks, while down below the flat Vale of Gloucester spreads westward around the knoll where the Roman city perches. Silver rivers lace their way through green forests and lush meadows, and in the west, seemingly close enough to touch, the blue hills of southern Wales offer protection. It is a world reduced to tabletop size, and I gasped at the sheer wonder of it while Vinnie stood speechless beside me.

'What did I say about Britain's beauty?' Agricola asked with a smile.

Whether it was joy and relief in reaching the crest of the Cotswolds or the fact that we had come into Arthur's personal kingdom of Logres, our progress soon took on the air of a travelling festival. People came from everywhere to join the procession, and they weren't just adventurous young men and local lords with their seasoned warriors; women and children had come to join the fun as well. Whole families were falling in behind us, laughing and singing and putting aside all other thought save that of escorting their king to his nuptials.

We made camp on the edge of a woods like none I had ever seen before. Agricola explained that the deep shade of beech trees prevents the growth of scrub or bracken underneath, so the trunks of the trees become tall columns rising from a clear floor. I thought of Kaethi's description of living temples for the Old Gods; with the late-afternoon sun dappling the fringe of new leaves and bluebells filling every path and open space, it was like a fairy woods, peaceful and pretty and untouched by worldly cares.

The bright mood was contagious, and the people took this chance to pay their own simple respects to their king. A piper played his music for us in the soft twilight, and a family of acrobats came to our fireside and offered to entertain us. They spun and leapt and tumbled in the meadow. When I asked the mother of the family if she and her troupe would perform during the wedding feast she blushed and stammered, but the oldest son bowed formally and announced they would be honoured to do so. Then they all went running back through the trees to their own camp.

I looked up to find Arthur watching me, and wondered suddenly if I should have asked him first.

My husband-to-be had seated himself on a nearby stump and Caesar, always at his side, dropped down next to him.

'You really do like people, don't you?' It was half question, half statement, and it caught me by surprise.

'Of course,' I said, unable to tell if he was teasing or not. 'Don't you?'

He thought for a moment, then answered slowly: 'Yes, but I don't seem to have the knack for making the common people feel comfortable the way you do. I can get them fired up over ideas, but that's not the same as making individuals feel good about themselves. It's a fine trait in a queen,' he added, 'along with Celtic pride and the ability to ride well. Now, if we can just do something about your wardrobe . . .'

He couldn't hide the grin, and I grabbed a bannock and lobbed it at his head. Caesar sat up with a sharp bark, hopeful I'd send one his way.

'You'll have to learn to duck quicker than that, M'lord,' called a familiar voice from the shadow, and Bedivere strode into the circle of firelight. He looked tired and dusty, but was obviously in good spirits.

'Well come, brother,' Arthur cried, jumping up and greeting his fosterling with a hug. 'You made better time than I expected.'

'Aye,' said Bedivere, looking quickly at the food that was piled on the makeshift table. 'We didn't exactly stop to dine with nobles, or even at inns. In fact,' he averred,

385

reaching for a roasted pigeon, 'I can't remember when we last ate.'

'I think,' Griflet said from behind him, 'it was at Palomides' parents', sometime last week.'

The boy looked every bit as weary and road-stained as Bedivere, but his eyes sparkled as he presented Arthur with the hand end of a leash that was attached to a second puppy.

She was a creamy-white copy of Caesar, and for all her skittishness from the long journey, the moment she and Caesar sniffed noses she was right at home.

'I already have a name for her,' Arthur announced, gesturing for the newcomers to help themselves to the food. 'A good Celtic name, to balance the blend of cultures in the kennel. Do you remember the story Merlin told when we were children, about the war dog named Cabal?'

Bedivere shook his head, and Arthur shrugged. 'No matter. It was a jumble of things, as I recall, about an animal that was a shape-changer – sometimes a dog, sometimes a horse, depending on which its owner needed. Anyhow, it was full of great spirit, brave and loyal and fierce, as all such creatures should be. I could have sworn it was one of Merlin's tales. Ah well, the name has been in my mind all this time, I think, so she shall have it as a homecoming present: Cabal . . . yes, that will do nicely.'

'But why should she bear a war dog's name?' I asked, expecting him to have picked something more feminine.

'Because she will be my four-footed warrior. Bitches are always the best attack dogs. Didn't you know that?' When I shook my head, he went on: 'Maybe they have more of the protective instinct. It's a male you want if you're hunting, or needing protection from wild animals, but it's the female that does best on the battlefield. Won't you, Cabal?'

The pup turned and looked up at him, focusing for the first time on the human who knelt down to greet her. She leaned her scruffy chin against his leg and drank in Arthur's presence, oblivious of all else. The gentleness and concern in Arthur's face were beautiful to behold, and I couldn't help smiling at the scene.

'Here we are – over here!' Bedivere called, waving to someone beyond the fire circle. 'It's Palomides. He wanted to wash up before being presented to you.'

'Ah, so you were successful on both missions! That's wonderful,' said Arthur, giving Cabal one last pat before standing to greet the dark-haired youth who made his way into the light.

I hardly recognized the boy with his hair combed back and a short cape of elegant brocade slung over one shoulder; the firelight accentuated his Arab features and he moved with a lithe, animal grace.

'M'lord, may I present Palomides, horseman extraordinaire and eager subject who would like to join your court,' Bedivere announced with a flourish that was both lighthearted and complimentary.

The lad came forward and knelt on one knee before his king, and when Arthur put his hand on the youth's shoulder, Palomides looked up with the same loyalty and devotion as Cabal. How eager they are for a leader, I thought, and how well Arthur meets that need.

'I understand,' my bridegroom said, smiling and motioning for Palomides to rise, 'that you have met M'lady Guinevere before. If it weren't for her, we wouldn't have known to send for you.'

The boy's dark countenance flushed, and he bobbed his head in my direction but was unable to meet my eyes.

'And,' I said quickly, 'if you hadn't thought I was just another page, I might not have seen what you could do

387

on a horse. So we are much indebted, and honoured that you have chosen to join us.'

Palomides looked up at that and smiled fully – a beautiful white flash of pleasure, his embarrassment gone.

The three newcomers began catching up on their food while the puppies nuzzled each other at our feet and we exchanged news.

Bedivere reported they had passed the Lady of the Lake on the Road, travelling with a full military escort and a number of druids and young priestesses. She had suggested they stay and accompany her, but Bedivere had declined on the ground of being needed to help with the wedding caravan; word of the masses of people following us had reached him long before he came within sight of our camp.

'Did Morgan say anything about her husband?' Arthur asked.

'Urien?' Bedivere thought for a moment, then shrugged. 'Only that he was coming down the eastern Road from York, and should make Winchester in time for the ceremony. Are you concerned?'

'No,' Arthur answered slowly. 'He said he would be present for the occasion, and I trust his word. After all, one has to start mending broken fences somewhere.'

Pellinore joined us, bringing with him a portion of ale a local farmer had contributed for the King, and soon political concerns were put aside as the drinking horns were filled and the evening turned to the merriment of toasts.

The next morning we were met on the Road by a group of men riding hard from the south as though hurrying to intercept us.

'By heaven, it's Cei!' Arthur cried, forgetting whatever we had been talking about.

He spurred forward, laughing and calling out greetings

388

to Gawain and Gaheris as well. They met with a round of jests, and suddenly I saw Merlin among them.

The Magician had not been in evidence for some time, but I was so used to his odd behaviour I had not thought to ask his whereabouts. Now it appeared that he had already been to Winchester, had conferred with Cei and was rejoining our party with Arthur's Companions in tow. Such a schedule would have meant hard riding even for an experienced messenger, and I wondered if Merlin had been using his shape-changing powers; only a bird could have covered so much distance so easily.

After conferring with them briefly, Arthur dropped back to explain that there had been a change in plans, and we would be turning onto an ancient track that crosses the Road near Liddington Castle. I glanced up at the ridge he pointed to, realizing that the long grassy lift of it terminated abruptly and boasted an ancient fortification at its top.

As we drew closer, the walls of the massive hill-fort came to life with cheering children and banner-waving women. At its base, where the Ridge Way met the Road, a contingent of warriors stood smartly at attention. These were the first of Arthur's home guard I had seen, and I eyed them curiously. Some wore bits of antique armour of the Roman style which had no doubt been handed down from father to son after the Legions left. A few had newer leather tunics, and the leader was garbed in a shirt of chain mail. They saluted smartly when we rode past and drummed their spear butts against the ground.

Arthur gave them a wave, and they fell in behind us as the caravan veered off across the grassy slope of the downs. Agricola's carriage was ill-suited for the rougher track, so I went back to riding Featherfoot, while he stayed on the paved Road and promised we would meet again before the wedding.

Arthur was busy with Cei and Gawain and others of the household who hadn't seen him for nigh on to a month now, so Bedivere came to ride beside me for a while. His eyes twinkled and he appeared to be genuinely pleased to see me again.

'And how does Logres seem to Your Ladyship . . . to you, Gwen?' he corrected himself, and I smiled.

'More exciting, more beautiful, more welcoming than I had expected,' I answered gaily.

I told him about the people we'd met and he nodded at my description of the whole procession dancing on the green beside the ancient well, and laughed when I contrasted Pellinore's hill-fort with Agricola's villa.

'And all the while,' I concluded, 'we've been riding into the very heart of spring. It's unbelievable.'

'And you're not disappointed with Arthur?' His gaze was so warm and confident it didn't occur to me that the question was impertinent.

'Good heavens,' I exclaimed, 'how could I be disappointed when he's so . . . so . . .'

I groped for words, and Bedivere reached across and laid his hand over mine. The smile that he gave me was slow and rich, rising from within rather than glancing quickly off the surface.

'I'm glad. It's just as important to have a happy queen as it is to have a contented king.'

I nodded happily. 'And what of you? How was your own trip, besides hurried and harried?'

'It was good. Busy but good. And Brigit's family welcomed us as though we were lost relatives. In fact, Sean's wife was delivered of a baby girl three days after you left, and they asked me to tell you they've named the child for you.'

It was an honour to be so remembered, and I thought of the young mother's eyes, bright and shining as she wished me many children and allowed me to touch her belly for luck.

'How is Brigit?' Bedivere asked. 'I didn't see her in the procession.'

It was a simple question, made casually from one friend to another, but of a sudden I looked at him more closely and realized that our growing confidence and trust was mutual. He had not hesitated to ask about my own inner feelings, and I knew it would be quite all right to ask about his.

'You thought of her a lot on the trip?' The look he gave me was so open, and so easy to read, I burst out laughing. 'She's doing fine,' I assured him, 'though I haven't seen her much except at bedtime and mornings. She's a very good, truly remarkable person, and a man would do well to treat her gently and woo her softly. She's quite devout in her faith, you know.'

'Aye, I am aware of that.' He sighed, but without rancour or sadness. 'It is a belief I have never thought to study, but perhaps she would be willing to teach me.'

'At least you could ask her,' I said encouragingly, and was glad to see him nod thoughtfully as he rode off to join Arthur and the rest of the Companions.

The richness of the day rose all around me, full of hope and excitement and the sweet, lifting song of larks. It was good to know that Brigit, coming south out of loyalty to me, was riding into a future that could include love and marriage for herself as well.

In the afternoon we left the old track and made our way down to the plain below.

'Avebury,' Arthur said as we headed for the entrance to the largest henge I'd ever seen.

'Everyone honours the sanctity of a stone circle, and there should be enough room here to accommodate this mob.'

We rode across the causeway which cut through the towering bank and crossed over an inner ditch that yawned both wide and deep. I was amazed to discover it was indeed big enough to embrace the masses who followed us. There were at least a hundred Standing Stones ranged in a circle along the edge of the huge ditch. Some were tall and slender, while others were broad and fat, but all seemed to be balancing on tiptoe, and I marvelled at the power the Gods had contained in such a place.

When the campfires came to life, pale streamers of smoke began to rise from half a hundred sites, filling the air with the tang of woodsmoke. I stood beside an immense boulder and looked out across the scene, really seeing for the first time the thousands who had gathered in our wake. It was a sobering sight, for all that it spoke well of the people's love for Arthur.

Arthur's Companions joined us for dinner and introductions were made all around.

Cei was dark and lean, more elegant than either of his foster brothers, but with a hard mouth and cool glance. He looked me carefully up and down and hesitated for a moment before bowing. There was only the barest of polite smiles and I wondered if he would be difficult to get to know. Do not look for trouble, I told myself; perhaps he is simply concerned that his foster brother choose well in taking a wife.

There was more pleasure in greeting Gawain, who had grown taller and thicker since our first meeting and was now well into his manhood. His hair was just as red as I remembered and he still moved with a kind of fierce, crackling energy.

He smiled when the formal presentation was finished and put one hand up to the noticeable bend in his nose.

'I haven't forgotten, M'lady,' he said with a smile. 'Best

riding lesson I ever had. There's neither horse nor jump I can't handle now.'

'Just wait,' I answered, 'until you see what Palomides can do! Soon we'll all be flying over streambanks like Greek gods on winged horses.'

'Ah, so Bedivere tells me. I haven't had a chance to meet the Arab fellow yet. What is it he calls those things for your feet?'

'Stirrups,' Bedivere put in, lowering his drinking horn and looking round at the different groups of people who had gathered near the King's fire. 'There he is, talking with Pellinore. Come, I'll introduce you.'

'Pellinore?' Gawain's voice was razor-sharp.

The smell of danger flickered in the air, and I wondered how many of us had forgotten that Pellinore had been the warrior who killed King Lot. I looked quickly at Gawain, seeing even in the uncertain light of dusk how flushed and heated his countenance had become.

'Remember, nephew,' Arthur said, his voice suddenly stern and forbidding, 'we are within the confines of a sacred place.'

He watched Gawain closely, and tempered his voice as the young warrior turned to stare unblinkingly at him. The youth's fiery colour began to fade and Arthur continued in a more conversational tone:

'Your father died in a fair fight, and is much honoured as a brave warrior. The victor in that battle is our ally, and has been invited to the wedding as my guest. I'll not have a blood feud mar the joy of these festivities, Gawain, and if you cannot abide by that, you do not have to attend the celebration.'

The Prince of the Orkney Isles was visibly struggling to control his rage.

'For the duration of this gathering, he shall be safe,' Gawain vowed at last, and turning to his squire, said pointedly, 'I give my word on that, Gaheris.'

The boy glared at Gawain, then dropped his eyes and nodded almost imperceptibly.

So the matter was left, and with a nod to the rest of us, Gawain and Bedivere went off to speak with the new horseman.

'And this,' Arthur said, gesturing towards the stocky squire who now stood before us, 'is Gawain's brother, Gaheris.'

No more than a year younger than Gawain, he had the sullen air of a boy who hasn't yet come to terms with his world. His bow was stiff with resentment, and I racked my brain for something that would put him at ease.

'Your brother spoke of you with pride when we were children' was the best I could manage, but it seemed to do, for Gaheris' troubled look vanished in a blazing smile.

'During his visit to Rheged?' the boy asked quickly. 'He told me often about your mountains and lakes, and how the women of Rheged are daughters of the Horse Goddess Epona.'

I smiled at the exaggeration, but was so glad to see Gaheris' manner change that there seemed no point in correcting him.

We chatted for a moment more, and I thought how mercurial the moods of the Orkneyans could be: all grace and open good nature one moment, and full of violence and rage the next. What had my father called them? Hotheaded and impetuous, with an undiluted dose of Celtic pride.

When Gawain had gone Arthur turned and gave me one of those private little smiles. 'I must tell Bedivere he has a rival for diplomacy within the court.'

'It's easy when things are calm,' I said with a shrug, 'but I always get into trouble when the words fly faster than the thought.'

'Thank goodness you don't wear a sword,' my husband-to-be said, 'or I'd be looking at the Celtic nature run amok within my own halls. You sure you're not related to Boudicca?'

Kevin's voice came suddenly into my mind, and the litany of warrior queens. 'Not directly, but perhaps in spirit,' I replied, and Arthur grinned.

'Much better than some fragile convent flower,' he said softly, and I blushed with pleasure and desire.

Merlin approached and introduced a druid from the Sanctuary up on the hill. He was a bright-eyed little man with a crick in his neck that caused him to hold his head on one side.

'We would be most gratified if Your Ladyship would come to our temple tomorrow morning,' he said, his voice as cheeky and chipper as a sparrow's. 'Our well is famous for its promise of fertility, and our doire has studied with the Lady. She is versed in the ceremony of the Bride's Blessing, and would like to take you through the rites of preparation.'

Although we had no doires at the wells of Rheged, I'd long heard tales about the wise women who were guardians of the sacred waters.

I looked to Merlin, wondering if it would be all right to accept this invitation, and the Enchanter nodded slightly at my unspoken enquiry.

'I think,' he said, 'the local people would be deeply touched if you honoured their shrine in this way.'

So it was settled that I would be escorted to the Sanctuary an hour before sunrise, and the druid withdrew with a respectful bow.

Arthur held a Council that evening to discuss the change in location of the wedding, for Cei and Merlin felt it best to move the ceremony from Winchester's small valley to the ancient hill-fort known as Sarum. It was

395

easily accessible, being at the hub of five Roads, and the open land that encircled it would provide room enough to handle the crowd that flocked behind us. It had a small but suitable church to meet the Christian needs, and although the spot was not unusually favoured by the Old Gods, there were enough sacred places near that the Lady should be satisfied.

When the question of Morgan's reaction came up, Arthur drew a deep breath and leaned forward with his elbows on his knees. 'I'm sure there won't be any trouble,' he said, tapping his fingertips together and frowning thoughtfully. 'She's shrewd enough to recognize the difficulties, and I know from experience she wants to keep her followers united behind me.'

So the plan was agreed to, and arrangements made to notify the travellers who had gone to Winchester that there was a change of locale.

'What of the Lady, travelling behind us?' I inquired. 'How will she know to come to Sarum?'

'I can head back up north tomorrow,' Pellinore offered. 'Wouldn't mind an extra day or so of travel . . . my horse could use the exercise,' he added, stretching his rangy frame against the night's shadows.

'Still questing?' Arthur asked, his face serious but his voice light.

'Always,' Pellinore affirmed, hooking his thumbs through his belt and heaving a deep sigh.

'So the travellers from the south are accounted for, and those who arrive at Winchester anyway, and Pellinore will go in search of the Lady,' Merlin was saying, carefully ticking off the items on his fingers. 'That leaves only the question of who will escort Guinevere to the preparation rites at dawn. It can't be the bridegroom, but it should be someone from her own family . . .'

My first reaction was to suggest Brigit. She was my

closest companion and the nearest I had to kin with me; but of course she was neither male nor Pagan and therefore would not qualify, so I kept silent.

'I'd be honoured, if M'lady will allow me.' Pellinore spoke slowly, his big face solemn in the fire glow as he turned to the Magician. 'I can present her to the doire at first light, and then leave for the Road.'

Merlin pondered the matter, his eyes cloudy with the unfocused look that Kaethi used to have when she was watching the future. An owl glided through the trees above, its silent progress noted only by the faint stirring of leaves. The Enchanter showed neither smile nor frown, and whatever he foresaw was not for others to know.

'Is that all right with you, Arthur?' he inquired, and when my bridegroom nodded, Merlin turned to Pellinore.

'It is a major responsibility, to stand for a bride on the Day of her Blessing, and betokens the next-closest thing to a kin-tie.' The Wise One stared hard at the warrior. 'Are you willing to be responsible for her welfare from here on?'

'M'lord,' Pellinore answered gravely, 'I was raised with the Old Gods and do not offer this lightly. But since the fairest lady in the land has been claimed for my sovereign's bed, the next-best thing I could hope for would be the chance to become as an uncle for all the future years.'

It occurred to me that I would rather have Pellinore as a kinsman sworn to my protection than a would-be admirer chasing me about a meadow, and it was probably in all our interests to accept this offer. So I consented gladly, and when the Council was finished and Arthur walked me to the tent, he said much the same himself.

'I would hate to have to defend your virtue and my rights against Pelli. I'm not sure that he couldn't best me yet.'

With that he reached out and gathered me in a full, possessive embrace, more fierce than tender, as though to place his mark on me for all time. I struggled to catch my breath, surprised but not displeased by his ardour.

Lavinia frowned in consternation when she learned what was planned for the morrow. She was convinced that heathen rites were dangerous to life and limb as well as soul, and nothing I said seemed to reassure her. Later even Brigit bent close beside me while she brushed my hair and asked if I wished her to accompany me.

'It is Pagan, Brigit, and therefore not allowed you,' I reminded her, touched that she would make the offer. 'I'm not afraid, really, for though it is sacred and not to be discussed beyond the Sanctuary itself, I have never seen a young woman who was hurt by the ritual. I've known the Old Gods all my life, and do not think they would harm me now.'

We left it at that, and I went to sleep feeling protected and well cared for by everyone, including Arthur himself.

34

Nimue

Pellinore and the druid came for me next morning while the earth still sighed in her sleep. The little man lifted the horn lantern above his head as Pellinore held the tent flap open and they both greeted me solemnly. Brigit gave me one last hug, while Vinnie crossed herself and muttered a hasty prayer for my well-being, and then we were on our way.

A soft haze filled the air, blurring the edges of the waning moon. The sight of a withering moon always makes me sick to my stomach, as though she had been wounded in some way, so I concentrated on how beautiful the land looked in the strange, diffused mist. It was neither the dense, heavy fog of Hardknott nor the layered, floating vapours of the fells, but rather a veil that brushed ever so gently against the earth, muting and transforming all things sharp and harsh.

Most of the camp still slept, though here and there a shadowy form stirred beside the embers of a campfire. No one noticed our progress, and we might as well have been invisible as we walked silently across the great circle of Avebury.

The gigantic ditch was full of shadow, gaping like a black pit on either side of the causeway, and I kept well to the middle of the beaten path so as not to get too close to the dark chasm.

Beyond the towering bank a double row of stones stretched before us in the pale light. They were ranged two by two, fat and lean, tall and squat, creating an Avenue that led off into the mists.

'Behold the power of all dualities,' the druid whispered, gesturing towards the stones on either side as we walked softly between them. 'Matter and space, chaos and order, male and female. You are following the Way now, child, from the womb of all Mothers to the bed of all Creation. Think on the Goddess, and do not be afraid.'

A medley of birdsong scattered through the trees, growing into an anthem of dawn. In a nearby glade a nightingale sang, its haunting melody rising above the rest. My heart lifted with the sound, remembering Arthur and the villa garden.

The Way led upward to a beech grove at the crest of the hill. Eerie, pale shapes glided within the darkness under the trees, and when we came to a stop at the edge of the woods the joy of the birdsong quieted into whispers all around us.

'Gwenhwyvaer, Gwenhwyvaer, Gwenhwyvaer . . .' they murmured, playing with the native version of my name. 'White shadow of the Cumbri, well come to this Sanctuary.'

It was a deep, resonant sound with echoes that rose and fell, for the Goddess was everywhere at once. I felt Her swirling around us, fluttering and hovering above Her people, slowly taking form in a white-robed priestess who came towards us with her arms extended in blessing.

When the naming of my presence had died away, the girl who stood before us spoke, her voice light and friendly.

'Who brings this woman for her Preparation?' the doire asked.

'Pellinore of the Wrekin,' replied my escort, his tone low and respectful as he stepped up next to me.

'And what is she to you?' the girl inquired.

'Kinswoman in trust, niece in spirit and soon to be Queen of the High King's Court.'

400

That was clearly not the expected answer, and the priestess looked back and forth between us curiously.

'Can you vouch for her?'

'Absolutely,' Pellinore responded with total confidence. 'By my own observation she is well suited for the forthcoming marriage. By Merlin's knowledge there are no encumbrances to the proposed union, and by the King's desire she is chosen.'

The young woman had been watching the warrior closely, and now she nodded. 'Do you agree to stand as surety should she prove to be forsworn?'

'In whatever manner the Goddess requires,' he said without hesitation.

I stole a look at my sponsor, struck by the fullness of his commitment. He must have seen the flicker of my glance, for he grinned down on me and added, 'Though I would prefer to keep my manhood intact.'

The doire laughed gently. 'You need not fear; our Goddess demands no such sacrifices as the Cybele.'

She gestured for Pellinore to kneel, and when he was on his knees before her she took both his hands in hers. Wide-eyed and solemn, she looked down at him, and her voice grew deep and vibrant when she asked, 'Pellinore of the Wrekin, do you swear to the truth of your statements, and vow to uphold the trust of the Goddess lest the earth should open and the sky should fall, and the sea retreat beyond our ken?'

'Aye, and by the Spirit of this Place, too,' he answered, adding the Latin phrase for good measure.

The girl was staring down at him, her eyes brimming with moonlight and perhaps tenderness. 'The Goddess is well pleased by the devotion of such a stalwart man. You may go on your way, and we will take the bride into the temple. When the rites are over, she will be escorted back to her party.'

Pellinore continued to look up at the priestess as though in a trance, and the two of them conversed silently with their eyes.

'May I come again?' he whispered huskily.

The girl shivered and gave a little start. For a moment I thought she tried to free her hands, but he held them imploringly, and at last she smiled.

'You will find the Goddess wherever you choose to look,' she said softly, her voice beginning to return to normal. 'But you will find me, Nimue, here at the Sanctuary above Avebury. I cannot say when the Goddess will visit you again, but I am here always.'

Pellinore kissed her hands reverently before letting go of them and getting to his feet. Turning to me, he took me by the shoulders and planted a paternal kiss on my forehead.

'Thank you for the honour, M'lady, and may the day go well for you.'

And then he was gone, striding into the dawn with swaggering shoulders and a jaunty step. I watched his form retreating down the Avenue, thinking he was one of the most truly solid men of any realm.

Nimue also watched him, a bemused expression on her young face. Slipping her arm through mine, she led me towards the circular temple within the screen of trees. 'Underneath it all everyone is vulnerable to the Goddess, but there are not many who show it as openly as that one does,' she said.

The day went by in a drift of colour and music, dance and prayer. There was a quiet ritual at the well and I found bits and phrases from my childhood interspersed with other, foreign ways. The details of such rites are not to be recounted – not because they are grotesque, as the Christians would have one believe, but because they are full of grace and power. They mark the line between maiden and mother, child and bride, and by early afternoon I had been bathed and robed in the white garment of the initiate, and I walked with the knowledge of the Goddess both within and without.

When I knelt for the final blessing Nimue placed the ivy wreath on my head.

'Remember,' she whispered, kissing me softly on each cheek, 'I am always here, if you should need me.'

'Won't you be coming to the wedding?' I asked, surprised at the idea she might not take part in the festivities.

'I do not know. My moira holds me here, at least until that one returns,' she said, nodding towards the Avenue as though Pellinore's shade still lingered there. 'What happens after that I cannot see. There is someone very important about to come into my life,' she added slowly, 'and if it is not Pellinore, then he will take me to him.'

A shiver ran down my back, and I envied the girl the assurance with which she spoke. Perhaps such confidence comes of giving oneself completely to the Gods; but though I knelt in tranquillity now, I suspected that the demands of the world would all too easily make a shambles of this inner peace. Certainly I was unsure that I could maintain contact with the calm majesty of the Goddess once I was Arthur's wife.

'Of course you can,' Nimue said clearly, and I started, for I had not spoken aloud. 'Do you think you would have been chosen to be High Queen if you were not right for it? It is what you have been groomed for since the beginning, regardless of whether you or anyone else knew it. Servant and sage and the seasons of the year have all combined to bring you here. You are to be Arthur's wife because you bring what is most needed to the marriage. It is as simple as that.'

Her voice was as deep and solemn as when she had

403

spoken with Pellinore, and I knew without looking up that the Goddess was upon her.

'Go now in confidence, for your Blessing is complete. It does not matter whether your wedding is now or a week hence; you have been found fit, and I will be with you.'

When I raised my eyes the girl was smiling radiantly. She put one hand lightly on my head, and for a moment I saw Mama standing there, looking down at me as when I was a small child, and my eyes filled with tears.

'I shall see you again soon, I think,' Nimue said, her voice reverting to its youthful lightness, 'so go with gladness, until we meet anon.'

The druid came forward then, along with a number of other Sanctuary folk, ready to escort me back down to the camp. But when we came down from the hill Bedivere and a small party of attendants were waiting beside the path that follows the river's course.

'Arthur and the Companions have gone on ahead to Sarum,' the lieutenant explained, carefully tying the bundle of my morning's clothes behind his saddle. 'The rest of the cavalcade is making the best time it can and will be camped at the foot of Sarum tomorrow. It's been arranged that you spend the night at the convent in Amesbury – if you're ready to go, that is,' he added.

I nodded and only then looked beyond him into the group of riders and mounts. There, amid the cluster of sturdy travel horses and warriors' steeds, stood the lovely white mare we'd seen at Chester. Her dark, lustrous eyes regarded me calmly, her long mane was plaited with ribbons and her hooves were as neat and polished as seaside shells. The reins were bedecked with bells and bronze bosses secured the halter. I gasped at the sight, and Bedivere gave me a crooked grin.

'Her name is Shadow and Arthur thought you would be

pleased,' he said. 'He wants the people to see by this gift how much he honours you, M'lady.'

I let the animal nuzzle my hand and hair, and admired the rich brocaded blanket that hung down on either side of the saddle. Tassels and bright fringes glowed in the afternoon sun, and when Bedivere lifted me to her back I felt as splendid as Etain the Beautiful herself.

We waved farewell to the druid and his party and began our trek towards the convent.

'What ever will the nuns say about my coming from the Sanctuary, decked out in all this pagan glory?' I asked, and Bedivere laughed.

'Very little, if they have any sense. Some things you don't tamper with, and the wedding of King and Queen is one of them! Surely they must know he is the Lord of the Land, and you are the living embodiment of the people. Besides, Brigit says not all Christians would be opposed to today's happenings.'

'You've talked with her, then?'

'With Brigit? Yes; we rode most of the way to the convent together.'

'Ah, she came out of the litter for you!' I was delighted at what certainly sounded like progress.

'It was just a morning's trip, and not too long, but it gave us a chance to chat. As you said, she's a remarkable woman.'

I was delighted, and made a silent little prayer to the Goddess for them before remembering how appalled Brigit would be. Ah well, if she could make Mama a saint, I could ask the Old Gods to look after her.

Amesbury is a tiny settlement named for Ambrosius Aurelius. An abbey has grown up on the bank of the Avon where the willows trail over the stream, and the choir which sings perpetually within the cloistered halls is one of the finest in the land. It amused me that so staunch a Christian centre should be associated with the king who had fathered Merlin, the greatest druid of all time.

The convent was a mixture of both Roman and Celtic skills. Although it was rectangular and divided into individual rooms, the thatch roof and wood interior made it cosy and pleasant. Bedivere allowed that there were many places being built like this, perhaps because it offered the best of both styles.

The people at the convent reflected a similar mixture of Roman discipline and Celtic naturalness. And they did not seem overly critical; Vinnie looked more askance at my day in the Sanctuary than the nuns did. But even she couldn't help admiring the mare and trappings Arthur had sent, and there was no argument when I said I wished to wear the white robe from the Sanctuary on my trip into Sarum next day.

We spent a quiet evening in my room talking about the journey now that it was almost over, and that led to reminiscences of earlier times.

'It's been a fine life you've shared with me,' Brigit said quietly, 'and I want you to know how much I've appreciated it.'

'Good heavens, it's not as though it were going to end now,' I said with a yawn. 'Why, I'll have as much need of your help now as ever I did in childhood.'

'Aye,' she answered slowly, plumping up the pillows. 'But it will be different from now on, M'lady. The wedding may still be a week away, but after you ride into Sarum tomorrow you'll belong to Arthur and the people, and there's no mistaking that.'

'Ride?' Vinnie piped up, suddenly taking notice of what we were saying. I had forgotten all about my promise to enter the city in the litter, and there was a sudden tension as the matron perceived that fact.

'I didn't even think to tell Arthur about it, and now

he's sent round that beautiful mare. What ever am I going to do?' I cried, seeing how distressed my governess was.

'You could let one of the men ride the horse, M'lady,' she suggested, 'while you are carried through the gates in a style that befits your station.'

'Now, Vinnie, that would never do,' Brigit scolded. 'You know how curious the people will be to see what their new queen looks like, and even with the curtains open they wouldn't catch more than a glimpse of her in the litter.'

Lavinia reached down to smooth the coverlet at the foot of my bed and I thought contritely of all the trouble she had gone to in having the litter made specially for this trip.

'I'm sure it will be very handy when M'lady's pregnant,' Brigit added gently. 'But you saw how beautiful she looked riding in here this evening with her hair long and flowing, and the horse prancing with fair pride to carry such a treasure. Surely the people should have a chance to see her for the first time that way too.'

'I suppose,' Vinnie agreed, then rounded on me imploringly. 'But you will promise to wear that dress, and not go skinning into a tunic and breeches at the last minute?'

'Ah, that I promise entirely.' I smiled, relieved that her feelings weren't more hurt. 'And as you've said often enough, from tomorrow on I'll be wearing dresses most all the time . . . I promise you that as well.'

My governess looked down at me with a mixture of fondness and exasperation and for a moment I thought she was going to lean down and kiss me good night, as Nonny would have. Instead she straightened her shoulders and muttered, 'It's about time,' then wished me good dreams and bustled from the room.

After everyone was in bed I thought of Brigit's comment about our lives' changing, and knew she was right.

The trip tomorrow was more than simply the last few miles of a long journey; it would be my first encounter with the people who from here on would think of me not as a person, but as their queen.

Regardless if that proved good or bad, there would be no changing it; I was embarking on a course from which there could be no turning back, and the finality of it loomed before me, fierce and unyielding.

With the sunrise my fate would be set. If ever there was a last chance to bolt and run, this was it; yet the thought held no attraction and I brushed it aside as childish nonsense.

Somehow, somewhere on the Road to Sarum my desire had shifted from a longing for freedom to the meeting of a challenge. And though I was awed by the magnitude of the change that was taking place and wondered how the people would accept me, there was nowhere I wanted to run to, nothing I wanted to avoid.

I was moving now with the structure of my moira as surely as if I were following the current of a river. The whisper of Kevin's litany circled round me: 'Of course you can . . . Heir to the great queens of the past, Celtic daughter of Rheged . . . of course you can.'

I smiled sleepily, hearing behind it all the message of the doire: I would marry Arthur because I was meant to be his wife . . . it really was as simple as that.

35
Sarum

The bells calling the nuns to Mass rang gently in the predawn hours, and I rose to join Brigit and Lavinia in the chapel. I had never attended a Christian rite before, but it seemed fitting and proper that as Britain's future Queen I should honour the different beliefs of the people, and this was a good place to begin.

The service was strange but not unpleasant, and when the priest offered a special prayer on behalf of the 'northern girl who comes to marry our king,' I wondered if he knew mine was among the veiled heads at the back of the chapel.

Afterwards we had a silent breakfast in the refectory, then returned to my room, where the simple white dress and ivy wreath hung waiting for the day to begin. By the time the sun was up I was mounted on the white mare and ready to leave.

Shadow sidled and pranced so that the bells on the bridle sent rills of music all about us like the benediction of gods long forgotten and still unknown. A light breeze of the sort that delights butterflies and honeybees slipped past and I lifted my face against its caress. The morning was undeniably beautiful.

At the last minute the abbess of the convent came hurrying across the paving stones gingerly carrying a large bouquet. The flowers, pure white and trumpet-shaped, were unfamiliar to me, and as she handed them up she explained they were lilies sacred to the Mother of God, and would bring me Her blessing. I thanked the woman for her thoughtfulness and carefully cradled the flowers in the crook of my arm.

The remarkableness of the day came home fully then: the meeting of north and south, Pagan and Christian, past and future. As in a bright counterpoint to Samhain, I could feel the division between mortal concerns and the eternals blur, as if the two realms overlapped and all things were possible, all contradictions acceptable. When Bedivere led the way through the convent gates, I was both calm and excited. It didn't even seem strange to be going to my new life crowned by pagan ivy and carrying the Christian seal of purity.

The river path was peaceful and quiet, and the few last-minute travellers moved to one side for us with a respectful nod or murmured greeting. But when we came clear of the woods and our destination loomed on the horizon, I caught my breath.

Sarum sits at the end of a high spur, a single white hill that rises smooth and glistening out of the surrounding plain. Around its base tents and camps and banners flourished in a sudden blaze of festivities, and they mingled and swirled through the campsites like birds along the Solway shore.

Word had spread that Arthur would welcome his bride this day, and as we came closer the crowd pressed in against the track, while children scrambled into nearby trees for a better view. Occasionally I recognized a face from the Road behind us, and here and there the banner of a Cumbrian contingent caught my eye, as reassuring as the smile of an old friend.

I asked Bedivere why Sarum's hill was so smooth, for even from this distance it was clear that its chalk sides had been stripped of any grass or vine or tree that might soften the outline.

'No point giving the enemy a handhold,' Bedivere said.

'To stand at the bottom of the ditch and stare upward at that smooth sheet of chalk is to be defeated before one even begins. Between the invincibility of the place and the fact that so many Roads meet here, it's a natural military centre. The town on top of it is fairly rough, I'm afraid, and not nearly so fine as Winchester; I hope you won't be disappointed.'

'But I can see pennants and banners flying from the towers,' I pointed out, and he laughed.

'That's for the wedding, M'lady. The people have decked it out like a Maypole to welcome you.'

'Oh, we must make sure they are part of the celebration too,' I replied, touched by their thoughtfulness.

'That's already taken care of,' Bedivere said with a grin, going on to explain there would be dancing and games and all the usual activities of a fair, and the wedding feast was to be open to all who wished to attend.

Bedivere also informed me that most of the guests had already arrived: Urien and Cador, the Cornish kings and the Queen Mother, Igraine. Morgan was apparently still on the Road, however.

Ahead of us there was a scudding motion like a cloud shadow ploughing across the plain. The crowd surged towards one particular spot and like everyone else I craned my neck and strained to see what was causing all the commotion. Then suddenly the throng opened and Arthur rode into view.

He came towards me on a fine black stallion with trappings of red and gold that were every bit as regal as those of my mare, and his garments were as simple in cut and material as my own, though his were bordered with the royal purple so dear to Roman hearts. The gold bracelets of a king's treasure adorned his arms, and Excalibur gleamed at his side. There was no mistaking either the man or his rank this time.

411

Merlin rode beside him, tall and elegant in black and silver.

Behind them Cei glittered with jewellery and bright colours as he wheeled his horse from side to side. I smiled to myself: in spite of his reputation for pinchpenny ways, the Seneschal's love of pomp and display was evident, and he seemed to be enjoying the occasion very much.

There were others in the train that followed: Gawain and his brother, Agricola wearing his ornate belt, and beyond them came Palomides. They were closing on us now and when I looked back to Arthur I found him staring at me with that wide, level gaze of his.

Merlin said something and turned aside, and Bedivere dropped back also, leaving just Arthur and me alone to pace proudly towards our fate.

The crowd fell silent, as though holding its breath, and all eyes watched us intently. We looked neither to right nor to left, but only at each other as the distance between us slowly closed.

Time shifted in its warp, and with each step I saw a different man before me: solemn, boyish, exuberant, thoughtful, battle-weary, optimistic, puzzled, powerful, grieving, majestic . . . as though Arthur embodied the whole range of human nature. We were being drawn steadily together by an invisible web and when he reached me I extended my hand, still without dropping my eyes.

He raised my fingers to his lips: then a fine, laughing smile lit his face and he turned his attention back to the crowd. With one eloquent gesture he offered me to the people and them to me.

The tension broke within me, overflowing in waves of love for him, for the multitude, for life itself, and I too turned to the throng.

A roar went up around us and even Merlin smiled. We made our way to the front of the procession still holding

412

hands, the horses pacing evenly and in perfect step while the people fell away before us with smiles and tears.

And so we traversed the last mile to the entrance of Sarum, smiling at each other and our subjects.

The town was as crowded as the Road had been, and the acrobats from the trip greeted us at the gates, spinning and leaping at the head of the procession while the drummers and pipers kept time with a merry tune. Everywhere there was shouting and cheering, and we waved and laughed and let the joy of the people carry us along.

Bedivere had been right about the town, for it was obviously more military outpost than fancy city. But the people had put up bunting and hung banners, and window boxes overflowed with flowers. Baskets had been hung from the corners of eaves and filled with blossoming plants brought in from wood and meadow for the occasion. The effect was one of riotous gaiety rather than thought-out elegance, and was the more dear because of it.

The wave of celebration swept around us and everywhere I looked the faces were wreathed with smiles and goodwill.

At the Square a Roman building had been turned over to Arthur and the Dragon Banner hung resplendent before the door. This would serve as headquarters and main Hall, with one room put aside for Arthur's personal use, while the Queen Mother and I were to be lodged in separate buildings nearby.

'I thought you might want some privacy, so I didn't put the two of you under the same roof,' Arthur explained as we passed the house where Igraine was staying. 'She expects you to call on her this afternoon, however.'

Smiling gaily, I glanced up at the window and saw a

413

shadowed figure behind the pane. Half-remembered stories of the sorcery and mystery that clung to Arthur's origins rose dreamlike round Igraine's name.

The masses of people behind us swelled out across the open Square, hurrying us along. Arthur turned down a narrow lane, to a house set well away from the noise and bustle of the Square. Here the High King called a halt and everything fell silent.

I blinked at the half-timber building, suddenly wondering what I was doing here. It was one thing to embark on a trip down the length of Britain, and quite another to come to a stop at so solid a destination. I had the giddy sense of slipping across ice and looked at Arthur for some reassurance, but he lifted me down from the horse without meeting my eyes.

The room we entered was large and comfortable. The hearth was at one end instead of in the centre of the floor, but the fresh rushes and newly plumped cushions made it familiar and homey. A pair of glazed windows let in a good light, and cupboards had been built around them, creating a niche with a padded seat under each opening. The lot was well supported by heavy beams, and though it was smaller, the richness of wood and alcoves made me think of the Great Hall at Appleby.

Vinnie began checking the cupboards while Brigit and Bedivere organized the unloading of the pack animals and Arthur guided me wordlessly to a window seat where we'd be out of the way.

'I hope you'll find it comfortable, since it's the best we could do under the circumstances,' he said awkwardly. His voice was stiff and formal, and I glanced at him sharply. Perhaps he too was feeling edgy and unsure.

'Have you heard me complain?' I asked.

'No, I guess I haven't,' he answered slowly. 'But it can't be half so elegant as you must have expected.'

414

The room was filling up with draymen and servants and people helping with our baggage, yet in spite of all the confusion a very special feeling was emerging, as though this were a place that had sheltered me all of my life. It was trustworthy and solid and to be appreciated just as it was, and I suddenly felt safe and happy and secure.

When I looked back at Arthur, I saw him in the same way: comfortable and familiar and very much to be trusted. He might also be lively, exciting, energetic and full of surprises, but on a level I could not question I knew him as thoroughly as I'd ever known anyone and found him to be as real and honest as the bolster we both sat on. Even his present shyness was understandable and the last of my doubts vanished with that knowledge.

'What I expect is to be with you,' I said slowly and deliberately, wanting him to see I was making my pledge without reserve or hesitation. 'Whether in a tent or a fortress, Roman hall or thatched roundhouse. It is you I am marrying, not the setting. And I will always choose to be with you, even in the roughest circumstance, rather than be set apart in some elegant but pointless "women's quarter."'

'I should have known,' he said with an embarrassed chuckle, 'and I apologize. If I treat you like some prissy stranger again, just remind me about Celtic queens.'

Relief was plain in his voice and face, and he rushed on to matters of practicality. He explained that we should plan to stay at Sarum for a week after the wedding, then move up to Caerleon till harvest time.

'They have some great horse lines there and the facilities for training are excellent. It would be a good time to start work on the cavalry,' he concluded.

I listened with growing bewilderment, wondering if he had even heard what I had said. I had just given over my life and freedom to him, and all he could talk about was horses!

Disappointment clawed at me and I struggled to put it aside, telling myself it was foolish to expect him to understand Cumbri ways. Perhaps he didn't realize I was making my vows to him; or knowing, preferred to wait for another time to give me his own pledge. This was not, after all, the most private of circumstances.

The broad assortment of our luggage was beginning to pile up around the edges of the room, and Vinnie fluttered about, pointing to this corner or that as the men brought more bundles through the door. Arthur glanced out the window to the street.

'That mob's so thick I can't even walk back to the Square,' he grumbled, 'and there's all manner of things to look after. With all these extra people it's as chaotic as preparing a military campaign. Worse, in fact,' he averred with a grimace.

'Is there anything I can do to help?' I asked, getting to my feet with him. The jumble of the day's emotions was threatening to exhaust me and I tried to focus on what would be expected from me in the near future.

A page came trotting in carrying a leather satchel, and recognizing the King, forgot to look where he was going. He collided with Lavinia, and there followed a flurry of indignant sputters and hasty apologies. Arthur was chewing on the end of his moustache and stared at it all as absently as if nothing had happened.

He sighed and shook his head. 'Outside of taking care of whatever you need to do for the wedding, I can't think of anything specific,' he said vaguely, then brightened as someone went through a door at the end of the room. 'I'm sure Ulfin said there was a back way out of this building.'

With that he dragged me through the kitchen and out

416

into a small garden that was planted with herbs and vegetables. A pear tree had been trained flat against the far wall. Arthur's spirits suddenly revived.

'With all the people to take care of at court, I doubt I'll get back to see you again today. But why don't I bring the dogs around tomorrow and we'll take them for a run?'

I nodded and accepted the hasty kiss he planted on my cheek, then watched him swing up into the branches of the tree and balance for a moment against the sky before he jumped down on the other side.

The idea of running away from one's subjects seemed outrageous to me, and I was both amused and shocked. Like so many other things it was full of contradictions, and the best I could do was shake my head and laugh as I returned to the house to prepare for my meeting with the Queen Mother.

36

Queen Igraine

'I can't find anything,' Vinnie wailed, standing in the middle of the bedroom and surveying the chaos of half-open baskets. 'I'm sure I put it in one of the hazel panniers!'

'It's all right, Vinnie, really it is,' I told her, running my hands along the plain wool girdle that graced the dark green dress. 'I'm more comfortable this way; it's only an afternoon chat, don't forget, not a formal audience.'

'Even so, you should be wearing your best,' my chaperone retorted, pawing through the jumbled contents of another hamper in her search for the silk belt with the little bells.

'At least,' she added, triumphantly hauling out Mama's jewel box, 'you can wear the gold fillet.'

Weariness and nerves were making me testy, and I took a deep breath to steady myself.

'Vinnie, there'll be a far greater crown placed on my head soon enough, and there's no point in hurrying matters.'

I didn't want to risk offending my future mother-in-law by flaunting my status, so in spite of Vinnie's protests, when Ulfin came to get me my hair was simply tied back with a ribbon. I felt a flutter of apprehension when I remembered he was Chamberlain of the Wardrobe, but he smiled approvingly and offered me his arm.

As we crossed the main room I spotted the lilies I had carried into Sarum that morning and hastily grabbed them up, vase and all.

'Does Her Highness like flowers?' I asked hopefully.

'I think she will today,' Ulfin said in an understated way that reminded me of Griflet.

So I marched out the door holding the flowers before me, trying to keep from spilling the water down the front of my dress.

After a minute Ulfin reached over and with a solicitous 'M'lady,' took the vase and carefully poured the water out on the cobbled street. 'They won't wilt between here and there,' he said, handing them back to me.

The Square had quieted considerably since the morning's excitement, though all manner of people lounged about in little groups. A cobbler with a shop on the corner looked up from his work and nodded as we approached. He eyed me curiously, as though trying to remember who I was, then with a shrug went back to his tapping, the bristle of tacks still carefully held between his lips. I remembered Rhufon setting me to look for a tack I had dropped once, with the admonition that one doesn't get careless with a commodity that's so hard to come by. 'Learn from a cobbler,' he'd said; 'they're the tightest-lipped people in the world.'

A flurry of questions hammered in my head as we passed: Would Igraine be friendly or aloof, resentful or critical or condescending? Had she watched my entrance and remembered the days of her youth, her years as High Queen at the side of a vigorous king? Would she view me as a stranger from a backward country who threatened to usurp her place in the hearts of the people? Arthur had said so little about her, I had no idea what to expect; the best I could do was try to remember the cobbler and keep my mouth shut.

At the Queen Mother's house, the door flew open before Ulfin had time to knock. The servant girl who stood there was all eyes and curiosity, and she couldn't decide whether to curtsy while I stood on the doorstep or wait until we had come inside. I smiled at her as reassuringly as I could, wondering which of us was more nervous: she in confronting me, or I in confronting Igraine.

The Queen Mother's quarters were much like my own, homey and unpretentious, and I noticed that she had done nothing to change them. Except for an ornate brazier, which even on this balmy afternoon glowed with fragrant embers of apple wood, the furnishings were undoubtedly those which normally filled the room.

Igraine was warming her hands at the brazier and she turned to stare at me as Ulfin and I approached.

She was a tall, regal woman, and the structure of her youthful beauty still showed beneath the parchment skin. Her hair, once fabled to be bright as gold, was silver now and mostly hidden by the black veil of her widowhood, and her dress was of sedate brown homespun. I was doubly glad I was not more formally gowned, for I should have felt a sorry upstart in anything fancier than what I wore.

Ulfin made the formal presentation and Arthur's mother watched me carefully, as though she were searching for the very heart of my soul. She might not have raised him, but it was obvious where her son came by his habit of looking the world fairly and directly in the face.

'These are from Amesbury,' I said hastily, making a deep curtsy and offering up the lilies. 'But they need some water.'

Igraine's eyebrows lifted slightly and she glanced over at Ulfin as though puzzled by what she had just heard.

'Well, get up, child. We can't remedy that while you're balancing halfway through a curtsy,' she said.

Red-faced, I scrambled back to my feet. The serving girl hurried forward and relieved me of the vase, then headed off towards the kitchen.

There were three chairs drawn up near a small table

and after Igraine was seated she gestured us to the other two.

'Would you like to have tea?' she asked, and this time it was my turn to look inquiringly at Ulfin.

'Chamomile tea,' she went on, not waiting for Ulfin to interpret. 'It's good for the blood, and quite tasty with a biscuit or two.'

I nodded my assent, feeling a silly fool. When the girl returned to put the flowers on the window ledge Igraine told her we would all take tea.

The presence of this august woman filled the room and I sat in silence while she and Ulfin conversed. They discussed the weather, the newest arrivals for the wedding and the fact that Morgan's party had not yet made an appearance. I stared at the long petals of the flowers, which glowed in the afternoon light with an impeccable whiteness, and wondered uneasily where this visit was going.

The tea was pleasant, but I found the biscuits to be odd little pillow things in a thick, brown crust. I munched my way through one cautiously, hoping it was the proper thing to do. I noticed the Queen Mother ate nothing, although she drank a cup of tea.

'They are delicious,' I told her when I had finished the little bun. 'But what are they? They are so . . . different.'

'Biscuits. Wheat biscuits,' Igraine said. Then, recognizing my confusion, she added, 'You were raised on good solid oat bread and barley, weren't you?'

When I nodded she leaned forward and carefully taking up one of the warm biscuits, very gently pulled it open. The crust tore with a crisp crunchiness and the bread inside stretched and seemed to expand as the layers slowly lifted apart. It looked like clouds caught within the golden casing of the outside, and I watched fascinated as she turned the two halves over and put them, crust down, on my plate. 'Only wheat does that,' she said. 'Now, try some honey on it and see if it isn't even more delicious.'

I did as I was told, drizzling the dark amber sweetness across the peaks and valleys of the bread and licking my fingers afterwards to make sure they weren't sticky.

When everyone had finished the tea tray was cleared away, although Igraine asked that the pot be left for us. Our companions were dismissed and the real encounter began.

'I understand you went to Mass this morning,' the Queen Mother said, making it a statement rather than a question as she picked up her teacup and curled her fingers around its bowl.

'Yes, Ma'am,' I replied stiffly, wondering how she knew.

'There's not much that escapes the wings of gossip in a High King's court, and that bit of news arrived in Sarum before you did. Were you born a Christian? Somehow I was under the impression that the people of Rheged had returned to Paganism.'

Her expression was one of polite neutrality, and although her tone was authoritative, I could not tell what her emotions were.

'I was raised in the Old Ways,' I ventured, 'but my foster sister was born a Christian, and my governess too. So I am not unfamiliar with the teachings of the White Christ.'

'That's good,' Igraine responded with a nod. 'You have no idea what terrible notions some people have about the Roman Church. I was hoping you would not come to the throne unduly prejudiced against it. I would never force my beliefs on another, but I hope, if you should ever need it, you could look to the Church for help. It has been a great solace for me, child. Particularly now, when I no

422

longer have a role to fill at court. Have they told you I live at a convent?'

'I had heard something to that effect,' I temporized.

The regal glance shifted to the flowers and she smiled slightly, though whether at my gift or at some inner thought of her own I couldn't tell. 'It's a very quiet, humble little place set within the curve of a small and unimportant river. My cell is shaded by a willow, which plays host to all manner of warblers; I haven't heard a trumpet, or seen a banner, or faced a crowd for more than four years now.'

'Oh, M'lady,' I said quickly, 'if you would like to come back, I'm sure there'll always be a position for you at Arthur's court, and he would want you to know that too.'

'Aye, and there's an equal place for me with Morgause in the Orkneys.' The flash of Igraine's response surprised me. 'Or possibly in Urien's court if Morgan ever gives up her priesthood and goes back to being a wife and queen. That is not a problem, my dear. After a lifetime of drama and majesty, with the surf pounding endlessly at Tintagel and the wind whipping up storms of every kind around King Uther, it's a pleasure to curl up in a small nest and be all but unrecognized.'

The Queen Mother was speaking freely now, in a relaxed manner, as though glad for a chance to talk with someone.

'I lost interest in court life long before my husband's death, and was relieved when Arthur did not expect me to stay on after his Coronation. My son and I are almost strangers, you know,' she added with a pause that might have been a sigh.

I started to say something, but she overrode me.

'No, I vastly prefer my little niche at the bend of the river to the tempestuous power of a royal household. The problem has not been what to do with a retired queen, but rather how to find a new one. For the most part people don't understand about queens. I'm sure every woman thinks she could be one, if given a chance, but very few are really equipped for it. I suppose what I am trying to say,' she added, jumping directly to the heart of the matter, 'is that I feel confident you will do a fine job . . . probably far better than I did.'

'What ever makes you think so?' I exclaimed, stunned by her unexpected endorsement.

She looked at me again, and this time there was a humour in her manner that I had not seen before. 'To begin with, there's no pretence or falseness about you; you are exactly what you are. And the people like that. They always see through pretence sooner or later. But more important, I watched you this morning, my dear. You were riding on that crest of excitement which comes with the first discovery of queenhood. The glory and wonder carry you along with them at first, and a certain majesty sustains you later, even when you are too weary to wish it. Or at least, it does if you're both strong and lucky,' she added, looking back at the brazier.

'It takes a particular kind of person to enjoy it. It helps if you are raised for it; bred to it, you might say. If you come to it as the consequence of passion, that's quite another matter. I was afraid that Arthur might pick some pretty but empty-headed little commoner who would love the notion of being queen without any concept of what it requires. Or that you would turn out to be an infatuated girl, full of romantic notions that would only break your heart later on, and cause no end of trouble once the honeymoon was over.'

Igraine was half-lecturing, half-reminiscing now, as if wanting to share a wisdom gained through hard experience.

She paused and stretching out her hand, felt the side of

the teapot to see if it was still warm. When I reached forward to lift it for her, she nodded and extended her cup, and after both cups were filled she leaned back in her chair again and went on.

'Then Arthur arrived night before last, raving about his bride-to-be, and I began to wonder if he was the infatuated one. He was full of talk about your horsemanship, and something called a stirrup, and how you took an interest in everything and everyone. He couldn't stop talking about all those qualities he was so pleased with, and I thought, Well, at least he's well satisfied. And that's important.'

Again there was a pause, but this time when she resumed she was looking directly at me.

'Arthur told me the people adore you already, and that's a good start. But that didn't tell me how you felt about them. So I stood here in the window this morning, waiting to see what you would be like.'

She raised her teacup and I caught a hint of amusement in her eyes as she stared at me over the rim. 'I think I half-expected to see a homely, gawking, horsey girl buffeted by that noisy mob and all but scared out of her wits. And instead I looked down on a handsome young woman who radiated back to the people the same devotion she was offered. One feels you love them every bit as much as they love you, and if that's so, it will make your task much easier. It is very difficult to be a High Queen if one is shy or private by nature,' she added very softly.

The Queen Mother put down her cup and folded her hands serenely in her lap as though she had forgotten my presence. But when she finally looked up, it was with a bright and twinkling smile.

'I could wish you no better wedding gift, my dear, but that you love the very thing your moira dictates. Better that than a grand passion, or a great ambition, or total devotion to another person. It would seem that the people are well blessed to have you for their queen, and you are blessed by nature with an enjoyment of your fate. And Arthur . . . well, whether he recognizes it or not, he is most fortunate of all.'

She laughed gently as though at the blindness of men, and I found myself laughing with her.

After that she insisted it was her turn to do the listening, and proceeded to draw me out about all manner of things in my life, both past and present. I told her about Mama, and Rheged, Kaethi and Nonny, Featherfoot and Ailbe, and of course Vinnie and Brigit and my father. We talked the afternoon away, and she insisted on sending a message to my house saying I'd be dining with her that evening.

For a woman who had renounced the world in favour of living in a convent she had a wonderfully quick grasp of human nature, and her assessments were shrewd and realistic.

'You were lucky, child,' she said when I told her of King Mark's inquiries into my availability for marriage. 'I've known Mark for many a year, and I would not wish any woman to his bed. He is a braggart and a coward, unloved by his people and unloving as well. So far no woman has met all his qualifications, and I doubt one ever will. Although,' she added with a mischievous smile, 'if I were Pagan still, I'd be inclined to think the Goddess will entangle him in his own net of demands, and in his old age turn him into the plaything for some young slip of a girl. It has happened before, goodness knows, and when a man starts seeking a wife who is young enough to be his own child, there's something chancy likely to happen somewhere along the line.'

The one subject I did not mention was Kevin or our encounter with the Lady, and though I was curious about both Morgan and Morgause, I hesitated to bring the subject up. I found it both pleasant and exciting to converse with this bright-eyed woman about so many things and didn't want anything to create tension for either of us. So I was unprepared when she brought the subject up herself.

'Have you been introduced to my daughter Morgan yet?' she asked suddenly. I shook my head. 'Well, no matter; it will come about soon enough. Morgan is rather . . . difficult . . . she's a hard person to understand. Oh, not that she's intentionally cruel or makes mischief the way Morgause does . . . no, I don't think one could call Morgan even consciously manipulative. Morgan gets into trouble because of the way she expresses her convictions. She's a deeply religious, fundamental, conservative Pagan with no time or patience for anyone who doesn't recognize the beliefs that she finds self-evident. She probably doesn't think the rest of us are deliberately evil . . . just too blind or stubborn to open our hearts to the Old Gods and accept Their grace. I'm sure she doesn't realize how much she puts people off.' Igraine sighed. 'Ah well, I suppose that's the problem with trying to make others follow your own beliefs: what starts out as spiritual ardour too often becomes arrogance and bigotry.'

I marvelled at the clarity with which Igraine tried to understand her daughter and thanked the Queen Mother for sharing her insight with me.

'Well, perhaps it will be a little easier for you if you're forewarned,' she responded.

I would have liked to hear about Morgause as well, but the soft spring twilight was deepening to dusk and I had to take my leave.

'My dear,' Igraine said, holding both my hands in hers and smiling sweetly, 'it's been years since I've chatted like this with a young woman. Uther sent my daughters away when they were not yet as old as you, so I missed the joy of seeing them move between maidenhood and queen-ship. I am delighted we've had such a nice visit, and I hope you've enjoyed it as much as I.'

'Oh yes,' I said, 'and I'll look forward to next time.'

On Igraine's insistence, Ulfin fetched a long cape for me, as I had not come prepared to stay so late. It was an elegant garment, richly trimmed with fur.

'Don't let her get chilled,' the Queen Mother admonished as he draped it over my shoulders. When I started to protest she laughed slightly. 'Our southern weather can be quite fickle, child, and it wouldn't do to have you go to your wedding with the sniffles.'

So I thanked her warmly, and on the way home I commented on how much more friendly she had been than I'd expected. Ulfin glanced over at me and chuckled.

'It's not her usual way, M'lady. She seems to have taken a real fancy to you, and there's many who'd say that's about the finest compliment you could have.'

We passed a tavern where the merrymakers overflowed on to the Square boasting and swearing and raising their drinking horns in endless toasts to their king. Not so different from the north, I thought, where it was well known that a Celt would relish any excuse to draw another cup from the cask. I wondered where Arthur was, and if he would be as pleased about the outcome of my visit with his mother as I was.

37

Palomides

'It's so nice not to be swaying along in that litter.' Brigit smiled over breakfast next morning. 'I couldn't believe how good it felt to wake up knowing we didn't have to *go* anywhere today!'

Vinnie and I agreed wholeheartedly, and we all concluded that sleeping late this morning had been a luxury well earned.

'Besides,' sighed the matron, surveying the remaining piles of luggage, 'it's only fair that we gather our strength when we can; it will take us days to get unpacked.'

'Just as long as we know where the dress is by Sunday,' I teased, stretching lazily and wiggling my toes against the rushes under the table. With all the time and work that had gone into the making of the wedding gown, I was quite confident Lavinia knew exactly where it was packed.

Back when the marriage was first agreed to, Vinnie had insisted I should wear white silk for the ceremony and had offered her own wedding dress for the cause. It had been her mother's bridal garment as well, and over the years the colour had mellowed to soft ivory, but the texture and sheen were still unmistakably those of silk. The dress itself had proved to be far too short, and the voluminous folds of the antique style hung like a tent on my lanky frame, but Vinnie and Brigit had taken it all apart and created a totally new garment. The braids and buckles, pieces of brocade and bits of lace that Vinnie had saved from Mama's fancier wardrobe were brought out and reassessed, and hours were spent embroidering the undergarment with flowers and birds and other symbols of fertility. The result was one of the finest gowns imaginable. I remembered Vinnie's determination to turn me into a 'proper Queen fit for any court' and was glad she had persevered.

We were still chatting about the wedding plans when Bedivere arrived with an invitation for all of us to come see Palomides demonstrate his riding technique. Vinnie wasn't interested, and Brigit demurred on the grounds that there was too much work to do, but I whisked into a dress and was ready in no time.

Sarum's flat top is quite sizable, and once we passed beyond the cluster of buildings and the fringe of kitchen gardens, a large green meadow spread out before us.

'There's not room enough for everyone in the main Hall,' Bedivere commented as we approached a circle of tents on the far edge of the grass. 'So a number of the Companions are camping here – close enough to be handy if Arthur needs them, but far enough away to stay out from underfoot. Don't forget, warriors and courtiers aren't the same beasts; they're more like dogs and cats, what with the soldier wanting to be out working and the noble looking for the soft spot by the fire. In this case it seemed best to let the visiting royalty share the Hall while the Companions rough it as usual.'

In Rheged the warrior and the noble were one and the same, and I pointed out to Bedivere that I thought that a much fairer arrangement.

'Oh, I quite agree,' my escort answered hastily. 'That's exactly the way Arthur and I were raised. But somehow, here in the south, there's grown up a class of privileged leaders left over from the bureaucracy of the Empire who do battle among themselves politically but don't bear arms in the common defence. They claim they are administrators, not warriors, and every southern king has to cope with them. They expect to be supported by others,

430

and give themselves as much power as possible. Arthur's trying to bring people around to the idea that the common good is more important than individual advantage, but the courtiers don't take well to the notion.'

I nodded, thinking that between his efforts to tame the wilder northern Celts and bring some sort of social consciousness to the decadent southerners, Arthur had his work cut out for him.

Beyond the tents a stand of trees denoted the presence of water and a small crowd of people had already gathered in its shade. The townsfolk were on foot, but the kings and warriors from the camps on the plain had arrived on their horses, and now they fanned out around a dirt patch that no doubt served as drill grounds for the men who regularly defended Sarum.

We made our way into the gathering and headed for a raised platform where Arthur and some of the Companions were taking their seats.

'Glad you could come.' My bridegroom beamed as he patted a place beside him on the bench, then looked past me to Bedivere. 'Why don't you introduce the boy, since you know best what he can do?'

Bedivere nodded and went to find Palomides, and Arthur turned back to his discussion with Gawain while I stared about at the people.

They covered the range of rulers, from the brightly dressed dandies of the south to the plaid-draped men of the Highlands. There were silk brocade and linen and homespun and old leather in great abundance, and their horses were just as diverse: stocky Celtic ponies from the north, big Shires from the Pennines and the elegant Welsh Mountain Ponies, like Featherfoot, from Caesar's own Oriental stud. Like their riders, they reflected the variety of men and cultures Arthur was trying to hold together.

Between the groups of gaudy warriors the common

people mingled, dressed in all the natural shades of homespun, with here and there a bright scarf or jaunty cap. A husky milkmaid had set up a stand with a wheel of cheese on it and was doing a steady business. An older woman, her greying hair wisping untidily out of the bun on the top of her head, carried a tray of breads through the throng, hawking her biscuits and portions of loaves with a harassed good nature. I wondered if the two boys who dodged in and out of the assemblage offering onions for sale were part of her brood, for they had the same ragged air and bright smile as she did.

Bedivere and Palomides rode into the centre of the oval, and Bedivere raised his arm for attention.

'I bring you Palomides of Ribchester,' Arthur's foster brother called out, his voice carrying well on the soft spring air. 'Where he comes from, the horsemen use a special kind of tack, and that innovation, so simple but oh, so effective, gives him a tremendous advantage. Watch him now, and see what can be done.'

Palomides looked nervously about the group, and it occurred to me the boy must be under tremendous pressure. A young foreigner not even experienced in court ways, he was being made the centre of all attention, and I wondered if we were doing him a disservice in exposing him to this sudden change.

He saluted Arthur formally, but though the High King nodded back, he didn't interrupt his conversation with Gawain. So I raised my own hand in salute, waving my scarf back and forth to be sure that Palomides saw me, and when I had captured his attention, I gave him the old Roman 'thumbs up' sign and a big grin.

With a flash of recognition and a broad smile he tossed his head back and surveyed the crowd, an eagle about to take wing. On command his horse moved out in loping strides and Palomides rose in his stirrups and went the length of the course balanced well above the animal's back. The crowd buzzed and murmured, watching curiously and commenting to itself, and the lad turned and came back down the oval, this time crouching low on one side, his purchase on his mount still secured by the leather loops.

A ripple of response ran along the course, and even Arthur turned away from Gawain to watch the exhibition. The boy went through the rest of his routine, and with each new manoeuvre the crowd grew more excited, clapping in appreciation as he went past them.

Then Bedivere joined him on the field, carrying two shields and a pair of lances from Ribchester, and gave a set to Palomides when they met. The crowd hushed while the horsemen withdrew to opposite ends of the oval, and turning, rushed at each other head on. The first time was a clean pass, with the horses holding firmly to the line and neither shying from the other, but passing with barely a foot between them. It was so smoothly done, I suspected that the two riders had been practising in secret.

When each had reached the far end of the track they turned and headed back at full gallop. The onlookers were watching avidly as the opponents couched their lances. The drumming of hooves was thunderous, and when they met there was a crack and thud that shook one's bones. Each man took the blow on his shield; but while Palomides kept his balance, the unstirruped Bedivere went sailing, none too gracefully, off his horse's rump.

The crowd gasped at seeing Bedivere so quickly put at the stranger's mercy, and there was a moment of tension while Palomides came back to the centre of the oval and kicking his feet free of the straps, leapt lightly to the ground beside his fallen friend. Arthur's lieutenant got shakily to his feet and embraced the boy, pounding him on the back and grinning as they turned to face the reviewing stand together. The onlookers, now thoroughly impressed, roared their approval, and after a deep bow Palomides turned back to his mount and swung easily up into the saddle.

The movement caught the audience by surprise, and at Bedivere's urging Palomides repeated it, leaping to the ground and then remounting without any assistance. Pandemonium broke out among the spectators. With a rush of excitement and clamouring voices, everyone converged on the pair to get a better look at the stirrups, and Bedivere had to call on a trumpeter to get the people's attention for Arthur.

'We have already modified several saddles,' the High King told them, obviously pleased by the reception of this new idea, 'and I invite every mounted warrior to try them for himself. It's an easy change to make to your own tack, but you should try it first, to be sure you want it.'

Most of the warriors had dismounted and all were trying to examine the stirrups at once. Gawain spoke briefly with Palomides and became the first to have a go at riding with them.

'If they accept it,' Arthur said, as much to himself as to me, 'we may have just secured Britain for the British!'

He turned and looked at me with a grin and pointed over to the greenwood where Griflet and the dogs were lounging.

'How about a walk?' he suggested, taking my elbow and helping me down off the platform.

'Sure,' I responded, waving to Ulfin's son as we headed across the grass. The boy was leaning against a tree, casually peeling something with his dagger, and he waved back as we approached.

'How goes it?' Arthur asked, nodding to the lad and squatting down to tousle the heads of the two pups. The animals wriggled close in against him, vying for his attention.

'Couldn't be better,' Griflet averred, carving a chunk from the onion he was holding. Spearing it with the point of his knife, he popped it into his mouth and began munching happily. 'It may not be as fancy as Winchester, but it's certainly a fine place for a picnic.'

Arthur laughed and got to his feet, and the pups exploded in a frenzy of wagging tails and excited prancing. We relieved Griflet of his charges and once we got their leashes untangled, headed through the patch of wood.

'How was your visit with the Queen Mother?' Arthur asked as we came out from under the trees.

'It went very well,' I assured him, stopping to wait while Cabal squatted in the weeds. 'She's a very dear person. It's a pity the two of you haven't had a chance to get to know each other.'

Arthur squinted up at the sun, and seemed to be calculating the direction of the wind. 'Hmmmmm,' he said noncommittally.

And that was that. We went on walking, the dogs went on sniffing and snuffling and marking the area, the conversation slid around the thin ice of an emotional subject and I told myself to stay out of the Pendragon family affairs. They were far too complex and uncomfortable for me to fathom, and it only seemed to make Arthur more distant when I brought them up. Clearly things would be smoother if I avoided the matter altogether.

'And how is it with you?' I inquired, slipping my arm through Arthur's and letting the mood of the day wrap us in leisure.

He grinned and sighed, and gave me one of his sidewise looks.

'Well, outside of the fact that we have half the country bivouacked on our doorstep, I guess everything is fine.'

435

Arthur laughed then and looked down at me. 'I know they think they're paying us homage, but they're also presenting a terrible headache!'

I laughed with him, appreciating the irony of the situation. We loosed the pups from their leads and found a comfortable spot to plop down in. I sat with my back against a stump, in the wind shadow of the rampart, and let the warmth of the sun soak in. Arthur threw himself down nearby, then turned so as to rest his head against my belly and continued his appraisal of the sky.

The pearly mirage of a cloud was sailing majestically overhead, and I told him about the merchant ship that had got stuck in the sand of the Morecambe when I was a child.

'Sounds like the ships that used to come to London,' he said thoughtfully. 'I hear the Saxons don't trade with the Mediterranean lands, so the big ships no longer ply the Thames, but in the old days they used to be tied up three deep along the wharves. Now they only occasionally find their way to the wealthy princes along the Welsh coast.'

I tried to imagine several of those giant boats in one spot, but the notion of it seemed totally improbable. I sighed and let my hand move smoothly across Arthur's brow and idly twine through his hair while we chatted.

The dogs made their way over to us and threw themselves down, one on each side. Cabal moved into the shelter of Arthur's arm and curled up comfortably there, while Caesar sat at attention on the other side of me, guarding us much as Ailbe might have. Not even the presence of a large and noisy bumblebee could lure him away, for he only snapped at it once and shook his head quizzically. Altogether it was a peaceful summer idyll, and I thought lazily of days and years to come spent in this kind of gentle luxury, as though it could go on forever.

When we rejoined the group at the drill field Arthur handed me the leashes, said something about having dinner together, then vanished in the direction of the encampment of the Companions. Most of the riders had left the field, heading down to their camps with the news about stirrups, and the freemen were wending their way back to town along the path across the meadow. I glanced at the stragglers by the edge of the trees and found the buxom cheese girl flirting outrageously with Griflet as she packed up her wares.

'If you'll keep hold of the dogs, M'lady, I can help carry Frieda's things,' he announced hopefully as I joined them.

The blond girl glanced at me archly, obviously piqued at my intrusion, but as Griflet's words sank in her look changed to one of open curiosity.

'You one of the nobles come for the wedding?' she asked.

'She's the bride,' Griflet said quickly, caught between being scandalized at her ignorance and wanting to impress her with the importance of his connections.

The girl flushed and bobbed a half-curtsy, and I grinned and reached out to take a small hamper from the load of things she was trying to manage.

'That's all right, Frieda, you couldn't be expected to know. You have a lovely name . . . are you Saxon?' I asked, equally curious about her.

'Ja,' she acknowledged, hefting the remains of the cheese on to her hip as Griflet picked up her folding table. 'There's many around these parts that are,' she observed.

'And Saxon women are known for their beauty,' I went on, remembering the story of Vortigern's marriage to the daughter of the mercenary leader he had invited into Britain. 'Even the old tyrant was captivated, and made Rowena his queen.'

437

'I'm not highborn,' the girl put in hastily. 'We're a good strong family among the Federates, and been loyal to the High King all these generations,' she added proudly.

We made our way single file past a stand of nettles, and when the path broadened out again Frieda was watching me intently. 'Without meaning to be rude, Ma'am . . . what is the High King like?' she asked suddenly.

Her bluntness caught me off guard, and for a moment I was tempted to answer her with the same open frankness, admitting that I knew as little of him as she did, at least where the inner things were concerned. Instead, I shrugged and gave her a general answer which was as honest as the other would have been.

'He's loyal and fair and always, always thinks of his people first.'

'Doesn't that make it dull for you?' she asked, much to Griflet's horror.

Not if you've been raised to be a queen, I thought, remembering Igraine's words.

We had come to a stop at the foot of my street and I looked at my fair-haired inquisitor and smiled. She stood sturdy in the noonday sun, determined to assess for herself just what the young King and Queen were all about, and I admired her forthrightness.

'Dull?' I repeated. 'Not really, because he's always so excited about ways to improve things and plans to make life better for everyone. And,' I added, seeing her look of scepticism deepening, 'he does know how to have fun.'

That was something the girl could understand, and she chuckled roundly. We all laughed together, and when we parted I took the dogs with me, since Griflet still had his hands full of Frieda's table and hamper.

Frieda made a full curtsy and wished me the best of luck for the wedding, and I thanked her and thought how different she was from what I had expected Saxons to be.

The more I grew to know Arthur and his countrymen, the more interesting they seemed, and I ran up the stairs to the house with the happy conviction that being High Queen of Britain was going to be much more enjoyable than I had imagined.

38
King Mark

The bright web of the afternoon's mood started to fray
and tangle before evening as intimations of darker, more
sinister shadows gradually intruded on my idyll.

When we stopped to escort Igraine to the Hall for
dinner the Queen Mother declined to join us. Her voice
was thin and weary, and her colour pale, though she
assured me she was only tired. She asked me to take her
young companion into my party, however.

'Ettard deserves something more than spending her
time with an ailing old lady,' Igraine said as the girl
stepped forward. 'It can't be much fun to come to the
Royal Wedding and never have a chance to participate in
the festivities.'

Ettard smiled shyly, her eyes shining with excitement
at the prospect, and she attached herself to Vinnie like a
lambkin reunited with its mother after shearing.

When we arrived at the Hall, Arthur was standing on
the steps carefully writing something on a tablet.

'There,' he announced, laying the stylus in its groove
and closing the wooden cover over it. A half-dozen
children lingered near the steps hopeful of running
errands for the King, and he handed it to one with the
admonition, 'Take it to the smith at the forge down by
the gate.'

Arthur looked up as the child trotted off, and seeing
our contingent, smiled a welcome.

'Do the smiths of Logres read?' I asked, thinking it odd
that a man skilled in one of the most important arts should
have bothered to learn the work of scribes.

'This one does,' Arthur confirmed. 'He plans to take Orders in the Church, and so has learned Latin. It's a handy skill to have,' he added, and I saw Vinnie nodding her head approvingly.

The high spirits of the afternoon were still much in evidence, and he bowed to Vinnie and inquired how the 'honoured lady from York' was feeling. My chaperone dimpled and made a formal curtsy as she allowed that everything was splendid, particularly now that we'd reached our destination.

Ettard stood to one side, all eyes and open mouth as she was introduced. Arthur gave her a gentle smile and said something about a garden of damsels blossoming at his court, and I asked if Bedivere had been giving him lessons in diplomacy. The girl watched our banter avidly, for it must have been very different from the convent life she was used to.

'Looks like we'll be eating with the Companions,' Arthur announced as Cei and Bedivere and several others joined us on the steps. 'The cooks have their hands full with plans for the Feast of Nobles two nights hence. Besides,' he added, coming down the steps and leading our group across the Square at a rapid clip, 'we'll be trapped in that stuffy hall soon enough, so we might as well enjoy the fresh air while we can.'

Bedivere contrived to walk with Brigit while Cei and an older man I had not yet met fell into step beside us.

'This is Sir Ector, my foster father,' Arthur said casually, never slackening his pace. There was no way for me to curtsy or the stranger to bow, so we grinned at each other instead.

Sir Ector was a man well past his middle years, his toffee-coloured hair all but gone except for a fringe around the bottom of his pate. Smile wrinkles creased his face and I could imagine him as a kindly and loving father.

He beamed at me with the good-natured smile of a man who is pleased at his son's prospects.

'You have no idea how much pressure Arthur had to withstand in order to find a bride of his own choosing,' he said. 'His mother and I used to worry that he'd be saddled . . .'

Flustered, he left the sentence unfinished, then shrugged. 'Well, no matter. It's turned out well, and Drusilla would have been pleased he chose a girl of the Cumbri.'

I thanked him, and commented on how proud he must be of all three of his boys, at which he smiled and nodded in agreement.

'It's nice to have the family together on such a splendid occasion,' he said softly. 'I do not know King Leodegrance except by reputation, but I gather he is not here for the festivities?'

I explained how hard it was for my father to travel and he nodded sympathetically.

'Well, my dear, I guess that will mean you'll return to Rheged to present him the first grandchild, doesn't it? You must plan to stop at our court on the way.' He gave me the same broad smile I had seen on Arthur's own face. 'Yes, I would say well worth the wait,' he affirmed.

Dinner was a noisy, boisterous affair around the cooking fire, full of the rowdy good spirits of warriors set to celebrate their leader's forthcoming marriage. When I caught sight of Agricola standing apart from the rest, I called him over.

The villa owner had brought no retinue of his own, so the Companions had temporarily adopted him and I wondered how such an elegant gentleman coped with the raucous nights that were typical of the young warriors.

'Arthur gave me a room in the Hall, next to Sir Ector's quarters,' Agricola responded when I asked him. 'It has made my stay very pleasant indeed. And how has the rest of your trip been, M'lady?'

'Wonderful!' I grinned.

'I'm glad,' he said, reaching out and putting his hand on my arm. 'If there is any way I can be of help to you here in the south, please don't hesitate to ask.'

I looked into his face, seeing the same reliability I had found in Pellinore.

'Oh,' I said suddenly, remembering my promise to Vinnie, 'there is one thing. I told my chaperone I would find a ring for her to replace one she lost . . . a Roman ring with a signet. She was most distressed, and I said we'd find another like it, if possible. Do you know where I could locate such a thing?'

Agricola pursed his lips and pondered the matter for a moment. 'There was a family of jewellers in Winchester my wife used to trade with . . .' His handsome face broke into a smile. 'I'll ask around and see if I can locate something, M'lady,' he promised.

Arthur was coming towards us, bringing with him a horse-faced, portly creature bedecked with furs and jewellery of the most garish kind. He was flanked by a pair of warriors who looked familiar, but it took a minute to remember my first encounter with royal suitors. Dinadan was still the same, wiry and wry of humour, but the champion with the Pictish name had filled out considerably and was no longer the gangling bumpkin of that earlier visit. I smiled at Tristan and thought how much we had all changed in the last two years.

'May I present His Highness, King Mark of Cornwall,' Arthur said smoothly as the rotund ruler bellied to a stop in front of me and went ponderously down on one knee.

I struggled to hide my revulsion, realizing that this was a man whom I might have had to marry. It appeared that he had no sense of moderation where any of his appetites were concerned, and I wondered if he was indeed as vulnerable to his lust as Igraine's sly remarks had implied.

His escort had to help him to his feet and Mark smiled broadly, his stubby teeth dark and rotten-looking.

'You're very fortunate, Sir,' he said to Arthur, one pudgy finger slowly stroking his lower lip as he appraised me. 'I can't imagine how my emissaries overlooked this jewel.'

'I'm afraid my Pagan ways made me unsuitable for your court,' I said hastily, hoping the truth would dampen his appreciation.

'Yes, well . . . perhaps we could have changed that,' Mark suggested, and I forbore to say anything further. There was no point in riling this ally, and I had no desire to get his giant of a warrior into trouble either.

Dinadan caught the byplay and after Tristan had knelt and paid his respects, the more worldly courtier went hastily to one knee. 'Well done, M'lady,' he whispered with a sardonic smile.

There was a sudden, violent commotion beyond the fireglow, and fingers closed on sword pommels while daggers flicked to hand. A rider came thundering into camp, bearing down on the Companions with no regard for life or limb as men jumped out of the way. The horseman brought his stallion to a wild, snorting halt just short of the fire.

The flame leapt upward in the draught and when it steadied I saw the rider was Pellinore. He carried a bundle before him on the saddle, and the smile on his face was sublime.

'I found her,' he cried, oblivious to the tumult he was causing. 'Behold, the object of my quest, the Goddess incarnate!'

The bundle stirred and resolved itself into a long, full cape, and when the hood fell back a girl's face appeared, wide-eyed and grave, staring at the gathered Companions.

'Nimue!' I jumped to my feet, amazed and delighted to see the doire of Avebury's Sanctuary here in Sarum.

At the sound of her name the priestess slipped from the horse's withers and came towards me, walking as if in a trance and totally unaware of the warriors who surrounded her. The men parted as she glided soundlessly past them, a beautiful and unearthly apparition.

'M'lady,' she said demurely, dropping to her knees in front of me, 'it appears I will be with you for the wedding after all.'

'I'm so glad,' I answered, bending down to be sure she was unhurt. The gaiety and laughter with which I started to greet her were deflected by her distant and untouchable air.

'I believe,' she whispered as soon as I was close enough to hear, 'that there is treachery afoot, and King Arthur should be warned.'

'Of course,' I mumbled, peering into her upturned face. She stared back with the blank look of one who is in another's power. Shock and surprise left me wordless, and a shiver ran across my grave. Whatever forces were shaping the future were living themselves out in Nimue.

I looked around for Arthur, only to find him on the far side of the circle. He had one hand resting on Gawain's shoulder, and from the look of it he was reminding the son of Lot that there was to be no reprisal against Pellinore during the wedding time.

So I sat back down, wondering how soon I could get my bridegroom's attention.

Pellinore had swaggered into the centre of the circle, laughing and boasting like any drunken warrior. He launched into some long, confused tale about a hunting dog and a white hart, and how he'd fought two other fellows for possession of this special girl.

'I had to deal with one of 'em right heavily,' he roared, unslinging the drinking horn from his belt and holding it out for someone to fill. 'But the other was her cousin, and seeing his companion felled by a single blow, he offered me not only the girl, but his horse as well.'

The warrior roared with laughter and gestured proudly towards the bay stallion. Draining his horn, he came round to his story again.

'Wonderful girl, just wonderful. Knew she was special right from the beginning, and wouldn't let anything distract me once I was on her trail. Met some poor creature beside a well wailing for help with her dying mate, but didn't have time to find out what all that dolour was about.' His mood suddenly shifted and the craggy face turned mournful. 'Pity, too . . . when we rode back that way both of 'em were dead and all the animals had left was their heads.'

'Oh Pellinore,' I cried, the picture of the lovers by the fountain dancing hideously in front of me, 'how could you have gone off and not even tried to help?'

'I do not know, M'lady,' he bellowed contritely. 'It must have been the fever of my quest.'

'Pellinore!'

Merlin's voice came out of the dark, crisp and clear against the fuzziness of the other's ramblings. There was no way to see him in the shadows, but his presence was so powerful it was as though a god were speaking. I felt a small pressure on my knee, and glancing down, discovered Nimue still knelt at my feet and had now raised her hand in an effort to slide it into mine. I took hold of her fingers and she clung to me tightly.

'Have you any idea who this lady by the fountain was?' the Magician asked.

'No, but she cursed me when I wouldn't stop. She was fair, with pale hair and violet eyes, and she knew my name and cursed me because I didn't help her . . . Now I cannot close my eyes without seeing that face, for she reminded me of someone . . .'

'I should think so,' the Wizard said, emerging from the darkness and walking towards Pellinore like a deed that cannot be disowned. 'She was your own daughter by the Lady of the Rule, and both she and her lord were on their way here for the wedding when they were ambushed by bandits. You could not have done much for him, but she would not have died if you hadn't deserted her.'

The huge warrior rocked back on his heels, stunned. There was a long, shuddering silence, and then a deep moan began to rumble in Pellinore's throat.

'What was her curse?' the Sorcerer demanded.

'She vowed I too would be abandoned by an ally in time of need, and die myself betrayed by the one I should have been able to count on. Why' – the bewildered man groaned – 'why didn't the Gods tell me who she was?'

'That would not have mattered, Pellinore,' Merlin countered, standing squarely in front of the trembling warrior. 'The Gods both bless and curse, and we do well to learn a few feeble lessons in between. By your own actions you have sealed your fate, and what is done cannot now be undone. But from now on, you need to think less often of that quest which you take such pride in and pay more attention to those who have need of other kinds of service from you.'

Merlin put his hands on Pellinore's shoulders, and the warrior went down on his knees, tears of contrition and remorse flowing down his face. Like a child, he had acted without thought; now he sought forgiveness with the same simplicity.

The Wise One made the prayer of forgiveness while the rest of us looked on in awed silence. When Merlin finished

Cei stepped forward and, helping Pellinore to his feet, led the sobbing man away.

Suddenly everyone began talking, stretching and laughing and speaking too loudly in an attempt to shake off the weight of what had just happened. I made a dash for Arthur and whispered that Nimue brought warnings of treachery. Someone had just finished proposing a toast to the bridegroom, and the crowd now was chanting his name, impatiently waiting for his bride to get out of the way. We hastily agreed I should take the priestess back to the Hall and wait for him there; it would not be possible for him to join us immediately, but I should keep this messenger of the Fates safe until he arrived.

Nimue came with me, mute and shivering, and finding the kitchen empty for the night, I seated the girl in a quiet spot next to a warm oven and began rummaging in the cupboard. There was some hyssop among the herbs, so I brewed up a batch of tea and added a dribble of honey to the pot while the priestess sat in her corner and stared, unblinking, into space.

She reached for the cup with both hands and began taking little sips of the warm, sweet stuff, then looked up at me gratefully and asked, 'Is he like that often?'

'Drunk and half crazy? I don't know,' I answered, thinking such an adventure with Pellinore would put anyone in shock for a while.

'No,' she said firmly, 'the White One, who stood in the ring of fire just now.'

It took me a moment to realize she was referring to Merlin.

'The Magician? No, I don't think so,' I replied, wondering what she had seen that the rest of us were not privy to. I pulled up a stool and sat next to her. 'At least, I've never seen him like that before, but I haven't known him very long.'

She took some more tea, and a small smile crept to her mouth. 'Now,' she murmured, her eyes grown very big and dark, 'now I know why Pellinore was sent to me. To bring me here . . . to bring me to him . . .'

Her words floated lightly in the stillness of the empty kitchen like the innocent confidence of a child, and their full meaning dawned on me slowly.

'Nimue!' I exclaimed, aghast at the notion, then froze in silence.

The girl was still her sweet-faced self, but it was the Goddess who looked out of her eyes at me.

'Do not question what you do not understand,' She said, Her voice a deep growl. 'It is not for mortals to choose where love shall flower.'

I looked away hastily, unable to bear the weight of that gaze, and a moment later felt the girl's hand slide into mine again.

'I told you,' she said in her own clear tones, 'something special was going to come of it. I just did not know who or what it was before.'

She sounded so happy I peered at her curiously. If I were being drawn towards such a passion, I'd be terrified.

'Aren't you scared?' I asked, thinking of the awesomeness of the Sorcerer.

'Of course,' she answered softly, looking down into her now empty cup. 'After all, he may not even notice me.' She faltered for a moment, as though heartbroken at the prospect.

I stared at her, dumbfounded. She who was so calm and sure in conversation with Pellinore, so gentle and firm in guiding me and so powerful when filled by the very presence of the Goddess now sat in the shadow of a hearth and worried that she would not be found desirable.

The idea was so preposterous, it was all I could do to keep from laughing. I could not imagine any man not being captivated by her, and if, as Arthur said, the Enchanter had a weakness for young girls, Nimue had nothing to fear. Seeing the priestess' wistful look, I threw my arms around her in a quick hug.

Surely the Goddess had been right; who was I to question the love between any two people? After all, love comes in many forms, and should be cherished and respected in all its manifestations, no matter how strange they appear to others.

So I sat with my friend until she ceased to shiver, and together we waited for Arthur to arrive.

39

Treachery

At last the party at the Companions' camp broke up and
knots of people began to make their way into the Hall.
The younger warriors were eager to be off down the hill
to the tent city that had sprung up on the plain below
where no matter what the hour one could always find a
game of chance, a cask of wine or a willing lady. The
older guests and those who held themselves separate from
such brawling were congregating in the Hall.

I peeked out of the kitchen doorway and saw Arthur at
the same time he saw me. He casually threaded his way
through the groups that milled about the Hall and when
no one was looking slipped into the dimly lit kitchen.

The air of jocular celebration dropped from him and he
turned his attention immediately to the priestess.

'What is this about treachery?'

Nimue faced him, tense and alert, and leaning forward
whispered, 'M'lord, I have reason to think there are spies
within your camp who mean you no good.'

'Spies? For whom?'

Merlin's voice, no louder than her own, caught us all
by surprise. He had simply appeared at Arthur's side and
was staring suspiciously at the girl beside me.

The priestess returned his look calmly. 'I'm not sure.
But I would prefer to talk about it in a more private
place.'

With a nod Arthur turned and led us down a passage to
the part of the building set aside for his personal use.

While he closed the inner leather draperies, which

muffled even the least sound from the Hall, I stared curiously about his quarters.

The room itself was comfortable, without pretence or decoration. The bed was a narrow cot, above which Excalibur blazed on the wall like a gold-and-silver flame. It hung at an angle, ready to be drawn should there be a disturbance in the night. The jewels on the pommel glimmered eerily in the flickering lamplight and the embroidery of the scabbard shimmered and moved with a life of its own.

Merlin was checking the shutters of the windows behind a long table that reminded me of home. I glanced at the items scattered across its top: maps and wax tablets, notes on possible posting stations and a rolled manuscript lay beside the inkstand. A chunk of red wax waited to be brought to life by the impression of the Dragon Seal.

'There,' said Arthur, once he was satisfied that all was snug and guarded from prying eyes or ears. 'Please, have a seat and tell us your story.'

Nimue sat down in one of the camp chairs across the table from Merlin and folded her hands primly in her lap.

'Well,' she began, 'when Pellinore and I were coming through the woods last night, my horse stumbled, and I was thrown to the ground. It was in the woodlands where the rocks lie like grey wethers sleeping in the grass, and I hurt my arm in the fall, so we decided to spend the night there, and not come on until daylight.'

She looked up, first at Arthur, then at Merlin. The Magician was staring down at her impassively, his high cheekbones and deep-set eyes accentuated by the shadows of the lamplight. To judge by the lack of interest in his expression, she might as well have been reporting the number of chickens hatched the week before.

'We were sleeping in a thicket not far from the track, and I woke before dawn to the sound of hoofbeats coming from different directions. The riders stopped and talked not a stone's throw from us. One had come from Sarum, and he gave a detailed report on the men gathered here, and what their disposition was, while the other laughed and asked if anything was suspected.

'The first said no, because everyone was absorbed in the celebration. Then he inquired how it looked "at home," and the second man allowed that with so many nobles and warriors gone off to the wedding, the time seemed to be ripe.'

A gust of air rattled the shutter, and the shadows of Merlin's face sharpened as the lamp guttered in the draft. I shivered involuntarily, but Nimue never flinched under his scrutiny, and after a moment she went on with her story.

'The men had turned away and there was more muffled talk; the only thing I heard clearly was the name Brychan. When they parted, however, they made a pledge for freedom from the British yoke; then each went back the way he had come.

'I do not know,' she concluded, 'either who the men were, or what sort of threat they represent, but it seemed wisest to tell you of it as soon as possible.'

Arthur had been listening intently and now he leaned forward.

'Can you show me where this meeting took place?'

I lit another lamp and brought it to the table as Arthur and Nimue turned their attention to the map.

'This is Sarum,' Arthur explained, 'and here is Avebury, so your Sanctuary should be . . . there,' he finished, putting his thumb down near a blot of ink.

'I think,' she answered, surveying the map and trying to decide upon distances, 'that it was about here.'

Arthur studied the position of her fingertip, then glanced up at Merlin. The Sorcerer was looking as much at the priestess as he was at the map, his expression unreadable.

'Certainly a spy could make it from Sarum to that spot and back in a single night's ride,' Arthur confirmed, and Merlin nodded. 'And whoever they were meeting could have come either from north, or east, or even west.'

'West seems most likely,' Merlin sighed, 'if the Irish chief Brychan is involved.'

The two men looked at each other speculatively, and Arthur straightened up.

'The point about all the warriors' being here at Sarum is well taken,' he mused, 'and one I've worried about, although I can't see how to send anyone home without causing ill feelings. If the Irish hope to capitalize on their ancestral ties with kingdoms such as Demetia, this would be a perfect time to do it.'

He paced to the end of the table and then back, chewing thoughtfully on the end of his moustache.

'We have to assume that the spy is still in camp, so we mustn't do or say anything that lets on that we've got wind of something.'

'Girl,' said Merlin, looking at the priestess again and suddenly blushing. 'Ah . . . that is . . . you must have a name?'

'Yes, M'Lord,' she answered levelly, 'I am called Nimue, and am one of the Lady's students.'

'Ah, yes,' the Enchanter muttered, staring down at the map. 'Well, Nimue . . .'

He stopped then and looked back at her. There was a long silence while the two of them stared at each other, and I held my breath. Arthur, quite unaware of what was happening, continued to pace, and finally Merlin cleared his throat.

'Nimue, are you practised in the Sight?' he asked.

She looked down at her hands, which were still clasped

454

quietly in her lap, and I marvelled at her composure.

'Not practised, M'lord, but I have occasionally seen things,' she answered.

'Will you try it in this matter, for the King?'

There was a gentleness in the Magician's tone I had never heard before, and I let my breath out slowly. Whatever their relationship was going to be, he was at least being patient with her and I smiled as Nimue nodded her assent.

A fresh rushlight was lit and Merlin held it up before the girl's eyes. Arthur came and stood next to me while Nimue stared, unblinking, at the flame. Her dark eyes grew fathomless, and I could see the flame of the light reflected in pupils as her concentration gave way to a blank stare. Her hands remained immobile but her breathing grew husky, and a beading of sweat appeared on her forehead.

'A boat,' she whispered. 'No, several boats. Tall as houses . . . and a man with a strange name, come from the Continent. Theo . . . his name is Theo, and he swaggers like an outlaw. He's lost . . . no, cut loose from past loyalties . . . his people are gone and he's searching for Arthur.'

She cried out sharply, closing her eyes and clasping her head with both hands. The beautiful face contorted in pain.

'There, there,' Merlin crooned softly, handing me the rushlight and laying both hands on her head. 'What else did you see, Little Nimue with the Goddess Eyes?'

The girl's face began to relax and the deep furrows between her brows melted away. 'I . . . I don't know . . . just the men with the boats . . .'

She opened her eyes and slowly focused on Merlin, whose fingers were gently massaging her temples. 'That doesn't help much, does it?' she asked.

The Enchanter left off smoothing her temples and ran his hand over her hair as a parent or a lover might. It was a gesture both soothing and protective, and I suspected he wasn't even aware of it as he tried to comfort her.

'That is for the King and me to decide. For now, you have done us a great service, and your vision will be of some use, somehow. The warning you brought about Brychan is, in itself, invaluable. I think now it would be best for you and M'lady simply to go back to your lodgings and get a good night's sleep. And, of course, not mention this to anyone.'

The Magician was actually smiling at the priestess and she looked back to her lap shyly.

'M'lord,' she said, 'I have no lodgings.'

'You can stay with me,' I blurted out, realizing too late that she might have been counting on a different invitation. 'That is,' I amended hastily, 'if you want to.'

She smiled up at me with relief and pleasure, and I was grateful to see that I had not spoiled some divine plan. If I had not seen and heard the Goddess speaking from her, I would have sworn Nimue was a guileless young woman, not given to intrigue. But knowing there was a greater scheme involved, I worried that I might inadvertently interfere with the Goddess' plans, for the Goddess Herself was no innocent girl.

'That is most kind of you, M'lady,' Nimue said, and when I glanced at Merlin there was nothing in his expression to indicate that he was disconcerted, so I decided no harm had been done and retreated into the safety of silence.

Arthur continued his pacing, totally unaware of anything except the threat to Britain, and I envied him his single-mindedness. Even after we gathered up our wraps and Arthur walked us home, it was obvious his mind was elsewhere. I kissed him gently on the cheek and sent him back to the Hall with a maternal pat, and I'm not sure he noticed either action.

Vinnie was already asleep, so Brigit and I made up a place for Nimue on the bench under my window. When we had tucked her in for the night the priestess looked up and smiled, murmuring drowsily, 'Bless you,' though I couldn't tell if it was the girl or the Goddess who was speaking.

The dark currents of implied treason were lulled by a good night's sleep, and I woke next morning to find the priestess had long since gone and my governess was prowling about the room like a cat on the track of a mouse. She came to a stop when she reached the niche where Nimue had slept.

'What ever is the matter, Vinnie?' I asked, yawning and propping myself on my elbow to watch as she lifted a corner of the mattress, holding it gingerly between two fingers and standing back the full length of her arm.

'I hear you brought a witch home last night, M'lady.' Her voice was carefully controlled, as though she were trying to hide a grievous disappointment, and she gave me a reproachful look.

'Witch? Well, I don't know about that,' I temporized, wondering what she meant by the term.

'Pagan mistress of secrets, that's what she is,' Vinnie announced, dropping the edge of the pallet. 'Ladies have no business in matters of religion,' she added with a sniff.

'But the Goddesses themselves are women!' I pointed out, amused at the matron's reasoning. 'And there have been druidesses ever since time began.'

'Heathen aberrations,' Vinnie hissed. 'Saint Paul told us what to think about that sort of thing.'

'Hey, where are you going with that?' I asked, suddenly

alarmed. Vinnie had wrestled the cushion to the floor and was tugging it towards the doorway.

'Taking it outside to wash it down for lice,' she replied resolutely.

'Oh, come now, Vinnie,' said Brigit, breezing into the room and opening the curtains that shrouded the window. 'One can be Pagan without being either the Devil or unclean. Look at Her Highness, for instance' – and she nodded in my direction. 'Would you say she is a direct relative of the Evil One?'

'That's different,' the matron flared back. 'She's not running around in the woods conjuring up Things best left alone. At least, not yet. But I don't trust these priestesses with their little gold knives and ancient spells . . . and with the Lady herself due to arrive today, who knows what will happen to Her Highness?'

'Today!'

I leapt out of bed and ran to the washbasin, all other thoughts wiped out by the spectre of the Lady keening in the woods beneath that pillar of skulls. No longer could the confrontation be avoided, and my heart began to pound as it had when we had come face to face at the Black Lake. The Priestess had only banished me then, tangling my life with mists and heartbreak; what vengeance would she work on me now that I had no place to run to?

But even while I splashed about at the washstand common sense took over. There was no proof that she carried a grudge for that childhood indiscretion; maybe she would overlook the encounter after all this time, and we could start fresh as adults, guided by the light of present circumstances.

'The Lady of the Lake is going to be my sister-in-law,' I said slowly, reaching for the towel Brigit proffered, 'so I

458

must be prepared to greet her properly and make her feel comfortable at Arthur's court.'

'What if Arthur doesn't feel comfortable about having her here?' my governess persisted, absentmindedly helping Brigit put the pallet back on the window seat.

'Arthur gets on very well with Morgan,' I answered, trying to reassure myself as well as Vinnie. Morgause, of course, was a forbidden subject, but he had made it clear that he trusted and relied upon the Lady. 'And I'm sure the Queen Mother will be glad to see her,' I added, remembering Igraine's effort to explain her daughter to me.

'The Square's in a turmoil already,' Brigit interjected, folding Nimue's blankets and patting the bolster into place. 'By the time Mass was finished, there were mobs of people outside the Hall. A party of foreigners was arriving and traffic was blocked in each direction, what with everyone stopping to gape at them.'

'How did you know they were foreigners?' I asked, thinking that I couldn't recognize more than a handful of the population as it was.

'By their clothes, and the fact they spoke something other than Latin or Celtic. They're rugged, weathered men, with scarves tied about their heads, and tight-fitting sweaters such as fisherfolk wear,' she answered.

They sounded fascinating, and I wished my window looked out on to the Square, but short of actually leaving the house there was no way I could see what was going on. So I had to be content with Brigit's description until I had a chance to ask Arthur himself.

He came about midday, bringing the dogs with him and insisting we take them for a run. Rushed and harried and vaguely distracted, he hustled me out the door with barely time to grab a shawl.

459

'Easier and safer to talk out here,' he explained as we loped across the meadow.

There was a tense excitement in his voice and a quick glance at his face confirmed the unease that was beginning to prickle around me. The reality of last night's news came fully awake, banishing the blithe cheerfulness of the morning.

Without further word we scrambled up the rampart, slipped the leads off the dogs and turned to look out over the parapet. On the plain below the makeshift camps spread out for miles, and Arthur pointed to the different banners whipping in the wind while I struggled to tie the shawl under my chin.

'It appears that the doire's Second Sight is more than a little accurate,' he said at last, ' – at least where the man named Theo is concerned.'

'The strangers who speak a foreign tongue!' I cried.

Arthur turned to look at me abruptly, one eyebrow raised in surprise, as though I had developed the Sight myself. I explained that Brigit had seen them this morning. 'But what are they like, and why did they come?' I queried.

'Theo is very much as Nimue described him: half military man, half pirate. He was a sea commander for the Visigoths, but since the Franks have driven them into Iberia, Theo's been moving from one coastal kingdom to another seeking a patron. When he reached Brittany, King Ban suggested he come see me, and since Bors was looking for a way to make it to the wedding, he volunteered to act as pilot and sponsor. They dropped anchor yesterday at Weston-Super-Mare; Bors says there are five ships altogether, and Theo is willing to swear allegiance in return for safe harbours and whatever military action might come up. Which gives me, I suppose, a navy.'

'Do we need a navy?' I asked, unsure even how such a thing would be deployed.

Arthur turned round, facing out across the top of Sarum, and squinted against the wind that perversely changed with him.

'Even if we don't need it now, there may come a time when a navy would be useful to keep the Irish quiet. It would certainly be easier to deal with the Saxons to the east if I didn't have to worry about the Irish in the west.'

We began to walk along the parapet, the dogs ranging happily ahead of us.

'I'm still not sure what to make of Nimue's warning about the spies,' Arthur went on. 'She and Merlin have spent all morning trying to determine more closely what she heard, but so far it's still unclear.'

I was shocked in spite of myself, for it hadn't occurred to me that Nimue's absence meant she was with the Wizard. I glanced at Arthur, wondering if I should warn him about what the Goddess had in mind for the Sage, but a cold band laid itself across my neck and I immediately decided to remain silent. The Goddess had already warned me not to meddle.

'I think,' Arthur continued as we came in sight of the Companions' tents, 'that we need to prepare for battle without seeming to . . . if that's possible.' He stopped to watch the individual riders practising on the drill field, then gave a short laugh and pointed to Griflet, who was pounding up and down the field at breakneck pace. 'Our young Kennel Master has a flair for fighting too, it seems. I'll wager he's more spirit than skill at the moment, but the day may come when he'll be a valuable warrior.'

Arthur knelt down to slip the leads back on the pups and motioned for me to join him. The two of us crouched in the lee of the wall, well hidden from sight or sound.

'No matter what form the treachery takes, you should

461

be better protected,' he said softly. 'Suddenly giving you a formal houseguard might arouse suspicion, but I could sent Griflet over. He's young enough to be viewed as a page put at your disposal, yet I daresay he'd fight like a lion if you were ever in danger. He doesn't know what the situation is, of course; I've told no one else except Bedivere. But from now on I want you to take Griflet everywhere with you, and find a place for him to sleep at your house as well.'

'Hmmph,' I snorted, 'between the priestess and Griflet, my household staff has doubled and taken on a pair of dogs to boot. I hate to think what it will be like in a week!'

For a moment Arthur was caught off balance by my banter; then he grinned and stood up.

'With any luck, by this time next week we'll all be under one roof, and then it will be up to Cei to find room for everyone.'

And so we left it. Arthur went off to talk with Griflet about his change of quarters while I took the dogs and headed for the house.

The wind was behind me now, capricious and unreliable, full of rough buffets and sudden whacks. The dogs were straining at the lead, pulling me along, and it seemed I was being propelled towards a future where the threat of battle and loss mingled with the festivities of the wedding. It was frightening and exciting at the same time and betokened a moira not even the Lady herself could have devised.

40

Morgan le Fey

By midafternoon the wind had turned to heavy gusts that whipped around corners and snatched at the bunting and banners of the town. Griflet, having moved his meagre possessions to my house, accompanied me and the pups on a visit to Igraine, and we fought our way into the teeth of the wind like fish travelling up a turbulent stream.

The Square was full of people, most of them clustered around a pair of stone-and-anvil men set up in the far corner. Their forge flared golden red when the capricious wind hit it, and the whine of the blade sharpener came and went like keening in the night.

'One of the King's gifts to the people,' Griflet explained. 'He's had the smiths set up both here and on the plain so that anyone who wishes can have scythe or knife or ploughshare repaired at the King's expense. Part of the wedding celebration, you know.'

Griflet's explanation was so ingenuous I looked at him sharply, but there was nothing to indicate he was dissembling. No doubt that had been Arthur's original intent, but it surprised me that Griflet didn't recognize preparations for battle when he saw them. Clearly sword and spear and weakened buckler would all be attended to in between the domestic items ordinary people brought forth. That it could be done under the guise of the King's largesse and without arousing suspicion was a stroke of minor genius, and I wondered who had thought it up.

We were windblown and breathless by the time Ettard answered our knock, and I felt very rumpled indeed while we waited for the Queen Mother to join us. The dogs lay

463

at our feet, rising quietly when we stood to greet our hostess. I introduced Griflet, and Igraine smiled indulgently.

'My dear,' she said, 'I have known this boy from the day of his birth. Don't forget, his father has been part of the King's household since before we were married.'

There was something in her tone that tugged at my heart, for she spoke as though Uther were not dead but, like the God King of old, merely slept somewhere while the rest of us kept the Court in trust for him until his return. Perhaps it is always like that if one has loved someone deeply; with that person's death time stops, and future generations are only shadows compared with what one remembers. Certainly it seemed to have been that way for my father after Mama died.

'I beg your pardon, M'lady,' I apologized, and she smiled softly.

'You can't be expected to know and remember what you have only heard about,' she said, seating herself next to the brazier and drawing a robe across her lap. The chancy wind was pushing against the shutters, and every so often a draught cut across the room.

'Now, tell me how you came by the Irish hounds,' she suggested.

'You know about these dogs, M'lady?' I asked as Griflet brought the pups to her chair. Caesar was all enthusiastic friendliness, but Cabal was barely polite. It was clear she was going to be a one-person animal, and that person was Arthur.

'Of course I know about wolfhounds, child, though from long ago,' Igraine said. 'A number of Irish settled in Cornwall, and Gorlois was very fond of his dogs, so he kept a wolfhound or two in the kennel.'

It was the first I had heard of Irish colonists in the south, and I wondered how they figured in the present situation. Was it possible they too posed a threat?

I looked at the Queen Mother and wished I could tell her about Nimue's warning. It would be so comforting to have a more experienced person to confide in, and I was sure she would know better than I how to deal with duplicity and treason. But remembering Arthur's caution not to mention it to anyone, I held my tongue.

We talked about the pups, and when I told her their names and how they had come by them she laughed with the light, high heart of a girl.

'I knew he'd do well to marry a Cumbrian,' she said, daubing at the tears of amusement that dampened her eyes.

A mad clatter suddenly interrupted us, followed by such a pounding on the door I thought the elements themselves were demanding entrance. Ettard no sooner undid the bolt than the door flew open and a dozen armed men rushed into the room. They wore a badge I did not recognize, and came to attention with their backs against the wall, filling the room with menace.

Griflet leapt to his feet, dagger drawn and both dogs alert beside him, their hackles raised and throats rumbling.

A swarthy man, barely taller than a child, strode into the room. His head and arms were of normal size, but his bandy legs were stunted, and one shoulder was hunched high and crooked. I caught my breath, thinking it was the Dwarf God Bilis Himself. He surveyed the situation within the room, then turned to the Queen Mother.

'Your Highness, the Lady of the Lake has come to pay her respects.'

I looked hastily at Igraine, hoping I should leave so that mother and daughter could meet in private. But the Queen Mother put her hand firmly on my wrist, pinning me to the chair, as she said, 'Tell Morgan we shall be happy to receive her.'

Igraine shifted her grip so that her fingers closed over mine in a reassuring manner. There seemed to be no sound but the roar of my heart in my ears and Morgan le Fey entered the room.

The Priestess was smaller than I had remembered, but her dark, pointed face and animal quickness hadn't changed. She surveyed the scene before her with a steady and inscrutable air. I would have risen to my feet out of sheer panic but for Igraine's hand over mine, and at last the Priestess came forward and curtsied to the Queen Mother.

'My Lady,' she said formally, her voice smooth and polite, 'I hope I find you in good health.'

'Indeed, child, as well as can be expected,' the Queen Mother answered, 'considering you've stormed in here like a marauding army. You needn't be so dramatic with me, you know.' With regal serenity she turned to me. 'Guinevere, may I present my daughter Morgan, Queen to King Urien and High Priestess of the Goddess.'

Igraine looked sternly at her daughter, and there was nothing for it but that Morgan must curtsy to me as well. The Priestess murmured some small formality and I attempted a wan smile, grateful that Igraine spoke again.

'I was just about to order tea, Morgan. Will you join us?'

The Lady nodded, and with a signal dismissed her dwarf lieutenant and the men who had escorted her. Griflet, looking as unstrung by this encounter as I felt, announced that he would like to take his refreshment in the kitchen, where he could also fetch the dogs a drink, and when the tea things arrived Ettard withdrew to the other side of the room and I was left alone with the two Queens.

466

Morgan accepted a cup from her mother, and reached for a biscuit.

'I believe having a cup of tea and a good chat is my mother's solution to every problem in the world,' she said amiably, sitting so as to face the two of us and making a point to include me in the conversation. 'When I was a child, no matter what else was happening, Mother always insisted we must observe teatime.'

Igraine nodded her head, but avoided the invitation to exchange reminiscences. 'Taking tea in the afternoon is a very civil habit to get into,' she said. 'It ends the working day well, provides a chance to gather the family before the evening activities begin and is a thoroughly beneficial custom. You might consider reinstating it at court, Gwen.'

'I'm sure the new Queen will have ideas of her own about what to do at court,' Morgan pointed out, her silky voice making light of the challenge behind her words.

I could think of nothing to say and was relieved when she went on chatting. She spoke about her trip and the need for an armed escort because the Roads were so crowded with riffraff on the move these days. I watched her carefully but could find no sign of emotion, even when she expressed pleasure at being in the south again.

'I left as a child, you know,' she said, not looking at her mother, 'and what with being schooled in the north and then married to a northern king, I don't get home often. Not that I dislike the area,' she added with a nod in my direction. 'Lakeland is one of the most beautiful and unspoiled parts of Albion, if you like oatmeal and mutton, but I do miss the sunnier clime, and all the flowers of Cornwall.'

She finished the last of her biscuit and turned to me directly. 'I understand that Cathbad was once your tutor.'

'Yes.' I nodded, feeling a fool as my voice stuck in my throat. Morgan's tone had become a little friendlier and I told myself it was absurd to be frightened of her. After all, Igraine had been remote and unapproachable in the beginning, and she had not proved to be an enemy. Perhaps the Lady simply needed some reassurance about my own motives and attitude. 'I was raised in the Old Ways, as much as any other,' I ventured.

'So you're familiar with the Wedding Rites?'

'Oh, yes,' I assured her. 'I've already gone through the Blessing . . .'

A draught slid icily around my ankles as Morgan's look froze my words. With a toss of her head she let out a curt expletive about amateurs dabbling in holy ritual.

'Just where did the Blessing take place, M'lady?' she asked, regaining her composure almost immediately. Her eyes were still full of anger, however.

'At the temple, near Avebury. I understand the priestess there is a pupil of yours, so I thought . . .'

'You did not think very well, I'm afraid. Those are rites sacred unto the Goddess, and should be performed by no one other than her appointed Lady. Who is this so-called "priestess"?'

'Nimue,' I answered, dreading the idea that I was exposing my new friend to Morgan's wrath, yet hoping that when the Lady knew who had officiated everything would be all right. 'She is one of your own students, isn't she?'

Morgan's eyes widened when she heard the name, then narrowed coldly, and she shrugged.

'She was one of my attendants for a time. But she lacked the ability to fit in, and in the end I had to ask her to leave.'

'I'm sorry to hear that,' I murmured.

'I am too.' Morgan sighed like a long-suffering parent. 'She had such promise, but took upon herself too many

468

. . . things. And now it is most regrettable that she should so have profaned your preparation.'

'Surely it's not profaned, M'lady,' I said quickly, trying to reassure her. 'I . . . I can't speak of the rites themselves, but the Goddess was present, of that I am certain. Who actually calls Her forth can't make that much difference, can it?'

I had completely misjudged the situation, and the Priestess turned on me scornfully.

'Are you that stupid, girl, not to realize that as the Lady of the Lake I am the only one through whom the Goddess speaks? I would expect such ignorance from some dull-witted Roman girl, but not a child of the Cumbri! Call yourself raised in the Old Ways? You might as well have grown up in a convent, for all you understand of life.'

Morgan was on her feet and pacing by then, moving with Arthur's sure stride from one end of the room to the other. One hand nervously twisted the black curl that hung down by her ear, and she was such a contrast to her mother's fair composure, it seemed likely the title 'le Fey' hinted at her being a changeling child. I remembered our first meeting and half-expected her to vanish in a fit of rage, with or without the magic of a Druid's Mist.

Igraine had been silent during our entire conversation, and now she settled back in her chair and took a sip of tea as she watched her daughter wear a path through the rushes on the floor.

'Goodness, Morgan,' the Queen Mother said, putting down her teacup. 'When I married Gorlois there was no great fuss over which priestess conducted the Blessing. I can't see that it matters all that much now.'

'But Gorlois was only a duke, not a High King,' Morgan flared, 'and besides, in those days the Old Ways were only just starting to come out of hiding, so there were undoubtedly exceptions made here and there. Now the rites have been reinstated and must be adhered to by all who seek the Goddess' favour.'

'Well, either way, it seems that what is done is done, and we should go on with the rest of the ceremonies as planned,' Igraine suggested sensibly.

'With all due respect,' her daughter snapped, still pacing, 'you are a Christian now, M'lady, and have no right to question the judgement of the Goddess. No,' she added thoughtfully, 'I will have to purify the girl and perform the rites all over again, as though nothing else had intervened.'

She whirled about and approached my chair, staring directly into my face with those cunning, savage eyes.

'It means you will be brought to me at sunrise tomorrow for exorcism, and we'll spend the rest of the day giving you a proper initiation. I'll send my people for you at first light.'

Without waiting for an answer she turned on her heel and would have left the house had her mother not spoken up.

'Am I to assume you are leaving, child?'

Morgan turned back, made a quick curtsy and replied, 'With your permission, M'lady. I have things to prepare.'

The Queen Mother raised one hand in a gesture that was a cross between a blessing and a shooing away, then sighed when the door banged shut behind her daughter.

'I haven't seen her for five years, not since Uther's death, and she hasn't changed a bit.' Igraine shook her head wearily. 'I had hoped that when she too became a mother she might soften some, but I didn't see my grandson Uwain until he was well nigh eight years old.'

Igraine held out her cup and I poured the last of the tea for her. She leaned back in her chair and looked speculatively at the door through which Morgan had just stormed.

'Uwain's a nice boy, and mannerly . . . takes after his father,' she commented wryly. 'Urien brought him to Uther's funeral, and I thought then he didn't even look like Morgan, much less act like her. I would say he'll become a prince to be proud of.'

It seemed unlikely that she knew he had been tendered as a possible husband for me, but I was touched by the idea that I would have married into this great queen's family one way or another.

'I know him and his father only by reputation,' I said, thinking it best not to mention the long history of border raids between Rheged and Northumberland.

'You'll be meeting them at the Feast of Nobles tomorrow,' Igraine mused, her voice lifting in the way I found so endearing. 'You'll have a chance to meet not only the client kings but almost all of the family under one roof, and on their good behaviour, at that! What a rambunctious brood they are, and as different from each other as could be imagined,' she added with a note of fond resignation.

'Will they all be there? I understood Morgause . . .' I hesitated, not knowing how much Igraine was aware of the tension between Arthur and his sister.

'No, my Orkney daughter is still on her islands, which is probably just as well,' the Queen Mother said slowly, smoothing the robe around her knees. 'Morgause has a way of causing trouble wherever she goes. Gawain and Gaheris will represent that branch of the family; of the five boys, they are the only two at Arthur's court.'

'Five?' I asked, puzzled. For the life of me I could only remember Lot boasting of four offspring, and wondered now whom I had forgotten.

'Gawain and Gaheris, Agravain, Gareth and Mordred,

471

who was born after Lot died. Had you not heard of him?'

I shook my head, surprised that news of a new Prince of Orkney had not reached Rheged.

'Poor dear, I think of him so often, being raised without a father in those strange, bleak islands so far away. Gawain says he takes after Morgan in look and action: dark and quick and brooding. What else could one expect for a child conceived on the evening of his father's death? I pray for all my offspring, but particularly for him.' she added softly. 'It can't be easy, especially with Morgause for a mother.'

I wondered what she meant, and might even have found the courage to ask, but Griflet and the pups came tumbling out of the kitchen just then, and the next thing I knew we were preparing to take our leave.

'Now you go home and get a good night's rest, my dear,' Igraine said, smiling directly into my eyes, 'so you'll be fresh and rested when it's time to be presented to the Nobles. It's bound to be quite an experience, and I want you to enjoy it fully.'

On impulse, I bent over her frail form and laid my cheek against hers with a light hug.

'Thank you so much, M'lady,' I whispered, and for a moment her hand rested lightly on my head.

'Bless you, child. It's nice to see someone in this family has some manners.'

I slept fitfully, with fleeting glimpses of Morgan flickering through my dreams, and came awake to the sound of Arthur tapping on my window. He gestured to me to let him in the kitchen door, and after waking Griflet to stand guard at the back of the house, led the way up the ladder to the loft. Hanging the horn lantern from a bracket, he sank into a pile of pillows.

I caught my breath in surprise, for he was grey with fatigue and looked as though he hadn't slept for days.

'Gwen,' he said soberly, taking my hands in his and pulling me down beside him, 'a colleague of Agricola's, a man named Geraint, arrived this evening with news of Wales. He says the Irish are indeed supporting a rebellion, in the belief that we are too busy with the wedding to notice. So it looks as though we'll be going to war tomorrow.'

'Tomorrow?' I choked. The lantern shadows wavered around the loft as I thought of the rites in disarray, the wedding called off, the chaos of a future neither confirmed nor denied.

'Aye, tomorrow.' He was watching me intently. 'Would you prefer to . . . postpone . . . the marriage? It is a hard thing to ask, but worse yet to expect you to accept a battlefield in place of a wedding night, and the possibility of a dead husband even before your life is rightly begun. Or I might come home maimed, or blinded, or crippled beyond repair. There are no certainties in war, and I would hate to have you spend your life with a husband who was less than whole . . . that is no future for a lively young lass.'

I thought of Mama, and started to tell him that wounds and crippledness need not make a difference in our love, but the bleakness of his expression stopped me. The words had been wrung from him by great effort, and I searched his face for some clue as to what lay behind them. Maybe the whole idea of marriage had become an encumbrance he needed to be free of at this time.

'Postponement? Is that what you want?' I asked.

He shook his head solemnly. 'No. I would have us wedded, and bedded, before I leave,' he answered, looking down at our intertwined hands and speaking in a low, husky voice. 'I would like to know the future rests already in your womb, and if I do not return, you will manage the realm and raise the next king for me.'

473

I gasped, stunned by the idea. He was not looking at me directly, but the gravity of his tone reinforced the importance of his words.

'And,' he added shyly, 'it would give me further incentive to know that I was fighting for wife and family as well as throne and subjects. Besides, if I die you are safer here as queen, with an army to protect you, than you would be as the almost-bride of a defeated king, trying to flee back to Rheged.'

'No, no!' I cried, the possibility of Arthur's death rousing me from personal panic. Freeing my hands, I put them on either side of his head. 'You will not die, I won't let you! I will be your wife waiting for you.'

He stared back at me with misery and hope.

Seeing him so vulnerable, I reached beyond my own fear to give him whatever reassurance there might be. Pulling his head down, I kissed him passionately.

'I am to be your queen, your partner, your mate and confidante, and together we shall rule Britain for years to come . . . Nimue and the Goddess have said so,' I added with as much authority as I could muster. His arms went around me in a life-seeking embrace.

'When will you know how bad the situation is?' I asked finally, sitting up slowly and straightening my dress.

'Tomorrow morning, probably. We're working on a plan tonight, but if it proves unfeasible, we'll hold the wedding on Sunday as planned, and wait to see what further news comes from the north. That would give us more time to prepare, but we'd lose the advantage of surprise. In the meantime, we must keep the people from getting wind of it and panicking.'

'How soon will you tell them?'

He shook his head and sighed. 'Not until we've decided what can be done. Once we're committed to battle we can draw upon the warriors who are here for the festivities, but until the plans are settled, the entire situation must remain absolutely secret.'

I nodded, standing up and stretching in an effort to dispel the sense of being stuffed into a narrow, black bag.

'I understand you met Morgan this afternoon,' he said absently, and I half-snorted in reply.

'She's upset that I've gone through the rites at Avebury. It seems she wants to do them all over again tomorrow.'

Compared with the importance of Arthur's problems, the Lady's attitude was petty and ridiculous. The more I thought about it, the less inclined I was to cooperate.

'This ritual Morgan has planned . . . it will take all day, won't it?' Arthur inquired, slowly getting to his feet.

'Probably. She wants to do some form of exorcism first.' I shivered at the very idea. 'I'm sure it isn't necessary; the important ceremony has already been done, so I could miss this one if something urgent came up,' I suggested, following Arthur down the ladder. 'Perhaps I need not go through the exorcism after all.'

We paused beside the hearth, and he pulled me close to him.

'No . . . no, I want you to go on with it as though nothing unusual were happening,' Arthur whispered. 'You mustn't cause any suspicion in your actions, and I need to know where to find you in a hurry.'

He put his hand under my chin and lifted it gently. Troubled, I stared up at him in the hope he would say something tender and reassuring, but he bent to kiss me instead, more roughly than he realized.

'Get some sleep,' he whispered, 'and I will get word to you as soon as it's clear what we must do.'

And then he was gone, and I stood looking down into the ashes of the cold hearth, wondering what it would all come to.

41
The Wedding

Unseen hands were scrabbling at my back, picking at my flesh through the cloth of the dream, and I watched with horror as Morgan's face began to melt and twist into something hideous and unreal. I tried to wrench myself away from her but the Priestess laughed with the high, shrill whine of a blade against the whirling stone . . . and then I was falling through aeons of darkness.

The hammering of my pulse became the sound of rain on the roof, and I struggled to wakefulness in a bed that had become a tangle of covers. Somewhere I heard a cock crow and the sound brought me fully awake. It seemed a night not made for sleep, and with a sigh I got up. At least there would be no more nightmares before I must face the Lady in person.

I slipped into the white dress as quietly as possible, but Brigit woke and rose to help, joining me afterwards in a silent vigil by the hearth in the main room. We huddled over the small blaze she coaxed to life, letting the warmth of hearthside friendship drive the demons of doom back into their corners.

The dogs leapt to attention when the knock came. Sleepily Griflet took them in hand, and Brigit opened the door as I reached for Igraine's great dark cloak.

A white form stepped through the doorway and when he pushed back his hood I recognized Cathbad.

'Is it still raining?' I asked him, coming forward to greet my old tutor.

'It looks to be starting to clear, Your Highness,' he answered stiffly. His tone was so cold I wondered if he now shared the Lady's antipathy towards me. 'I have been appointed to stand for you in your father's place, if you have no objections,' he added.

'I would be honoured,' I assured him carefully, and after a hasty farewell to my household, followed him outside.

An armed escort stood at attention and I looked slowly from one to another in dismay. The men and women in white robes posed no threat, but the guards and warriors bristled with purpose. Perhaps the Lady thought I would have to be brought to her by force.

To the east the sky was lightening, but overhead the stars were hidden by clouds, and the torches that smoked in the damp air cast a lurid red reflection off paving stones and puddles. Huge shadows danced about the walls, and as we made our way through the streets the low rumble of a muffled hand drum gave cadence to our steps.

When we reached the fields the druids began to chant, at first soft and plaintively, then more loudly as the drum became more insistent. It was so different from the trip to the temple at Avebury, where the nightingale had welcomed us and the Gods had sent my name whispering all through the trees; by comparison, this morning's music was heavy and ponderous, like an ominous, guttural dirge.

The prospect of spending an entire day in the Lady's hands loomed ever more terrifying. Though Nimue had led me gently through the initiation, it was clear the High Priestess had a very different manner, and while the grandeur might be more impressive when conjured up by Morgan, surely the result would not be half so beautiful. Then too, there was the unknown rite meant to erase what had already been done. I could not imagine what it would entail, and the throbbing drum echoing around me underscored my growing panic.

Even Cathbad's presence offered no solace, for a quick glance at his hooded face convinced me there would be no help from him. And physical flight was out of the question, for there would be no escaping so many pursuers if I gave in to the panic and bolted. Certainly I had no desire to be dragged to Morgan's feet like a runaway slave. So whether I ran or stayed, the result would be the same, and my stomach heaved at the realization.

The Lady stood waiting at the edge of the woods, wrapped in her black hooded mantle like the spirit of night. We came to a stop in front of her, the escort fanning out to form a circle in the gloom as the chanting slowly died. The drum, however, continued its relentless rhythm.

A smile of satisfaction played about Morgan's mouth, and when she extended her arms, I saw the glimmer of the armband she had been wearing when she raised the unspeakable goblet at the Black Lake.

'The time has come, my sister, when we are at last well met,' she said, her voice purring with triumph.

Behind me, unseen hands began to tug at Igraine's cloak, as though to strip me of all defence, and the nightmare rose while the drums pounded until they shook the ground.

'Hold!'

A horse and rider burst through the ring of druids as the drumming turned into hoofbeats, and my captors froze. The steed came to a rearing, whinnying halt in front of Morgan like some ancient god unleashed by her spell.

'How dare you?' the Priestess demanded, stepping back to glare up at the intruder. Her wrath filled the glen and focused on the unknown element. 'Who are you to command the Lady of the Lake?'

'It is I, Arthur Pendragon!' the horseman roared, fighting to gain control of the situation.

The words ripped through my terror, shredding it like rotted fabric, and I went limp with relief. Arthur swung down from the saddle and handed me the reins without even a glance. All his energies were concentrated on the Priestess.

'M'lady Guinevere and I must be wed this morning, and I have come to ask your blessing. Will you perform the ceremony now, here, on the spot?'

Morgan took a step backward as though physically assaulted.

'Of course not!' She spat the words out, her voice full of outrage at such an idea. Drawing herself up to her full height, she announced, 'The bride must first undergo the preparations.'

'But that has already been done at Avebury,' Arthur pointed out, 'and we cannot wait another day.'

'I have reason to think they were not done properly,' Morgan retorted coldly.

There was a moment of silence while brother and sister assessed each other in a naked confrontation of power.

At last Arthur turned on his heel and reached for me. 'Then we shall be wed by the Archbishop,' he announced flatly.

He gave me a boost up on to the stallion's back and, finding the stirrups, swung up behind me.

'You'll do what?' The shrill edge of disbelief made Morgan's smooth voice ragged. 'I forbid it!' she screamed, fists clenched and eyes burning with fury. 'As the High Priestess of Albion, I forbid it.'

'And as High King of Britain, I say there is no time to argue!' Arthur replied, wheeling the stallion round and spurring him down the track.

The animal, trained for war and quick as mercury,

sprang forward as the Lady's people drew back in a flicker of white robes, and within seconds we were free of the circle and racing for the town.

I crouched low on the horse's neck, and Arthur slid one arm around my waist, lying close above me so that the two of us clung to the flying steed like two burrs on a blanket. The stallion plunged and rose beneath us, his hooves throwing up clods of grass and damp earth. I closed my eyes and let the rhythm of the gallop and the warmth and firmness of Arthur's hold on me replace the recent terror.

The wind was whipping my hair into a cloud around both our heads and Arthur had to bury his face in it to make himself heard.

'Sorry about that,' he said, but when we pulled up to a more respectable pace at the edge of town, I twisted round to look up at him and the gleeful grin on his face was neither contrite nor apologetic.

'I'll make it up to her, somehow,' he promised. 'Loss of face and all that. But last night's plans went perfectly; we have three boatloads of warriors halfway to the coast this morning, and I've promised Theo a kingdom for his trouble. Cador and Pellinore and all the others are getting their men together, and we're set to march come eventide. There's nothing left now but finding a priest for the ceremony. And collecting witnesses,' he added, laughing at my expression. 'Who really has to be there?'

'Well, Vinnie and Brigit, and Nimue and Merlin, and of course your mother . . . and Agricola and Pelli if they can make it, and Bedivere and . . . whoever else can come, I guess.'

I burst out laughing at the realization that this State Occasion was turning into a cross between an elopement and a May-dance. Waves of relief and surprise and joy were surging through me.

'Are we really going to get married right now?' I asked, leaning back against Arthur as he guided the stallion between the houses.

'Unless you've changed your mind,' he whispered, nuzzling through the tangle of hair around my ear. I gasped and scrunched my shoulders happily.

We came trotting into the Square to find it full of people scurrying about in the early-morning light. Spits were being set up and coals banked in open fires which had been lit well before dawn. Vast arrays of meat and fish, game and fowl were already spitted and waiting to be cooked.

'What's a wedding without a feast?' Arthur grinned. 'We've just moved everything up a couple of days. This way everyone will have eaten by the time we're ready to leave tonight, and we'll take whatever's extra with us on the road. We can make better time if we don't have to forage and cook, and there'll be no need for fires that give away our position. Travelling by night, we could get as far as the Severn before they realize we're on the move. Thank goodness the moon will be new.'

He was happy as a child with a whirligig on a breezy day, and the youngsters who ran to surround us where we came to a halt in front of the church were laughing and smiling as well.

Swinging lightly down from the saddle, he handed the reins to one of the bolder lads who stepped forward. The boy proudly accepted the honour, shushing his colleagues and talking softly to the stallion, who continued to prance and tremble with excitement.

Arthur stood at the foot of the church steps, looking up at me with a confidence and gaiety that were irresistible. I grinned back at him, amazed that all trace of the tension and stress from the night before had vanished. It was unclear whether his rejuvenation came from getting some rest or because he was finally able to take action, but I suspected it was the latter.

'Did you get any sleep last night?' I asked as he raised his arms to me.

'Sleep?' he queried. 'That comes later, once we are man and wife.' He put me on my feet and gave me a quick hug.

The curate came to the doorway of the small wooden church and scowled at us for causing such a commotion. He would have shooed us away if he hadn't been in such a hurry to get back to the altar, where the Archbishop waited to begin the Mass.

'Sir . . . uh, Father,' Arthur called out, taking the steps two at a time and pulling me along behind him. 'We need to see the Archbishop immediately.'

'What about?' asked the priest, obviously unaware who we were.

'A marriage. Our marriage. It's urgent.'

'I suppose you've been celebrating the Goddess under the hedgerows and only just now realized the consequences,' the holy man said testily, looking suspiciously at my cape, which certainly could have covered a multitude of sins.

It was all I could do to keep a straight face, and Arthur was grinning from ear to ear.

'Not at all, Father. Just tell the Archbishop that the King wishes to see him . . . now!' he added, holding out his hand with the Dragon Ring on it. After staring in open-mouthed amazement, the priest bowed hastily and went skittering off into the church.

Arthur was waving to a familiar figure who loped across the paving stones towards us.

'It's good to see you here, M'lady,' Bedivere commented, giving us a sweeping bow as he came to a stop at the base of the stairs. 'I gather the Priestess wouldn't listen to reason?'

He and Arthur exchanged quick news about what had happened with Morgan and the progress of the spits; then Arthur laughed cheerfully.

'You'd best send a page round to the Queen Mother, and to Gwen's house, to tell them if they want to attend the wedding they'd better come quick. And be sure to tell Merlin too, and Nimue. I think you'll find them together.'

Bedivere cocked an eyebrow and I wondered if he was aware of what was happening to our Magician.

'Oh,' I added as he turned away, 'tell Vinnie to bring the veil, and a comb as well.'

'And the smith,' Arthur added. 'Be sure he knows he's welcome too. Poor man, he's been at his forge a day and a night; seems the least we can do is invite him in for the ceremony.'

Bedivere was already running down the steps, and he waved an acknowledgement, then whistled to the flock of children, who rushed to follow him towards the Hall.

In the middle of the Square, a woman with a tray full of breads paused when she saw the horse, then cautiously made her way around him to come and stare up at us. She looked vaguely familiar and I tried to remember where I'd seen her before.

'Lor, if it isn't the King!' she exclaimed, recognizing Arthur and dropping a quick curtsy.

The motion upset her tray of goods, sending buns and biscuits tumbling helter-skelter to the ground. It was a moment before the disaster came to her attention, for she stared at Arthur just as Cabal had when they first met, absorbing his presence as though it were life itself.

At last she glanced down at the scatter of her loaves and with a rueful grin began picking them up. It was then I recognized her as the woman hawking bread at the stirrup demonstration. Her frazzled air and general good nature had struck me on that day as well, for she gave the impression that no matter how many disasters might trip her up, she would rise above them with a kind of unflappable humour at the ludicrousness of life.

I hurried down the steps to help her, joining in the scramble to retrieve the errant rolls. She accepted my help without a second throught, though at one point she sat back on her haunches and tried to poke a flyaway strand of hair back into the knot on the top of her head.

'Ain't he grand?' she marvelled, staring up at my bridegroom.

I was no sooner on my hands and knees than the Archbishop arrived at Arthur's side, huffing and puffing in amazement as he looked first at his king and then down at me. Arthur made the introductions and I bobbed my head in respect, deciding that true dignity lay in continuing to help my subject without question.

The bread lady stopped to gawk at me while Arthur conferred with the holy man, and by the time the Archbishop nodded in agreement, the bread had all been retrieved.

Arthur turned to our subject with a wonderful smile. 'Go tell your family, and neighbours, and anyone else you meet, they're all invited to the Royal Wedding,' he said, carefully not looking at me as I stood up and dusted off my hands. 'The whole town is invited if they can get here in time.'

The woman stood there staring back and forth between the two of us, her face reflecting amazement, disbelief and sheer delight as she grasped the situation. With a joyful shout she threw her tray in the air and went running back the way she'd come. I watched the loaves go bounding across the pavement a second time, then looked up at Arthur, who grinned and shrugged and reached out for my hand.

And so it was that we were married before a stunned and sleepy congregation that damp April morning, by an Archbishop who decried the loss of the glorious event he had so carefully planned, but wasn't about to make the same mistake as the Lady of the Lake had.

Vinnie and Brigit arrived just before the service began, and since the veil hadn't been unpacked yet, Brigit took a wreath of dried flowers from the altar and put it atop my head.

Acolytes brought out extra candles, making the little chapel glow with light and warmth as townspeople came streaming through the door. A skimpy choir got off to a shaky start, but as more members arrived the voices blended in harmony and the sound became rich and elegant.

When the Archbishop asked who brought this woman to be married, Merlin stepped forward and gave me away. Between Pellinore and Cathbad and now the Sorcerer, I must have been one of the most often offered-up ladies in the country, though never by my own father.

Standing in a cloud of Christian incense, my eyes watering and nose twitching, I wished he might have been present. And while I wasn't sure what he would think of all this, I could see Kaethi's wry grin as clearly as if she had been with me instead of hundreds of miles away.

Sometime during the ceremony I heard Vinnie sniffle, and at one point caught a glimpse of Nimue, her eyes huge and dark, and knew the Goddess was attending. Halfway through, Pellinore came striding in the side door, buckling his belt and all but tripping over Griflet and the dogs, who were standing in the shadow.

There was a moment of confusion when the Archbishop asked for a ring. The holy man turned to Bedivere, who looked startled and then crestfallen and finally shook his head. Arthur let go of my hand and carefully pulled the Dragon Ring off his own finger and gave it to the priest. Someone, perhaps Igraine, gasped, but the ring was blessed, and then Arthur slid it on to my thumb and carefully closed his fingers over my hand.

I looked up at him, appalled, seeing a light of triumph and satisfaction and perhaps love shining in his face. The Archbishop pronounced us man and wife. Arthur's arms were close around me and we were drowning in a kiss mixed with laughter and joy.

Public event or not, hasty and confused and full of chaotic excitement, we'd made our vows before the people of the land and were now officially and forever wedded, Arthur and Guinevere, High King and Queen of Britain.

As we turned to the congregation, the chapel dissolved in a prism of music and candles and the faces of our subjects. I saw the Saxon girl standing next to Griflet, her smile solemn and respectful; an enormous mountain of a man with the arms and shoulders of a blacksmith looked me up and down, then gave Arthur a knowing wink; the bread lady and her brood stood to one side, basking in the chance to take part in history, while the pursed-lipped cobbler gave us a big, toothy grin and didn't once glance at our feet.

People barely met, casually passed or quickly spoken to mingled with the dear ones already loved: Vinnie, dabbing at her eyes; Bedivere, staying quietly in the background as usual: Igraine, with her elegant bearing and sweet smile – and of course Brigit, making the sign of the cross and then smiling that knowing-laughing-encouraging smile which had seen me through so many scrapes. My eyes brimmed with tears, and I wanted to embrace all of them, even Merlin.

486

We made our way up the aisle with friends and strangers all falling in behind and the dogs barking excitedly as Griflet ran along to catch up with us.

Hordes of people were streaming into the Square, all running towards the church as we emerged, and for a moment there was pandemonium everywhere.

'Are we too late?' someone cried, and the answer flew back, 'Naw, they've just come out the door, can't you see?'

Those who were outside came rushing to the steps while those who were inside were trying to get out, and we were in the middle of it, an island of calm in a ripping sea of enthusiastic subjects.

'We can't go back to the Hall,' Arthur whispered, surveying the crowd. 'It's a military headquarters now, and there's no place for privacy.'

'My house?' I offered, looking over the swelling mob and wondering how we would ever get there.

There was an eddy of movement by our feet and Gawain pushed his way to the front of the throng, his ruddy face covered with sweat and a tattered bouquet of wildflowers clutched in one hand.

'I couldn't make the vow-taking, but wanted you to have these,' he said breathlessly, offering up the posies as if they were a royal treasure. Some had been plucked up roots and all, but at that moment they were the sweetest gift I had ever seen, and I took them solemnly and buried my face in them.

The crowd began to cheer, and Arthur put one arm around my shoulder, waving exuberantly to our subjects with the other. Then, without any warning, he picked me up bodily and started down the steps.

The startled populace parted to let us through, 'oohing' and 'ahhing', all the way to my house until we were safely inside, with the door kicked shut and the crowd outside singing and laughing.

He put me down, and we looked at each other in silence.

'Well,' he said awkwardly, turning to check the already closed door. 'I guess it was a bit unorthodox.'

'A bit,' I agreed as the shyness rose between us.

'And in years to come they'll undoubtedly claim it was much more grand and formal. You know how the bards like to exaggerate.'

I nodded and looked down at the field flowers still clutched in my hand. Someday they would no doubt say I had been draped with jewels, and kings of great renown had attended us in a fine cathedral setting. But I knew better . . . I knew the truth of the matter and found it much more exciting.

I glanced back up at Arthur, wishing he would say something loving and tender, but he was looking at me with that fixed, level stare and I turned away, embarrassed.

'Do you want some tea?' I asked preposterously.

He laughed then, and I caught the sidewise sweep of his glance, merry and mischievous and no longer constrained.

'You sound like the Queen Mother,' he teased, grabbing me by the hand and heading for the loft. 'We can have tea later, if there's time.'

We made a great heap of pillows, then flung the fur robes over them, and he pulled me down in a laughing, romping roughhouse. I barely had time to slip the dress over my head before he was ready – thick and hard and insistent, his own knowledge and need making up for whatever experience I lacked. With one fluid movement he rolled me over on my back, his thighs pressing eagerly

488

between mine, his manhood questing and then finding its goal.

Confused and surprised, I tried to follow the rhythm of our union, waiting for the waves of desire I had felt for him during the last few weeks to well up within me again. But there was no time, no chance to build in longing, no opportunity to share and trust the closeness of our bodies. Arthur reached the peak of his passion with a deep, sustained groan and slowly lowered his forehead to my shoulder.

Baffled, I lay quiet beneath him, holding this stranger in my body and wondering at the absence of the kisses and caresses I had so looked forward to. He, at least, seemed satisfied, and I ran my hand gently up and down his back as his breathing returned to normal.

At last he raised his head, and I searched his face for even a touch of the tenderness I'd seen when he was talking to the dogs.

'I've looked forward to this since the moment I realized you were about to beat me in that horse race,' he said slowly, reaching out to brush a flower petal out of my hair. 'You're a remarkable woman, Gwen, and I want you to know how glad I am you're my wife and not someone else's. Besides, you're the best queen material I've seen in years,' he added fliply, 'and I think I'd better take back the Dragon Ring before you decide you can do the job all on your own.'

His jesting made it easier to accept the lack of endearments and tenderness. I smiled solemnly and unclenching the fist which had been guarding the symbol of Britain, took his hand in my own and carefully returned the Ring of State to its rightful position.

We parted then, stretching out next to each other in a quiet, languorous way, and as he drifted off to sleep he mumbled, 'Bedivere will be coming round at midday . . .'

I lay beside him for a long time, wondering if all weddings ended this way, and if we would always have this sort of bantering, good-natured play rather than the touching of two spirits. Perhaps this is really all there is to it, I thought; but the memory of Nimue's eyes when she had looked on Merlin told me there could be much, much more.

Arthur settled into a heavy slumber and after a while I rose quietly and tiptoed down to the main room. There was singing in the street where a small group of revellers had positioned themselves outside our door, offering a concert for their king and queen's repose. They began a Cumbrian lullaby, and my eyes grew misty as I turned away from the window, touched by such devotion.

The coals in the grate were still warm, so I brought the fire back to life and curled up in a chair in front of it, bone-weary but too keyed up to sleep.

Images of the past whirled through my head, shifting from one to another as in a kaleidoscope: Igraine staring silently at the lilies and the abbess of Amesbury handing them up to me; Nimue blessing the ivy wreath before turning to place it on my head; Gawain, so proudly offering his gift of wildflowers; Arthur's expression as he stroked the petals from my hair.

Yet for all the blossoming of spring and hope, dark shadows crept silently round this day's horizon: war was surging across the Irish Sea, bringing death and dismemberment and terrible, throat-swelling grief. The knowledge of it lurked beyond the fire's glow and cast a bittersweet edge to the moment's joy.

Climbing silently back to the loft, I stood looking down at Arthur, trying to reassure myself it was all happening, it was all real. Lying there with one arm thrown carelessly across the pillows, he looked more like a child than a king, wandering in a land far more innocent than the one he would wake up to. Surely no one who knew him could help loving him.

I stayed there a long time, watching over his sleep and trying to memorize his face. I wanted to have a picture to recall across the years if need be, so that if he didn't return from this coming battle I would be able to describe him to his child.

When I could close my eyes and still recall his face, I began to note little things like the cowlick by his temple or the scar on his shoulder. I could imagine Drusilla trying to make the wayward hair lie flat when he was a boy, and wondered what misadventure had caused the scar . . . perhaps a fall from a horse, or a tumble out of a tree?

Fear clawed its way into my throat and I moaned silently. How many things we had yet to learn about each other, and how little time . . . how precious little time!

42
The Parting

When Bedivere came to the door at noon I let him in and caught his look of surprise that I was up and dressed while Arthur occupied the bed alone.

'I thought he should get as much sleep as possible, if he's leading an army out tonight,' I whispered.

Bedivere nodded, and I climbed slowly up to the loft.

Arthur looked so peaceful I paused, unwilling to let the world intrude on this precious scrap of privacy. Another hour or two . . . until he has rested and we have a chance to talk and snuggle and explore being together . . . is that so much to ask before the needs of the kingdom tear us apart?

But even as I resisted waking him, he opened his eyes.

'Bedivere's here, isn't he?' he asked, stretching and reaching for me at the same time.

I nodded and sank down on the bed, too close to tears to speak.

He sat up and gave me a half-hug. 'Here, now' – he gestured towards the warm nest he was vacating – 'why don't you go back to bed for a nap? You'll feel better for the sleep, and I'll wake you before we leave.'

'And miss all the excitement?' I exclaimed, sentiment giving way to bravura. The fact that we hadn't known the sort of intimacy I wanted didn't mean I wasn't his helpmate. And there'd be time enough for sleeping once he and the men marched off to war; in the meanwhile, I was jealous of every hour that remained.

'Ah yes, the Celtic queen . . .' he joked, looking about for his breeches. 'Tell Bedivere I'll be with him shortly.'

The heavy grey clouds of morning had lifted, and the day turned fresh and bright, full of the loveliness of spring's promise. People thronged to the Square, for word had gone out that the wedding feast would be held in spite of the sudden change in plans.

I looked over the gathering, thinking of the dancing and music and happy celebration that should have filled the air. Instead, warriors from every camp were readying their weapons while leaders conferred, medics collected their supplies, cooks filled hampers and baskets, and the ever-important smith packed up his anvil for transport to the field.

On the far edge of the crowd a supply train was making its way towards the gate. The wagons creaked and groaned as the drivers prodded the lumbering oxen, trying to get a head start on the faster-moving troops who would overtake them within the first few hours of the march. It was all the reminder I needed that dreams of laughter and gaiety and the sharing of sweet secrets must give way in times of war. There was, after all, no other choice.

We settled down to work in the privacy of Arthur's room, where maps and inventories and hasty sketches of potential routes were spread out on the long table.

A small but steady parade of people came through the leather curtains bringing information and questions, taking away answers and orders. Cei checked in from time to time, and Bedivere too, but Merlin stayed with us constantly, and Nimue sat silent as a shadow next to me.

I made lists for Arthur, keeping track of the problems as they arose and crossing them off as they were resolved.

A platter of fresh-roasted fowl was brought in and we munched on it casually, not having time for a more formal meal. Arthur had just picked up a drumstick when Tristan and Dinadan sought admission, and he gestured towards the food as he made them welcome.

'Sorry it's not more elegant.' He shrugged. 'But you understand how things are right now.'

The Cornish champions nodded, and Tristan cleared his throat. 'I hope you understand how things are with us, too,' he began.

'We want you to know,' Dinadan interjected, 'it is not our idea to return to Cornwall. King Mark does not like to risk battles outside his own land, and since we are sworn to him we cannot stay and take the field with you, though we would both like to.'

It was the first I had heard that Mark was defecting, and I caught my breath and looked quickly at Arthur. He nodded slowly.

'I understand it is a matter of honour,' he said, tossing the chicken bone aside, 'and I want both of you to know you're welcome at my court any time you choose to come. As for King Mark, well . . .' He sighed, looking for the most tactful way to phrase it. 'I was not totally surprised when I heard of his decision.'

'I'm sure his absence does not connote disloyalty,' Dinadan put in discreetly, and Arthur smiled at the man's efforts to soften the insult. I wondered what this would mean in terms of men lost, and how it would affect the other kings; it could be disastrous if it triggered a string of desertions.

There were a few more words of apology and good wishes; then the warriors bowed to us and departed, and Arthur stared after them.

'Someday,' Merlin said, watching the High King shrewdly, 'they'll leave King Mark, and possibly even come to you . . . but with a taint of scandal, I'm afraid.'

He sounded so much like Kaethi, I was sure he knew more than he was saying, but a messenger from the north arrived just then and, after a hasty bow to Arthur, began reporting the number of curraghs that had landed at

Carmarthen, who had resisted and what skirmishes appeared to be shaping up. The lad was pale with exhaustion, but he relayed his information without stumbling once, and Arthur listened gravely and thanked him when he had finished.

'So many Irish!' I whispered, appalled at the figures.

'Don't forget, Theo's ships carry a great many more people per boatload. I don't think we'll be as outnumbered as it sounds.' Arthur's voice was calm and assured, and I smiled at him hopefully.

As the afternoon wore on things began to sort themselves out, and a kind of order emerged from the confusion. It even appeared that we might have a few minutes to ourselves before Arthur had to leave. I remembered the wedding present I'd made for him and sent a page hurrying to the house to fetch it.

The boy returned and slipped into our chamber behind Cei, who came in carrying a pitcher of wine and a clutch of goblets. I gestured to the page to leave the package by the doorway as Cei splashed the wine into the glasses and handed them around.

The Seneschal lifted his goblet to the light and squinted at it thoughtfully.

'King Mark has turned tail and run south.' His voice dripped with scorn. 'And Pellinore has left for the Wrekin.'

I gasped aloud, unwilling to believe that the giant warrior from the Marches would so readily follow in Mark's footsteps. Pellinore was the furthest thing I could think of from a coward.

'Seems he thinks he can get home, gather up an auxiliary force and still meet us outside of Caerleon. Cador and Geraint went off last night with Theodoric and a handpicked group of men, and everyone else, including Urien, is preparing to leave this evening with you.'

Cei raised his glass in tribute to Arthur and took a sip of wine. I watched him roll the liquid around his mouth, wondering if he was checking it for poison, for I'd never before met a person who fancied himself a connoisseur of the grape. In the north wine is drunk with much gusto and appreciation, but without such elaborate rites beforehand.

'There's only one detail left,' Cei said, taking a further sip from the goblet, but grimacing afterwards. 'Who stays behind with the Queens?'

There was a brief discussion, and it was decided that Bedivere should stay in Sarum to provide us with adequate protection in case the Saxons decided to take advantage of Arthur's involvement elsewhere.

'I think that's the last of the details,' Cei concluded, 'but I'll come fetch you when it's time to leave.'

The Seneschal finished his wine with a gulp, then put the glass down on the table. 'Pheeww, what a bunch of vinegar!' he exclaimed, making a terrible face as he strode from the room.

Arthur rose and began to pace restlessly about, his sober expression deepening into an outright scowl. Finally he stopped and appealed to Merlin.

'I'm still not happy about taking Griflet,' he said. 'He's only a well-meaning boy who's spent more time in the kennels than with the swordmaster. And if, as you say, he's likely not to survive his first encounter . . .'

He sighed and turned away, angry and perplexed by the situation. I knew exactly how he felt, for it seemed brutally unfair that the eager young lad who had accompanied me south should pay for his loyalty with his life.

The Enchanter spread his hands above the table and moved them slowly apart, as though smoothing out a wrinkle in the air.

'Even those with the Sight do not try to play God,' he

said. 'The boy must follow his moira, and if that means death at this time, that's between him and his gods. He would follow you on this mission with or without your approval, and at least this way there's a bit of glory attached as well. If he survives, he may be the better for it.'

He glanced over at Nimue. 'And now I suspect the newlyweds,' he added, solemn as ever, 'would benefit from a few minutes alone, so I think we'd best get on with my packing.'

There was a bit of tense laughter as we all stood up and stretched, making halfhearted jokes as though loath to leave the comradery of the moment. As long as we were all together, going over plans and arranging details, we were sharing an exhilarating challenge; once it got down to the specifics of what one was to take or leave, perhaps forever, it became a solitary and frightening business.

Merlin and Nimue filed through the door, and Arthur began throwing clothes on the bed, then went rummaging for his saddlebags. I retrieved my package from the doorway and was undoing the straps when I realized that my husband was standing immobile, staring at something suspended from his hand. It was a talisman like the one Kaethi had given me, old and worn and obviously much used.

'When I was child,' he said softly, not looking at me, 'this was the only thing I knew about my parents. Drusilla told me my real mother had put it around my neck before I was taken away, and I've kept it with me ever since. I had no idea then that it was a gift from the High Queen herself, but I used to look at it and wonder if the woman who'd given me up had hoped it would keep me safe.'

He stood silently watching the little embroidered pouch as it swung slowly on its thong. I crossed the room, coming to a stop in front of him, and reaching out, laid my hands over his.

'Knowing your mother, I'm sure she did,' I said, lifting the amulet and solemnly putting it over his head. 'And it's worked so far.' I was careful to keep my voice light and playful as I turned back to the table. 'I brought you a little magic of my own, by the way.'

The cloak shook out full and rich and heavy under my hands. I had not made it to serve as a battle cape, so there was no padding across the shoulders or upper torso, but it would keep him warm at least. And it was the best thing I had to send with him, except my love.

He stared at it with admiration and ran his fingers gently along the embroidery that spilled over the shoulders and down the front panel. Stars and flowers and symbols of the Goddess burned bright against the dark green wool, and I held it up for him with pride and hope that he would like it.

'It's absolutely superb, Gwen . . . like fairy work. And much too elegant to wear on a field of blood and muck and gore. I should not like to see it shredded and defiled in battle.'

'Nor would I, if you're inside it!' I joked, draping it carefully over his shoulders and checking the length of it. 'But it will bring you luck and victory and the blessing of the Goddess . . . or at least, of your wife,' I promised as his arms went around me and we came together in a hasty embrace.

Suddenly he pulled back and looked down at me, a sheepish expression wrinkling his brow.

'With all this confusion, I forgot to get you a morning gift,' he said contritely.

I smiled and leaned my forehead against his chest, trying to keep my voice balanced somewhere between tenderness and teasing. 'If you gave me a child this morning, it's the finest gift I could want.'

'Spoken like a true queen!' he jested, breaking into a smile at last. 'And when I come back we'll take that trip I promised. We'll tour through the entire land, M'lady, and you can pick whatever spot you'd like for our very own retreat! Maybe a Welsh hunting lodge, or a manor in the Highlands, up beyond Dumbarton. Or a villa like Agricola's if you'd prefer, with heated floors and a bath that works all the time!'

'How long do you think you'll be gone?' My voice betrayed me by sinking into a whisper, and I was careful not to look at him. Running my hand along his shoulder, I remembered I still didn't know how he'd got that scar.

'As long as it takes!' Arthur's response was typical. 'It depends on what we find when we get there. Most of the coastal kings swore fealty to me at the Coronation. If they've defected and joined with the invaders, I'll have to battle each one down, and replace them with British rulers . . . men I can trust. We may be at it until autumn, if that happens.'

He turned away and began gathering last-minute items from the table, so I stuffed his clothes into the saddlebags. All the while he went on thinking out loud, much as my father used to do.

'If the client kings stay loyal to me, we may be finished within a week or two. Of course, Theo is an untried factor; he talks military strategy well enough, and if he and his men are as good in combat as they sound, they may be able to hold the south shore for me. If he's not that good . . . well, I'm confident I can count on the men who went with him, so even if Theo just supplies a ferry service, our advance troops should give the invaders something to think about!'

I looked up as he lifted down Excalibur. The gold and silver flickered with an inner fire, still filled with the Power as in the morning at Hardknott. Keep him safe, I prayed to it as I knelt to buckle the sword belt in place.

Cei was knocking at the door with the news that the Companions had gathered in the Square. Arthur cleared his throat and promised we'd be right out.

'Merlin says he sees much bloodshed at the River Usk,' he said in a low voice, pulling me roughly to my feet. 'He also said to tell you not to worry – I'll be returning home in one piece and muleheaded as ever.'

'You'd better,' I whispered, no longer attempting to keep up the banter.

We looked at each other in silence, trying to say with our eyes the words that would not cross our lips, then came together in a crushing embrace . . . thighs, mouths, hands, tongues and breath all intertwined. For a little moment that was all there was in the world, filling and consuming at one and the same time, until Cei's voice cut sharply through the air.

As though on cue we turned from each other's arms, grabbing up map case and saddle bags and heading for the door. Neither of us looked at the other but we both strode through the archway with only one thought: to meet the moments ahead with as much verve and courage as possible.

News of the impending departure had spread rapidly through the town, and the Square was a riot of noise and light. The late-afternoon sun was gilding everything with a hard brilliance, flinging its illusion over warriors and townsfolk alike. We stood on the steps of the Hall and squinted against the glare.

People and horses milled about uncertainly, forming little knots of kinship. The Companions stood next to

500

their mounts, while those who would be left behind fussed nervously at husband and father, son and brother. There was much adjusting of battle gear or exchanging of mementos, admonitions to stay out of draughts and efforts to be sure that lucky charms and amulets were carefully tucked under the folds of tunics.

I watched the little rituals meant to keep the finality of such partings at bay, and understood them fully for the first time. Sad, poignant, brave, honourable, they eddied around us like a great, silent sob.

Arthur stood on the steps of the Hall and called for Bedivere to join him. As the crowd grew silent, the High King formally gave over the Seal of Britain to Bedivere's keeping, announcing loudly and in front of hundreds of witnesses that if he was killed and if there was a child born of our morning's union, Bedivere was to act as Regent until the child was grown.

Stripped of all pageantry, it was so simple and so heart breaking: life and death in one and the same sentence. I stood there numb and tired and very close to tears.

'M'lady,' came a familiar voice. 'M'lady, I have a favour I would ask of you.'

Agricola was pressing forward and I looked at him blankly, unable to imagine what boon I could grant to this man whose life was so rich and well ordered.

'I was remembering your need for a ring of Roman workmanship for Lavinia,' he explained, 'and it occurred to me that my wife had had just such a piece. I'd like to give it to you now so that you can pass it on to your governess. It's not particularly valuable, but if I do not return from this battle, I'd rest easier knowing it graces the matron's hand rather than some Irishman's purse.'

He carefully laid a gold-and-jet ring in my palm and closed my fingers over it while I stared at him, stunned by the recognition that no one was safe on a field of battle.

'Oh, sir,' I blurted out, 'surely nothing can happen to you!'

'There, there, M'lady,' he said, taken aback by my reaction. 'Of course nothing's going to happen to me, and I'll be doing whatever I can to make sure the High King comes back in one piece as well. He's the kind of leader one finds but rarely, and none of us will let him down.'

I slid the ring on to my finger and mumbled a thank-you to the villa owner, more grateful for his reassurance than I could say.

Arthur had turned and, seeing Igraine, made a point of bowing deeply and bidding her farewell. Then he was looking around for me, and I stepped forward to his side.

He slid his arm around my waist, and we turned slowly so as to take in all the people in the Square. He brought his other arm up and I did likewise, saluting the subjects who had just that morning saluted us at our wedding.

'To victory, and the cause of peace in Britain!' he sang out, and the throng roared its approval.

The ringing clatter of hooves on stone broke through the crowd and a stableboy came running ahead.

'Make way . . . make way for the King's stallion!' he cried, dodging through the press of people.

The animal himself plunged and pranced excitedly, half-dragging the groom to the foot of the steps. His coat gleamed like black metal and both mane and tail had been braided for battle. The trappings glowed in the late-afternoon light, and the people drew back in awe as the great beast snorted, impatient for his master to be done with politics and get on with the journey at hand.

After that, everything spun and fragmented and blurred around us; we dropped our arms as the war horns were sounded, the deep, belling notes of the aurochs horns making the hair on my nape rise, for it is a call to arms and death that every Briton knows. Arthur lifted my hand silently to his lips, acting out a parting for the public's sake and giving my fingers a last, quick squeeze. And then he was striding down the steps and swinging into the saddle and the moment of separation had come.

The Dragon Banner was lifted into place, and the crowd opened up to let the warriors through. Bedivere and I ran along at Arthur's side, though I doubt he even knew we were there. The enemy had landed, his troops were ready and all the last-minute things at home had been attended to. Arthur was already living on a different plane, heading for a rendezvous that was miles away on another day, and we who were to stay behind were as unremembered as seaweed left stranded by the tide.

The mob bunched as we came to the gates, waving and weeping as the men marched away, and Bedivere helped me climb to the parapet. We stood at the top of the sheer chalk wall, poised between earth and sky, triumph and despair. Arthur was clearly visible as he led the men across the causeway, riding straight and proud and elegant in his new cape while the Red Dragon leapt and whipped above him in the twilight.

The men along the Road saluted as he passed, then fell into line behind him. New banners joined the cavalcade as the different kings brought up their forces until it looked as though the land itself were moving, funnelling into the future.

It was only when Urien's Raven Banner streamed out in the dusk that I remembered Morgan le Fey. I had neither seen nor thought of her since the morning, and the realization that she must still be at Sarum filled me with apprehension.

I shivered and Bedivere slung his cape around my

shoulder, steadying me in the crook of his arm. I leaned back against him, suddenly too tired to think about anything. The tears began to course down my face, and now that Arthur was safely off, I let them all pour out.

Cathbad appeared on my doorstep bright and early next morning with an invitation from Morgan suggesting that we meet in her quarters that afternoon. His manner was unexpectedly pleasant, and I stared at him in astonishment.

'Is she very angry about yesterday?' I asked cautiously.

'The Lady is a woman with a deep commitment to re-establishing the rights of Paganism,' the druid replied, his rich voice swelling up out of my childhood. For a moment I was back in Rheged, preparing to hear some fabulous new legend. 'She is also a woman with a very quick temper, and sometimes her zeal gets the better of her patience. If you are willing to overlook her outburst yesterday, I'm sure you'll find her one of Arthur's most devoted, and influential, subjects.'

A gentle stress on the word 'influential' brought me back to the present, and I reminded myself of her importance to Arthur while Brigit helped me dress for the afternoon meeting.

'Don't forget, Morgan has no other choice than to befriend you, now that you are Britain's High Queen,' Brigit said pointedly. 'It's up to her to make peace with you.'

I hadn't thought of it that way, for although I now carried the highest title in the land, I didn't feel any different inside and had little notion of the power my position gave me over others. When, I wondered, would I begin to feel like a High Queen? At the moment all I could think of was healing the rift between Morgan and myself before Arthur returned, so that he could come home to find wife and sister well in accord.

Morgan had moved into Agricola's room, with a bright, sunny exposure and remnants of painted plaster decorating the walls. Silk pillows and rich tapestries were spread across the bed, and her servants had put fur rugs upon the floor. Compared with the surroundings I was used to, it was royally sumptuous.

'My dear,' she cried, breaking away from the flock of young women that surrounded her. Coming forward, she greeted me with a kinsman's embrace. 'I'm afraid you must think me a terrible boor. I do apologize for that scene in the grove yesterday . . . it was just a shock. If I'd had any idea that matters were so tense and time so short . . . ah, well, I only hope you'll understand.'

Her voice was honey-smooth, her manner all open friendliness. I made some comment about the pressures of the moment, and she laughed gaily.

'The Queen Mother said she was sure you wouldn't hold a grudge. But come now, let's put all that behind us. What with the men going off to their war, we'll finally have a chance to get acquainted as sisters should. I've been trying to meet you for months now, but something always seemed to get in the way.'

Morgan made some signal to the white-robed girls, who melted out of the room, and slipping her arm into mine, guided me towards the window where an embroidery frame stood. A blank piece of linen was stretched within the hoop, and she gestured towards a sewing basket that contained a jumble of bright-coloured thread.

'If I'd known I'd be trapped here at Sarum indefinitely, I would have brought the work I have at home. As it is, I've sent messengers around to the markets to get whatever flosses they can find. Embroidery is the one domestic activity that I really do find soothing.'

506

I thought of the scabbard she had made for Excalibur, and nodded appreciatively. Certainly her touch was magical.

'You must have a talent with the bodkin as well,' she went on. 'That cape Arthur was wearing when he left was hardly the product of the usual sewing room.'

It pleased me that she had noticed and I smiled, glad we had a common ground of communication.

We sat where she could continue her stitchery, and I studied her surreptitiously. The same intensity that made her such a formidable opponent also made her a charming companion, and she seemed genuinely eager to put the tensions of the past behind us.

The conversation turned on stitches and designs, yarns and colours and recipes for dyes while her sleek bodkin poked into and out of the fabric.

'My stock of dyes at home is quite complete,' she confided. 'I've even learned how to extract the Royal Purple from Northumbrian whelks; the colour is quite rare and hard to come by, you know. Most people don't associate the Sanctuary with dyer's arts,' she added casually. 'We're too well known as a healing and spiritual centre.'

I shied at her reference to the Black Lake, afraid it would lead to the subject of our first meeting.

'And of course, the school that Vivian established is justly famous,' Morgan went on, deftly twisting a piece of blue thread between her fingers. 'Our first students are reaching an age when they are ready to go out into the world. Fine young men, all of them.'

I smiled nervously when she glanced over at me. Nothing in her manner betrayed any anger over my parents' refusal to let me attend that school; maybe Cathbad had not told her.

Uneasiness was making my palms clammy, and I cast

507

about for a way to find out how much she knew without a direct confrontation.

'Are there no girls there?' I queried, wondering for a moment which of us was cat and which was mouse.

'No, and I gather there never have been. Originally Vivian planned to have more students, but I have chosen to concentrate on quality rather than quantity.'

There was an edge of defensiveness in her voice, as though she found it difficult to follow in Vivian's wake. Perhaps that accounted for her appalling single-mindedness as Priestess.

'Occasionally one or another of the local farm children blunders in on us,' she went on, plucking fiercely at a snarl in the embroidery thread.

The breath stuck in my lungs and I sat very still, sure she was leading up to our encounter at the Lake.

'But it's easy enough to scare them off.' She shrugged. 'After all, they can't be allowed to wander around the Sanctuary at will . . . it would be bad for the discipline among our students, and who knows what sort of misunderstood notions and tales they would take home with them?'

With a sharp tug she got the knot out of her floss, and the tension inside me snapped. It was suddenly clear that I had lived for years in terror of an event that was so common to the Lady, she didn't even realize that I had been one of those children. It seemed unbelievably funny, and a riotous giggle welled up inside me, and I had to fight to keep from breaking into peals of laughter.

For a moment I wanted to share the story with her, but the memory of her anger the day before stopped me; that had certainly not been the guilty imaginings of an adolescent girl. So I curbed the gleeful giggle, and let the conversation go wherever Morgan chose to lead it, convinced that nothing stood in the way of friendship with my sister-in-law.

Returning to the house in a light and buoyant mood, I found bags and baskets and hampers all being carted out the door.

'Bedivere's orders,' Vinnie said tersely, martyrdom written all over her face.

'He says it will be easier to provide for all three queens under the one roof of the Hall,' Brigit explained. I nodded, thinking it a logical safety precaution, if somewhat chancy, given the different personalities involved.

Vinnie came round to liking the new arrangement in spite of herself, for it approximated the kind of 'women's quarters' she expected in a proper court. It allowed us to eat separately or together, depending on our inclination at the time, and made it easier for me to drop in on Igraine whenever the Queen Mother felt like having company.

Nimue moved with us, as did the dogs, though Bedivere said one of the local girls who worked in the kitchen had volunteered to look after the pups. That turned out to be Frieda, and I teased the Saxon wench about keeping up her contact with Griflet.

'Well,' she allowed in her slow, rough accent, 'the dogs are used to me from all the playing and romping we did together, and I'm fond of them as well. Besides,' she added earnestly, 'if Griflet's going to become a warrior, I'd better show I'm able to be something more than a scullery girl.'

I suspected the Goddess was weaving some kind of moira between these two, much as She had with Merlin and Nimue.

Life at Sarum settled into a quiet, mindless routine with everyone trying to keep from unsettling anyone

509

else. Morgan and Nimue avoided each other entirely, and though I visited Igraine every day, the two priestesses seemed to alternate the afternoons spent in our company. Igraine's companion Ettard was always there, watching and listening, but never saying a word. I began to wonder what, if anything, went on inside her head.

After a fortnight news arrived that the invasion was much bigger than even Arthur had expected, and a major battle had been fought near Caerleon, beside the River Usk. This was the city where Arthur had received the Christian crown, and it seemed a pity that he must re-establish his right to rule from that same centre these four years later.

The High King himself had not been hurt, though many on both sides had been killed or injured. It appeared that those who had gone over to the Irish cause would have to be chased from kingdom to kingdom, so we were to stay at Sarum for the rest of the summer.

I sighed, saddened that Arthur was busy hunting the Irish when we should be getting acquainted and starting a family, for it was evident that I was not pregnant from our bedding following the marriage rite.

Morgan reacted vehemently to the war news, throwing her hands in the air and proclaiming she'd die of boredom if she must stay here until harvest. It took Igraine and Bedivere both to convince her that it would be foolhardy to attempt the trip back to the Lakes with only her dwarf and the cadre of adoring acolytes for protection. In the end the High Priestess agreed to stay with us, though not without strain and irritation on her part. More and more she retreated into the company of her followers.

By the beginning of June the soft, lazy afternoons had begun to run together in a continuous scroll of sameness,

510

with little to mark one day as different from another. So bland was our existence that the day Ettard actually said something at teatime stood out as vividly as though it were a feast day.

Nimue had been commenting on Merlin's generosity in sharing his knowledge with her, a subject that she returned to often, when Ettard suddenly leaned forward, a small frown of concentration on her pretty face.

'Aren't you frightened, being with Merlin?' she asked with a mixture of awe and curiosity.

'Frightened?' inquired the doire.

'He's so . . . important. He's the second-most-powerful man in the kingdom, after all,' Ettard pointed out. 'Why, I wouldn't have the slightest idea what to say to him, even.'

Nimue laughed gently – a rich, knowledgeable sound that contrasted notably with the virginal timidity of the convent girl.

'No matter what kind of power a man has, he's still a male animal, and the Goddess never forgets that,' Nimue said. 'But I don't love Merlin for his power . . . I love him for his humanness.'

Looking at the priestess, I realized that somehow she had changed. This girl, younger even than I was, had blossomed in a way I didn't understand, and the promise of a fine, wise woman hovered over her like an aura. It was unclear whether it resulted from being loved by Merlin or was simply a manifestation of her own inner nature, but either way, it was clearly noticeable. I smiled at her, wondering if I would ever be as confident a queen as she was a priestess.

Later that evening the two of us went strolling along the parapet, looking out at the pearly sunset and wishing the heat would break. The summer lushness cloyed the senses after a while, and I longed for the high, crisp blue of a northern sky instead of the dreamy opal mirage of Sarum's clouds.

'Do you hear directly from Merlin these days?' I asked restlessly.

'Only through the messages Bedivere gets,' the priestess answered. She turned and looked at me, and for a moment I wondered if she could read my thoughts.

'I'm sure they are both all right,' she assured me, laying her hand over mine. 'It's just going to take longer than they expected.'

Soon after that the first groups of wounded began to arrive at Sarum, those strong enough to travel but too severely hurt to be of any use in camp. They came by cart or litter or holding each other up with cane and crutch and comradery. They reported that the enemy had fragmented and Arthur had split our men into different groups to pursue them across South Wales.

The organizing of a temporary hospital gave Morgan an outlet for some of her energy. Brigit volunteered to help, quite willing to overlook religious beliefs when it came to saving lives, and the two of them made an odd but effective pair as the days wore on and a working routine was established.

By midsummer, Morgan had finished the third pillow cover in a row. Even the hospital wasn't enough to keep her occupied, and her nerves were strung taut and sharp. I remembered the question of whether a fox kit could be tamed, and concluded that Kevin had been right: you can't tame something that doesn't want to be tamed. The Lady hadn't wanted to stay with us, and even though she tried to accept it gracefully, her very nature was at odds with the situation.

And then Accolon rode up to our gates, arriving during a long dusk that lasted well past the sunset. The guard routed Bedivere out of bed to come identify the

512

young man, and by morning every girl and woman in town knew we had a visitor from the Continent.

Morgan focused her attention on him like a kestrel hovering above a promising tuft of grass.

'All the way from Gaul to help my brother?' she marvelled over dinner the next night. 'My goodness, what a fine show of commitment.'

Accolon was an elegant young fellow, lean and well muscled, and he flushed now under the stroking of Morgan's attention. He wasn't much past Gawain's age, and the Lady was rather turning his head.

'Arthur will be sorry not to have had you on the battlefield with him,' I said, 'but you are certainly welcome to stay here with us until he and the Companions return.'

'Or,' Morgan suggested silkily, 'perhaps you could come up to the Lakes with me. The men who normally accompany me are off with the High King, but I'd feel quite safe with you as an escort . . .'

Our visitor was suddenly beyond his depth, and he glanced around the table to get his bearings.

'I believe,' Bedivere said, turning pleasantly to Morgan, 'that your brother expects you to stay here and continue to treat the wounded as they come home. M'lady Morgan is the finest healer in all of Britain,' he added in explanation to our guest.

'How very fortunate for the King.' Accolon responded, and Morgan took the compliment graciously.

'Well, at least you can accompany me in gathering herbs and such from the plain. I'll even take you to Stonehenge,' she suggested, her eyes full of invitation.

I had never seen such a smooth seduction before, and it both fascinated and repelled me. Infinitely older and wiser than the young warrior, the High Priestess played with him adroitly. Perhaps if they had been nearer in

513

age, or if there had been some aspect of play and mutual flirtation, it wouldn't have seemed so sinister. As it was, all I could do was smile at our guest and hope he realized what he was getting into.

They took to riding out together at all hours of the day and night; as Morgan pointed out, some plants must be gathered before dawn while others need the spell of a new moon to be effective. At first they were accompanied by her ladies, but as time went by they more often rode alone. Bedivere worried about ensuring their safety, but decided it was better to let her have her way in this and avert a major explosion than to tether her too close and see her break all constraints.

Then one day in August I was having tea with Igraine when the Queen Mother collapsed suddenly, her skin going pale and clammy and one hand tightening into a fist.

Ettard jumped to her feet and began chafing the Queen's hands while I ran out of the room in frantic search of Morgan. Brigit said she hadn't been at the hospital for several hours, and after sending a page to see if her horse was still in the stable, I raced down the corridor towards her room.

'Morgan, Morgan . . .' I called, pushing aside the curtains without knocking. 'Morgan, are you here?'

The movement on the bed stopped abruptly and Accolon rolled to one side as my eyes adjusted to the gloom.

'Must you be so crude in your spying?' the Priestess sighed, languidly pulling the sheet up to her hips.

'It's Igraine,' I panted, reaching out to steady myself against one of the high-backed chairs. 'She's having some sort of an attack and needs you . . .'

'I'll be there shortly,' came the terse reply, so I took a quick breath and ran back down the hall.

By the time I returned to the Queen Mother she was looking better, though Nimue insisted she stay bundled up and warm. When Morgan arrived a few minutes later, she banished the rest of us from the room and set about working her arts on her mother. Whatever she did, Igraine responded well and soon was resting comfortably.

I assumed that as long as I didn't bring up my intrusion into Morgan's bedroom it would be ignored. As a Celtic queen she had a right to bed with anyone she chose, provided that she did not desert her people. I saw no reason to mention the subject to her or anyone else, and so was surprised when Cathbad came to my room that night with a curt message from the Lady summoning me to her quarters.

I was tempted to send him back with a reminder that even High Priestesses can't command royalty. But for Arthur's sake I held my tongue and went off to see what she wanted.

Morgan was sitting in one of the high-backed chairs, her hands clenched on its arms. She dismissed her attendants and turned to glare at me.

'I allow no one the right of judgement over me, except for the Goddess,' Morgan announced, not even waiting for me to sit down.

'I have neither need nor desire to judge you,' I answered, nettled that she should speak so harshly without cause. She obviously had as little understanding of me as I had of her.

'Oh, come now!' The scorn flicked along the edge of her words. 'Don't expect me to believe you aren't going to tell Arthur, and possibly my husband, about what you no doubt think you saw. And certainly it's too tasty a bit of gossip not to be delivered to the teatime circle.' She rose and began pacing around the room, full of the same indignation I had seen on the first day of her arrival. 'Between the men thinking treason and the women tut-tutting in moral righteousness, it will be impossible for Accolon and me to stay on here.'

'Nonsense,' I flared, vexed by her attitude but still determined to smooth matters over.

'Oh, don't try to deny it,' she interrupted. 'I know your type . . . just like my mother, always doing the "proper" thing and criticizing those of us who are more honest in our responses. What a dull, boring lot you are . . . goody-goodies looking for the best side of things, or Christians looking for sin and corruption! Between the bunch of you, you'll dissect every word and action and make our lives miserable without even understanding whom you're dealing with.'

This time when she glared at me, I glared back.

'That's all your own imagination, Morgan, and if you'll let the subject drop, I promise you I won't tell anyone . . . I haven't yet, nor will I in the future.'

'I don't believe it,' she stormed. 'Not considering how cosy you are with that Christian Irish lass, or the upstart doire from Avebury! I'll just thank you not to mention it to my mother; with her health as poor as it is, it might kill her.'

Thunderstruck, I stared at Arthur's sister. For the first time I saw clearly and fully how arrogant, insecure and egocentric she was. Threatened by anything that might interfere with her ability to control the world, she reacted constantly to her own prejudices instead of the reality around her.

Her assessment of me might be below contempt; I could shrug that off as her prerogative. But that she thought I would jeopardize Igraine's life for a bit of bedroom tattle was another matter entirely.

My anger overrode any desire to maintain a peaceful

relationship, and rising with all the dignity at my command, I spoke slowly and firmly:

'When you have got yourself under control, Morgan, I shall be willing to receive you; meanwhile, I don't have time to deal with your histrionics.'

I turned and walked out of the room, catching only a glimpse of the disbelief on her face.

Surely, I told myself, a good night's sleep would calm her down; when she remembered I too was a Celtic queen, she would see that there was no need to fear my undermining her with anyone at court.

But once again Morgan surprised me, stealing away with Accolon in the middle of the night. When Bedivere told me early the next morning, I was shocked and appalled, for this was far more dangerous than simply bedding the young warrior. Ill-considered and foolhardy, it was a deliberate flouting of the King's command during wartime. Morgan's action was so close to treason it could set the entire court in turmoil.

Fortunately, the Lady's defection was totally eclipsed by the arrival of a messenger later that morning.

The Irish campaign was over and Arthur was returning home.

44

Glastonbury

The world turned grey and flat and I felt the horizon contracting around me, leaving nothing but Bedivere's voice.

'A wound, Gwen . . . only a surface wound, not a broken skull or a lost arm.'

The lieutenant was holding both my hands, and I concentrated on his face, desperately trying to see if he was hiding worse news.

'I tell you, Arthur would not dissemble. And if it were a bad wound the messenger would have said so. You can't hide that sort of news from these people. A king who's fainting while he's dictating his message isn't going to be reported as simply "inconvenienced" . . . and that's what the report said.'

It was tempting to believe his soothing tone and reassuring words. Colour began to creep along the edges of things, and the smell of fresh-harvested hay came through the open window as the world took proper shape again.

'The campaign is over for the year. The war has gone well, with only a last few remnants of the enemy remaining in Wales . . . and now your husband will be coming home aboard his own naval vessel.' Bedivere's voice was bold and confident. 'He'll be coming into harbour at Glastonbury like a proper world traveller.'

'And we'll give him a hero's welcome,' I cried, swinging from panic to euphoria. Pulling my hands out of his grasp, I clapped enthusiastically. 'We'll have pipers and drums, and a parade, and – '

'I don't think he really wants that,' Bedivere interjected

quickly. 'Arthur's always said triumphs should be for the soldiers who did the fighting, and since most of them are coming home by land, he wouldn't think it fitting to hold a celebration at Glastonbury. Besides, it's just a sleepy little fishing community, even smaller than Sarum.'

'Don't play with me, Bedivere!' I rounded on him, my voice gone hard and firm as the truth dawned on me. 'He's too badly hurt to sit a horse, or he'd be leading the men home himself. How bad is it, Bedivere . . . how bad?'

My friend glanced down at his hands, then nodded slowly.

'Bad enough to lay him up for most of the winter, I suspect. They say it's starting to heal already. He was always in command of the men . . . no need for heavy drugs. Thank goodness it happened at the end of the campaign.'

'How long have you known?' I asked, trying to keep the fear under control with good solid information.

'I heard just this morning, Gwen.'

He looked at me with such candour, I had to believe in his truthfulness.

'So when do we meet him?' I asked.

'Well, they should be in Glastonbury by the end of the week. I'll just slip over there with a couple of wagons and – '

'And leave me behind? Oh, come, now, do you really think I'd be willing to stay here and wait for him to be delivered like a load of hay?'

Bedivere grinned at that, and though he made a halfhearted attempt to persuade me to stay at Sarum, he finally agreed to let me come. I suggested we take the litter, because it was more private than the cumbersome wagons and the curtains could be closed if we didn't want the people to see how 'inconvenienced' their king was.

519

Instinct told me not to be too obvious about this trip, so I went to the stables early the next morning to saddle Featherfoot, preferring not to take the showier Shadow.

Nimue was already there, also wearing tunic and breeches, as if planning on travelling herself.

'You need someone to attend you, M'lady,' she said calmly, 'and Ynys Witrin used to be a centre of worship in the Old Days. There's a holy mountain there, with a Spiral Sanctuary at the top that is sacred to the Mother. I would like to perform certain rites in honour of Arthur's safe return . . . and ask Her blessing on your own fertility,' she added gently.

Whatever objection I was going to voice melted at her last comment, and I smiled at her, grateful for her thoughtfulness and glad of the companionship.

We made good time on the Road, and it was just coming on night when we reached the causeway that crosses the marsh separating Glastonbury and the Tor from the rest of the world. In the dusk a mist was rising, floating low over the silent waters. It came no higher than the horses' bellies, and the animals waded through it as though gliding effortlessly towards some appointed future.

In the distance a light took shape as a group of riders came towards us, torches held high against the encroaching night. Featherfoot's ears flicked nervously towards them, and I wondered who would travel in so strange a fashion.

The doire and I dropped back next to the men at the litter, turning away from the oncomers lest we be recognized. Bedivere had trotted out to challenge the approaching party when Nimue suddenly lifted her head, a glad smile brightening her features. Reining her mount sharply around, she rode quickly towards the newcomers, for Merlin had come out to meet us with an escort.

The Enchanter led us to a small, rustic inn at the foot of the Tor. We shared a light supper, and I questioned Merlin about Arthur's condition.

'He will be home by the hearth for some months,' came the answer. 'But after a summer of campaigning, it will do him good to rest for a while . . . probably plan the tidying-up operations needed next year. Don't worry,' he added, looking off into some other space, 'his tide's still coming in strong, and won't be turning to ebb for many more years.'

It was a simple statement, made without drama or fanfare, but Merlin was Britain's Seer and Arthur's personal Sage, so I accepted his reassurance gratefully.

The next day dawned crisp and fresh, and I woke up filled with anticipation. Grabbing a chunk of cheese from the sideboard, I went outside to do some exploring.

The inn was situated at the mouth of a small, steep valley that nestles between a soft hill on one side and the sharp conical rise of the holy mountain on the other. Apple trees heavy with fruit covered the lower flank of the Tor, and as I entered the orchard, Nimue's laughter came lightly from a little house hidden within it. It seemed that Merlin had chosen a fitting spot for his nest.

After picking a pair of apples, I began to climb the long, angled ridge that leads to the top of the Tor. Partway up a rock juts through the turf, and I sat down to enjoy my breakfast.

Shiny as polished silver, the waters of the marsh and lake stretched in front of me as far as I could see. The new gold of autumn was reflected along the channels, where alder and willow marked the river courses like a tangled maze. Waterfowl of all types made their homes here: tufted ducks and dabchicks, moorhens and occasional herons. The presence of such large flocks made me think of Solway's wintering hordes; truly the Gods had blessed Logres as richly as Rheged, and I sighed happily at the realization.

When both apples were eaten I got up and stretched, noting the broad terraces that lie along the sides of the Tor. Clearly they formed a pattern of some kind, though they didn't cross the ridge I was standing on. For a moment I was tempted to follow them, until I remembered that this mountain was the scene of ancient rituals. I scrambled up the steep ridge instead, leaving it to Nimue to follow the paths that called forth the Goddess and Her Otherworld temple.

From the summit of the Tor the world spreads out below like a map laid flat for reading. Here and there, other hilly islands poked up through the water, the fields along their tops rich with ripe grain. Some were reflected in the glassy lake, while others stood with their feet shrouded in mist. Across the water a flock of lapwings and golden plovers rose thousands strong, frothing the air with their wings and banking into and out of sight as the sunlight held or lost them on some gliding turn. They were so joyous I raised my arm in silent salute, glad of the fine omen for the day's beginning.

It was then I saw it, the ship that was coming slowly through the waters in the northwest. Shading my eyes, I peered fixedly at the vessel. Tall and wooden, it looked like the one that had got stuck in Morecambe's sands, and appeared to be heading in our direction. When a puff of wind lifted the flag and the Red Dragon slowly bellied in the breeze I let out a wild yell and went racing down the ridge.

'It's here . . . Arthur's ship is here,' I cried, dashing towards Merlin's retreat without thought of discretion.

Nimue and the Wizard were standing together at a table scrutinizing a scroll covered with antique writing. They were so engrossed in their study I stopped in the doorway, suddenly shy about rushing rudely into their world.

'Well, come in, M'lady, and close the door, please. No point in heating the whole outdoors.' Merlin gestured towards a seat by the hearth, and Nimue poured a cup of cider for me as the Enchanter rolled up the scroll. 'It will take another hour for them to reach the wharf at Wearyall Hill, so you may as well sit down and wait.'

After the first wonderful excitement of knowing Arthur was truly almost home, our actual meeting was anti-climactic. Surrounded by a cadre of young men, my husband was carried ashore on a stretcher, looking grey and spent and terribly weak. When I reached his side and dropped down beside him, he took my hand, but he focused all his attention on Bedivere. They exchanged greetings, the most immediate of news and a few words of welcoming banter before we began the slow march back to the hostel. I continued to hold Arthur's hand, and from time to time he squeezed my fingers sharply when some misstep jarred the stretcher, but that was all. It was only later, when he was well settled in a clean bed and everyone else had left, that he looked specifically at me and smiled.

'I was not wearing the cape,' he noted drily, 'so it's still quite presentable. In better shape than I am, as a matter of fact.'

I took his hand again, pressing it to my cheek.

'It's just so good to have you back home alive,' I whispered.

'Are you . . . that is, are we . . .?'

I had so many months before dealt with my own disappointment at not being pregnant, it took me a minute to realize what he wanted to know.

'No,' I answered.

'Pity,' he sighed, closing his eyes as if for sleep. 'With this wound, I won't be able to remedy that situation for some months, I'm afraid.'

'That's all right,' I reassured him, reaching out to stroke the hair back from his forehead. 'There will be more than enough time for a whole flock of bairns come spring . . . Well, maybe not all at once,' I added when he raised one eyebrow. 'Now, you go on to sleep and we'll talk of the future when you're more rested.'

He nodded, still without opening his eyes, then murmured, 'Did Morgan come with you or is she still healing those at Sarum?'

'No . . .' I temporized, wondering if he considered his own wounds bad enough to need her special touch and confused as to what to tell him about her departure. I didn't want to mention her dalliance with Accolon, for if the High Priestess and I were ever to repair this most recent rift, she would have to have recognized that I was not a meddling, judgemental tattletale. As to the question of her defiance in leaving, Bedivere would be the best one to report that to the King. So I simply said that Nimue had come instead, and planned to perform a special rite on the Tor.

Whether Arthur heard me or was already asleep I couldn't tell, but the subject of Morgan didn't come up again, much to my relief.

When Arthur had rested fully and was better able to handle the sway and lurch of the litter, we travelled back to Sarum. Things were much as we had left them, though on our second day home, Igraine asked permission to pack and return to her convent, and nothing that I said could dissuade her.

'Bedivere can spare an escort now, and with Arthur back, the two of you will be needing time alone to get into the habit of ruling together,' the Queen Mother said firmly.

By the end of the week she was all packed and came to Arthur's chambers to say a formal farewell. I tried to leave them alone, thinking that privacy might give them a way to express their feelings more openly, but both raised such a cry when I excused myself, I ended up staying. Later, as I walked with her to the litter, Igraine reached out and took my hand.

'There is probably no way to make up for the wrongs my children think I've done to them, all in the name of love. But it helps to know that you're beside him, and that you at least don't think ill of me . . .' She smiled at me sweetly. 'You're not only going to be a fine queen, you're a delightful daughter in my old age.'

We hugged each other then, like true mother and daughter, and I begged her to let me know if she needed anything, ever.

'Of course,' she answered, 'and you must promise the same.'

After she was seated in the litter and the horses started forward, she waved one last time. Beside her, Ettard wept silently, unable to hide her sadness at leaving court. When the entourage had left the Square I hurried off to find Brigit, my own face wet with tears.

With Morgan gone, Brigit had taken over the running of the hospital and had recruited Frieda to assist her.

'If I can work with Morgan's Celtic gods, I can certainly work with Frieda's Saxon deities,' my Irish friend announced. 'Besides, the girl has been here day and night since Griflet was brought in. She needs something to keep her occupied, and we need the additional help.'

'How is the boy?' I asked, taking one end of a newly washed bandage and rolling it up for future use.

'Bad . . . very bad. I'm not at all sure we can save him.' Brigit spoke briskly, having no time to decry the unfairness of fate, then looked over at me with a wry smile. 'But we'll not give him up without a fight.'

As matters turned out, Griflet mended more rapidly

than Arthur, and by Samhain he was up and walking about, coming in to visit the High King every day and working constantly with the dogs.

'Makes me feel old,' Arthur grumbled one morning after such a visit.

'Broken ribs are different from body wounds,' I replied, plumping up the bolster I had made for his chair.

'And boys are quicker to mend than men,' he averred crossly.

I got the draughtboard out and was setting up the pieces, hoping the game would improve his mood, but he pushed the thing away with an oath.

'I'm fed up with games and idle chatter! Damn it, I should be about the business of ruling this country, not sitting here like some invalid, unable to mount my horse or my wife or even a diplomatic mission to my enemy's camp!'

'You have been working,' I pointed out. 'Why, we've drafted treaties with the Irish settlers in Wales, giving them new governments with men like Agricola in power; men whose loyalty you can count on. Geraint is keeping things under control in Devon, and both Theo and his lieutenant, Marcellus, are commited to making sure the Bristol Channel is free of invaders. The different kingdoms have accepted their new leaders and are sending their best warriors to fight under your banner. That's pretty impressive progress for having been home only a little more than two months now.'

'Ah, but it's not enough, Gwen . . . it's not enough,' he fretted. 'Treaties are only as good as the will of those who sign them . . . and they don't mean much if I can't get the kings to understand The Cause . . . the need to solidify into a working unit. Merlin says it will take a new ideal, a new concept to bond the people together; religion won't do, because the people's beliefs are too diverse.'

526

He sighed wearily. 'If we don't find a solution pretty soon, the Saxons will recognize our weakness and pick up the offensive again. I know they have more plans for claiming the British heartlands; I can feel it in my blood. I don't know which among the Federates I can trust and which have expansion on their minds. My information comes piecemeal, and then it's generally only from observation, not from inside knowledge. What I need is someone who speaks the language.'

'Frieda . . . Frieda does, and she can teach us,' I suggested. 'We can both learn, and then when you have to deal with them we'll be on firmer ground.'

There was a long pause while Arthur thought the matter over, and finally he sighed and nodded. 'It's a good idea,' he admitted, grudgingly pulling the game board back into position. 'A really fine idea, actually. If I can't meet them on the battlefield, at least I can prepare to best them in their own tongue.'

So Frieda began tutoring us, trying to shape our fluid Welsh tones into the guttural growls of Saxon speech. Arthur was far worse as a student than I would have expected, and the Saxon girl far more patient, so between us we made steady, if not spectacular, progress. And it kept him occupied during the winter months. He even continued the lessons after he was back on his feet and able to join Bedivere at the drill field each day.

Plans for the cavalry had blossomed after the Irish campaign proved the importance of stirrups, and our troop of horsemen had grown from a handful of Companions to an impressive fighting force. By the time Arthur was able to observe the practice sessions, Bedivere and Palomides had perfected a number of techniques essential to making the mounted unit effective. It was fascinating to watch, and Arthur's spirits picked up immediately.

The fact that we had begun to have sex again also

helped. We drifted into that just as we drifted into administering the kingdom together; it was comfortable and productive (though not yet in terms of children), and if there was none of the grand passion and deep emotional communion I had expected, neither was there dissatisfaction. Arthur simply approached bed the same way he approached everything else: directly and openly, without dalliance or diversion. I hoped with time we might grow closer on a romantic level, but was content to accept the present as it was.

'The new horsemen are looking better and better,' he mused one night as we lay cuddled together before sleep. 'I'm thinking we should give them a chance to show off what they can do now. Maybe,' he added, propping himself up on one elbow and staring out the window at the half-moon, 'it's time to move the court to Caerleon and stage a kind of tournament. In fact, we can combine it with a celebration of my recovery, and a chance to impress on the Irish that I mean to keep Wales well in hand!'

He bounded out of bed, all thought of sleep evaporating as the fire of his idea took hold. At the table he unhooded the lantern and tossing me a tablet and stylus, began dictating a list of all the people who should be invited. We debated the importance of each name on the list, and in the end it sounded much like a regathering of the people who had come to the wedding, except for King Mark, whom we both chose to ignore.

When we got to Morgan's name I glanced over at him, wondering if the Lady would accept. Honour forbade that I mention the cause of her leaving, and Arthur had never brought the subject up; he probably had no idea of the animosity she bore me.

'We'll present you to them with all the formal ritual due a High Queen,' he announced, pacing eagerly back and forth, 'just as we would have if the Irish campaign hadn't interrupted. Also, Merlin once told me it was a good idea to have the client kings reaffirm their loyalty every year. We'll include it all in a proper Feast, at Pentecost, in the spring. What do you think?'

'I think it will be a madhouse.' I laughed, wondering if we were tempting fate to bring together so many rival factions once again.

'Aye,' he said with a nod, putting on a robe to combat the chill. 'There's got to be some way to rise above all those "royal egos." Who sits where, indeed,' he snorted.

'That part's easy enough to fix.' I shrugged. 'Just set the trestles out in a circle, the way the Cumbri do at Council.' I drew my knees up under my chin and tucked the down quilt in around the edges. 'That way all the guests are equal in status, and if you leave spaces between the trestles the servants can move in and out easily enough.'

Arthur stopped dead in his tracks and, thrusting his hands deep in his pockets, stared at me. It was hard to know whether he was looking at me or through me, but I stared back, wondering what he was thinking up now.

'We did it on the trip south, only without the tabletops,' I went on, 'and my forefathers have been doing it for generations. If it works for the touchy Celts, it should work for the Romano-Britons as well.'

A wonderful broad grin was stealing over Arthur's face, and his eyes began to sparkle mischievously.

'By Jove,' he swore in Latin, 'Bedivere said I would do well to listen to you! A circle . . . like a great round table where there isn't any "head" or "foot." What a marvellous device; it'll keep the politicians among them scratching their beards for weeks, trying to decide whether they've been insulted or complimented!'

He grabbed up the lantern and headed for the door.

'Arthur, where are you going?' I cried, scrambling out of bed and running after him.

'I've got to tell Merlin about this,' he said, tugging impatiently on the ties that fastened the leather curtains.

Throwing myself in front of him, I pointed out of the window. 'It's long past the middle of the night . . . look, even the moon has set. Goodness' sake, love, let the Magician enjoy his sleep. You can discuss it with him tomorrow.'

The nip of the night air was sharp against my skin, and I started to shiver even as I laughed up at my husband. He stood there looking down on me, really and truly seeing me this time.

'Maybe you're right,' he said slyly, hanging the lantern on a hook by the doorway and sliding both arms around me. 'Who knows what other ideas you might come up with if given a further chance?'

I laughed again – the deeper, growling laugh that comes from the Goddess – and thought happily that Arthur was now at last finally and completely himself again.

45

The Round Table

The idea of the Feast at Caerleon swept through the winter court with visions of colour and pageantry and all the gaiety such occasions create. Messengers were sent out across the realm with writs inviting the Kings of Britain to join us for Pentecost, and at the bottom of each scroll the Dragon Seal blazed in its crimson glory.

Merlin called on the best craftsmen and cabinetmakers in Logres and took them with him to Caerleon, where they built the special trestles to be set in a circle at the Feast. Every woman at court picked up her needle and thread to help with the embroidering of the noble names of our guests; the horsemen spent hours polishing their trappings, and the cooks set about planning elegant menus that would do us all credit. Cei even scoured the countryside looking for caches of the prized Mediterranean fish sauce that might be found in nearby larders, and the amphoras he came up with were duly loaded on packhorses and carefully sent on ahead. By the time we left for Caerleon ourselves, no one had thought of anything but the Feast for weeks.

Glad to be on the Road again, Arthur was everywhere at once, riding with Bedivere, jesting with Gawain, conferring with Merlin. For my own part, after a year of living with the long sea swells of the green downs, the chance to see a different face of Britain was a blessed relief.

We travelled at a leisurely pace and on the second night set up camp on a hillside overlooking the steamy, fetid valley that had once been the Roman resort of Bath.

Cei stared down at the ruins of the town, his tax appraiser's eye taking in every crumbling column and broken arch.

'What are the chances of repairing it?' Arthur asked, gesturing towards the heaps of rubble and fragments of stone arcades that glowed golden in the late-afternoon light.

'Drain the swamp . . . see what we can do to shore up the buildings?' The Seneschal considered the matter. 'There's too much to try to rescue all of it, but perhaps the baths could be salvaged . . . probably not enough people living here to keep up the old elegance, but a place with naturally hot water shouldn't go to waste. I can look into it, if you want.'

Arthur grunted noncommittally, continuing to stare at the remnants of another age. Reeds and rushes now clogged the watercourse, and in the standing pools masses of water lilies floated, soft and fleshy and languid. The toppled masonry and broken statues around the hot springs were wrapped in vapours, sometimes plainly visible, sometimes hidden in clouds of steam. It was like a dream of remembered glory tugging pitifully at the cuff of the present.

I made the rounds of the camp with Arthur that night, and we stopped afterwards at a rocky outcrop to look down on the ruins again. They shone in the moonlight with a strange, eternal lure.

'A sense of identity in the here and now . . . that's what Britain needs,' my husband mused, as much to himself as to me. 'The belief in something honourable and honest and real . . . This habit of looking back to the days of the Empire, or even the older time of Heroes . . . that's fine, but it's like a meal remembered: you can recapture the flavour mentally, but it doesn't fill the stomach now. The people need to take pride in what they are doing now,

532

today . . . with a chance to recognize their present worth. There's nothing in Britain that isn't salvageable if the people just put their minds to it, and that goes for everyday life and trade as well as clogged drains and decaying buildings. As long as they feel beaten and frightened and unable to fix things, they will be unable, and they'll skulk like rats in the ruins of their own making . . .'

He sighed, frowning into the night. I had learned that there were times when Arthur wanted nothing more of me than silent support, so I listened quietly, confident that when the time was right the solution to the problem he wrestled with would take shape, itself clear and whole and purposeful.

The ferry crossing at the Severn went smoothly, and we rode into Caerleon on a bright afternoon with all our penants flying in the June breeze.

The town was resplendent with flowers, and banners and bright awnings adorned the buildings, while the outlying meadows bloomed with the tents of the nobles who had come to join us. Jugglers performed on the corners, and a dancing bear entertained the crowd outside the amphitheatre.

The arena had been prepared for cavalry demonstrations, with smiths and leatherworkers, horse doctors and military men all meeting to exchange tips and information, new remedies and the most recent tactical developments. The tournament itself lasted for two days and included displays of individual riding skills, group manoeuvres and mock battles, and that favourite of Celtic feats of bravery, the single combat between two heroes. Arthur and I sat under a canopy erected on the reviewing stand, applauding the various participants and hoping there was some way to balance out the awards so that no one faction became discontented and testy.

Even the Queen Mother had come for the festivities, though it was obvious that her health was failing. She looked paler and more drawn than before, but her eyes still twinkled with a bright humour when we talked, and I was sorry there wasn't more time to visit her.

'That's all right, child,' she remonstrated gently. 'You're busy being a queen, after all.'

I nodded, appreciative of her understanding, and hurried back to my chambers to dress for the Feast.

Later, when Vinnie had finished piling my hair up in waves and braids so that the fillet rode proudly on a mass of apricot swirls and the long gold earrings from Brigit's family swung free against the length of my neck, I picked up the elegant gold torque Igraine had given me as a wedding present. The piece had been in Cunedda's family for more generations than anyone knew, and I stared at it now while the little animals on the knobbed ends peered back at me in pop-eyed surprise.

How many other women had held it thus, thinking of the lives it linked together? The ancient badge of the freeborn, a treasure in itself, it would have been worn at times of great honour and ceremonies of deep grief, as well as State Occasions and the high holy days of magic and dancing. Down through the ages the braided strands glimmered like the intertwined moira of destinies: proud, untarnishable, symbol of the dignity and courage of all who had the right to wear it.

I slipped it easily around my throat, then stood up to check the effect in the mirror. I might never have Mama's striking beauty or serenity of nature, but the green silk dress had been remade to fit my taller, lankier frame, and the golden jewellery gave my reflection a regal air.

Standing behind me, Brigit whispered loudly to Vinnie,

'Looks like a regular High Queen, doesn't she?' and the matron turned to stare at her, shocked.

The mischief on the Irish girl's face made even Vinnie smile, and after a moment of exaggerated reappraisal my governess nodded. 'I think she'll do . . .' she whispered back.

I laughed with them, remembering how long I had tried to fight off just this fate. Somewhere in the gaiety that filled the room I heard Mama's voice as well, and hoped that she would tell Nonny I'd turned out to be a credit to Cunedda's line after all.

Arthur gave me his own nod of approval when we came together outside the Great Hall, and I grinned up at him. Perhaps someday I'd tell him how I'd planned to run away rather than become his bride, but for the moment it was delicious just to slip my arm into his.

At the entrance to the Great Hall I caught my breath. Merlin had insisted on laying out the room himself, saying that I would be far more useful helping Cei than setting up the trestles. So like the rest of the nobles, I was dazzled by my first sight of the Round Table.

The room had been decorated with banners and shields and all manner of bright hangings on the walls. Towering sconces held great blazing torches, and on every table miniature suns floated in pools of crystal light, their wicks close-trimmed and neat.

The tables were draped with white linen cloths which hid the sturdy trestles. They were ranged in a circle as for any feast at home, except that there was no fire pit in the centre, so we could look directly across the intervening space without a forest of firedogs and hanging pots. Fresh rushes covered the floor and wildflowers were laid out before each guest's place.

Every noble at the table had a chair of his own, over the back of which hung a panel of embroidery proclaiming his name and rank, while his retinue was ranged behind him. Most of the guests were already seated, and I noted that the Companions had been carefully interspersed between client kings and notables of other realms.

Merlin had created a splendid setting far beyond my expectations, and I mentally congratulated him on a job well done.

The trumpeter raised his instrument and at a nod from Arthur, gave us a fanfare that brought our subjects to their feet. We crossed the Hall together, stride for stride. Arthur moved smoothly now, without a hint of limp or stiffness, and there was no way to tell he had been so seriously wounded. I stole a glance at him, noting that he looked wonderful: proud, eager, and sure of his world.

When we were seated, Merlin moved to the centre of the circle and raised his arms in the classic position for prayer. He invoked all the gods, Christian and Pagan alike, and then turned his attention to our guests.

Slowly scanning each section of the gathering, he drew the audience's attention as easily as a weaver draws his threads together when warping a loom. The room became absolutely silent, and the Magician's amazing voice stole, softly at first, among the guests in the Hall.

'Companions of Arthur, allies and rulers and heroes of many realms, you have come here in one of the finest of peacetime gatherings Britain has ever known. King and duke, count and warrior, freeman, noble, druid and bishop . . . you are the best flowering of this land, gathered to honour the High King and his Queen. Thus, in the name of Arthur and Guinevere, I bid you well come, Lords and Ladies of the Realm.

'Note well this union of all Albion, invited specifically at the request of your High King,' Merlin went on, spinning out the importance of the moment like thread from a distaff. 'Are you not Cumbri and Cornish, Breton and Pict, Scot and Irish and Roman: freemen all, powerful in your own sovereignty, yet willing to put aside personal differences for the chance to participate in this great celebration? And do not your gods look down and smile on this fair couple who have brought you together thus?'

The Magician paused, and I thought of how much my father would have liked this moment, and wished he were here.

Merlin was speaking again, his voice rising to fill the Hall, rich with the timbre of prophesy and import.

'Be it known to all men here that you are taking part in the creation of a new order. Throughout the whole of the Empire the barbarians have brought death and savage destruction to city and villa alike. Governments have cowered in the face of marauders, and holy men of all faiths lie slaughtered in this most wretched of convulsions. Yet it has been written in the skies that Britain will rise to defend herself. A powerful king will rally his countrymen against the tide of invasion that floods our eastern shore, and he and his followers will keep the torch of civilization alight as the rest of the Empire reels into darkness.

'Behold, the promises of old have come to pass, for Arthur Pendragon is that king, and this meeting of the Champions of Britain is but the first unfolding of that destiny. From this day forth the allies of Arthur shall be special to the gods, drawn together under the banner of the Red Dragon. Therefore,' he intoned solemnly, 'I propose a toast to you.'

There was a pause while someone filled a goblet and passed it out to him. The audience barely stirred, awed that the Sorcerer should pay them such honour. Arthur was sitting forward on the edge of his chair, his fingers so tensely intertwined the knuckles had gone white. When I glanced about the Hall it was clear that there was not a single leader who was not similarly enthralled. Captured

537

by Merlin's vision, the noblemen were all defining themselves in a new way, and the fire of enthusiasm was taking hold of their souls.

'To the Knights of the Round Table,' Merlin intoned, raising his glass in the traditional salute. 'To that mystical alliance of leaders in both war and peace. The Gods are forging, even now, your place in history. In Brittany and Spain, as close as Scotland and as far away as Constantinople they shall hear of Arthur's court and will come to pledge their honour to The Cause of Britain. So I, Merlin the Mage, salute you, the first of this great fellowship. As members of the Round Table you will become part of a glory that shall be sung of for all time . . . May your courage shine forth, your honour be assured, your loyalty be rewarded by eternal fame.'

He poured out the libation for the Old Gods, then drank the wine in one long quaff, like a warrior in the prime of his career.

A roar went up from the guests, heady with excitement and proud to pay him honour.

I found Arthur grinning from ear to ear, applauding like any other noble. He leaned close and hollered over the tumult, 'I think we've done it! We've given them an identity!'

'You planned this?' I queried.

Without another word he nodded, then, rising, led the assemblage in a standing ovation for his old tutor.

When the accolade died down, the Enchanter gestured towards us. 'Now,' he declared, 'it is time to pay homage to Arthur and his new queen, Guinevere.'

A hum of happy comments filled the Hall as people settled back in their chairs. I noticed that Lavinia had contrived to be seated with Agricola, and I smiled, hoping that such companionship made up for all the years of tried patience and endless endeavours to make a lady out of

538

me. Surely the good matron deserved something in recompense.

Igraine, who was seated next to me, had taken up quite a conversation with Brigit, and when I looked about for Bedivere, I found him seated with Gawain and Palomides; no doubt he intended to contain our hotheaded young champion should the need arise.

Even Morgan was there, though when she had arrived I was not sure. She sat in aloof majesty, not speaking to anyone, and I wondered if she'd left Accolon behind. Only later did I recognize him among the young warriors in the Gaulish contingent.

Merlin turned and bowed deeply to me, with the smooth motion of a practised courtier. For a moment I thought he might even smile, but then he was facing the Fellowship again, his fine voice tolling out the name of the first noble to be presented.

What a signal honour, I thought, to have your name called forth by the magic of the Sorcerer at this, the first meeting of the Round Table. Surely somewhere that unforgettable sound would linger, forever part of the music of time, so that generations later people would hear it and whisper in awe, 'What kind of wonder was this?'

Arthur and I sat in majesty upon the flat hard seats of the carved chairs and greeted each as the nobles were presented. Some I had met already, of course, but there were many I knew only by reputation. Cador, Duke of Cornwall, was a rangy wolf of a man, both leaner and older than I had expected, with grey hair and a face seamed by battle scars and seasons in the wind. He had an air of antique courtesy that was charming, bowing low to the Queen Mother before being presented to me. It was only later that I remembered Igraine had been his stepmother in the days when Gorlois was still alive.

Urien of Northumbria was smaller and more placid in

539

demeanour than I would have guessed, considering the troubles he had laid at Rheged's doorstep when I was growing up. He knelt proudly before me, offering the homage that is due the High King's wife, and I smiled graciously and thanked him for his allegiance. Clearly I heard my father's voice saying it was better to have Urien as an ally than an enemy, and I was glad it was now possible.

His son Uwain was a lad barely old enough to be a squire, but already he carried himself with the dignity of a young man who knows that someday he will lead a major kingdom in Britain.

Arthur grinned broadly as Merlin called up Bors of Brittany. A large blond man who wore his moustaches in the same downward droop as King Ban, he bounded forward with an abundance of hearty goodwill. Even if he hadn't brought Theo and his sailors to our shores, Arthur would have been glad to see him, for he was boisterous and hardy and full of the same open comradery as Arthur himself.

There were others whom I hadn't heard of, and their names and faces became a blur as the time went on.

When the last of the guests had paid homage, Merlin bowed low and retreated to his seat next to Nimue, who was radiant in her white dress and crown of ivy leaves. The smile she gave him was grave and admiring and though the Magician's back was to me, I was sure that we were seeing the God and Goddess looking upon each other.

I rose then, thanking our guests for coming just as Mama used to do at the feasts in Rheged. A murmur rippled through the court and then became a chant. Arthur got to his feet, so that we stood together while the bravos and acclamations filled the room. I looked slowly around the gathering.

Someday, I thought, you will all be as familiar to me as the warriors and nobles of my childhood. Someday I will know all your histories, the stories of your hopes and dreams, broken bones and lost promises, deeds of daring and stupidity, loves claimed or lost, children raised or buried . . . great and small, triumphant and tragic, our lives shall run together. Like a tapestry of human endeavour, woven on a god-held warp, dyed with the glories of each individual's action, we shall be remembered and sung of for generations to come.

I smiled at my husband and my court, then signalled to the pipers standing by the kitchen door and called out, 'Let the Feast begin.'

The best of romantic sagas in paperback from
Grafton Books

Parris Afton Bonds

Mood Indigo	£2.50	☐
Lavender Blue	£2.50	☐
Deep Purple	£2.95	☐

Barbara Taylor Bradford

Hold the Dream	£3.50	☐
A Woman of Substance	£3.95	☐
Voice of the Heart	£3.95	☐

Rebecca Brandewyne

Rose of Rapture	£2.95	☐
Love, Cherish Me	£2.95	☐
And Gold was Ours	£2.95	☐

Monique Raphel High

The Keeper of the Walls	£3.50	☐
The Four Winds of Heaven	£1.95	☐
Encore	£1.95	☐

Anne Melville

The Lorimer Line	£2.50	☐
The Lorimer Legacy	£2.50	☐
Lorimers at War	£2.50	☐
Lorimers in Love	£2.50	☐

Diana Stainforth

Bird of Paradise	£3.50	☐

To order direct from the publisher just tick the titles you want
and fill in the order form.   **GF1482**

All these books are available at your local bookshop or newsagent, or can be ordered direct from the publisher.

To order direct from the publishers just tick the titles you want and fill in the form below.

Name _____

Address _____

Send to:
Grafton Cash Sales
PO Box 11, Falmouth, Cornwall TR10 9EN.

Please enclose remittance to the value of the cover price plus:

UK 60p for the first book, 25p for the second book plus 15p per copy for each additional book ordered to a maximum charge of £1.90.

BFPO 60p for the first book, 25p for the second book plus 15p per copy for the next 7 books, thereafter 9p per book.

Overseas including Eire £1.25 for the first book, 75p for second book and 28p for each additional book.

Grafton Books reserve the right to show new retail prices on covers, which may differ from those previously advertised in the text or elsewhere.